D1541446

# The Music Teacher

◆ ◆ ◆

"Music is the tie that binds all during love and war in Sennett's debut novel, which opens in Dublin in 1910. Joe Dooley's life is devoted to music and the strength of connections formed during his coming of age. As he rises in the ranks of the British military, he searches for meaning in his friendships as well as for that one special person with whom to share his life."

—*Publishers Weekly*

◆ ◆ ◆

"Laurie Odell, hero of Mary Renault's classic *The Charioteer*, would recognize a kindred spirit in Bob Sennett's Joe Dooley. *The Music Teacher* provides a deeply affecting window on Catholic Ireland before the Easter Rising and Europe destroyed by the Great War while being always a novel of ideas and ideals, and a portrait of one thoughtful romantic in a world that dishonors all he holds dear."

—ALEX JEFFERS, author of *Deprivation* and *The Abode of Bliss*

# The Music Teacher

◆ ◆ ◆

# The Music Teacher

◆

*a novel*

◆

# BOB SENNETT

◆ ◆ ◆

Lethe Press · Maple Shade, New Jersey

*The Music Teacher*

Published in 2014 by Lethe Press, Inc.
118 Heritage Avenue, Maple Shade, NJ 08052 USA
lethepressbooks.com / lethepress@aol.com
ISBN: 978-1-59021-145-8 / 1-59021-145-6
e-ISBN: 978-1-59021-153-3 / 1-59021-153-7

Set in Garamond, Rechtman, and Jenson.
Interior design: Alex Jeffers.
Cover design: Fred Tovich.

LIBRARY OF CONGRESS CATALOGING-IN-PUBLICATION DATA
Sennett, Bob (Research bibliographer)
The Music Teacher : a novel / Bob Sennett.
    pages cm
ISBN 978-1-59021-145-8 (pbk. : alk. paper) -- ISBN 978-1-59021-153-3 (ebook)
1. Music teachers--Fiction. 2. Gays--Fiction. 3. World War, 1914-1918--Fiction. I. Title.
PS3619.E6593M87 2014
813'.6--dc23
                                        2013029555

For John,
*Tá a fhios agat cén fáth.*

◆ ◆ ◆

# Chapter 1

❖ ❖ ❖

## The Rabaiatti Pilgrimage

❖ ❖ ❖

Joe Dooley loved music; of that, there was no doubt at all. Each day's dawn might be met by the clang and blare of the unoiled cars of the tram which passed directly beneath Joe's second story window but all he heard were the grace notes, metal tones in the cold Dublin air. All through his walks about town he would hear it. If a flock of chirruping sparrows alighted upon an oak in Mountjoy Square, Joe would naturally sort the notes in his head until they emerged sounding like a harmony lesson. He would hear Mr. McBride naming the vegetables in his corner stand, "marrows and butter beans and peas in the pod," as a waltz all the way home. Even the Liffey suggested a song. As Joe crossed the river he recalled a rhyme from his earliest days:

> *Ferry me across the water.*
> *Do, boatman, do.*
> *If you've a penny in your purse*
> *I'll ferry you.*
>
> *I have a penny in my purse,*
> *And my eyes are blue.*
> *So ferry me across the water.*
> *Do, boatman, do.*

Joe's window looked out upon a brownstoned stretch of Talbot Street that commonly impressed anyone making their way to Amiens Street Station—should they accidentally step off the tram one stop too soon—as poor in the necessary qualities for the raising of a child. From his bed, he could just make out the top of the window of the law offices at no. 8 on the one hand and the vacant shopfront at no. 12 on the other. Joe was too young to comprehend the reasons businesses fail and proprietors revolve (being not quite three months shy of his tenth birthday) but he felt the apprehension which swept across the da's face at the mention of it and the mention of it receded in time for that.

There was not always such reticence. At least once every day in the silent leavings of the classroom or his walking to and fro, Joe would surrender to his memories: a fading image of a great cathedral on a hill—not Dublin—where his sister would challenge him to a race to the top or a day when the da was not so poor in health that the two of them, father and son alike, could scuffle on the green and no dark warning would come. There were even buried, joyful memories of the Dublin of the past four years, for despite the need for more money than could be garnered and constant fret that filled the room, as long as Joe could hear the birdsongs and the hawkers singing to him he would find the time to sing right back.

Now that summer was over Joe's day was refitted to the rituals he had previously established to protect himself from the usual assaults of the world. Without prompting, he would awaken at seven each school morning and wash his hands and face in the bowl of water he had brought up the evening before. There was usually a sufficient assortment of clean clothes to choose from, although Joe preferred the worn-out green-striped muslin jersey which he had received as a gift for his eighth birthday and which since he had outgrown it made his small frame look fuller and more defensible.

Ablutions complete, Joe would climb downstairs, counting the steps because the fifth one down from the top was loose and had even come out one morning and nearly killed him. He would take down his brown worsted jacket from its place upon the row of pegs in the hall and bound out onto Talbot Street. It took him twenty minutes to make the round-trip to Sackville Street to buy an apple for his breakfast, six seeded rolls from Boland's, and an *Independent* for his da. Joe liked the seeded rolls although his sister Kathleen complained that the seeds stuck in her teeth.

By a quarter to eight Joe would be out the door again, book bag in hand, on his way to his schoolroom in the basement of St. Mary's, where Sister Aloysius taught thirty boys and seven girls how to multiply by fives and tens and what Jesus taught the world. Joe felt it was very good that Jesus taught the world but he remained uncertain exactly what it was He taught. No amount of questioning of Sister Aloysius seemed to ever advance the cause. It was an uncomfortable coincidence that Joe's teacher's name was the same as his saint's own and that she knew he was Joseph Aloysius Dooley Jr. and might expect more from him, a flaw forevermore.

Joe liked his schooldays. He felt comforted to know that his pencils and pen would be in the same place every morning and that the assignment that he had completed the night before about the War of the Roses would greet him in his notebook. Still, he wondered what if anything the War of the Roses had to do with the life of a poor Irish boy at the dawn of the twentieth century and worried that his wonderment might not stand him well in the eyes of his teacher should it somehow be revealed.

To no one's surprise, including his own, Joe's favorite class was the music lesson. Sister Aloysius had no musical abilities but she was clever enough to know this. Every Wednesday and Friday right upon lunch she would conduct her pupils to a room in the basement where Sister Agnes would accept them and arrange them in as neat a semicircle as possible about her piano. The music room, such as it was, also served as the boiler room of the church, which meant it was oppressively hot and clangy, but Joe had long learned to force ignorance of these things as the wavering bell-tones of Sister Agnes's triangle and the uneven notes of two dozen singing children overrode them. His only mistake was to be talented.

"Joe Dooley, what a beautiful voice you have," Sister Agnes exclaimed, making the class giggle and embarrassing Joe. "I have a mind to let you lead the class in 'Hail, Redeemer.'"

"Thank you, Sister Aloysius," Joe answered into his sleeve with the hope that his lack of enthusiasm wouldn't count against him.

"Perhaps tomorrow," Sister suggested, allowing the moment of crisis to pass. Joe breathed a perceptible sigh of relief that Sister fortunately overlooked. But the principle had been established: Joe had a talent. He was certain that he would never live it down. And so it happened that Joe was selected to lead the music class in a new hymn every week and with that Joe's favorite moment became the point of a nightmare.

ⵕ

ON THE THIRD WEDNESDAY OF SEPTEMBER, AFTER A PARTICULARLY humiliating day of hymn-singing, errors in mathematics, and uninspired game-playing Joe came home to find an incident taking place at the previously vacant no. 12. From the back of an open carriage, two large men were carrying a barber's chair into the building. These men had all the appearance of being capable of lifting a tramcar but their efforts to relocate the overly wide and bottom-heavy chair were humorously frustrated. The conglomeration of leather and iron crashed to the ground accompanied by a Babel of oaths.

"*Du Idiot!*" one of the men shouted at the other. "*Vorsichtiger sein.*"

At last, one of the men shoved the other aside and lugged the piece of furniture into the building. Joe sidled up to a trio of women whom he vaguely recognized as neighbors and listened in.

"They say a German family has rented the shop."

"More of them come over every day. Pretty soon we'll be outnumbered."

"That may be, but at least my husband will have no excuse not to shave every day."

Joe registered interest in the business being established and was about to continue on his way when he spotted a boy about the same age as himself standing apart on the other side of the threshold. He was tall with red hair and pale blue eyes. Something about the look on the boy's face ignited Joe's pity and without preparing his usual defense-laden opening lines he walked up to the boy and introduced himself. "Hello. I'm Joe Dooley. I live at no. 10."

Joe extended his hand. For the briefest of moments, the boy looked only at the hand. Then he smiled, took the hand, and looked at Joe. "My name is Heinrich Vogeler. My papa has taken no. 12. He wishes to open a barbershop."

His English was nearly perfect. The only evidence in his speech of the boy's foreign origins was the sharpness of the first syllable of his first name, for in the open "o" of the first syllable of his last name and the almost thrown-away quality of the second syllable it might have been an Irish name.

"That's grand," Joe answered. "The nearest barber is halfway to Dromconda and I always look like a savage. Where's your ma?"

The boy looked away. "My mama died. In Germany—years ago."

"I'm sorry".

"'S all right."

Just then, an older-looking man came up to Joe and Heinrich. "*Ist das ein neuer Freund, Heinrich?*"

"English, Papa. Please. This is Joe. He lives next door."

Joe shot out his hand. "I'm pleased to meet you, Mr. Vogeler."

"One day in Dublin and already my boy has made a friend."

"Can I help you with anything, Papa?"

The old man smiled, as if this was a usual and usually dismissed request. "Not now, my son. It will be a while before all the boxes will be inside and then I will need your help turning these empty rooms into our home. Why don't you go exploring with your new friend?"

"Yes, Papa."

Joe tried to be helpful. "I like to walk by the river."

Heinrich turned a hopeful eye in his father's direction. "May I, Papa?"

The old man beamed. "Of course."

THE VOGELER BOY SOON BECAME JOE DOOLEY'S CONFIDANT. HE was the kind of friend that Joe never knew was needed until he arrived. Somewhere deep inside himself Joe acknowledged without really ever spelling it out that he enjoyed a sense of superiority to the boy, who was after all a Lutheran in a universe of Catholics and a German ivy in a field of Irish moss. Joe also sensed his own world was more one of ideas whereas Heinrich's world was filled with things. The boy was six months older, and bigger. Their physical differences made the push-weight that balanced Joe's native advantages. They attended separate schools of course and their chores prevented them from playing together every day, especially now as the autumn deepened and the weather turned. Still it would be a long week in which Joe Dooley and Heinrich Vogeler would go without at least one late-afternoon walk by the Liffey or a stroll up Sackville Street for a sweet and a gawk at the crowd in front of the GPO.

Joe diligently unraveled the threads of the Vogeler family history and tucked them into the weave of his own. Herr Vogeler had only the one son; Heinrich's mother was always ill and tragically died of consumption before the boy had turned seven. Father and son abandoned the small farm in Saxony which they had rented and moved first to London and then to Dublin, bringing two suitcases, a dozen boxes of books, photographs, and mementoes, and that one enormous chair—with the hope that making a living as a barber would be easier in Ireland, where the prejudices are strong but the people are friendly, than in the more church-bound and imperial England.

Joe tried to communicate to Heinrich how his own sense of displacement harmonized with his friend's. For Joe, too, had lived like a vagabond in his own still-short life: exile from Dublin to Queenstown (when the money ran out, to stay with his ma's sister), then back to Dublin (where his da found work in a print shop that twice was raided by the constabulary), only to have the da's health fade, leaving his ma to take in piecework). It seemed to Joe that he only had to look at his friend's smiling face and all the cares of this world would slide away as dew on a window pane, leaving behind a clear if distant view of someplace beautiful and better.

By mid-October, the boys' friendship had settled into the pattern with which Joe was most comfortable and to which Heinrich seemed generally accommodating. After school if the weather was fine the boys would meet in the middle of the O'Connell Bridge and shoot peas into the Liffey or venture entirely into the South Side and watch the students in their dark suits glide in and out of the gates of Trinity College. When the sun started to set chores would intervene, but on most evenings the boys would convince their families to let them study together and they would reconvene upstairs at no. 10 or in the broom-swept corner of the parlor of no. 12 where the smell of talcum powder would scent the Lambs' *Tales* or Keats.

Whatever the time and no matter how exhausting the day's adventures, Joe and Heinrich would always make certain to allow time for music. A stranger might compile an entire directory of differences that separated the boys by size, coloring, or faith; those with a more intimate knowledge of them might discern the subtle character traits that distinguished them, such as Joe's shy nature and intellectual curiosity and Heinrich's physical ability to command a room. But no one could doubt that in the end it was a love of music that brought the two friends their highest and most intimate happiness.

When Heinrich discovered that Joe's family owned a piano there was less of the smell of talcum and more of the sound of music. Each night after the lessons had been memorized and the home assignments filled out and pushed into the corners of the book bag Joe and Heinrich would take out a sheet of music and put it on an improvised stand. Mr. Harrison owned a music store on Sackville Street Upper and out of pity he would give Joe any misprints for him to take home.

Joe suggested that they try to read along with the music. Sister taught Joe the names of the notes but the Dooley piano was woozy and Joe could never be certain of them. Nevertheless, he and Heinrich were so enthralled with the italicized tempo indications and inky rubrics scattered across the paper that they made a pact then and there to learn how to read music and someday Joe would be first violin and Heinrich would play second and conduct.

"If we're to have a quartet, we'll need a third and a fourth," Heinrich intoned. 'Peter Malin and Tommy Doyle like music. We could ask them to read along with us.'

"Peter Malin is a stuck-up fool, and Tommy Doyle's ma never lets him out of her sight. We'd be better off mining your school, don't you think? Especially if we're going to learn Beethoven—that's something where you're better off with the Germans."

"I'm not German," was the boy's retort. "It's always Heinrich this and Heinrich that—you'd think I'd just stepped off the boat from Bremen."

"Your da doesn't mind, Heinrich."

"Papa is different. He spent his whole life in Germany. His accent will never go away. But I'm not like him. I'm Irish."

"If you're Irish, you've got to have an Irish name."

"What is Irish for 'Heinrich'?"

"There is no Irish for 'Heinrich.'"

'That's not true. I can read, you know. There was an English King Henry. Why can't I be Henry?"

"It's bad enough being German. Do you want to be German and English? The boys from the University College would dump you in the Liffey."

"You're being contrary."

"Fine, then. We'll christen you 'Harry.' There's a 'Harry' in Shakespeare and Shakespeare's all right. No Irishman would mind being called 'Harry.'"

"I like that. 'Harry' it is."

"Nothing I can do about the 'Vogeler' bit, though. Unless you want to go around town being addressed as 'Harry the Birdcatcher.'"

"I don't mind Vogeler."

"Harry Vogeler," Joe opined to no one in particular. "I like it. It has a distinguished air, like a professor of chemistry or an international spy. Well done, Harry Vogeler!"

The boys laughed and laughing knocked the music to the floor.

"Mary and Joseph," Joe exclaimed as he dived across Harry's lap to rescue the paper. "Mary and Joseph."

This caused Harry to laugh even harder, set him to sputtering even, which sent Joe into a torrent of hysterics as well. For no reason at all, they broke out a chorus of "Little Tommy Murphy":

> For Little Tommy Murphy was a soldier bold,
> And he sang as he marched away.
> Tow di-lough, di-lough, di-lum,
> Tow di-lough, di-lough…

"What in the name of the Lord is going on in there?" Mrs. Dooley shouted at them. "Would you please play some decent Christian music and be done with it?"

"Harry, Harry, Harry…" Joe said between verses, curled up on the floor, laughing.

"Harry, Harry, Harry," Harry repeated, as if the act of saying the name made it his.

And so it did.

⌒

THE MORNING OF ALL SAINTS' EVE HARRY INVITED JOE TO JOIN him and his Papa for Reformation Day service. St. Finian's was located on the south side near the Grand Canal and it took the three of them nearly half an hour to walk there from Talbot Street. Joe thought it was unfair for a family to have to travel so far to worship but he didn't want to say anything about it to Harry for fear of hurting his feelings. Joe was wearing a new shirt that fit poorly but he imagined the discomfort was part of the ritual. The day was fine and the walk was pleasant but Harry's Papa was in a contemplative mood and not inclined to conversation. The silence struck Joe as mysterious and holy.

When they arrived at the church, Herr Vogeler greeted several old men in German and introduced his boy and Joe as if they were both his sons. St. Finian's was old and small and constructed of weathered stone that looked cold and uninviting. The three of them crossed the threshold and walked down the aisle until Harry's Papa directed them to sit side by side on a worn wooden bench halfway to the altar. Joe was comforted by the clatter of the voices in the foreign tongue and the dark and unfamiliar atmosphere. He felt as if he was attending a show instead of a service and that at any moment the lights would be turned down and a singer would take to the stage.

The minister approached the pulpit and the congregation rose. The German phrases flowed out and although Harry had taught Joe a little of the language it was still incomprehensible to him. Joe moved his mouth in silent affirmation and hoped that the old woman standing next to him didn't notice his dissembling. Finally, the Lord's Prayer came around and Joe latched on to a phrase he recognized:

> *Vater unser, der Du bist im Himmel. Geheiliget werde Dein Name. Dein Reich komme. Dein Wille geschehe, wie im Himmel, also auch auf Erden...*

Harry had tried to explain Reformation Day to Joe and how they were celebrating the anniversary of the day Martin Luther nailed his debate about indulgences to the door of his church in Wittenburg. Joe tried to be patient because he truly loved his friend and he thought it was polite to be tolerant of other people's beliefs but in his heart he had to admit it didn't really make sense. What good was any deed at all if in the end it wasn't to be weighed in the balance? Where did God's grace come from if not from everything Joe could see and especially hear? And, most of all, if it was all sorted out a long, long time ago, why would God grant salvation to some men and not to others?

Joe looked at Harry. He was sitting next to his Papa with his hands neatly folded over the open Bible in his lap. The minister was leading the congregation in prayer and Joe watched Harry speak the rejoinder in loud and firm German. Joe transformed the sound of the words, with their sharp consonants and their variant rhythms, into a kind of music. In this manner Joe understood that Harry's invitation had very little to do with the liturgy and much, much more to do with communion. By sharing his faith and his heritage with Joe, Harry was sharing his soul.

The service ended and the congregation slowly made their way from the cool dark of St. Finian's to the paved walk of Adelaide Road. Harry and his Papa were pulled aside by a young couple and Joe thought it would be best if he stood apart. At just that moment, another boy about the same age as Joe came up to him and introduced himself. *"Mein Na-men ist Steffan. Wer bist du?"*

"I'm sorry, Steffan," Joe replied. "I don't speak German."

"That must be difficult for you."

"I am Herr Vogeler's guest. My name is Joe."

"Welcome, Joe. I'm very glad you could come."

The boy looked at Joe for a long time, as if he was waiting for Joe to say something, but Joe had no idea what was expected of him. All he could think of was how uncomfortable he was and how awkward it was of him to try to make conversation with this German boy. Just then Harry came to his rescue. "I see you've met Steffan Weiss."

"Yes."

"Recruiting Catholics again, Vogeler?" Steffan began.

"I'm doing nothing of the sort," said Harry. "Joe is my neighbor."

"Again?" Joe asked. "How often do you invite heathens to your temple, Harry?"

"Every chance I get," Harry answered, running his hand through Joe's hair.

"I bet."

"Nice to meet you, Joe."

Steffan ran off and rejoined his party. Harry's Papa returned.

"Thank you for coming with us this morning, Joe," Herr Vogeler said. "You have made my son very happy."

"I'm glad I could oblige, sir," Embarrassed, Joe tried to push his disheveled coif back into place. "Very, very glad."


THE FIRST OF DECEMBER MRS. DOOLEY SAT WITH JOE AND KATH-leen in the parlor and told them in a soft unsteady voice that there was no longer enough work to be had in Dublin and they were returning to Queenstown to live with her sister. From the back room, the da's cough resounded like the bark of a trapped animal and the echo of it hovered in the air. The poor man couldn't even be present at the ceremony and Joe felt the pang of the sadness of it all. Mr. Dooley had always blamed his failed health on an illness he called "sorting dust" but Joe knew it was not the materials of the print workshop but the literal letterpress it produced that was his downfall. He heard his father's violent protestations against the police raids and he felt his father's determination when the editors and the typesetters would reconvene in their kitchen and carefully plot to reconstruct the machinery that lay in anarchic ruin below. Joe Dooley Sr. was going to beat the system or die and Joe Jr. knew that the crossroad was coming.

"Now, Joe, we've a lot of laying out to do and your poor da is not up to it. I am counting on your helping me and your sister in this matter," Mrs. Dooley said.

"Of course, Ma. All that and more."

"To begin, there's Christmas," Mrs. Dooley continued. "I'm not having our circumstances interfere in any way with the joy that rightly belongs to the season. I want the two of you to go on as best you can as if nothing was really the matter and we'll make the best of it, we will."

Kathleen nodded in assent and promised that she would be both a boon and a blessing to her mother and father's trials but Joe resented her equanimity and felt the pressure inside his head building like too much air in a carnival balloon. He tried to find the words but when it came his turn to speak he found he could utter no protest nor make any gesture in sympathy but only held his hands to his side and stared at what he now knew was soon to be all that remained of his family.

THAT SUNDAY AFTER MASS JOE ROUNDED UP HARRY AND TOMMY Doyle and set out for Capel Street. Everyone knew that Rabaiotti's made the best ice cream on the North Side and it was a bit of a holiday tradition for the boys of St. Mary's to make a pilgrimage of it for Advent. Joe's friends had heard the news about his imminent removal and the day had something of the air of a send-off.

"We'll make you sick with the sugar," Harry cried as the boys dashed in front of a tram barreling south down Sackville Street.

"I'm glad to hear you are thinking foremost of my health," Joe answered, forcing a smile that considering the company couldn't dally long as forced.

"Do we have to go all the way to Capel Street?" Tommy remonstrated.

"What? Does your ma never cut the strings?" asked Harry.

"I'm not supposed to go farther than the river on my own."

"Well, you're not on your own," Joe said. "That's evident. And we have no intention of crossing the river at all."

Just then, a formation of bigger boys elbowed their way between Harry and Tommy, sending Tommy spinning into a crowd of well-dressed patrons congregating in front of the entrance to the Hotel Metropole.

Tommy lost his balance and fell to the pavement with an undignified arabesque.

"Brava," one of the boys shouted backwards. They laughed.

"Are you all right, Tommy?" Joe asked, extending his hand.

"Of course."

"We'll spare your ma the details," Harry retorted.

"Spare all."

The boys switched their attention from the vicinity of the altercation to the lights and sounds of the street. Slight, translucent veils of frost edged the window of a sweet shop, making the rows of candied fruits, chocolate nuts, and Christmas cakes waver in their trays like figures in a dream. The thin layer of ice in the roadway glittered from the reflected light of the electric candles. Joe heard the sound of the streetcars as they glided by and the murmur of the crowds of people walking up and down beside them and suddenly he felt safe and insulated as though here—in the most crowded place in the most crowded city in the whole of the island of Ireland—he was independent and free. The world revolved like a polar axis around him and no matter the size or scale so long as he was at the center of it he was not afraid. It was isolation and unfamiliarity he feared the most. No open spaces, no dark path, no turn in the road dissuaded Joe from investigation as long as he was with company. He cursed his da and the fate that was to draw him away from this and trap him in the south where like Gulliver he would be pinned and poked, his every move and even his every thought numbered and thus exposed.

It was nearly five o'clock when they finally arrived at Rabaiotti's. There was a queue out the door. Joe joined the line and took the inventory of his pockets. "Four pence and three," he intoned, counting out the coins in his gloved palm. "That's enough for a penny cup and a small box to take away."

"How sporting of you," Harry said. "I've got five and I have no intention of taking home any of it." He laughed mischievously and felt compelled to add, "I'm joking with you. Papa would murder me if I came home with anything less than tuppence. Get me a penny choco and be done with it."

The line had moved inside the store now and the room was filled with the smell of sweet fruit and warm sugar. The little trays that held the ice cream were smoking in the heated air and the boy behind the counter was moving frantically from well to well filling orders.

"What do you want, Tom?" Joe asked.

Tommy surveyed the choices. "A lemon."

"A lemon 'tis."

Joe ordered a penny vanilla, a penny chocolate, a lemon, and a box of Neapolitan to go. The boy put the box in a small paper bag and Joe carefully folded down the top so he could carry it. The three friends stood on the street outside the shop. The sun was gone so they licked their cups by the light of a street lamp.

"I think I lost a penny," Tommy cried, pulling his pockets inside out.

"I'll give you one if that's the case," Joe answered. "We won't want Mrs. Doyle to hold a debt against us for the rest of our days." He fetched a coin from his own stash and handed it to the boy.

"Thanks, much."

"Get off it."

"I've got to get home now," Tommy said. "Don't you have to get back, too?"

"So says you," Harry replied.

Joe advanced a plan. "I don't think I'm quite ready yet," he said. "If it's all right with you Tom, I'm going to skate on the Liffey for a bit."

"You'll fall in and catch your death," Tommy admonished.

"You idiot," Joe laughed. "I'm not going to jump into the river."

"But you said…"

"Do you always believe everything you hear, Doyle?"

"I don't mind keeping you company, Joe…" Harry said. "…so long as Tommy can make his way back on his own."

"I'm not a baby, if that's what you mean, Vogeler."

"I didn't mean a thing," Harry answered. "As for me, if I didn't stick to Dooley here they'd be fetching me out of the Grand Canal at dawn."

"Suit yourself."

Tommy lit out toward Abbey Street and disappeared into the crowd.

"I hope that box of Neapolitan of yours enjoys the river view."

"It's cold enough. It'll keep."

At the foot of Capel Street, the boys intercepted a band of carolers. There were approximately ten of them and their ruddy cheeks shone in the cold and gave evidence of pocket flasks for warmth. Their leader apparent, a tall old man wearing a black top hat with a worn fringe, was reviewing a sheaf of papers in his gloved hand. He stopped and cleared his throat.

"Ladies and gentlemen, '*Adeste Fideles*' if you please."

The revelers broke into uneven song. Joe cast a conspiratorial eye toward Harry, who dramatically cleared his throat in imitation of the old man. Joe giggled and then in his clear boy soprano brought the ensemble up to snuff:

> *...ergo qui natus,*
> *Die hodierna*
> *Jesu, tibi sit Gloria*
> *Patris aeterni...*

The effect of the boy's singing, so natural if untrained, stirred the ranks of the carolers. Severally they turned in Joe's direction and lowered their voices in harmony. Harry smiled and put his arm around his friend as Joe took over leadership of the choir and directed them in a final chorus:

> *Venite adoremus,*
> *Venite adoremus,*
> *Venite adoremus,*
> *Dominum!*

The old man beamed and applauded in muffled admiration. "Why, what a lovely voice you have!" he said.

Joe beamed. "Thank you, sir"

"You must continue on with us to Grafton Street. We are meeting up with a band from St. Mark's."

"It would be lovely, sir, but my friend and I—we're overdue at home."

"Of course, of course." The old man shook his head, beaming. "Your ma and da must be so proud of you."

"Thank you, sir."

"Thank you. Thanks to both of you. You are very pleasant and polite young men."

At that, the carolers still full of murmur walked on ahead.

"That was quite a show, Joe," Harry said.

"Can I help it if I'm one of a choir of angels?" Joe smiled.

"Apparently, no."

They crossed at the Grattan Bridge. The Liffey ran slow and black beneath them. From here, the north and south quays appeared relatively distant. The middle of the river was the only place in Dublin where you could step back and see the city with any sort of perspective. Joe stopped there and leaned over the iron railing. "Lookat. You can see all the way to the Custom House," Joe began.

"I'm afraid you're making it out better than I am, Joe," said Harry. "Papa thinks I need spectacles."

"Oh, Harry," Joe said, smiling, "What will you do without me?"

"I'll get along just fine."

"Queenstown is only one hundred and sixty-two miles from Dublin. I looked it up in the atlas in the library."

"I could come for a visit in the summer. People get fewer haircuts in the summer"

"That would be grand. There's a bathing pool by the sea and there's an enormous port where they build the most tremendous ships."

"Will you miss Dublin?"

"Ah—well, I've left it before, haven't I? I've had some practice."

"You were three years old. This is different. I bet you didn't have a lot of friends when you were three."

"I don't have a lot of friends now," said Joe. "Only you."

The river flowed silently past. A solitary seagull drew a circle over their heads and then landed on the railing opposite. It seemed eager to watch the boys and then changing its mind lifted up its wings and sailed off into the dark.

"That box of Neapolitan isn't going to survive, is it?" Harry said.

Joe opened the top of the bag and peered in. "S'pose not." He laughed and tossed the melted contents into the murk.

"What a waste of fivepence."

"What the Hell," Joe said, relishing the curse.

"What the Hell," said Harry.

JOSEPH ALOYSIUS DOOLEY, SR. DIED THE THIRD WEEK OF JANUARY. The funeral was held at St. Mary's and the experience was doubly strange because the queen had died the same day and there was black bunting hanging in every window. It was hard for Joe to feel singled out for sorrow with everyone else moping around with sad looks keeping their speaking voices low. He was curious to find that he felt more sympathy for the anonymous faces he passed on the street or in the pews with their practiced expressions of grief than he did for his family sitting there beside him. After all he had been expecting his da to die for years now. His death was not sudden, and now there was the queen. He had rarely thought about the queen. It was a small measure of satisfaction which actually drew a smile across his face and which he had to hide when he approached the coffin to remember that his dear, departed da hardly ever thought about the queen either and that when he did you were sure to know they were unkind thoughts. Joe helped his ma and Kathleen box up what they needed from no.10. They said goodbye to Mr. O'Connell, the man who owned the shop and was now retired, and to his son who had taken over the business. They promised Joe a spot on the press line should he come back and need work. A car came to the door to transport the household to Kingsbridge Station and the train that would deliver them to the south. It was at that moment that Joe relived the argument between him and his mother which had taken place the day before the funeral when Joe realized that the piano was to be left behind.

"How will I practice my lessons, Mama?"

"There are pianos in Queenstown, Joey. I'm sure we will find one for you."

"Not like this, Mama. This is the only piano I know."

"And how many fathers did you have, Joe? One. You will play another piano."

Surprising even himself, Joe began to sob. "I'll pay for it too, Ma. I'll work to pay the movers."

Touched, Mrs. Dooley reached around and pressed the boy to her chest. "We don't have enough money, son. I had to leave my sewing table and the bureau your father gave me as a wedding gift. If I can leave my table and bureau behind, why can't you abide to leave your piano?"

"The music, Mama…" Joe said, between stifled tears. "What will I do without the music?"

"Joseph Aloysius Dooley, my son. Your poor father suffered terribly and for a terribly long time so that you—and your sister, might I add—had enough to eat and a place to sleep. But he knew that was not enough. He knew that children need more than food and sleep. Children need dreams. And that is why we had a piano. Now, you are the only Joseph Aloysius Dooley I have. And no one, certainly not I, wants to leave your dreams behind. So look at me, and listen to me, and remember—we may be leaving behind the piano. But we are not leaving behind your dreams."

After all the boxes had been taken down and loaded into the car and the room was swept clean, Joe went back into the house one last time. He stood in front of the piano. He lifted up the cover and played "*Für Elise*" from memory. The past floated up with the notes and filled the room. Joe took a large breath of it and held it and held it all the way to the station, letting it out in small draughts as he called out the quays and on the edge of the train platform, and again at the window before he offered the window seat to Kathleen, and at last as the train rose over the hills and dove toward Kildare and to the new and promised land.

# Chapter 2

◆ ◆ ◆

# *A Rainy Afternoon at St. Colman's*

◆ ◆ ◆

THE CHURCH WAS UNFINISHED. A PATH OF BRICKS LED AWAY FROM the south portal only to fall upon a bed of daffodils that the flower committee was intermittently successful at raising. It concluded with a plank scaffold where a team of plasterers scraped and lathed the Dalkey granite that was intended to be a part of the foundation. Whoever wrote "a mighty fortress is our God" had evidently never set foot inside St. Colman's.

This April morning Joe was climbing the hill on his way to his catechesis with Brother James. Dark-bottomed clouds sped across the sky and threatened rain. At each street crossing Joe would stop and turn his face into the wind that blew cool and damp with the sea-air and look down at the town below. The whole of Queenstown seemed to be arrayed before him, fancy box upon fancy box of three-story houses nestled like a sinking balustrade, their mottled wood facings fading to pink, pine green, and ivory in the indifferent daylight. As he approached the cathedral Joe turned into the wind one final time and looked for Crosshaven dim in the mist on the opposite side of the harbor with the channel beside that led to the open sea.

Joe loved this view; it nearly lacked a vanishing point. With the stones of the church at his back and his Aunt Maeve's house out of sight below him, Joe felt unfettered and he could almost believe he had something to say about his own destiny. The thought of it inspired him. In the four years that had passed since his da died and his ma brought him and Kathleen to live in Queenstown nothing Joe said or did felt like something on which he could put his name. His tiny bedroom had no room for a desk to write or even a shelf for books. Joe had to walk seven blocks to the Carnegie Library if he wanted to read about the Restoration and five blocks in the opposite direction to the Misses Ryans' parlor where he took piano lessons after school two days a week.

Joe had a hard time adjusting to the family move. He made friends easily if not deeply and that and his lessons were sufficient to fill his days but as he grew every aspect of his existence seemed diminished. Queenstown harbor was picturesque but entirely without any of the capital city's unburdened sense of importance. His aunt's home was pretty, faced with purple wooden shingles, but it was no more or less interesting than the Burdicks' place next door or any one of the identical parti-colored homesteads running up and down the sea-faced streets. There was no piano he could call his own. Even as his church expanded it seemed smaller.

⌒

THE LESSON WITH BROTHER JAMES WENT WELL. JOE WAS CAUGHT up on his Bible stories and felt no particular need to act disputative with the brother. Winter was hard behind them but the heat was turned on and the room in which they were reciting was stifling. Today's assignment was Matthew 10.

"...Heal the sick, cleanse the lepers, raise the dead, cast out devils; freely ye have received, freely give," Joe read.

"Very good, Joseph," James replied. "Go on."

"Provide neither gold nor silver, nor brass in your purses, nor script for your journey, neither two coats, neither shoes, nor yet staves, for the workman is worthy of his meat."

Joe stopped. "What are staves, Brother?" he asked.

"I believe Matthew is referring to a walking stick, Joseph. Tell me, what is the meaning of this passage?"

"Well, the only staves I know are the printed lines on a sheet of music. I knew that was wrong."

"Indeed."

"So I suppose the prophet is referring to the dignity of work."

James paused to consider the boy's answer. "A rote reply but a fair one," he said, finally.

"I'm sorry, Brother".

"No, I meant that as a compliment, my boy. Most of my other students would have bogged down with 'gold and silver' and gotten no further than the Third Commandment. At least you were listening to what you were reading."

"I could hardly do elsewise, Brother."

"Elsewise is not correct, Joe. I believe you meant to say 'otherwise.'"

"'Otherwise.' Thank you, Brother."

"You're welcome. Is there anything else you might care to add about the significance of this passage?"

Joe searched his mind for a clue as to what Brother James was looking for. He felt it was always best to anticipate what adults wished to hear, for if you could do that and put it in a complete sentence he found more often than not they were completely satisfied and would thereafter leave you alone.

"It means if you do good work for any reason, work can be its own reward."

"Very true, Joseph."

There was a pause. The warm air flowed back into Joe's lungs and he felt the rise of perspiration at the edges of his temples. The smell of the hot dust made him feel nauseated.

"May I take some air, Brother?" Joe asked.

James looked up from the Bible.

"What? Oh, yes, of course. We've read quite enough for this afternoon. Why don't you head along home now?"

"Thank you, Brother."

JOE LEFT THE RECTORY OFFICE AND WALKED OUTSIDE. A GENTLE rain was beginning to fall but instead of bothering the boy it cheered him. Rain fell from Heaven after all and what could be more beneficent than dew from Heaven to bless his Bible reading and all that he had learned that day. Joe felt that he had indeed learned something but when it came time to try to make sense of it the precise meaning of the lesson eluded him. He sat down upon one of the unplaced carving stones that the masons would soon attempt to turn into a suitably frightening gargoyle and thought about the monster-to-be. He imagined a stoneworker flinging the finished sculpture onto a pulley and hoisting it up to the corner of the façade where it could glower at the sea serpents that dared to threaten

Queenstown's sailors and he surmised that men were not nearly as powerful as they believed themselves to be.

The cool drops of water beaded up on the leather binding of Joe's
Bible and edged down the sleeves of his jacket but he didn't mind at all. It
was nice to sit out in the rain and the cold spring air and feel something.
Inside the church and especially within the confines of Brother James's
stuffy office it was hard for Joe to feel anything. Most of the time, Joe felt
like an actor in a school play in which no one particularly cared about
what you were saying as you got on and off without embarrassment. He
longed to find meaning in the words and was even covetous of it. He
wished that he had thought to ask the brother about this at the time for
now that the moment had passed there was nothing really to do about
it.

Joe had whisked the water droplets away from his book and was about
to start downhill when a boy who looked a year or two older than himself came out from under one of the eaves of the building with a small
pane of decorated glass in his hands. Joe was immediately attracted to
the triangles and rectangles of red, blue, and emerald green. The blaze
of light, so sudden on such a colorless day, seemed to emanate not only
from the glass but also, strangely, from the boy. He was taller than Joe
and his long black hair hung heavily across his forehead and over his ears,
making him look like a beautiful girl. His hands were bruised and laced
with tiny cuts from the shards of glass as if Christian suffering was part
of his job description.

"What's that, mate?" the glassworker asked, a question that seemed less
of a question than an exclamation.

"Sorry," Joe muttered.

"Sorry, what? Just saying hello. I don't climb out of the darkness often
enough. I didn't think I would see any soul hanging about today." He put
down the glass and put out his hand. "My name's Severin."

"I'm Joe."

"You here for a lesson?"

"My lesson's done"

"Never done, my friend, never done."

"What are you here for?"

"I'm helping with the windows. There'll be bloody well over a hundred
of 'em when we're finished—if we're ever finished. I've been cutting glass
and pouring lead since I was twelve."

"Twelve?"

"I'm sixteen now. Can you do sums?"

"That's four years. I've lived in Queenstown for four years. I never saw you until today."

"My luck."

Joe scowled.

"I'm joshing you, Joe." Severin reached down and pulled Joe up off the rock. "Come, take a break with me."

"Don't you need to tell someone where you are going?" Joe asked as Severin stowed his tools.

"Did you see that man loitering by the West Portal—the one who's six foot two and looks like a devil?"

"Yes."

"That's Mr. Murphy, our Head of Works. You'd never tell from the look of him but he's a fair employer. We'll be grand."

The boy was now several feet ahead of Joe and Joe almost lost his footing keeping up. There was a strange urgency about everything that Severin said and did as if whatever idea he had but crossed his mind and it was tried, accepted, and executed then and there. Joe felt ambivalent about this. He usually liked having enough time to reason with the facts before committing himself to any action. Something about the choices that were now being presented to him and the framework for his decision was skewed but Joe surprised himself by discovering he did not care.

"How long have you lived here?" Joe asked as the boys reached the foot of Harbour Row and entered Mrs. Shanahan's establishment.

"You're full of questions." Severin led him to a table by the open window that looked out over the cove.

"Sorry."

"'S all right. Where's 'here'?"

"I asked you first," Joe said, smiling.

"There, now I've got a smile off you. That's more to the point."

The girl came up to them and took their orders. Severin asked for a cup of tea and two scones. She looked at Joe.

"I'm buying, if that's what's giving you pause," Severin said.

"But…"

"Don't argue with me." He looked up at the girl and grinned. "Two teas." Then, to Joe: "You can have one of my scones."

"Thanks, much."

There was a lull in the conversation. A gull cried out and swerved above in anticipation of the crumbs which custom would scatter to the pavement. A trawler sounded its horn but the air was so thick that nothing could be seen of it. Joe felt nervous as if he was being auditioned and he was underprepared. He tried to make out something of Severin behind the sweeping strands of hair and his beamy smile but he found nothing he could take hold of.

"Don't be thinking this will be a regular treat, like," Severin said. "I'm not earning that much money."

"I didn't think that," Joe answered.

"With the damned few shillings the church pays me, I'd surely starve if I didn't come down to the quay three days a week. Thanks to God the stevedores need spellsmen every now and then."

"Don't you have a ma or a pa to help out?"

"Gone with the mist of the morning."

"I'm sorry."

"Not your fault, Joe. My name's Coole and I come from a long line of Cooles who have made it on their own. I never knew my parents. Seems I washed up here like Moses in the bulrushes and that's been my story ever since."

"How do you take care of yourself?"

"I take care of myself all right."

Just then the girl returned with their tea and tray of pastries. She busily arranged the sugar bowl and creamer in a corner of the table and banged the cups together as she put them down. The awkward pause in the conversation and her small lack of grace embarrassed her and she smiled awkwardly and bowed and retreated from the table with a giggle.

"You seem to have affected the help," Joe said, smiling.

"Is it me? I thought it was you. I was guessing you do that to all the girls."

Joe blushed and blushed at the thought of blushing. What was it about Severin that Joe found so disconcerting? He wasn't like the other older boys at school who were moody and ignored Joe if he stayed out of their way. But he hardly resembled the boys his own age, the few that Joe knew well enough to call friends, who were—there didn't seem to be another word for it—uninspiring. Severin struck Joe as someone who had at least put a toe out into the sea-swell of the world.

"So tell me, Severin Coole, how do you take care of yourself?"

"You want an answer, Joe…Joe what?"

"Joe Dooley."

"Dooley. Must be a long line of them as well."

"You're changing the subject."

"So I am."

The boys laughed and tore at the scones. The way Severin talked past things, the unthrifty way they were spending the time—it all seemed to Joe a very grown-up thing to do and it made him feel happy.

"Mr. Murphy keeps a bungalow for all the boys who are working on the cathedral. It's just a wood shack at the back of the property but it has a roof that doesn't leak and a bed that I fit in. The sacristy makes us breakfast and dinner each day and I do the work that's needed. Three or four days each week, I attend the call-out on the quay and they have me repairing the ship's woodwork and hauling now and then. I like it, I'm good at it, and it's a living. What more do I need in the world?"

"I don't rightly know."

"What do you do?"

"Me?"

"Um," Severin grunted, stuffing the last of the crumbs into his mouth.

"I'm fourteen years old. I don't do anything."

"You're breathing. You're sitting here with me, finishing your tea. What else?"

"I study my catechism. I read my English history."

"English history—ugh. You're off to a bad start."

"I help my aunt around the house."

"That's chores. What do you do for fun?"

"I like music. I sing and I play the piano."

"That's better. I like music." Severin reached into his pocket and pulled out a shilling. "Now I do have to get back to work," he said. "Come on."

HALFWAY UP THE HILL THE BLESSING MIST INTENSIFIED AND RAIN began to fall. Peals of thunder filled the air. The gutters overflowed and the water gushed down the center of the street. The torrent was unavoidable; the boys' faces grew wet with rain as their shirts dripped and their footfalls squeaked. By the time they had reached the entrance to the cathedral, the boys were giddy from running and laughing.

"I've got to go back to the bungalow and change," Severin cried as they dove under an eave. "I can't go back to work this way."

"All right, then," Joe said, "Thanks again for the tea."

"Where are you going?"

"Home."

"You're not going anywhere in this storm," Severin shouted as another roll of thunder burst over them. "You'll drown with the rats. Come along with me. I can stash you until the weather clears."

"If you think it's all right…"

"'Tis."

Joe and Severin made another dash around the corner of the church. There was a small wooden building nestled against a buttress, all of twenty feet square with a slightly angled black tar roof and beams of stained timber. Joe had climbed up and down the hill to St. Colman's a thousand times and he had walked around and around the grounds of the church after services or to fly a kite and he had never seen this obviously out-of-place structure. It looked both mean and cozy at the same time, more like a clubhouse than a residence and quite inviting for all its plainness. Severin pushed the door open and he and Joe tumbled in.

Joe peered into the darkness. The room was filled with narrow beds, five along each wall with barely enough room for one person at a time to walk down the aisle. There were two windows at right angles to the door. Another door at the back led, apparently, to the W.C. The walls were bare, except for a calendar that still read March. Each boy had a wooden chair next to his bed and box beside in which they could keep their belongings. But Joe's eyes truly widened when he saw what was sitting on a small wooden table in the corner of the room—a Victor Talking Machine. It was unmistakable; its brass horn gleamed in the dull light and the dark walnut veneer looked more holy to him than any altar.

"You have a talking machine!" Joe exclaimed.

"That's Mr. Murphy's. He lent it to us so we'd have something to do at night other than to get into trouble."

"My piano teacher Miss Ryan owns one. They're amazing."

"All Murphy ever wants to listen to is John McCormack."

"John McCormack is wonderful."

"I tell you he's not that wonderful the hundredth time around."

"If Miss Ryan lets me borrow one of her recordings, can I bring it around? Wouldn't you like to hear Nellie Melba?"

"The English singer?"

"She's from Australia."

"A colonial? That's good, 'cause I don't know about anything English being rightly played around here. Don't you ever follow politics?"

"Not really."

"Hang around us, you will."

Severin stopped in front of third bed on the right and took off his shirt. He rummaged through his crate, pulled out a blue cotton jersey and threw it on the bed.

"Here, put this on," Severin said. "I'm not letting your ma think your friends would leave you to perish of cold."

Joe reached for the shirt on the bed and started to unbutton his own. Severin stood in front of him, half-naked. Joe had seen other boys without their clothes before, of course, in the changing room at the bathing pool or in medical inspection at school, but he lived in a family of women now and he was unsettled by the intimacy and air of conspiracy that his being alone with Severin created. He tried to look at the boy and not look at him at the same time and this anguished deal that he made with himself had the inevitable consequence of making him even more aware of their near-nakedness. Severin's years of laboring in the glass yards and on the docks had helped his chest and arms fill out and Joe found himself making note of the fact in contrast with his own pale adolescent form without ever actually allowing the image to enter his mind's eye. It was a thing, a thought, independent from him and without causation.

Severin reached down and took out another white shirt identical to the one he had just taken off. He threw his wet shirt on his bed. Joe picked it up and hung it over the back of the chair. He did not know why he was suddenly seized to perform this task but it seemed to him the kindest and most natural of acts and it made him very happy to do it. Then Joe picked up the blue shirt that Severin was lending him and pulled it over his head.

"My shirt looks very nice on you," Severin said as he buttoned up.

"It's too big," Joe said, the only thing he could think of saying.

"You're two years younger than me," Severin answered. "You'll grow into it."

"I'll have my sister wash it and bring it back tomorrow."

"Wash it yourself, you lazy *slaba*." Severin gave Joe a shove and Joe fell back on the bed. Severin hovered over him and Joe thought that Severin was about to hit him or kiss him, he didn't know which. The indecisive moment thrilled him. But Severin didn't hit him and he didn't kiss him either. He laughed and smiled and pulled the boy to his feet. A faint beam of light fell upon the floor.

"Lookat, the sun is coming out," Severin cried.

"I best be getting home," Joe said. He picked up his wet shirt and rolled it up into a ball. "Thanks, again for the loan."

"Bring it back when you can."

"I will. I want to come back."

Joe wasn't sure about his tone. He wanted to let Severin know he was eager to visit with him again but wanted to go about it without giving the boy the wrong impression. I've got other friends, Joe thought. He needs to know that. But in the tangle of his thoughts Joe hadn't noticed that Severin was already out the door, examining his arms in the light.

"Now, what am I going to do about all these cuts?" Severin asked, but before Joe could answer or even be certain whether or not he was being addressed at all Severin turned around and smiled at him.

"Come Tuesday at five. We'll take out a skiff."

Joe smiled back.

☌

The boys' friendship grew naturally, like everything else that season. Joe would stop at home after classes and remove the pages for *Heiden-roslein* from his music book, taking care to wrap them between two blank sheets of paper. At the bungalow, Joe would read along as Severin played the Minnie Nast recording that Mr. Murphy loaned him. It pleased Joe to look up from the page as they listened and watch Severin close his eyes and lift his head when the highest notes filled the room:

> *Röslein, Röslein, Röslein rot,*
> *Röslein auf der Heiden!*

Later in the afternoon if the weather was fine Severin would lead Joe down to the quay and show him his work, fine knots pulled tightly against the scraping tide and shiny, clean joists with fresh sawdust like ladies' powder on the surface. It always seemed to Joe that he was doing the watching and Severin was having the experience and he longed to learn how his friend so easily assimilated the world. Time stood still for Joe then. Their relationship was closely calibrated upon fragile exchanges and unspoken affinities; it was a piece of delicate lacework that neither cared to fret.

ONE SOFT LATE SPRING EVENING WHEN THE SUN BURNED UNUSU-
ally hot in the harbor and a stillness lay upon the heat, Severin failed to
turn up for an appointment at the bungalow. Joe tried to go out of his
way not to have anything to do with the other boys on Mr. Murphy's
work crew and as a consequence of this he found he had no coin to cast
upon them in his search for information.

"How the blazes am I supposed to know where Coole's gone to?" one
of the boys replied to Joe's inquiry. "Am I his ma?"

"You might find him at Jem Rogers," another boy shouted, laughing.
Joe guessed at the reference but he felt shamed to think of it and fled.

The six o'clock bells were rung and then the sevens and still Joe could
find no sign of Severin. Joe was out past his time and his ma would be
concerned but he felt as if this last, great mystery had to be solved and
damn the consequences. He walked the length of the harbor and was
now feeling both exhausted and lost but he did not care. He would walk
out to sea before giving up, he would. Just then he saw the crumpled
form of a boy propped up against the sea wall and knew that it was
Severin. He ran to him.

"Severin? Severin!"

The boy looked up. There was a stigma of blood across his nose and a
blot of it had formed upon his shirt. "Is that you, Joe? I'm sorry I missed
you."

"Severin—what happened to you?"

"Don't be worrying about me, Joe."

"You're caked with blood. Your shirt…your shirt is torn. What is it?"

"Bloody stevedores is what. My turn for a beating is all."

"Why did they beat you?"

Severin looked at Joe directly now. His eyes were black and wet. He
took Joe's hand and pressed it hard against his chest. "Do you feel that,
Joe?"

"It's your heart."

"Yes."

"So?"

"That's the answer to your question, Joe."

"I don't understand."

"There's a change coming, Joe—a change in the world. Those of us
without aren't going to be without forever and those that have everything

can lose everything in the blink of an eye. It's written in the Bible; it's written in the stars."

"What are you talking about, Severin?"

"I was beat because I refused to sign the steamship company agreement. They wanted me to swear I would never join the union."

"This is because of the union?"

"It's all because of the union. The company makes the men work ten hours a day for six days a week with no extra compensation and no right to make a collective bargain. They throw the weak ones to the wolves and beat the ones who refuse."

Severin stopped and held his hands out, palms facing the heavens. "They think this is all I have, Joe—my hands to cut the glass, my arms to plane the wood. But I have my eyes to see the world. And I have my heart to feel its pain."

"And you have me, Sev."

"Yes, Joe. You're a good friend. And we do need our friends."

"What are you going to do?"

"I'll keep to St. Colman's, Joe—you don't have to worry about that."

"But look at your face—your shirt..."

"I have other shirts, Joe. And as for this face—it'll stand me, I guess."

"Don't ever go down to the dock again, Severin."

"Oh, Joe—don't you see? The dock is the one place I've got to be. Not for me, mind you—but for the rest of us. There's a principle at stake here and I can't be bending my conscience to gain a contract. I know you understand. You'll help me."

"Not for getting beat up, I won't."

"There are ways of getting what you want without a beating, I tell you. Now..."

Severin tried to stand up. He was unsteady. Joe put his arm around Severin's waist and held tightly and together they stepped away from the wall.

"That's good," Joe said.

"Thanks, Joe."

"I just want you to be well, Sev."

"I'll be grand. How's about you pretend you have some money and stand this poor maligned dockworker a drink?"

"Lend me two shillings and I will," Joe answered, smiling.

"My money's at the bungalow."

"Let's go then."

As they climbed up the hill, Joe heard the sound of the sea splashing below and he wished it would wash clean the world with the tide. Even as he knew it wouldn't, he felt just then it might.

# Chapter 3

✦ ✦ ✦

## *Under a Field of Stars*

✦ ✦ ✦

ONE MAY MORNING JOE WALKED OVER TO THE BUNGALOW TO MEET Severin.

"You're Severin's friend, aren't ye?" a boy asked when Joe came in. He was sitting on his bed, untying his shoes.

"Um, yes."

"Sev's gone down to the quay. I don't think he'll be back till supper."

"That's all right then," Joe said, and started to go.

"All right enough for you, to leave me all alone here just because my name's not Severin," the boy went on. "Pity you came all the way up the hill just to climb back down. Stow yourself. My name's Dermot."

Joe took his hand off the door. The boy looked to be younger than Severin, closer to Joe's age. He was tall and stocky, with short auburn hair and a face wide with freckles that still hadn't faded.

"I'm Joe. Pleased to meet you, Dermot."

"The same. Now we're settled."

Joe did not expect to meet a stranger. For all the time he and Severin had been friends, Joe had grown inured to the callous indifference of the St. Colman's boys, but it had at least been a known quantity. This was something new and unmeasurable.

"Your reputation precedes you, Joe. Welcome!"

Dermot stood up and literally drove Joe into the center of the room with the sweep of his arm.

"Thank you," was all Joe could think to say.

Dermot was set upon conversation. He asked Joe about his studies and Joe went on about Bach until the other boy's evident disinterest forced him off. Out of politeness, Joe asked Dermot about his library of books on sailing and received a brief lecture on backstays and headsails. There was no one else in the bungalow and such accidental intimacy made Joe nervous. Still, there was something exceedingly attractive about Dermot's cheerfulness. As he listened, Joe caught himself looking at Dermot and thinking that his smiling, handsome face was not uninteresting and he wondered what it was about himself that attracted Dermot. It couldn't be the Bach.

After ten minutes or so, Joe excused himself and asked if he could use the W.C.

"Help yourself." Dermot waved toward the door.

Joe walked to the back of the bungalow and pushed through the little door that led to the latrine. The room was dark, even in the bright of the morning, and very tiny. The sink was practically on top of the toilet so Joe didn't have to move to wash his hands when he was done. When he turned to go out Dermot walked in.

"You don't mind, do you, Joe?"

"Mind what?"

"You know," Dermot said. "Me."

"'S all right," Joe muttered, helpless.

"I like you," Dermot said, touching Joe's belly.

"'S all right."

Dermot laughed softly. "Is that all you know how to say?"

"No."

"Shall I go on?"

"If you wish."

"'If I wish?' Are we at Oxbridge?"

"Yes, then."

"Are you scared?"

"Why should I be scared?"

"You're right. Maybe I should be scared."

That got Joe to laugh.

"Good, I've gleaned a smile. Don't you like me, Joe?"

"Yes."

"Good. Now, relax a little, won't you?"

Joe closed his eyes. He imagined himself leaving the W.C. and going back into the bungalow and watching himself. He thought it might be a useful memory. It was strange to see himself not in a mirror but the way he thought others might see him. This Joe had a presence, a glow, something like an electrical current that drew upon all that surrounded him. But when he opened his eyes, he was still there and Dermot was looking straight at him.

"Now this isn't anything we need be telling Severin Coole about," he said. "Is it?"

In June Joe received his letter of admission to the University College in Dublin. The future loomed large; even to think of it made Joe anxious. Seven years had passed since his da died; the city he knew in his boyhood was certain to be transformed. His acceptance to the college had taken him by surprise; he only applied at the suggestion of his music teacher, who apparently recognized a scholarly streak that heretofore to Joe had remained obscure. But now as the promise of it rose to the surface—a chance to gratify his love of music and his earnest desire to understand an incomprehensible world—he embraced it and grew alarmed by the intensity of his desire.

A scouting trip to Dublin was planned. Joe needed to make arrangements for the fall term and Severin had never set foot in the city. By the end of July, they had enough money to finance their adventure. Joe managed to convince his ma of both Severin's personal responsibility (in which, truth to be told, she already had confidence) and the necessity of experience. Although Joe was now nearly seventeen years old, his mother was still certain, as all women who raise children must be, that her young charge would be lost without her and it was upon this last point that Joe needed to wage his most vociferous battle. Finally, with a leap of faith and a gift of five pounds, Joe's ma offered him her blessing.

It was Severin's idea to continue on to Belfast. All that summer he had been listening in at the docks. He overheard whispers of a great fight. The men talked of dockhands prohibited from joining a union and workers threatening to strike. The Belfast Steam Company was recruiting blacklegs from the south and the laborers needed all the bodies they could get. And not just the dockhands: there were carters who took the goods from the quays to the rails and miners who loaded their coal on the carts. Joe listened with wonderment as Severin told him about Jim

Larkin, the great union organizer, and the movement to unite all the working classes of Ireland from the north to the south and from the east to the west—along the docks, in the mines, and everywhere between. There was something intensely romantic about Severin's political fervor that drew Joe in and made him wish to enlist. Joe felt that his own passions were personal and internal and it made him feel a part of something to fall in with his friend.

"Don't be shy now, give me your hand." Severin shouted to Joe as the train whistle shrieked and the gears unlocked with a heavy, low groan. The train had started to move; Joe had one instant to act. He heaved his leather suitcase on to the top step of the doorway and flung out his right arm in supplication. Severin took hold of it and pulled Joe on board. Joe was panting and sweating and his chest swelled and ached. There was nothing Severin could do but laugh.

"That's right," Joe gasped, "Make a mockery of me."

"If you hadn't been so doddering with your shirts and toiletries we would have had enough time to make the train without risking a limb, you know."

"You don't need to remind me."

"Apparently I do."

Severin picked up Joe's suitcase and his own, smaller bag. "What have you got in here, anyway? We're only to be gone a week and I'm feeling enough weight for a transatlantic voyage."

"'Tis only the necessities."

"Says your ma."

"Says no one."

Joe pushed the car door open. Queenstown was a terminal station and there were free seats on both aisles. Severin lifted the bags into the overhead compartment and threw himself next to the window. "Here will do."

"Don't get too comfortable," Joe warned him. "We have to change in Cork."

"I'll get as comfortable as I wish, thank you."

"You're most welcome."

By the time they reached Cork station they were running ten minutes late. The boys collected their bags and rushed down the platform, scanning the signboard for the indicator. Track three. Off. Back up the iron steps, hoist the bags above, all settled in—a hiss, a squeal, onwards. The carriage lurched and clanged and inched down the incline.

"Forty winks and all, chum?" Severin asked.

"Don't let me stop you."

Severin made a few dramatic attempts to claim a larger allotment of the seat than was his due and then curled up against the window and fell asleep. Joe watched him intently and claimed temporary guardianship of their domain. It was his portion of the relationship the two friends had forged across the years. Severin was always the more adventurous of the pair, suggesting mad dashes to unexplored places at unusual hours and demonstrating his superior strength by taking down ripe fruit with a rock or volunteering to carry a larger share of the day's quarry of spoils. But behind this braggadocio, Joe was allowed to see subterranean rivulets of insecurity. There was the time when Severin had a fever and allowed Joe nurse him back to health with cups of tea and borrowed recordings of Puccini. They listened together, Severin tucked in his cot and Joe on the floor with the tray and the sheet music:

> *Diedi gioielli della Madonna al manto,*
> *e diedi il canto agli astri, al ciel,*
> *che ne ridean più belli.*

> *Nell'ora del dolor*
> *perchè, perchè, Signor,*
> *ah, perchè me ne rimuneri così?*

As Joe watched his friend sleep, he thought about this and took advantage of the opportunity to review his feelings about Severin and see if they could be sorted into categories. They could not. Joe didn't consider himself much of a lothario, but he often imagined Severin in the role. He would watch his friend plant a kiss on Sheila Connor's cheek or even put his arm around her. Joe thought about Severin's success with girls much more than his own and with this discovery he concluded that he wasn't himself that interested in the subject unless it directly affected his friend. To be strictly honest, it was his own cheek he longed to have Severin kiss and his own chest he wished pressed under Severin's embrace.

As if taking his cue from Joe's unconscious, Severin shifted his position in the seat and leaned his head and chest upon Joe's shoulder. Still, the boy slept deeply. Joe reassured himself that Severin had no palpable knowledge of his longings and was merely sipping at the comfort he felt in the company of a pliant and pleasant friend. Opportunities to escalate the emotional temperature of their friendship presented themselves to Joe many times and at each turn things remained at their usual simmer.

There was a day quite recently when Severin turned up unexpectedly at Joe's aunt's door at eleven o'clock in the evening and asked Joe to come out with him for a walk. The household was asleep and would have never taken notice of it but it alarmed Joe to think of the impropriety of it all and it thrilled him nonetheless. They ended up at the end of the quay and sat side by side with their bare feet dangling in the cold water. An inexplicit disillusion lay across Severin's brow as he talked about how poorly his bosses on the docks treated him, how he wished he'd taken better care of his schooling, and how he longed for a family of his own. At the end of his speech, Severin leaned over and Joe thought that he was going to kiss him but instead he just laid his head down on Joe's shoulder and left it there, his soft breathing audible in the surrounding silence.

Just yesterday, when Joe came by the bungalow to help Severin pack for their trip, there was yet another chance for him to do something about their tenuous physicality and force it to be expressed or quenched. In fact, Severin's action was so overt that Joe felt it had to be deliberate, except for the fact that he knew his friend well and knew him to be so forthright and confident that he could not believe than in this matter alone his friend would be indirect.

They were alone in the bungalow. Severin was arranging his shirts in his duffel bag, taking out one and putting another one in for no good purpose. Finally, he threw one of his shirts at Joe, of lovely green linen with a white-stripe pattern. "I hate this shirt," he announced. 'See if it fits you."

"What, so you can hate it on me instead?"

"Don't be a donkey. Here." Severin started to unbutton Joe's shirt. Joe shivered and fretted but let him continue. "Hold still."

"I can take my own shirt off," Joe protested.

"Sometimes I wonder."

Severin took the gifted shirt and unfolded it and threw it over Joe's head to help him put it on. They were standing in the middle of the floor in front of Severin's cot and their position meant that Joe was face to face with Severin and separated from him by a few inches. Severin was taller than Joe and his mouth was exactly opposite Joe's nose and just as Severin was looking down to button the first button on Joe's chest he brushed

Joe's nose with his lips and if not exactly kissed it seemed to offer some sort of benediction. It was all done within the instant that the buttonhole was closed and the space was cleared, so quickly and without emphasis or even notice that afterwards Joe could not even be sure if it happened at all. That was twenty-four hours ago.

THE TRAIN ARRIVED AT KINGSBRIDGE STATION AT HALF-PAST TEN. They had three hours in Dublin before their departure to Belfast and Joe wanted to make the most of it. Severin was a novice in Dublin and one hundred and eighty minutes from now Joe was determined to make a convert of him. Their first stop was Talbot Street.

"This is where we lived until the da died," Joe said, as they dropped their bags on the sidewalk. Joe pointed to a window on the second floor. "That was my view."

"Constricted, no?" said Severin, peering up at the small and chalky window.

"Not to a ten year old."

Joe had written to Mr. O'Connor, his landlord at no. 10. Mr. O'Connor remembered him fondly. The shop was long gone, replaced by a respectable linen store, but his old room above was vacant and if Joe wanted it, it was his for five shillings a week. Joe needed a place and it was only a half hour walk to St. Stephen's Green and his classes at the college. The deal was struck and Joe was to come by to sign the lease and see what he might need.

Mr. O'Connor answered the bell. "Lord almighty, will you look at you?"

"*Conas atá tú,* Mr. O'Connor?"

"*Tá mé go maith.* The last time I saw you, boy, you came up to my waist. Haven't you turned out to be a fine young man?"

"Last I looked, sir." Joe smiled. "This is my friend, Severin Coole."

"I'm pleased to meet you, Mr. Coole. And now it's nearly time for lunch. Would you and your friend care to join me for a sandwich and a beer?'

"That's a lovely offer, Mr. O'Connor, but we're on our way to Belfast and we have to catch the 3:10 out of Amiens."

"Belfast, eh? Well, there'll be plenty of time in September."

"Yes, I'll be back. September fifteenth."

"Take a look-see?"

"Yes, that would be grand."

Joe climbed up the familiar staircase. Mr. O'Connor turned the key in the lock on the door and let the young men in.

"It's tiny," Severin said.

"Welcome to Dublin," Mr. O'Connor answered.

The room was the same as it last appeared to Joe seven years ago, minus the furniture and the piano, of course. Even the crack in the wall over the sink was still there, although Joe's memory must have played tricks on him for he recalled it being bigger.

"I can find you a better desk and a decent lamp to read by."

Joe smiled. "It'll do fine, Mr. O'Connor, just fine. Where's your pen?"

ON THE WAY OUT, JOE PASSED TWO WOMEN SITTING ON WOODEN chairs in front of no. 12. The storefront was vacant and he couldn't help but wonder.

"Whatever happened to the German family that lived here?" Joe asked.

"Is it the barber you're asking about?" the first one replied.

"Yes," said Joe. "Vogeler."

"Vogeler, Vogeler," she said, turning the word over in her mouth looking for clues to its meaning. She turned to her companion. "Whatever happened to them?"

"Oh, the shop closed up years ago…aught four, aught five, was it? I was here then, wasn't I, Mrs. Shea?"

"I do believe you were, Mrs. O'Hanlon."

"There was a boy…" Joe began, hopefully.

"A boy—yes, a madder-haired lad. Poor boy, with no mother in the world."

"Yes, that was he."

"The old man wanted to go back to Germany, he did. And the boy would have nothing of it. There was a terrible row."

"Oh, no."

"Oh, nothing violent, mind you. A vivid disagreement, you might say. I do believe they went their separate ways. Herr Vogeler packed up his combs and scissors and sailed back to the continent, and the boy…the boy…"

"His name was Harry."

"Ah—yes. Harry. I believe Harry went by himself to America."

"By himself, to America? But he must have been barely fifteen years old."

"You knew the lad?"

"He was my best friend."

"Ah…" said the first one, spanning the years in her mind.

"Water under the bridge, sir," said the other.

"Joe, the time," Severin interrupted.

"The time," Joe muttered. "The time."

THE TRAIN PULLED IN TO GREAT VICTORIA STREET STATION AT HALF-past six. From there it was a half-mile walk to Corporation Square. They heard the rally before they saw it—muffled cheers and chants chased in turn by a hurrah and an angry roar. When Joe and Severin turned the corner of the Custom House and peered down the street they were greeted with a scene straight out of a medieval woodcut. On one side of the square there was crowd of approximately two hundred strikers armed with barrel staves, rakes, and pikes. Across the square, in the opposite corner, a nearly equal number of police officers and militia stood at arms. In the middle, there was a haggard assembly of blacklegging men looking like a flock of sheep lost in the balance between pasture and slaughter.

"Union people, down this way," a bearded man with a megaphone shouted. That was a good enough clue for Severin and he grabbed hold of Joe's arm and pulled him over.

"We're up from Dublin to swell the ranks," Severin said to the man as another volley of chants rose up from the men. "What can we do to help you?"

"Have you nothing but those satchels to defend yourself with?"

"Would I be needing anything more?" said Severin. "I've my hands and my wits and that's good enough for any Irishman."

"Right now I'd advise you to keep both close at hand, son."

"What is going to happen?" Joe asked.

"If I knew, I'd tell you. Jim Larkin's coming and he's going to speak. That's what all the excitement's about."

"Jim Larkin himself," Severin said.

"He comes in no other form that I know of. Here…" The man handed Joe a packet of papers tied up with a piece of string. "Do something useful. Hand these out."

Joe looked at the sheet of paper. It was a broadside for the strikers, an exhortation in uneven letterpress of the kind that Joe saw being carried out from the basement of Talbot Street all during his boyhood and it was strange to feel himself on the giving end of history for a change.

"This is what we came for, Joe, isn't it?" Severin asked. "The good fight."

"If any fight is good."

Joe attempted to distribute his stash of papers. A middle-aged man in an ill-fitting suit pushed the sheet back at him and called him a papist and an old woman startled him by spitting at his feet but otherwise he was greeted with respect and at times with genuine appreciation. It was cumbersome to try to hand over the paper while kicking his suitcase along the pavement in front of him but there was nothing to be done about it. Severin had been the smarter of the two after all, hooking his bag over one shoulder and carrying it about him like a gleaner's satchel. It gave him an authoritative look although Joe surmised he met less resistance merely because he looked older.

At a little past eight o'clock as the sun was setting behind the spires of the university the crowd began to jostle in the manner of fanatics at a football match when their team is making a move. Then the jussive voice of Jim Larkin floated out above them all:

"My colleagues, my fellow patriots, my friends…I thank you for coming out here tonight and demonstrating in such a strong and forceful manner your overwhelming commitment to the hard-working dock men and their allies in our attempt to gain fair representation and decent wages for all working men in Ireland. There is no limit to my love of the cause. Tomorrow, I return to Dublin to continue our fight but I felt it appropriate to spend my final night in your beautiful city out here in the warm summer air, by your side, with you, as I will be with you in spirit. We will fight on together until the victory is ours."

The crowd cheered. Severin poked Joe's arm and smiled. Joe felt light-headed from exhaustion and the heat and by the closeness of the crowd. He found his attention drifting as Larkin built to his climax. He thought of the words that burst out from the podium as things that would drift down upon the audience like balloons and he followed them as they settled. There was the word "commitment" landing on the outstretched arm of a young man with red hair, tears of anger streaking down his cheek as his drove his stave into the sky. And there was the word "victory" sailing down to touch the brim of the hat of another man, his eyes fiery at the thought of it and his fists clenched in anticipation.

Joe's reverie extended to his friend standing beside him. He heard the word "love" and he thought of Severin's stubbled cheek resting against his arm on the train. He heard the word "together" and he imagined the rest of the time they had—these few days in Belfast, another month along the quays or in the bungalow before Dublin and schooling and a separation for who knew how long. It was not just the parting which upset Joe but the long trail of emotions which emanated from it—all that music to be heard alone, all those teas where he was the only one at the table, and the Liffey flowing indifferently past everyone, friend and stranger alike.

And then, as one waking from a dream, Joe realized that Larkin's speech had ended and the crowd of strikers had flowed into the center of the square. The police and soldiers moved into position, pinning the blacklegs between them. Joe saw the staves flash in the gaslight above him and come down on the heads and the backs of the blacklegs. The police raised their clubs in defense and the pickets crept behind. The sound of the space which only moments ago had been filled with the ringing tones of rhetoric now hushed with the whisking of air and the soft wail of injured men. Joe heard the deadened thumping sounds of legs and chests and even heads being hit.

As the wave of bigger and heavier men flowed into him Joe let go of his suitcase and linked his arms around Severin's chest. Severin tucked his bag into his stomach and the two boys fell to the ground. The bodies tumbled over them and someone's broken stave slashed the back of Joe's hand. The hurt flashed like lightning and then, dulled, rolled into Joe's stomach and made him feel sick. It was not fear he felt but abandonment, as if there was no more surety in the world. And still the crowd marched over him. They crossed like a cavalry, these riotous men, now all mingled together into one undifferentiated army—the soldier and the worker, the guilty and the innocent. Then, like a rolling wave, they sank, leaving bodies in their breach. The square grew quieter still, and then silent.

"Joe, are you all right?" Severin whispered.

"I'm bleeding. I've lost my suitcase."

"They're arresting people. We've got to run. Can you run?"

"I think so."

"Do you see that street lamp, over there?"

"Yes."

"Run with me for it. We can get out from there."

"Severin…"

"Do you trust me, Joe? We don't have the time for any doubts."

"I do."

"Now."

Severin stood up. A policeman shouted at him to halt. He started to run. "Let's go, Joe."

"But…"

"Only the soldiers have guns. The police can't stop us. Run."

Joe fell in behind Severin. Two dozen or more other men who were uninjured were running across the square. Police orders filled the air but there were no gunshots.

"This way, Joe. Here."

They turned toward the quay and ran north. Three men ran after them, but they were strikers not policemen. Joe could hardly breathe for the exertion. He found strength in never letting Severin out of his sight. Finally, the street light faded and the pursuit ended. Severin unhitched his bag from his shoulder and flung himself down along the dock's edge. "We can rest here, Joe. It's safe."

"I've lost my suitcase, Sev."

"My God, Joe—is this all you care about?"

"Right now it is."

"Lookat. I've got my stuff. We'll be fine. It's the workers we've got to concern ourselves with. We're outnumbered and this is war."

"Isn't that always the case?"

"We did our part, we did."

"We did something, all right. I was scared at first, but then I found out I wasn't nearly so scared at all."

"You know what, Joe? So was I. But we're grand now, aren't we?"

"Yes."

"We came through, no fear." Severin smiled. "And look at the shape of you."

"You're no better."

"A couple of scrapplings, aren't we? How's your hand?"

"The bleeding's stopped. Hurts, though."

"Let's see if we can make our way back to Victoria Street and find ourselves a bed and some grub. What d'ye say to that?"

"I say aye and I second it."

"Meeting adjourned."

A FELLOW AT THE STRIKE HEADQUARTERS ALLOWED JOE TO HELP himself to a bandage and gave them each a glass of water and a piece of bread. "All our cots are spoken for, but if you don't mind the stars we can give you a pair of blankets and put you on the roof."

"Offer accepted."

Joe found a sink and washed his hands and face. The dried blood melted under the stream and he felt dizzy at the sight of it. In the mirror he noticed a bruise on his forehead that he hadn't felt before. Suddenly the strength and the courage drained out of him and he fell to his knees on the floor. Severin, who had been searching through his bag for something clean to sleep in, saw Joe collapse and ran to his side.

"Joe? Joe? Are you all right?"

"I'm grand, Sev. Just tired is all."

"Up to the roof with ye."

Severin pointed Joe toward a metal ladder in the corner of the room that led to a trap door. They climbed up together, Joe first with Severin behind holding Joe's legs to steady him. Then Severin climbed back down and returned with two green felt blankets.

"Here you go, mate," Severin said, laying out the blanket for Joe and smoothing it down for him.

"Thanks."

Joe liked being on the roof under the stars. The heat of the day might have lingered on the pavement but fifty feet above the street you could smell the sea and feel the air cooled by the breeze off the water. It was pleasant and it eased his pain.

"So, what did you make of today?" Severin asked.

"How d'you mean?"

"Walking into a riot and all."

"Well, I don't rightly think it's fair to give a man employment and tell him because of that he has to act like a slave."

"'Tis true."

"On the other hand, I don't see how threatening a man with a stick will ever solve anything."

"Way of the world, Joe, way of the world."

"I'm sorry. I do try to see all sides of a situation."

"Don't let them hear you talking that way at the headquarters."

"Don't worry. *Entre nous.*"

"What's that?"

"It's French, for 'just between us.'"

"Well, just between us, Joe, I'm sorry I talked you into coming here." Severin avoided looking at Joe as he laid out his blanket. "I never expected you'd get hurt."

"It's nothing one expects," Joe answered. "I told my ma and my aunt I needed to have some experience and I guess I was right about that."

"You'll heal before you get home, you will."

"Yes, I think so."

"It's nice up here, ain't it?"

"Nice to get away from the heat, sure."

"I meant nice being up here with you."

"*Cara macree.*"

"Thanks for coming with me, Joe."

"I wouldn't have stayed home for all the tea in China."

Just then, the moon started to rise and Joe saw Severin's face reflected in its light. He had forgotten how beautiful Severin was to him but it was hard not to credit it at a moment like this. Joe looked straight into Severin's eyes. He hoped that what he was thinking could not be read in his own eyes for he was thinking how much he loved his friend and even more he was thinking how much he would like to kiss him. But Joe often underestimated how clearly he communicated and this was one of those instances.

"Lookat, Joe. We need to clear the air about something."

Joe held his breath.

"We've been best of friends for—how long?"

"Going on three years, I suppose."

"Three years, then. Don't you think I've thought a lot about our friendship all that time?"

"How d'ye mean?"

"You know perfectly well what I mean. I'm nineteen years old, Joe. I'm not a kid anymore. I want to get on in the world, do something with my life, find a girl and settle down."

"Is this something I don't want to do?"

"I think you know you don't."

"Sev?"

"Do you really want to find a girl, Joe?"

"I don't know what you're talking about."

"I think you do."

Joe turned away from Severin and sat up with his arms crossed over his knees. He looked up at the stars arrayed above him and took in the beauty of it all as he felt himself shiver. Funny, he wasn't cold. It was something else. And he knew if he didn't face it down here he might never be able to face it down again. He was challenging the deepest part of his courage.

"Please kiss me, Severin."

Severin climbed up from his blanket and walked around to face Joe. He crouched down before him and took Joe's face in his hands. Then he pulled Joe toward him and kissed him. Joe reached up with his good hand. "Thanks, Sev."

"I love you, Joe. But this is all I can do."

"I know. I've known."

"So have I."

"You have?"

"It's all right. I'll always be your friend. Always."

"Sev…"

"Now let's not go and ruin everything by turning it into a novel, shall we?"

Joe smiled.

"You're a spectacular guy…and not only that. You're brilliant and talented and—as evidenced by your behavior this evening—a very brave and principled person to boot. That's pretty much all of the Joe I know."

"Would you shut up now?"

"Sure."

Severin leaned over and kissed Joe again. "How's that for shutting up?"

"'Twill serve. Now go to sleep, Severin."

"Good night, Joe."

"Good night."

The two young men lay in silence for thirty seconds or so. Then Joe started laughing softly.

"Fine, then," Severin said. "I'll bite. What's so funny?"

"I was only thinking of the poor girl you are going to marry."

"Poor? How so?"

"I wonder, will she ever know until it's too late how really bad a kisser you are."

"Good night, Joe."

"*Codladh sámh.*"

"*Codladh sámh,* Joe. Indeed."

# Chapter 4

❖ ❖ ❖

## A Kin of Song

❖ ❖ ❖

JUNE 1, 1911

Dear Severin,

It is hard to credit, but I graduate in less than two weeks. Wasn't it a moment ago we were in Queenstown cheering my admission? Now Chronos has me in his maw and I am struggling to break free. Yesterday I sat my chemistry examination; it is a wonder no.86 is still standing. One of my formulae was sufficiently inaccurate to the point of filling the laboratory with pale yellow smoke and we were forced to temporarily evacuate the building. I was reassured that this happens with clocklike regularity but I was unnerved nonetheless. And this is only the first leg of the race. In order to gain my diploma, I need to dazzle the professoriate with my knowledge of Johnson, prove worthy of Spinoza, climb a ladder rope, and secure a position on the Dublin Board of Trade (this last, alas, is an exaggeration). You should be glad of your craft.

I would like to see you. It has been too long since we have been 'at ease' together and now that I am soon to be sprung from the clutches of college life I fear that my standing will only become more precarious. There seems little chance I can afford to go home this summer but perhaps you can shake yourself loose for a weekend and we can languish together on the strand at Blackrock. "Home." Does it seem curious to you that I still call Queenstown "home"? After all, I haven't lived with my family since 1907. But they say "home is where the heart is" and after all only my brain is in Dublin. What's left of it, anyway.

Time to put down my pen and pick up my books. Smile when you read this, and I'll do the same when I read your reply.

Your friend,

Joe.

THERE WAS A PILLAR-BOX ALONG ST. STEPHEN'S GREEN AND JOE carefully deposited his letter there. Little rituals comforted him and this was one of the most important ones. He never failed to pass the pillar-box whether he had a letter for it or not. It was his preeminent superstition.

Joe was due at the College four days of each week. Tuesdays and Thursdays he would stop on Grafton Street for a sticky bun and some tea; on Wednesdays and Fridays his first class was an entire hour earlier and he only had time for an apple. Joe liked the calm and quiet of the green at that hour of the morning; he would sit on a bench there and admire the façade of the Bank of Ireland gleaming in the mist before turning around the corner and climbing the steps to his classroom.

This lifeline to Severin Coole was maintained because Joe was unsure of the strength of his local affiliations. Other students were exiled on the North Side; it wasn't merely a function of geography. It was as if all his fellows were speaking a language for which he only grasped the approximate translation. Joe postulated two reasons for this; the first, which he could readily admit to himself, was that he did not share their interest in women. This being unspoken of in mixed company remained unnoticed. The second, which in truth was far more distressing to him, was what he called his sympathetic imagination. In the company of Jesuits, he defended the Church of England; amongst recruits in the Brotherhood, he found common ground with the R.I.C. When a student committee proposed requiring knowledge of the Gaelic language as a prerequisite for granting a degree Joe signed up at once and drafted their charge. He was always straddling an issue and always striving for amalgamation. If he could never guess at anyone's intentions at least he could leave them guessing as to his own.

The Choral Union was his sanctuary. Over the years Joe had risen to serve as the principal tenor and with his position came influence. One morning this past winter just before the beginning of the term, Joe had knocked on Dean Stephen's door.

"Who's there?" the dean cried.

"It's Joseph Dooley, sir."

"Ah, come in, Mr. Dooley."

"Thank you, sir."

"And how may I help you on this fine, cold morning, Mr. Dooley?"

"I've come as a representative of the Choral Union, sir," Joe began. "We wish to make a few adjustments to the Spring Concert Program."

The dean pulled down his spectacles and looked over them at Joe.

"Tell me about these…adjustments."

"Frankly, sir, we want to present an entirely new program."

"How ambitious," the dean said, smiling. "But I'm hardly an expert in choral music. I would think you would be better off speaking directly with Prof. Moreland about any recommendations."

"It's not for recommendations we're approaching you, if I may say so, sir."

"Don't be redundant, Mr. Dooley. 'If I may say so' is redundant."

"I'm sorry, sir."

Joe's rhythm was ruined by Dean Stephen's rhetorical interjection. There was an uncomfortable pause.

"What is it, then?" the dean asked.

"We would like to present a program consisting entirely of Irish music…"

"Hmmm…"

"…I mean songs written by Irish-born composers or representing the national spirit. And if…"

"I know what you mean, Mr. Dooley," the dean said, interrupting Joe. "I had been under the impression that the entire repertoire of the Choral Union was not incompatible with the national spirit."

"The Irish national spirit, sir."

"Get to the point, Mr. Dooley. Show me your proposed program."

Joe pulled out a sheet of paper from his jacket pocket and handed it to the dean. The dean took longer than he should have to read it.

"You can see…" Joe began.

"I can see," said the dean, nodding. "The folk songs are fine. I appreciate the inclusion of 'The Bard Of Armagh'—the Ulster boys will be happy. But I find the preponderance of Thomas Moore frankly a little too politically charged."

"Begging your pardon, sir, but I think it is necessary to include Mr. Moore in any program of Irish music."

"That is precisely my point, Mr. Dooley. I think your whole idea is politically charged and I will only allow it if Mr. Moore's name is left off the program."

"Not sing any Moore?" Joe asked.

At this, Dean Stephen removed his eyeglasses and smiled. "I said his name must be left off the program. I didn't say anything about his songs."

THE CONCERT WAS A SUCCESS. THE LORD MAYOR OF DUBLIN, HEAR-ing of the nationalist bent of the program after one of the more sly boys in the choir leaked the handbill to the *Irish News*, invited the singers to perform at Mansion House. Joe was used to the shabby Georgian pillars of the College Green buildings with their peeling paint and crumbling steps and he was amazed by the glitter of the gold trim on the stair rails and the tiny chandelier bulbs in their copper trellises. He borrowed Timothy Freeman's suit for the evening and it did not fit him well; the trousers were too long and the jacket was too tight and Joe feared that if he tripped and fell his strangulated cry for help would never be heard.

The front of the room was filled with ladies and gentlemen from the mayor's office. They were seated on brocade-covered chairs and fanning themselves against the unusual spring warmth. Behind them, a number of the student body had arrayed themselves in uneven rows that spread to the bowfront windows. A dozen or so of the boys had brought their girlfriends. These women were dressed in gowns of pink and aubergine that helped to soften the black and white of the men's wear, the pattern of which spread to the grand piano, the whitewashed walls and the marble tile floor. Even the music was presented most decorously, brought out by the page-turner, a third-year student named Donal McCormack with whom Joe had intermittently been sleeping.

When the moment came to perform, the Lord Mayor entered to gentle applause.

"I want to thank you all for coming, and I especially want to thank Dean Stephen of the University College for arranging this concert and for allowing their Choral Union to perform for us. It is a font of civic and even national pride to me, as it should be to all Irish men and women. Gentlemen…"

The choral master held his baton. The first notes of "The Last Rose Of Summer" echoed around the room:

'Tis the last rose of summer left blooming alone.
All her lovely companions are faded and gone.
No flower of her kindred, no rosebud is nigh
To reflect back her blushes and give sigh for sigh…

Joe raised his voice in celebration. The sound of his own voice always calmed him and as he sang he found his heart filling with sweetness and happiness. How beautiful a room to hear music! How wonderful, to be standing here surrounded by these sounds, these walls, these people! He forgot entirely about his cuffs, the chafe on his neck, the silent swallowing of nerves that consumed him as the boys assembled in the hall. He found he didn't even have to look at the printed sheets anymore. This was his life, his family, his kin of songs. He wanted to share this moment with Donal but the boy was intently focusing on the music and didn't look up.

After the concert Joe shimmied his way into standing next to Donal on the receiving line. As each of the guests took his hand and said thank you, Joe turned to Donal with a conspiratorial smile. Finally, the line broke up.

"Brilliant," Joe said, taking Donal's hand.

"I turn the pages with the best of 'em, don't I?"

"That you do."

"I'm certain you'd rather watch me turn them than hear me sing them."

"I give lessons, you know. I would love to teach you."

"I'm sure you would."

Just then, a young man came up to Donal and embraced him forcefully.

"Dick, you made it!"

Joe stood aside.

"Joe, this is my brother, Richard. Dick, this is Joe Dooley, our tenor potissimus."

"I'm pleased to meet you, Joe. Donal sings your praises."

"Better I sing praises than sing, right, Joe?"

"Harmony is not one of your attributes."

"Thanks to God, I have many others."

"Lookat," Richard McCormack said to Joe, "I'm up from Wicklow for the day. It would be my pleasure to buy you dinner. That is, if you don't already have other plans."

"I do not."

"Grand."

THEY ATE AT THE SHELBURNE AND JOE HAD A STEAK AND TWO glasses of wine. It was not the fare he was accustomed to and it loosened his tongue. He went on about his future or lack thereof and described in detail the adventure of living from hand to mouth in a North Side flat. At some point in between his recounting of the month he had to practice minus his F below middle C because he couldn't afford to pay to repair the string and the confession that his borrowed suit of clothes had to be back in Timothy Freeman's closet before ten o'clock Joe understood that he was losing his perspective.

Richard McCormack was a businessman. He owned a newspaper in Ballydowling and lived with his wife in a cottage in the mountains. It struck Joe as very rational and he wondered aloud what he would have to do to secure such a peaceful and relatively prosperous arrangement for himself.

"Have you ever given any thought to military training?" Richard asked Joe. "The English Army pays quite well and if you sign up for the reserve you can have a steady income."

"I don't rightly think it ever occurred to me," Joe answered.

"I'm certain if more artists knew about the opportunity they would embrace it," Richard continued. "It's an elegant solution to the problem of earning money and carrying on with your work. You spend a few days each week palling around in the barracks in a uniform. They throw five pounds a month at you and you have the rest of your time to write or teach or do whatever it is you want to."

"You make it sound like a holiday," Joe said.

"…a holiday where you get shot," Donal added.

Richard ruffled his brother's hair and gave him a cuff to the cheek. "No one gets shot," he said. "You shoot at targets."

"Assuming you can aim," Joe said.

"There's hard work involved. They teach you how to clean, load, and shoot a rifle. You learn signaling, transport, and strategy. You drill and drill and drill. And you owe them your skin, there's no ambiguity about that. But it's focused and every man is in the same boat and you've a real sense of doing something for the common good."

"Plus that fiver," said Donal.

"Plus that fiver."

"I could use the money."

"You could use the time, too. Find yourself a full-time job and you'll be sleeping straight through your evenings."

"I could teach on my free days."

"Think about it, Joe. I've volunteered and I love it. Tell Donal if you want to do anything about it and he'll get in touch with me. I'll introduce you to the right people. We can get you a non-com at Beggars Bush. It's five blocks from the Green; if you tutor at the college you won't even need to get on a tram."

"But the British Army?"

"I can't see you trading your capeen for the khaki, Joe," Donal said. "My brother is an *amadan* for the empire but I expect more of you."

"Lookat, I understand there are a lot of good reasons not to do it," Richard responded. "But I can assure you, you won't be shooting at any Irishmen. You won't be shooting at anyone at all. And when we do have to defend your country—be it England or Ireland or just an incident in Ballsbridge—wouldn't you rather know how to do it than not?"

"I suppose so."

"Think it over and keep tight with my brother."

"I will," Joe said.

"No problem doing that," Donal said, smiling.

JUNE 16, 1911

Dear Joe,

It was grand to hear from you. Congratulations on your attaining your diploma! It is a great accomplishment by any standard and you know we share the highest ones.

I have not neglected to write you out of lack of love. My work on the cathedral has ended and all my waking hours are filled with thoughts of how I might get on. There's a man comes down to the docks each week with a new paper they call the *Irish Worker*. They've got a plan for organizing us and you know how much I want to be a part of that but there's no money in it, I fear. I may be a man on the loose after all. Can you really stand a visit from your poor Cork cousin this summer? How about August? It has been too long and I'd love to see you.

I'd be telling you about the girleens I was getting and all but I'd be making it up knowing how easily you're impressed. You can count on me for trouble. Take care and write back if you can afford the stamp.

Your pal,<br>
*Sev.*

JUNE 24, 1911

Dear Sev,

You must imagine how happy I was to receive your letter. I hope you're sitting down when you're reading this because I am sharing some news with you that may knock you over. I am training for special reserve status in the army. Are you still there or have you fallen unconscious? Let me fill you in.

After graduation I was completely adrift. I owed Mr. O'Connor two months' rent and my old piano was so out of tune that I couldn't play it myself let alone think of giving lessons and who would want a lesson on that anyway? Think, Joe, I says. You need a new piano and you need to eat and a degree from UCD isn't going to get you either. Then I remembered a man I met at the spring concert who told me the army pays you five pounds a month to train you. Five pounds, Sev! If I could put one away every month I could have the down payment on a spinet in a year.

You know we've a Republican strain at the college. They're rightly suspicious of me. So are you, I bet. But this is an Irish regiment I've joined. We're largely County Meath men and most of us are Catholic. I feel right at home. And I can bring down a partridge with a single shot. A new Joe, eh?

It's not the same telling you all this in words. I long to
have you with me, you know that. Come in mid-August
if you can; the weather will be fine and I get relieved for a
long weekend. Tell me you will.

All my love,

Joe.

THE BARRACKS AT BEGGARS BUSH WERE A RAMSHACKLE AFFAIR with
only enough bunks for half the population and no training grounds to
speak of; when recruits drilled they were marched along the Grand Canal
like driven animals or, even worse, set up along the periphery of St. Stephen's Green for the amusement of the picnickers. When he first signed
on, Richard McCormack was the only man in the regiment Joe knew
but he found that the common ridicule they faced and the relentless
pressure for precision and order they were under formed a bond between
them that surprised him with its elasticity. The petty inequalities of class
rank or grade were gone; the biases of favoritism and prejudice were sup-
pressed and everyone's misery was a shared resource.

Joe discovered he had an aptitude for army life. This fact was revealed
to him one June afternoon. Their drill leader had impetuously and perhaps deliberately ordered the men to march with haversacks filled with
a three-day supply of dry clothing, food, and water, "for emergency preparedness," he said, despite the knowledge that they were in central Dublin in the middle of an unusually fecund summer. The skies blackened
just as the troop hit Lower Mount Street and opened to a downpour a
minute later. There was nothing for them to do but proceed according to
orders along the mud and grass down to the banks of the flooding canal
and around to the entrance to the barracks, all the while being soaked
and grimed and blinded by the water which engulfed them in a nearly
biblical manner.

"It's the Irish Sea come to reclaim the four provinces," one of the men
cried out as they funneled their way into the barracks.

"Let her have them," was the reply from one of the others as he started
to strip out of his wet clothing. Joe was allowed to keep his changes at
home and always walked to drill in uniform and thus had nothing to
switch in to. He was standing like a drenched rabbit on a watercourse
in a room full of naked men. But now he felt no shame, no fear, and no
self-consciousness. A liberation of a sort had occurred and it took place
in the mirror of Joe's imagination. If I can't see them, Joe thought, then

they can't see me, or rather: if I see them as mates in a barracks room then they see me the same way. No class, no rank, no filled-out chest or curled fist, no seductive smile or defensive stare could separate him from his men or them from him. His heart filled with the pride of it and with the pride he felt for the feeling of it and he now knew he had found a company to which he truly belonged. It was a game and not a game and you could float above it or live it and either way was up to the mark. Joe understood this outlook completely. This was for him.

In July, his old friend Tommy Doyle from St. Mary's joined the Dubs. He came in on a Tuesday as Joe was reading through the roster. "Joe Dooley as I live and breathe," Tommy cried as he pinned up his cap badge and closed his locker.

"Tom," Joe said. "I saw 'Private Thomas Doyle' added to my list but who would have thought it?"

"I'm one in a million, Joe."

"That's Corporal Dooley now, Private Doyle…"

Tommy shot Joe a look.

"…and that'll be the last time we'll need to stand on ceremony, Tom." Joe ran his hand through Tommy's hair and Tommy smiled. All that mother's milk had not spoiled the boy, Joe thought. Tommy Doyle had turned out thin but muscular; his energy could prove admirable if properly directed.

"It's grand to see you again, Joe."

"All those years, Tommy. What have you been doing with yourself?"

"This 'n' that."

"That sounds exemplary."

"I haven't seen the world, if that's what you mean."

"You'll see it now. Grab your kit and I'll introduce you to your mates."

"Yes sir, Corporal Dooley," Tommy answered, offering a crisp salute.

"At your ease, Tom. At your ease."

⌒

August 1, 1911

Dear Sev,

Should you wish to take advantage of it, the opportunity has arisen. I have been granted leave from the 9th through the 16th—eight entire evenings without the anticipation of

a 6 a.m. call and seven entire mornings full of the knowledge that I will be able to stand upright at the end of the
day. My mates warned me that summer training is a bear
but I was a babe in the woods about it. I'll be glad of the
autumn and the switchover to part-time rifle cleaning.

Do say you'll come and share this time with me. My flat
isn't very spacious but I know you're used to playing the
tramp. The ma and Kath are conveniently up amongst our
Derry cousins so I'm off the hook for them.

I'm writing this in the dark as the sun has yet to come
up on dirty old Dublin but as soon as it does I'm off to
Boland's and Beggars Bush and another day with my Lee-
Enfield. I await your word.

Affectionately,

Joe

AUGUST 4, 1911

Dear Joe,

Received yours of the 1st. All is arranged. There's a drive
on here to deepen all the channels so the transatlantic
trade can lay anchor at a practicable distance and they've
put extra men on every detail, my luck. A week in the
harbour and I will be provisioned. I'll be at your door
afternoon of the 10th and if you want me to be precise look
at your timetable. Just kidding—we'll have supper together.
Then the world will be our...well, I hate oysters so let's
make it something palatable. Until then,

Your pal,

Coole

THE TRAIN PULLED INTO BLACKROCK STATION JUST PAST NOON. The
boys looped over the tracks and headed for the bathhouse where they
could change into their bathing suits. The day was fine and warm and the
crowds were already beginning to fill in at the baths and along the strand.
Far away out to sea, a pair of spidery black trawlers sounded their horns
and the seabirds returned the greeting with a grace note. Joe was pleased
with the musicality of it all, a harmony that elided the space between the
land and the water.

The old stone hut had been built in the 1840s and it was cold even on the hottest days but after the stifle of the railway car it was a pleasant pang to their senses. Severin pulled off his cotton jersey and brown twill trousers and stuffed them roughly into the bag and he jumped into his red-striped suit and wrapped his towel extravagantly around his neck. Joe was more circumspect and took the time to arrange his clothing as if he was leaving for a holiday and Severin mocked him for it and yanked it away, mingling the contents. Joe protested and laughed at the same time and at that moment for a reason he couldn't explain he felt overwhelmed with sadness. The sadness flooded him like the water rushing in with the tide and when it receded he understood that he was sad because of his happiness and because of his freedom, out in the open air with the friend he loved. It was a time which had come and which was passing by as he watched it and he wanted to reach out and reset the clock.

Severin found a spot a few feet short of the tide line. They planted the bag and towels and raced into the sea. The water hit Joe's thighs and then his chest with a wildness that made him shiver and shout. Then its peacefulness and permanence rolled over him and he felt as he did when he was just waking up from a dream, half in and half out of consciousness. Finally he adjusted to the rhythm of the waves and brought his body back on top, up and down in the ceaseless pattern of time, his friend floating beside him like a nautilus. Joe was always at home when he was in or near the sea. Although he knew from looking at a map that the water was bounded by land it inspired him to think of the limitlessness of it, to scan the horizon and imagine eternity.

Joe liked to lie there and kick his feet gently in the tide and feel the water flowing beneath him. Severin was a much better swimmer than Joe and as Joe floated Severin turned around and dove under a wave, reemerging on his other side. It pleased Joe to look at Severin as he swam, to see his body taut and flowing and shining in the Irish sun. There was a great beauty in this boy, Joe thought, a beauty beyond his looks and having more to do with his confidence and enthusiasm and as he watched him he said to himself over and over again like an incantation, "This is my friend. This is my friend."

THE SUN HAD MOVED FAR TO THE WEST AND THE SHADOWS FELL long and sharp in front of them, their profiles black and elongated against the tawny sand. All too soon the air would grow cool from the sea and the beachgoers would begin to roll up their towels and walk back to the baths and the street. Severin reached into the bag and pulled out a cigarette.

"Where did you get that?" Joe asked.

"I thought I'd add a continental habit to my repertoire." Severin struck a match and pulled on the cigarette until the tip started to glow. "Some fella I worked with filched a whole box of 'em and he gives 'em out as he sees fit."

"You look like an idiot."

"No less of one for smoking," Severin said. "Why the hell not?"

"There's enough smoke in Dublin as it is."

"We're not in Dublin."

"I'm not going to argue with you."

"No, you're not."

The boys sat together in silence. Severin puffed contentedly.

"Now what?" Severin asked.

"I suppose we should gather up and head home."

"I meant with the world, you donkey. What is my little tin soldier up to next?"

"I resent your attitude."

Severin whacked Joe in the side of his head with his balled-up shirt. "That's attitude for you if you want it, you eejit."

"Stop it."

"So answer my question."

"What? Do you expect some new answer? I'm to go back to my reserve duties. I'll tutor at the College. I could give lessons for an extra penny or two but there's nothing doing until I get a new piano."

"God, I wish I was unprincipled enough to steal twenty pounds for you. Then you could buy that goddamned piano and you could quit squawking about it and stop working for the crown."

"I wouldn't take your stolen money and anyway I'm not working for the crown. I'm training to defend my country."

"And what country is that?"

"Ireland, you idiot."

"I don't see a harp or a field of stars on that uniform of yours. Don't you remember Belfast? There's men being brutalized and men being killed to defend Ireland and it's English soldiers doing the killing."

"Don't talk that way, Sev. You know that's not forever the case. Half the men in my regiment are republicans. They'd never shoot an Irishman for any reason whatsoever."

Severin hooked his arm around Joe. "Now lookat, Joe. You know I love you. And one of the things I love you for is your idealism and your dedication. I'm glad—I'm really glad that you like what you're doing and that you have a goal in life. I'm just trying to warn you that the path to righteousness is not always straight and not always easy."

"I know."

"Sometimes I think you do, and sometimes I think you don't."

"You may be right, Sev. But part of living a life of principle is hewing to it when the challenge seems greatest. I hear all the talk on the green about the Brotherhood and "A Nation Once Again." Don't you think I do? And I hear all the talk in the barracks about the war to come. So I hold my tongue and I do my job and I try to be fair and honest with everyone. I don't rightly see what more I can do."

"Just be careful who you go shooting, Joe," Severin said. "You just might be shooting at an Irishman."

"I told you no one has said anything about shooting any Irishmen," Joe said, angrily. "That's absurd."

"And how often do the words 'Irishmen' and 'absurd' end up in the same sentence? Daily, I tell you."

Joe smiled.

"You talk about living a life of principle," Severin continued. "You know me. I was not the first man to be beaten for saying what he thinks and I won't be the last. But there are other ways to get what you want besides fighting for it."

"What do you mean, Sev?"

"A pair of real jackeens came down to the docks the other day. They said they represent a consortium of businessmen who are raising money to outfit a ship to be the first to circumnavigate the African continent under an Irish flag. To beat the English at their own game, don't you see? Let the world know that Irish patriots can do more than shoot straight."

"I already knew that."

"But the world, Joe—the world…"

"Haven't we heard this before, Sev? To gain the world and lose your soul…"

"Nobody's losing their soul on a forty-foot steamboat, Joe."

"It's dangerous."

"This coming from someone who's about to pick up a rifle—that's a laugh. I think it's a grand idea and I'm proud to say I was the first to put my name on the dotted line."

"How soon?"

"We ship out on the tenth."

"Two weeks?"

"It had to come sooner or later, Joe. Better sooner, don't you think?"

Joe looked out to sea. Their shadows were almost gone now, faint in the last rays of the sun. An old man wandered up and down along the water's edge wrapped tightly against the cold and a dog barked in the distance.

"Our separate ways at last," Joe said. "We've talked about it for seven years. I guess the time has come."

"We always knew it would, Joe. It was a sign of our friendship that it took so long."

"*Aimsir agus taoide fa no se duine.*"

"What's that?"

"'Time and tide wait for no man.' It's an old Irish saying."

"True enough."

Severin stood up. In the failing light, Joe wasn't sure if this was meant as a signal for them to go or if his friend was just looking to shake few more cares from his frame to leave behind in the sand.

"Let's say our goodbyes here, Joe."

Severin took Joe into his arms and kissed him. Joe put his arms down at his side and took a step back.

"You didn't have to do that, Sev."

"I did so. I don't want to wait until we had traveled all the way back to Talbot Street and then we'd have the weepies and the dinner wouldn't be sitting right and then you'd follow me to Kingsbridge like a puppy and there'd be this whole scene out of a melodrama. It's easier here."

"'Tis."

Joe tiptoed forward and reached out to take Severin's face in his hands. Then he leaned forward into him and let his body rest against Severin's legs and chest and kissed him gently on the cheek. The dark had settled and the beach was deserted.

"I expect great things from you, Joe. You're going to get that piano and you're going to dazzle the world."

"I think you are the one more likely to do the dazzling."

"I'm always dazzling. But you're the chrysalis."

Joe liked that. He was a chrysalis, a moth fluttering alone in the dark at the edge of a vast and impersonal sea and waiting for the beacon that could either guide him to safe passage or end it by crashing him against the light, searching forever for home.

# Chapter 5

✦ ✦ ✦

## *Circumnavigation*

✦ ✦ ✦

THE FIRST LETTER ARRIVED THAT AUTUMN.

CAPE TOWN, OCTOBER 19, 1911.

Dear Joe,

I know you well enough to know that you are fussing over this letter, both for the amount of time it took me to get it to you and for your inability to wait patiently for it to reveal its contents. (In fact, I am chuckling to myself right now at the vision of you reading the letter backwards if only to find out how it ends before you commit yourself to it—typical, safe Joe Dooley). So to spare you the exercise I will tell you straight at the top that I am having a grand time and still have both arms, both legs, and at least a portion of my wits about me.

The men in our crew are a bunch of old salts; I'm the youngest by several years. In consequence I am the first on the deck when it comes to the burdensome chores but truly I'm not minding it (yet). We steamed out from Queenstown on schedule but it took us three weeks to get to the Canaries. This was not due to any difficulty with the weather or even poor planning (Irish tars might be an exploitative bunch but they're nothing if not up on the latest

in seamanship) but because every sack and store seemed
to need to be newly discovered, sorted, and registered. If
this is the way we are going to run a republic God help us.
Eventually we found our routine and everything since then
has been smooth as silk.

We've called at Dakar, Libreville, and Cape Town, the latter from which yours truly managed to post this commu-
niqué. Europeans are less and less like exotic flora here and
I think you'd be amazed at how relatively ordinary these
former outposts of civilization have become. There's the
heaps of exotic goods loaded on the docks and the uniden-
tifiable meats in the stewpot but really, how much different
is that from my experience in the kitchen at St. Colman's?
For me, the many purposes of this voyage are being realized: I am learning to be a better mariner; I am meeting
people from all different classes and backgrounds; and I am
advancing the cause of the Irish people around the world.
That, plus taking a lot of exercise. You would not recognize
me anymore with my dark skin and developed chest.

We are waylaying in Cape Town for two weeks while
the *Aran* (for that is the name of our little vessel) gets her
holes patched up and her turbines refitted. The men have
organized a hunting expedition to Mafeking but I'm no
sharpshooter and I'd rather see the tusks and the antlers
with the animals attached to them the way God intended
them to be. I might like the opportunity to climb out from
under everyone else's shadow for a few days and take a
boat out on my own. My own tackle, my own fish, and my
own time—the words ring like chimes as I write them and
almost bring tears to my eyes in anticipation.

I am sorry that we will not be able to correspond. As you
rightly suspected, it is not possible for the *Aran* to receive
mail. We have no port schedule and it is truly impossible
to predict one. If all goes well, we will be up the eastern
coast by the end of the month and chugging our way
across the Mediterranean come winter. That puts us in a
position for a homecoming by the spring of next year. Wait
for me.

I hope that your music and your soldiering are advancing apace (although not in tandem, for I despise military
music) and that you are cheered by my news and my

determination to sustain our friendship. Now it's back to the plane and the hammer and my kettle of fish.

Yours,

*Sev Coole.*

ONCE JOE'S APPETITE FOR NEWS WAS WHETTED IT WAS HARD FOR him to fast. Despite Severin's very clear warning not to expect a letter from him anytime soon Joe made it a source of anticipation and thus a reason for disappointment at regular intervals. Month upon month passed without any further correspondence. Joe would circle the block at the GPO and conduct an argument with himself but inevitably he would go in and sort through the usual meager pile of solicitations: nothing. By Christmas, Joe was down to checking only once each week and by the spring he had entirely stopped looking for Severin's hand on the envelope. A summer passed and Joe was convinced he had been abandoned. Then it came:

KHARTOUM, SEPTEMBER, 1912.

Dear Joe,

I left you in the lurch and for this I am truly sorry. As you might surmise from the top of this letter I am no longer on my Grand Tour. As far as the *Aran* goes, things have fallen apart. Our equipment kept malfunctioning and I discovered too late that my colleagues were great sailors and patriots but not so accomplished as mechanics. I consider myself a quick study and was fully prepared to do my part to make our voyage a success but by the time we reached the Suez I was beginning to appreciate that I was not considered an equal on our crew and in fact was little better off than the Somali slaves that I witnessed being whipped along the shore in Aden. As you well know, I have little tolerance for this. I don't blame my friends in Ireland for this state of affairs—after all, if it hadn't been for their generosity I never would have had this chance to see the world. Still, I surprised myself with my own naïveté. One would have thought that by the age of twenty-four I should have anticipated my cynicism. Not so, my friend, not so.

I left the ship in Egypt with little more than the clothes around my waist (it was too hot to hang anything on my back). My first thought was to work my way home to Ireland as quickly as I could but when I thought through the situation with a little more determination I realized that although my attempts at nationalistic pride and nautical fortitude had been dashed my education was still incomplete. I took a long walk along the canal and watched the scenes unfolding before me with hungry eyes. It didn't take me long to see that a man with basic business instincts, a benevolent but disinterested knowledge of his fellow man, and the ability to defend himself with words, fists, or (if necessary) bullets could become rich. The riverbank was overrun with traders and I was determined to join their profession.

At first I borrowed a little six-foot boat from an Egyptian lad who took a liking to me. The damned thing leaked from the bow and I could barely fit a week's worth of goods into it but I had no money of my own to afford to be a true competitor. It took all of my first season in the ranks and a good part of the second one before I had accumulated the down payment on a skiff but once I got going there was no stopping me. You'd be amazed at how I've added engineering, accountancy, connoisseurship, and management to my previously meager collection of skills.

The sights and sounds of the Sudan are fantastic. I think the little bands of musicians who stroll up and down along the quays playing their ouds and riqs and xelamis would mesmerize you. (An oud is very much like a guitar, a riq a tambourine, and a xelami is a pipe and if you close your eyes you might think you were in the middle of a *sessun*). For all its weirdness the bittersweet harmonies do more than any familiar accent or glimpse of a passing colleen to remind me of home.

For the past six months, I have been sailing up and down the Nile from Cairo to Khartoum hauling dyes, cloth, quinine bark, bronze ingots—whatever material treasures that can be pulled from the hills and caves of the Sudan and be turned into coin of the realm in the city. I'm hardly prosperous (now there's an image which could shake you in your boots) but I have a roof over my head (admittedly, it's made of straw, but it keeps out the rain) and—more to the point—a real address at last: Box 868. This means that not only can you continue to listen to my prattle, but now I can hear yours. I cross the path of a random Irishman every two months or so but that's not the same thing as a friend. Please write. This is an order.

I hope you receive this letter and have not shipped out to Hong Kong or some other farflung outpost of empire to defend our George. I'll put aside a jalabia for you (it's an article of clothing).

Your African correspondent,
*Coole.*

THE LETTER TOOK NEARLY A MONTH TO BE DELIVERED. JOE PUT PEN to paper for his response the same day.

DUBLIN, OCTOBER, 1912.

Dear Severin,

You must imagine how happy I was to hear from you. Although I am sorry to hear of your dashed hopes for the circumnavigation it appears as if the Severin I know has persevered and even thrived. I think of you often and always wish you the best, be you a sailor, a trader, or even the old vagabond I recall from our salad days. I am glad to read that the heat has not yet wilted your sense of humor or need for adventure.

I think you might find me similarly if not equally entrepreneurial. You know the few pounds I gain from my army service fail to keep me as well-fed and as well-habited as I would like to be, so I have started trawling for gullible pupils who might pay me a few shillings to show them the elements of musical composition or learn enough about the sonata form to make a presentation at their ladies' club tea. Dublin is bustling but never quite prosperous and so far my efforts have produced one seventy-year-old pensioner with hearing difficulties and the two teenaged daughters of my lieutenant who took pity upon me. Such is my world of business.

I've grown quite fond of my army friends and my army
service. I hope you will not judge this attachment too
harshly or mistake my love and admiration of my fellows
as wholesale support of things monarchial. I do believe I've
made it clear to you and to everyone else that I do not as-
sociate my desire for companionship and my development
of a sense of responsibility with the excesses of violence in
heart and in mind which seem to be sweeping the world
these days and threaten all the progress I thought mankind
had made.

As I reread this letter, I see that I have wandered far from
my initial emotion of joy in hearing from you. Instead, I
have ended up burying you under my philosophy. My day-
to-day life of drill, lessons, and the occasional mates' night
out is deeply unsatisfying, the more so for the sense that
somewhere just beyond my vision (and very likely lying
directly in front of you) something really vital is happening. My fears of what this may be and the consequences it
might have for me and for all my friends are not enough to
dilute my longing for it. All I can hope for is that someday I will have the opportunity to act upon these desires
and that there might be some way for us to share in their
execution.

Now from the sublime to the ridiculous: time to cook
an egg. I hope you stay put long enough to receive my
letter and even more so that you have the time and the
opportunity to reply to it and allow us to have our first real
exchange in over two years.

Until then, I remain

Your loyal(ist) friend,

Joe.

IF JOE FELT THE FRUSTRATION OF HAVING TO WAIT FOR A LETTER
from Severin when he had no idea where the letter was coming from, it
was double now that the reference point was known. Beyond this there
was the possibility, hiding in a distant corner of Joe's imagination, that
Severin didn't think that writing to Joe was truly important. Finally, in
the spring, Joe made one last try at gauging the depth of his friend's
commitment:

DUBLIN, APRIL, 1913

My dearest Sev,

I checked the address you gave me three times over; it was always correct. Why have you not answered me? You must know I am distraught over this and not because of any personal sense of disappointment but only because I am certain that your failure to write must be due to some disaster that has overtaken you. At my moments of greatest lunacy, I imagine you imprisoned by pirates or wounded and suffering from amnesia in some overgrown corner of the Congo.

I have calmed down now. Perhaps you are merely so busy taking the inventory of your wares and wiring the funds to Leinster Street that you have forgotten to put pen to paper. Or, more likely, you have addressed page upon page of detailed narratives to me in your customary indecipherable hand and each and every one of them has been lost at sea or misdirected to some confused Dooley in Lisburn. Whatever the reason, Sev, do know that I am in poor condition without word from you and long to be restored.

Not knowing if you are ever to read it, I am somewhat unwilling to fill this tablet with unimportant incidents. Nothing that I could write to increase the length of this letter would improve upon it; I have already told you all that you need to know. Write, or come back, or do something that would let me know you are well.

Ever faithfully,
Joe.


SIX MONTHS LATER, SEVERIN'S RESPONSE ARRIVED.

DAKAR, NOVEMBER, 1913.

My dear Joe,

At last, I have the chance and opportunity to correspond. You see that I have abandoned my nib and am corresponding via the civilized machine known as the typewriter. I am in my office in Dakar. It is ten o'clock at night and still nearly eighty degrees Fahrenheit. I'd go home to bed but for the fact that this is my home and I am in bed. That's how it's been for some months now.

Things got hot for me round about the time I received your letter a year ago. First the pressure was on from the colonials in German East Africa and we suffered a sequence of armed raids on our storehouses. I've been shot at twice (and missed twice—I don't know how much longer my luck will hold up) and I never thought I'd see anything more ridiculous than a British officer in full military dress until the Hessians started to don their plumage in the forlorn hope of intimidating us. Then the local authorities decided to get in on the deal and they started asking for ridiculous duties on everything we were exporting. And if that wasn't enough, some tribe living deep in the heart of the Sahara picked just that very moment to start a war with their neighbors and all my traders were either shot or pistol-whipped or quite sensibly quit.

There was very little for me to do but close up my Khartoum enterprise and pack my trunk again. A pair of French traders with a serviceable motor vehicle were heading across the continent, aiming for this port and a chance to escape by boat to Marseilles. You know me—I say "yes" before I even look at a plan and before I knew it I was being driven across the Sudan in a military-issue Renault whose engine kept cutting out at the most inopportune moments. I could rival Stanley with my memoirs but for the sake of your sanity I will spare you. Needless to say, we made it to the coast and as noted above I have established a bit of a communications beachhead here in Senegal as we wait for the right amount of money and goods to bribe our way on to a merchant marine vessel headed for Europe.

At this point, I long for the boring stability you complained of. I think of you in particular tonight because—I haven't forgotten—this week is your birthday, Guy Fawkes Day, the ultimate irony. So much water has gone under the bridge (and over the bow and everywhere else) since that fateful day in Blackrock when we parted. I had so much more I wanted to say and have wanted to say to you since then but, as you put it, time and tide wait for no man. (You see how that line resounds in my memory). Certainly it didn't wait around for us. I do not fear that we have grown apart, because I know the ties that bind us are stronger than anything that distance can sever, but I think that experience is marching us in different directions. I can only hope that someday we will have the chance to look at that map together and check the proximity of our hearts.

Either tomorrow or the day after or next week or next year the money will come and the boat will be ready and I will be out on the open seas again. Until then, I need to lay low and keep to myself the best I can. If I am stuck here for too long a time and have the wherewithal to do so I will write to you again. If not, know that I love you and that I am thinking of you. When I'm in a praying mood, I'll even pray for you, knowing you will have done the same for me.

*Go gcasfar chéile sinn arís,*
*Severin.*

JOE WAITED. CHRISTMAS CAME AND THEN THE NEW YEAR AND still there was no news. By the spring, Joe had given up hope. He believed there were to be no more letters from Severin Coole.

# Chapter 6

◆ ◆ ◆

## *Lessons at No. 10 Talbot*

◆ ◆ ◆

TODAY'S LESSON WAS NOT GOING WELL. JOE HAD ACCEPTED THOMAS Davis as a favor to the boy's father, the caretaker at Beggars Bush, but now regret was beginning to overtake courtesy. The boy was ten years old and more interested in learning how to throw a sliotar than uncovering the intricacies of Liszt, all the more in emphasis on this glorious June afternoon.

"No, that's B flat," Joe said as the boy attacked the keys. "You've no reason for making that sort of error." Joe immediately regretted his tone and apologized. "I'm sorry, Tom, but you need to pay more attention to what you are playing."

The Davis boy fidgeted on the stool and dutifully put his hands back in position, leaving them hovering silently above the keyboard.

"Shall we try it again?"

Thomas attempted the variation with excessive enthusiasm, banging out the notes as if he was aiming for the back row of a music hall. The notes lurched and careened and finally meandered to the tonic, a victory lap more than an artistic gesture but no less sweet for ending. When he was done, Thomas folded his hands neatly on his lap and turned to Joe. "Was that better, Mr. Dooley?"

Joe thought for an instant about lying to the boy but decided that Thomas would see through it and that not only would such a lie fail to improve the boy's skills but it would lower his confidence in the teacher as well. "Not really, Tom, I'm sorry to say. Maybe we should stop for today."

"If you say so, Mr. Dooley."

"You are not lacking for attitude, Thomas. I admire your determination. But there is the matter of communication. Remember, music is another way of speaking. You want to make sense as well as sounds. Think about what you are playing."

"In all fairness, Mr. Dooley, it's all I can do just to play it. I can read the notes all right but when it comes to getting from one end to the other it's all like a parade to me."

"I know, Tom. You'll get better, I'm sure. Just practice your lessons and try to remember what I have taught you."

"I will, sir."

"Very well, then. I'll see you next Tuesday and give my regards to the da."

"Thanks much, Mr. Dooley."

Thomas grabbed his book bag and skittered down the stairs like an animal released into the wild. The sound of the boy's footfalls on the staircase was tremendous and Mr. O'Connell's girl peeked out into the vestibule with a startled look on her face. "Is everything all right, Mr. Dooley?" she asked.

"Yes…yes, Clara. I'm sorry. Tom is one of my more boisterous pupils."

"Is that all?" the girl said, shaking her head as she went back into the shop. "I thought it was the elephants come marching to the circus."

JOE KNEW HOW TO BE ALL THINGS TO ALL PEOPLE AND HIS HELP-fulness was his camouflage. Everyone at the University College knew Joe Dooley was the man to call upon if you needed someone to transpose your Haydn and Joe was smart enough to recognize that the beneficiary of this day's assistance could be tomorrow's paying pupil. In the same spirit any Royal Dublin Fusilier knew you could tap Joe Dooley for a bailout should your best girl be coming up from Dundrum and you needed to be spelled for a shift. This perfect transparency also served Joe well when it came to politics. He looked so unlikely a conqueror in his British Army uniform that he was spared the derision and disrespect aimed at his more martial peers and was so recognizable a figure about the town that he could confidently hand out his union pamphlets while in full military dress and not a soul would think it contradictory.

Although Joe certainly fit into the category, he never thought of himself as poor. If his army pay ran out he could always go to the club at the barracks and cadge a potpie and a pint. He was a corporal in His Majesty's army and the perquisites that came with this were more than handy at times like these. Furthermore although he lived alone Joe was never really lonely and he felt that loneliness was a great symptom of poverty. Between his colleagues in the Fusiliers, his neighbors on Talbot Street, and his pupils Joe Dooley could honestly say he never lacked for company. Intimacy was another matter entirely. Joe was nearly twenty-four years old now and still he had not "settled down." He himself did not find this exceptional but whenever he was reminded of his situation he took the point as being that it was.

Joe did miss Donal McCormack. Just at the moment that he was willing to admit that he was in love with Donal, the young man decided that he was serious about becoming a medical doctor and took off for Heidelberg. Unsatisfactorily as their affair ended, Joe supposed it was all for the best as he was now Donal's brother's superior in rank and he genuinely liked Richard and didn't wish to have any sort of complication arise which could injure his standing or perhaps even cost him his job. But no one filled Donal's place. Joe allowed himself to flirt with friends he found attractive but the safety switch was always at hand, with the excuse that the hour was too late, the whiskey too expensive and the schedule too full.

Without a doubt, Joe's closest companion was his piano. Precisely one year to the day after Joe enlisted he talked Mr. Harrison into loaning him an Ajello upright for two pounds a month. The day it was delivered was the crowning moment of Joe's life. He stood in the street and watched like a nervous father as the delivery men hoisted the machine from the back of their truck and swung it over the walk on a harness. Earlier that day, he and Mr. O'Connell had removed the window from its frame so that the instrument could be swung up and through it into Joe's room but now that the time had come Joe thought the opening was half as large as it needed to be and he held a vision of the dark wood case in midair splintering against the wall and clattering to the paving stones. By the time the piano was twenty feet off the ground, a crowd had gathered below. Joe closed his eyes and only opened them when he heard the cheer.

THAT FREE AFTERNOON JOE WAS WALKING ALONG THE GRAND CANAL taking in the flower beds and saluting the swans. He sauntered as far as the tramway and then turned north on Aungier Street where the union headquarters were located. He had two hours to spare. Less than a week ago a man there had told him a membership push was starting up and they'd need someone to canvass at the South City Market. Would Joe come by and pick up the materials when he had the chance? Well, now was the chance and who was he not to do what he could for his fellow man? We are all workers now, aren't we? — the man who works the switchyard and the woman who frets the lace and the lad with his doss-bag are no less entitled to their dignity and no less oppressed by their work than is he in his uniform or his fellow soldiers in the map room or his colleagues at the college in their laboratories.

It was Severin who had taught him to think this way. Joe liked to incorporate Severin in his thoughts and especially in his actions. It was his way of staying close to him even though he had no idea where he was or what he was up to or even if he was still in the world at all. Keeping his friend in his mind's eye was Joe's way of underscoring his own ideals when it would have been very easy to abandon them and it helped him to square his commitment to the Dubs with his larger and more personal desires. For Joe dreamed of a great achievement.

Joe was thinking all this as he left the union office with his sheaf of papers and he decided to stop in at the Carmelites next door before beginning his promenade. The cynicism of adulthood had not overwhelmed Joe's spiritual nature and he still prayed to the Jesus his soul had been entrusted to even if there were times when he was not completely certain of his faith. Joe noted with especial irony that it was not his Catholic but his Protestant friends in the barracks who were interested in hearing about his beliefs. It was they who felt that if you followed a path—any path—toward salvation you were taking steps in the right direction. All the St. Mary's boys Joe knew were convinced that sin was cash-and-carry and so long as you confessed you could pour that extra Guinness, Hell be damned.

The Carmelite Chapel was dark and narrow. An old woman was at her beads in the first pew, singsonging softly to herself. Joe crossed himself and bowed and tapped the font of holy water with his finger. The water was warm. He moved slowly down the east aisle toward an empty row and sat there, laying his army bag on the seat next to him and placing the union papers on top. He fell to his knees and tucked his head and said a prayer for Severin. He thought of his ma and Kath and added them to his prayers as well, remembering his family was still if not near and if not completely dear at least his and for that he felt some responsibility. Then he got up, brushed the dust from his uniform, walked around to the nave to light a candle and turned back along the corridor to the street.

As he pushed open the heavy wooden door, Joe saw a young man sitting on the ground in the corner, propped up against the stone. The boy appeared to be between twenty and twenty-two years old. He had once been beautiful but now his hair was long and dirty and his complexion was sallow. Even though it was early summer and he was wearing two shirts, he looked cold. His eyes were closed but when Joe emerged into the sunlight he opened them and took Joe in, a piteous look of fear that showed no sign of being caused by a lack of understanding of his situation.

"Please, sir," the young man said to Joe. "I'm starvin'."

Joe reached into his pocket and took out a shilling. He handed the coin to the boy. It fell out of the boy's hand and Joe had to rescue it as it rolled away.

"God bless you," Joe said, this time slipping the coin into the boy's shirt pocket. As he did this, he felt the boy's chest beneath the thin cloth and it shocked him with its hardness and its heat. It was as if the Holy Spirit burned inside him and was trying to escape.

"God bless you, sir, and thank you," the boy said very quietly.

Joe wanted to heal the boy, to actually take him up in his arms and embrace him and calm his soul with his pity. It was the kind of love he most knew how to give, a love of sympathy and understanding which united the giver and the receiver in a way that transcended their physical connection and inoculated them against pain and suffering. But there was only so much money to spread around and only so much time to give and Joe remembered the greater good which came from the uniform he wore and the pamphlets he carried and as he wished he had another shilling he smiled one last time at the boy and continued up Aungier Street.

WHEN JOE REACHED HOME THERE WAS A YOUNG MAN WAITING FOR him on the sidewalk.

"Joe Dooley?" he asked.

"Yes. I'm he."

"I saw your flier at the GPO," he said. "'Lessons at No. 10 Talbot.'"

"We can arrange something if you're interested. I'm not free this afternoon, however."

Joe eyed the man more carefully. He was about five foot ten, strongly built, with red hair and blue eyes that refracted bluer behind a pair of round, gold-rimmed spectacles.

"Hello, Joe. It's Harry Vogeler."

Joe stood speechless.

"Well, don't just stand there, man. Invite me in."

"Jesus, Harry—how was I…"

"I'm still waiting for my invitation."

"Come on up. I'll put on a cuppa."

The boys climbed up the stairs. Joe dumped his bag in the corner and filled the kettle. Harry pulled up two chairs, one in each hand. "Look at you in full military dress and all," he said. "I'm shocked. I had expected to see you in a college capeen, is what."

"Talk about your shock," Joe began. "What are you to make of mine?"

"I do suppose I arrived a bit out of the blue."

"You could put it that way. I thought you were in America."

"I was. Ten years."

"I heard about your split from the da and all."

"Well, that's permanent now. My papa died last month."

"I'm sorry to hear that."

"We ended up friends. I went to Germany for the funeral and there were loose ends to tie up here. I was about to make my way back across the ocean and I thought to myself: If I was Joe Dooley where would I end up? So I checked in to the Metropole and crossed the street to the GPO to look up all the J. Dooleys in Dublin and what do I see hanging all raggedy from one of the ancient pillars but your tiny flier? 'Lessons at no. 10 Talbot, contact J. Dooley'. Well, I knew there are a dozen Joe Dooleys in town but I bet there was only one giving piano lessons on Talbot Street. And I was right."

"My accommodations aren't nearly as enticing as the Metropole but if you're looking to save a pound or two I know of none better."

"I'm only here until Tuesday," Harry answered. "But I suppose I could tolerate you until then. Let's collect my luggage and see what the last fourteen years have wrought."

JOE WAITED FOR HARRY AS HE CHECKED OUT OF THE HOTEL. THEY walked over to Juno Donovan's and wended their way across the years over pints of ale and a pair of steak-and-kidney pies. Joe caught Harry up on his schooling and his lessons but the bulk of the conversation was dominated by the far more intrepid and cosmopolitan ramblings of his friend. After the split with his papa Harry indeed had sailed to America; in that detail the neighborhood was correct. But Harry was far from an immediate success. After failing to find work in Boston or New York, Harry ended working for a brewery in Saint Louis. It was steady work but evidently unfulfilling and there remained a touch of the Lost Boy hanging around Harry's eyes.

Harry asked Joe if he was married yet.

"Did you take a look around my flat?"

"I take that as a 'no.'"

"You are correct."

"Why not, Joe? You cut a fine figure in that uniform of yours."

"I'm penniless, that's why."

"I never knew love required a salary."

"You know what I mean."

"Do I? Whenever I thought of you, I always imagined you sitting by a fire reading poetry to your wee ones or having a sing-along over the breakfast table, conducting a veritable choir of little Dooleys."

"Did you think of me, Harry?"

"I did so often. I never understood why after you moved away you never found the time to return for a visit or put pen to paper and let me know how you were. I was hurt by it and I thought about it a lot. For the longest while I wanted to forget about our friendship. Did you ever think of me?"

Joe was about to sip at the last of his draught but he put the glass down untasted. "I did. I don't know why I never acted upon it. It was something I never understood myself. Sometimes I do things even I don't understand and once they're done I can't figure out how to entangle them. I languish and then I feel it's too late to repent. Please forgive me. I guess I was angry at my fate and in my anger I exiled everything that was being taken away from me—my music, my home, my friend."

"You returned to the music. You came back home."

"And now I've found my friend."

"And now you've found your friend."

Harry ordered another round and proposed a toast. "To the old Talbot Street Gang."

"Cheers."

As the beer warmed his spirits and the room grew close, Joe wanted to find a way to bring Harry all the way back to the place he had occupied in his heart when he was ten years old but he found that the distance was not as easily negotiated as he wished. Something of Harry's childhood openness and cheerfulness remained but it had been layered over by a thin but impenetrable coating of circumspection. Perhaps the years of struggle had dimmed his optimism, that or the shadow of the recent passing of his only kin. Whatever it was, it held Joe back.

"I knew when I stopped in Dublin that I was going to find you again," Harry said.

"It's not that big a city," Joe answered.

"I suppose after America it's not."

"Did you like America, Harry?"

"I liked Americans. Everywhere I went, everyone I met, all of us were just fellows from somewhere else trying to make a go of it."

"All they wanted was to exploit you to make some money."

"Ah, that's the socialist in you talking now."

"But that's what they did, Harry. Don't you see?"

"It's a mutually exploitative world, my friend. They got the heart and soul out of me and I got my steak-and-kidney pie out of them."

"Actually, Harry, you got it out of me. I'm paying for it."

"I'll let you do that for me now, Joe, because I'm your guest. But sooner or later you're going to have to let me pay you back."

"You're doing it already, Harry."

TUESDAY PASSED AND WEDNESDAY, TOO, AND HARRY STUCK AROUND. Before he knew it, a week had passed. Harry got in touch with the shipping company that had hired him and asked if he could switch to another boat going out. He could, but that boat was loaded and departed and still Harry was reluctant to board. There was the worry about his standing. Harry was a German subject and had never taken out papers either in Ireland or America. Now it was too late. Upon application, Harry discovered that the Castle had discontinued all nationalization for German-born immigrants. It was all good for Harry to sail with the breeze from continent to continent when the world cared little about him, but now at the very moment when the world was starting to pay attention Harry truly wished for it to go away.

Joe was blithe about this, for he was beginning to enjoy the fruits of Harry's domesticity. On drill days, Harry would be solicitous, putting an apple in Joe's pack and coming round to the barracks every now and then at the end of the day to accompany him on his walk home. At other times, when Joe would be late at the college with his tutoring Harry would make sure to have some leftover stew on the stove and enough money left for them to go down to the corner for a nightcap. Joe was inordinately grateful for Harry's help and not at all suspicious of his motives, for he had concluded that in matters of attraction Harry was not like him. The evidence was subtle but convincing—a look between Harry and the serving girl at Neary's, for instance, or the night that Joe was home with a cold and Harry went out by himself and didn't come back until long after closing time. "He knows and doesn't want to hurt me," Joe would think to himself as he admitted what it was that Harry knew and imagined how the hurt would feel if it was delivered.

On nights when he was free Joe would bring Harry down to Fleet Street and sit in on the *sessuns*. It was inevitable that at some point in the course of the evening one of the regulars would hand over his squeezebox to Joe. Harry himself was getting fairly adept at the spoons. There, accompanied by a box flute, a bodhran, and the complementary pint the boys would shake out a passable version of "Ned Of The Hill":

> *Cé hé sin amuigh*
> *A' bhfuil faobhar ar a ghuth*
> *Ag rébahd mo dhorais dhún ta?*
> *Mise Éamann a' Chnoic.*

Joe was in his happiness here. He lost himself in the enveloping sound, one hand running up and down the keys while the other crushed the bellows and all the while he was beaming with the joy that naturally came to him while making music in the company of his firm and devoted friend.

ONE NIGHT A FEW DAYS LATER HARRY AND JOE WERE SITTING AROUND at home when Harry idly hit a few discordant notes on the piano.

"Try an E," Joe said, not looking up from his book.

"What's that?" Harry replied, but when Joe started to answer he could see that Harry was joking. "Look at the look of you. You think I've forgotten our salad days. Not true, my friend, not true." Harry turned around on the stool and played an inexact but recognizable rendition of "*Für Elise.*"

"Sounds to me like you've forgotten everything," Joe commented.

"I didn't show up on your doorstep looking for a handout, you know. I'm willing to pay you for lessons if you have a mind to teach me."

Joe laughed. "Pay me with what? You've barely a tuppence to call your own."

"If I'm to stay with you, I've got to pay my own way. I'll find the funds somewhere."

"Until then, I think you'd better remain untrained."

"I'll show you." Harry ransacked his suitcase and pulled out a sheet of music paper. He began to sing in a wavering tenor:

> *Du holde Kunst, in wieviel grauen Stunden,*
> *Wo mich des Lebens wilder Kreis umstrickt...*

Harry's voice might have been untrained but to Joe it was lovely, rich in feeling what it lacked in precision. Joe dropped his book and ran over to the piano.

"'*An die Musik*'! Where did you get that?"

"I'm not as stupid as you think, Joe. I passed by Harrison's the other day and introduced myself. Mr. Harrison made the connection at once and thanked me with this lovely German misprint."

"It's Schubert. He was from Vienna."

"It sounds like German to me."

Harry picked up where he left off but Joe stopped him.

"No, no—like this..." He tried the notes on the piano and began to sing:

> *Hast du mein Herz zu warmer Lieb' entzunden,*
> *Hast mich in eine beßre Welt entrückt!...*

"That's beautiful," Harry cried.

"You want a lesson. Here. Follow me."

Together, they finished the song:

> *Oft hat ein Seufzer, deiner Harf' entflossen,*
> *Ein süßer, heiliger Akkord von dir*

*Den Himmel beßrer Zeiten mir erschlossen,*
*Du holde Kunst, ich danke dir dafür!*
*Du holde Kunst, ich danke dir!*

"Appearing on our stage tonight," Joe said. "Heinrich Vogeler accompanied by Joseph Dooley."

"At least I get top billing."

HARRY DECIDED TO TAKE UP CYCLING. A MATE FROM A PUB WAS selling an old wreck of a Raleigh and Harry's affair with the machine took off from there. Each evening just before sunset, Harry would take the bicycle down from the hallway and plant it on the sidewalk in front of the building. He would oil the gears and tighten the chain and then he and Joe would walk down to the Liffey and along the quay to the park. Joe had no taste for riding and no interest in making a spectacle of himself so he set upon the task of turning himself into Harry's trainer. Harry had laid out a course that ran along the army athletic grounds and around the zoo. It was Joe's job to take the antique stopwatch that Harry had inherited from his papa and keep a record of the times in the hope of improvement.

"Why don't you just join a cycling club?" Joe asked one evening as they arranged themselves in their usual spot just inside the park gate. "Wouldn't that be more fun for you than dragging me out here with your timepiece day after day?"

"I was under the impression that you enjoyed our little outings," Harry said, sounding offended.

"I do, to a point. But I hardly see how you are entertained by my endless reporting of your little circles. Wouldn't you care for some competition?"

"You're not about to start in on the G.A.A., are you now? I wouldn't be caught dead working up a slather for that pack of sycophants."

"I thought you were sympathetic."

"I'm all for political freedom but I don't see my musculature having anything to do with a free Ireland."

"I don't see any musculature at all," Joe interjected.

"Very funny. It's my own self-improvement I'm after, not the Gaels. By the by, what time do I have to top this day?"

"Twenty-two minutes, ten."

"I won't quit till I'm under twenty."

"Then I suppose we'll be here in December."

"You'll see."

Joe watched Harry cycle away toward the open fields. The image had all the elements of a Landseer—Harry in his sleeveless racing shirt and short pants pedaling over the rise in the road. Joe believed there was something in this vision that was truly idyllic in the Greek sense of the word. He drew inspiration from the sight of Harry at his labors—the long muscles of his legs flexing above the pedals and the full reach of his arms with their tight grasp of the bars with the whirl of the spokes of the wheels and the silent flow of air trailing behind. Sometimes Harry would take a second lap without stopping and he would sail past Joe shouting at the sky as Joe ran alongside him, winded and happy.

"Twenty-one and forty," Joe cried although he was certain Harry never heard him. Joe pushed the stopper on the watch and secreted it into his pocket. It would be another twenty minutes at least before Harry came around again. Joe was on his own. These solitary opportunities came often during their long midsummer evenings and Joe discovered that he was enjoying them. Something about Harry's companionship made Joe less alone always. It was as if an infinite and invisible tether connected the two friends and no matter how long it grew or how far it reached a true separation would never be effected. As he waited for Harry to return Joe realized that he had never felt this way about anyone—not his family, certainly, and not even Severin Coole. With Severin, all of Joe's longing was in the present tense. When he was not around, he seemed to Joe as distant as a figure in a history book. But somehow Harry was there, even when he was out of sight.

Then the flash of red hair and the long, pumping legs rode out of the haze and Harry came about, scraping to a stop in the dirt. Rivulets of perspiration ran down Harry's neck and chest. Harry ran his hand across his brow and wiped the sweat away. "Once more unto the breach…" he said.

"Isn't that enough for today, Harry? You've taken thirty seconds off already."

"Then let's take another thirty more."

"I'm hungry. I'm thirsty. Aren't you?"

"Yes, but hunger and thirst are great motivators."

"They may be your motivation, Harry, but to me it's merely sustenance. And I don't know about you, but I can't live without it."

"If I can, you can. Set the time."

"Harry—"

"Set it, Joe."

Joe pulled the watch out of his pocket and held it in his hand.

"Ready?"

"Ready."

Joe pushed the release. The ticking sound was louder than usual.

"Go!"

Harry raced off into the blaze of the setting sun. Joe lost him in the light and by the time he had found a position in which he could see his friend was gone. Joe felt he had not been as adamant about his desires as he should have been but the time seemed endless and it hardly mattered enough for him to make an issue of it. Instead he walked over to a bench on the side of the path and patiently waited for his reward.

It came soon enough. Harry pedaled his way down the incline and breathlessly awaited his judgment. Joe pushed the stopper and checked the time. But something was wrong. The timer read fifteen and eight. Joe pushed the starter and the hands stood still. "It's broken," Joe cried.

"'S all right," Harry said. "I can have it repaired."

THAT JULY WAS FULL OF BLUE-DAPPLED DAYS AND IMMOTILE EVE-nings. Although Dublin was a much busier city now than when they were boyhood friends, Joe and Harry acted as if the quays and the alley-ways and the stone-faced streets were their private property. Even in the middle of a crowd surging along Grafton Street or making their way to the trams after last call the two of them felt deliriously alone. Joe reveled in this. He would stand apart from Harry under a street lamp and look back at his friend's face flush with the glow of beer and joy. Harry's hair was growing out now and the red of it had become tinted the color of old copper. Harry's eyes glistened behind his shiny spectacles and Joe knew without saying that to at least this border he loved Harry and Harry loved him. Beyond that frontier his thoughts could go no further.

One night, the two friends' adventures found them wandering along the southern edge of Phoenix Park. The hour was late and the park was abandoned and the path lights threw weak shadows on the lawn. Harry was pulling blossoms down from the bushes.

"Don't do that," Joe said.

"Do what?" Harry answered.

"Disfigure the trees."

"These aren't trees. They're hydrangeas. And I'm not disfiguring them. I'm merely giving them a trim."

"Well, whatever you call it, it's unpleasant. You should let nature lie where it may."

"If you say so."

"Forget it, Harry. Where are we, anyway? Are we lost?"

"Only if you think we are."

"Phoenix Park at night gives me the shivers."

"Why so?"

"There's trouble in dark, abandoned places."

"The only trouble you'll run into here are the prostitutes. Is that what you're afraid of?"

"I'm not afraid."

"There's better women to be had, if that's what you're angling at, Joe."

"I wasn't angling at anything."

Harry swatted Joe in the vicinity of his crotch and laughed.

"I can see that, Joe."

"Stop it, Harry."

Harry was feeling his drink and this was one of those nights when Joe was going to have to take responsibility for steering him home. Harry chuckled softly to himself and then sat down and rolled over on the grass. He started to sing:

*Hoppe hoppe Reiter*
*Wenn er fällt, dann schreit er*
*Fällt er in den Teich*
*Find't ihn keiner gleich…*

"Hush, Harry. Let's try to keep you on your feet and get you home."

"There'll be time enough for that," Harry said. "Can't we just stay here a while longer and listen for the nightingales?"

"There won't be any nightingales at this hour of the morning, Harry. They've all gone to bed as any sensible person would have."

"They're not persons," Harry said with emphasis. "They're birds."

"Come along."

Joe extended his hand but Harry pulled him down on top of him. Joe lay entangled with Harry for an instant and felt Harry's weight. It was pleasant to be comforted so and feel safe and surrounded out in the open this way. But he had to know that Harry was only opening up to him because he was tipsy. Then he saw that Harry had passed out.

"Mary and Joseph, Harry—what am I going to do with you now?" Joe cried out to the night. "You're far too heavy to carry and we're a mile from home."

Joe attempted to wake Harry but it was nothing doing and it was not possible he would leave him here alone. So he pushed him aside and propped his frame against a willow trunk. Harry grunted but did not stir. Joe lifted Harry up and took off his own jacket and used it as a cover to keep him warm. Then he sat down beside him and leaning into Harry's chest he fell asleep.

In late July Toby Caulfield invited the Royal Dublin Fusiliers to a garden party at his father's house in Marino. Toby's father was the seventh Viscount of Charlemont and their house overlooked the whole of Dublin Bay. The invitation included a guest and Joe decided to ask Harry. The evening of the party Joe pressed his trousers and pinned up his regimental cap badge. Harry wore his only suit of clothes in Joe's honor.

They took the tram to Dollymount and then walked up the hill to the gate. The night was warm and already Joe felt the perspiration rising on his forehead. The sentry announced them ostentatiously. Joe noticed the torches were lit even though it was only seven in the evening and the sun wasn't due to set for another hour. The gravel path from the gate to the rotunda where the party was arranged was nearly a quarter of a mile in length.

"Shall I take your arm?" Harry joked as they made their way toward the casino.

"I knew this was a bad idea," Joe answered. "I don't even like Toby Caulfield."

"It's not for Toby Caulfield's sake you accepted."

"That's true. But if I'm going to keep my position I have to play along with the politics."

"Aren't there any rich Catholics in your regiment?"

"The only rich Catholics are in the clergy and none of them are fool enough to send their kin into the army."

"None of them are fool enough to have any kin in the first place."

Once the boys passed the maze of hedges they could see two tables of food spread out to the left and right of the entrance. An ensemble was playing under the tent.

"Beethoven, string quartet number 12 in E flat," Joe said.

"I wouldn't expect any less from you, Joe."

"Let me see if there's anyone here I know. Otherwise, we'll have to hang back behind the cheese tray until Toby makes his appearance."

Joe scanned the crowd. It was not yet fashionably late; only two dozen or so people were there to mingle on the lawn or dance. Six of his fusilier comrades were present, including Richard McCormack and his wife. Three of the soldiers were married men as well and their wives accompanied them. Joe noted with humor that all the women had chosen similar white evening gowns with colored sashes that set them off beautifully alongside the garden flowers—in fact, it made them look like garden flowers, part of the scenery. The other three soldiers stood together unaccompanied next to one of the tables, sipping champagne from narrow goblets.

"Hello, Joe. I'm glad you came," Richard said, striding up to him. "This is my wife, Mary."

Joe took the young woman's hand. "I'm pleased to meet you, Mary. Richard speaks of you often."

"As does my husband of you, Corporal Dooley."

"Thank you." Joe turned to Harry. "Mrs. McCormack, this is my friend Harry Vogeler."

"I'm pleased to meet you, Harry," she said.

"Not an army man, Harry?" Richard asked.

"No, sir."

"Well, I'm pleased you could come."

Just then, Toby Caulfield arrived in a flotilla that included his father, his mother, his two sisters, and an unidentified woman who Joe assumed to be his escort. A grand huzzah went out from the crowd and the band stopped and saluted.

"Thanks, all," Toby began. "And that's the end of the formalities. Here's to the Dubs!"

There was another cheer. Now that the host had made his entrance the room quickly filled up. By nine, you needed a card to get on to the dance floor. The good champagne had run out and the staff resorted to uncorking poor vintages. Joe waited in vain for the opportunity to thank his host personally and settled in a striped lawn-chair in the southeastern corner of the garden that gleaned the last rays of the sun. Harry had wandered off in search of some punch and a young man in a yellow suit came up to Joe to fill the gap.

"You must be Joe Dooley," he said, offering his hand. "Toby has told me all about you."

"I don't believe we've met," Joe said, for in fact he had no idea who this man was or why Toby, of all people, would have ever mentioned him.

"I'm Robert Caulfield, Toby's brother."

"I'm pleased to meet you."

"Quite a martial assemblage we have here today, what?"

"I take it you're not in the army."

"Good heavens, no. The British Army is large enough without me crowding my way in. I'll leave that to my brother. He seems quite dedicated."

"*Spectamur agendo.* That's our motto. But I'm curious—why would Toby have mentioned me to you at all?"

"It's not every day one meets an I.R.B. man in the British Army."

"I'm hardly a…"

"Don't get me wrong, Dooley. I admire your political stance and I think it's a very gallant thing to do when you're paid in English pounds."

"But how…"

"One never gets very far in the King's service without a lot of questions being asked. But really, I only wanted to congratulate you and wish you the best of luck."

"I'm not sure what luck has to do with…"

"Wrong word, sorry. What I meant is 'success.'"

"And why do you keep cutting me off?"

Just then, Harry returned with his drink. The cherry-colored liquid looked vivid in the failing light. Joe thought about cutting Caulfield and then reconsidered.

"Harry, this is Robert Caulfield, Toby's brother. Robert, this is my friend, Harry Vogeler."

Harry put out his hand, but Robert didn't take it.

"Vogeler, eh? That's a German name."

"Excuse me?"

"Haven't you been reading the news? We're about to go to war with Germany."

"I'm an Irishman."

"Are you a soldier, like Joe?"

"No."

"Then I wonder."

"Robert…" Joe implored.

Harry took a step forward. "Do you always insult your guests before you greet them?" Harry asked.

"You aren't my guest."

Joe turned to Harry. "Harry, let's go."

"No, Joe. I'd like to hear more of Mr. Caulfield's views on the world situation."

"You needn't pay attention to my views, Mr. Vogeler—there's nothing extraordinary about them. If you asked anyone here what they thought about Germany you would receive the same response."

"I think you should apologize to me," Harry said, loudly. Turned heads greeted his raised voice.

"I will do nothing of the sort."

"Come on, Harry," Joe implored.

"Hold this, Joe," Harry said, handing Joe his glass.

Joe took the glass and then understood that the reason Harry handed it to him was so he had his hands free to slug Robert Caulfield in the jaw. Caulfield fell to the ground and a cry went up from the vicinity of the punchbowl.

"Now we can go."

Joe put the glass down on the table and followed Harry as he walked away across the lawn. He kept his eye on Harry as he heard a commotion erupt behind him. Someone—he thought it was Richard—called out his name but he was determined not to turn around. There will come a time when all this will be explained, he thought, when he would have to square the circle around his badge and his men and acquiesce to the sacrifices that will be required of him but now was not that time. Now he wanted to be by his friend's side and there he would be. Sure as the last shadow of the day would sink into the sea, he knew it.

# Chapter 7

✦ ✦ ✦

## *Channel Crossing*

✦ ✦ ✦

JOE COULDN'T SLEEP. THE ROCKING OF THE BOAT WAS A SOPORIFIC but the close quarters and the fearfulness that ranged in his stomach militated against it. He tried the bedtime games he had played since childhood, cycling through the names of all his mates and spelling them backwards or following a path in his memory up and down the streets of Dublin. All failed. He looked over to the men sound asleep beside him. He wondered how they managed to burn off their cares until there was nothing left to them but a core of pure instinct. His wonderment relaxed him.

Joe remembered the time in Beggars Bush when Mick Kennedy improvised an Irish flag using a green towel for the field and building a harp of butter beans upon it, all arranged on Corporal Dooley's desk.

"Now there's a useful Republican gesture," Mick cried out to the amusement of the ranks. "You can tuck in a towel and have your lunch."

"Better bring your own corned beef," Tommy rejoined.

"That's for the M.T., don't you think?"

Joe was the M.T., short for the Music Teacher. He earned this sobriquet not for his pedagogy but rather for his careful adhesion to the rules and his reticence in joining in the section's boisterousness.

"Bother you get a scrap of meat out of Dooley."

That was Joe's cue. He tramped in through the side door and sniffed at the still life that covered his paperwork. "What's all this, then?" Joe asked.

Mick was grinning. "An idle gesture, sir."

"If I gave you a warning you'd put up a pot of broth and throw me in it. So we'll skip the lecture this morning and try to keep the beans in reserve until you're hungry."

"Begging your pardon, Corporal Dooley," Tommy said, "but I'm always hungry."

"That's just growing pains, Tom." Richard laughed.

"Don't go complaining to the M.T. about your rations," Billy said, "Or we'll all starve."

Joe didn't mind the comic disrespect because he knew his men loved him and he loved them in return. Mick Kennedy took the lead in the give and take; he was a hard Cork man who had landed in the Dubs due to a last-minute sorting. Mick wasted no time letting Joe know he was not going to let any city-soft fella push him around. He was the first one to call Joe the M.T. to his face and once Joe let him get away with it he knew it was going to be all right.

Tommy Doyle was a favorite as he was an old friend and the only man in the section younger than Joe. Billy Macready switched with the tides; one day he would play Puck roasting the potato skins with Mick in the kitchen and the next he would be the father figure teaching Tommy the quickest way to pack his kit. Then there was Richard McCormack. For some reason unknown, Richard had accepted a low rank, making Joe nominally his superior. In his heart, Joe knew this would not stand in the way of their friendship. It was Richard who first tipped him off to the Dubs—and he was Donal's older brother.

JOE SPENT HIS PENULTIMATE NIGHT IN IRELAND IN A BED WITH Donal McCormack. How this happened is its own tale of overcrowding, willfulness, and plain luck. Mobilization had begun. It was the second week of August and the Dubs had been training at the Curragh for a week. Joe could tell from the way the battle orders were arranged that their brigade was next in the line. The men were encouraged to take care of family business before shipping out, so that Saturday Joe issued a leave. Most of the section headed for home but Richard McCormack could afford to put up his wife, his parents and his brother at the Albert Hotel in Newbridge, less than two miles from camp.

"Thanks much for the chance, Joe," Richard said as they walked out of the barracks. "It means a lot to me."

"You're welcome," Joe answered. "Everyone's entitled to a bit of a leave before deployment. It's my job to see that it happens."

"Still and all, you didn't have to care."

"It's all part of my duties."

"What are you going to do between now and Monday?"

"I think I'll stay put, get things ready."

"Why don't you come with us?"

"I wouldn't think of interfering."

"Nonsense. I can't think of you stuck here in the Curragh with a slice of dried beef in one hand and your order books in the other. We'll have a grand time and Donal would love to see you."

"I would be imposing on you."

"What are another few pounds among friends? Maybe you'll remember me when it comes time to assign sentry duty."

"Richard, I…"

"That's the old M.T. again. I'm kidding you, Joe."

"All right, then."

"Good. Grab your overnight kit and let's get out of here."

Joe packed his bag and he and Richard changed into their dress uniforms and took a car to Newbridge. The lights not yet come on at the Albert and Mary McCormack was waiting in the shadows to greet them. Richard's parents were beside her and Donal stood next to them.

"Dick!" Mary shouted the instant she saw him. "Oh, Dick." She was dabbing at her tears with a handkerchief.

"You look fine, son," his father said, taking his hand.

"Mom, Dad, this is my C.O., Corporal Joe Dooley."

"It's a pleasure to meet you."

"Nice to see you again, Joe," Mary said.

"Hello, Joe," said Donal.

Richard went to talk to the concierge about Joe and returned with a frown on his face. "No surprise here—the hotel is full-up. War orders and all."

"I am imposing on you," Joe said. "I'll go back to the Curragh."

Donal shot him a look. "Don't be a donkey. I've a perfectly good double room and as far as I can tell I'm only one person. Why don't you stay with me?"

"I couldn't…"

"That's a fine idea, Donal," Mr. McCormack said. "Poor Corporal Dooley is going to be sleeping in a field in Belgium before too long. Your sacrifice will be his gain."

"No sacrifice at all," Donal said, smiling.

At dinner, Richard and Mary understandably spent most of the meal engaged in semi-private conversation. Richard's da displayed the geniality that derives from wealth and Joe found his deference to his wife extremely sweet. This combination of benign indifference and casualness helped calm Joe's nerves. A good part of the uneasiness that lay just below Joe's skin when he first saw Donal in the hotel lobby had been vanquished, replaced with an evening's glow caused in no small part by a measure of exceptionally good whiskey. *Bonus adveho ut is quisnam exspecto,* Joe thought, smiling to himself. His Latin proved useful after all and it was pleasant to play the schoolboy once again.

"How was Heidelberg?" Joe asked Donal as they tossed their bags on the bed.

"You'd love it, Joe. The city's ancient and everyone behaves as if they're in a mystery play. But the labs are scrupulously modern and my professors write for all the medical journals. Hopefully this war madness will be over by spring term and I can get back to my anatomy."

"'Tis a shame."

"'Tis more than a shame. I never doubted your commitment and all, Joe, but if you asked me I would have told you the British Army was just looking for a fight and you should only be glad it's the Germans you're shooting at and not Padraig Pearse."

"Didn't we go through all this years ago, Donal?"

"Yes, and look at where it brought us—me in exile in my own parlor and you in full military dress. It's not the kind of world we set out to make back at no. 86, is it?"

"No, I suppose not. But I never thought I was making a world. All I ever wanted to do is to make music."

"The old M.T."

"You heard about that?"

"I think it's clever. There are a million Joes, anyway. Why wouldn't you want to be different?"

"Sometimes, Donal, I really do think you're an idiot."

"Sometimes? Well, that's progress."

Joe was impressed with Donal. The boy he had loved was turning into a man worthy of admiration. Donal was shorter than his brother but still tall—taller than Joe—and the features which so interested Joe back at the college had matured but not been revised. There was still the gleam of delight that flooded his pupils when a really good joke was told and the naturalness that came from a perfect sense of how to place his body in relationship to everything in the world. To Joe it was a form of grace.

Joe stifled a yawn.

"You must be tired, Joe."

"A permanent condition, I'm afraid. It's a big strain, you know, all this preparedness without any real course of action."

"Do you really think you'll prefer racing over a field under fire?"

"I've done it in drill."

"Do I need to remind you that in a drill no one is trying to shoot you?"

"No, you don't."

"Funny, ending up here like this. When I took off for Germany, I figured our little chapter had come to an end. Now here you are."

"We don't have to talk about it, if you prefer not to."

"No, I'm not the diffident type. Talking isn't going to get us anywhere. Get undressed."

They made love quickly and carefully. As it was happening, Joe felt as if he was experiencing a correlate of death, that slow negotiation. Donal represented the part of his life that trailed behind, all the shyness and security and the sound of the pages being turned both literally and figuratively and with the smoothing out of his fist along the ridges of Donal's chest Joe was bidding farewell. With every kiss upon Donal's lips or on the nape of his neck where the soft hairs curled or down below his sternum where his belly lifted and sank quickly with each breath, Joe felt the world of the living receding from him and the world of the dead and dying rushing forward. He was frightened of it and terribly, terribly calm as well. This is the world, Joe thought as he turned over on his side and let Donal wrap his arms and legs around him, and this is what I must do to remember it.

THE WINDOW WAS SITUATED SO THAT THE SUNRISE SHONE DIRECTLY through it, a typically Irish consideration that brooked no opportunity to delay the harvest, postpone the building of a fire, or leave the cattle lowing. Joe awoke with the light. Donal was still asleep, curled up beside him with a pile of pillows stuffed under his head. Joe climbed out of the bed, washed up, and started to put on his uniform.

"I'll meet you downstairs," Joe whispered in Donal's ear.

"Mm."

Joe stepped into the hall and closed the door behind him. He met the McCormacks in the lobby and over tea they joked about Donal's sleeping habits and finally Donal arrived and they went off to mass together. A picnic in Bodenstown and delivery back to the Curragh by nightfall was part of the plan. Throughout it all, Joe sensed he was in a bit of a trance and each time he looked over at Donal and they caught each other's glance he felt as if the two of them were in a funhouse and everyone else was on the opposite side of the mirror. At one point, Mary McCormack asked Joe how he was feeling. Joe believed it was a well intentioned but boilerplate question and that no one, not even Donal, expected him to answer it truthfully.

"I'm very well, thank you, Mrs. McCormack."

"Mary, please."

"Thank you, Mary."

As he unloaded his bags from the car and bade his last farewell, Joe didn't feel much of anything anymore.

"Goodbye, Joe."

It was Donal offering his hand.

"Goodbye, Donal."

"Take care."

"Come on, Joe," Richard said. "I'm exhausted."

"Me, too," Joe agreed.

"Goodbye, son," said Mr. McCormack.

"Goodbye, Da. Thanks for coming."

As he walked back to the barracks, his bag slung over his back, Joe felt as if he couldn't turn around. One turn would finish him. He blinked to wash out his tears and the salt momentarily blinded him. Then he saw Richard holding the door for him and he went in.

THE WEEK BEFORE, JOE HAD VISITED HIS FAMILY IN QUEENSTOWN. His ma embraced him and cried of course as soon as he entered the house. Kath was smiling. He put down his bag but held on to the bouquet of asters he had brought for his aunt. "Let me bring these up to Maeve," Joe said.

Maeve was housebound now. She had difficulty sorting through things and spent most of her time upstairs in her bedroom.

"Hello, Aunt Maeve," Joe began. "I've brought you flowers."

"Is that Joe?" she asked.

"Yes, aunt. It's me."

"Could you get me a glass of water?"

"I've come to see you before I go away."

"Kathleen said she was going to bring me a glass of water."

It went on this way for several minutes. Joe tried to steer the conversation in the direction of an exchange and Maeve added Joe to the list of people in the house who for some reason or another were not doing her bidding. Eventually, Joe resigned himself to bringing Maeve her glass of water and receiving her grace in the form of a weak kiss. He rejoined his family in the parlor below.

"Maeve's feeling poorly," his mother said as Kath brought out a tray with a pitcher of lemonade and three sweet rolls and placed it on a wooden table.

"I suppose she doesn't do well in the heat," Joe said.

"No one does well in the heat," said Kath.

"Look at you in your uniform and all," Mrs. Dooley said.

"It's my job, Ma. But will you look at you?" Joe said to his sister. "What a fine figure you make."

"Thank you."

"How long can you stay, Joe?" Mrs. Dooley asked.

"Only until tomorrow, Ma. I'm in command of my section now and I've got to have everything ready."

"Ready," Kath said. "Everyone has to be ready, as if fighting a war is like having a party. All you have to do is make sure there's enough punch and the sitting room is clean."

"It isn't really all very different from that, I'm afraid."

"Don't make this any harder for your brother than it is already, Kathleen."

"I'm sorry."

"It's all right, Kath," Joe answered. "It's just as difficult to explain to myself and I've been thinking about it for a year."

"We missed you, Joe," his ma said. "With Maeve failing it was all your sister and I could do to keep house."

Joe skipped around this attempt at an entrée and tried to redirect the conversation. "How's your teaching, Kath?"

"I love the children. The pay is poor. Have you ever heard a teacher say otherwise?"

"No," Joe answered, smiling. "I can't say I have." He turned to his mother. "I missed you too, Ma. But I have real responsibilities now. My men depend on me and I depend on them."

"Your first responsibility should be to your family…"

"Ma…"

"…and now you're going to go get yourself killed in a war." The tears started to stream down her cheeks.

"Ma…"

"Drink this," Kathleen said to her, handing her a glass.

Mrs. Dooley took a few cautious sips and handed the glass back to Kathleen. "Thank you."

It was always this way, Joe thought, as he looked around him. Nothing ever changed. The same plaster saint sits on the table near the front door, the same chintz-covered armchair is pushed into the corner and the same Turner mezzotint hangs on the wall above it. Always, the ma made Joe feel as if he was a disappointment to her, as if with just the smallest bit more effort he could have been the son she wanted.

"I'm not going to get myself killed," Joe said, as if this made it so.

THE NEXT MORNING JOE MADE BREAKFAST. HE PUT MAEVE'S TEA and toast on a tray and carried it up to her room, and then he sat with her as she nibbled on the piece of bread and sipped her tea. She smiled at him when she was finished but Joe was never really sure if she knew who he was. Then he set three bowls of oatmeal and three cups of tea on the kitchen table and he sat there with his ma and Kathleen. No one knew what to say and the absence of conversation filled the room. Joe cleaned the table and started to wash up but Kathleen shunted him aside.

"Let me do that," she said as Joe backed away.

It was time to go. He went and fetched his bag from the hall and stood in front of his mother with his arms straight at his side. Tears began to well up in his eyes and he found himself wondering if the tears were from sorrow over the possibility of never seeing his ma or his sister again or if instead they were due to the sadness he felt over the great chasm that separated him from their love and his from theirs.

"Goodbye, Joseph Aloysius Dooley," Mrs. Dooley cried.

"That's me all right, Ma."

"Ta, Joe," Kathleen said.

"I'll be home by Christmas."

"By Christmas, sure," added the ma as she gently closed the door.

THERE WAS ONE FINAL THING TO SETTLE BEFORE CATCHING THE train back to the Curragh. Joe walked toward the sea in the direction of St. Colman's. The spire of the church was finished now and it shone in the summer sun like a vision. The stone yard that he had come to know during his years here was replaced with a playground and the road leading up to the entrance to the cathedral had been paved. The shed where Severin and the other boys lived had been dismantled. Only the ghost of the outline of it remained, a dead border around a small rectangle of grass.

This was where Joe knew to look for what he hoped to find. The summer sun was at its apex and the strong light raked the ground. Joe kicked at the stones and the detritus of the building materials. It only took a minute or two and he saw it—a tiny piece of colored glass, no more than two inches wide, jagged on one side and mostly ultramarine but with tiny flecks of cerulean and crimson. Joe picked up the shard and polished it with his shirt and it gleamed in the sun. Pleased with himself, Joe put the piece of glass in his pocket and started down the hill toward the harbor.

At the bottom of the hill Joe crossed Harbour Row and walked out on the pier. There was a little wooden staircase that led to the strand and at the top of the steps Joe sat down, took off his boots and his socks, and rolled up the cuffs of his trousers. Then he climbed down to the sand and padded out as far as the edge of the tide. The cold water felt good splashing over his feet. The sky was a creamy blue and the water seemed to go on forever. A pair of seagulls dove and screamed as they skimmed the surface. Soon enough my friends, Joe thought, I'll be out there with you.

Joe took the piece of colored glass out of his pocket and gently turned it over and over again in his hand. After some time in the water, he thought, the jagged edges will be smoothed away and the color will be bleached out. Eventually the glass itself will return to the sea, transformed into the sand from which it was born. This is for you, Severin,

Joe thought. Since the water of Cork harbor flows into the Irish Sea and the Irish Sea mingles with the ocean, this piece of glass will reach you and we'll be together again.

Then Joe threw the piece of glass as far as he could and watched it sink into the sea.

⌒

THE DUBS WERE LOADED ON TO A CROSS-CHANNEL FERRY THAT HAD seen better days. It was far too low in the water due to the excessive weight of the men and matériel crammed on the decks and in the hold and the waves crashed over the railings and sloshed everything stored there. As if this was not enough that morning the weather turned and the crossing was punctuated by bursts of lightning, rolling thunder and torrents of rain.

Joe settled his section in a relatively secure corner of the lower deck. It was hot and close but at least it was dry. The sweat drenched his shirt and ran down his forehead. He crumpled to the floor and tossed his kit against the wall. He thought of opening it and taking out the biography of Mozart which he had stowed but between the heat and the rocking of the boat Joe was not confident he could focus on Vienna just now so instead he tried to close his eyes. Then he heard Tommy Doyle cry out. "Corporal Dooley," Tommy said. "Corporal Dooley, sir."

"What is it, Tommy?"

"I think I'm going to be sick."

"Didn't you take the medicine they gave you before we boarded?"

"I did, sir. It made me sicker."

"I understand, Tom. But how can I help you?"

"I don't know, sir. I just thought you should know."

Just then, Mick Kennedy popped in and stirred the pot in his own helpful way. "Why don't you just spew it out and get it over with?" he said. "It might make an appetizing mix with the rest of the smells on this boat."

"Thank you for your advice, Private Kennedy."

"You're welcome, sir."

Mick slid down next to Tommy. "Don't mind the M.T., Tom. You'll be fine."

Tommy tried to smile and closed his eyes.

"Where's Richard and Billy gone to?" Joe asked.

"Either the latrine or the canteen, I suppose," said Mick. "Unless they decided to chuck it all and throw themselves into the channel."

"I haven't felt right since Gravesend," Joe said. "Maybe there's something wrong with the food."

"It's feeding Irishmen English rations that's the problem. Did you see what they called bacon? It looked like something pulled out of the side of a dog. I can't wait until we get to France with people who know what a decent meal is."

"We still have to eat our own rations in France," Joe said.

"Says you."

The boat took another tumble and a cheer went up from the 4th Lancashires opposite.

"Gravesend was a lousy pun," Mick complained. "Who ever heard of sending an army to train for a war in a town called Gravesend? They might have well named it Death's Door."

Joe smiled.

"I'm glad to see your spirits are holding up, Mick. I guess if you can make it through Gravesend and the bacon and this boat ride you'll stand up well enough against the Uhlans."

"I guess I will, Joe."

Joe thought that he should pay closer attention to wherever it was that Billy and Richard were off to but then he figured that all in all they couldn't go too far so he allowed the rumble of the engine to lull him and finally he drifted off to sleep. In his sleep, he dreamed of Harry.

THE DAY AFTER THE PARTY AT THE CAULFIELDS', HARRY WAS UNDER-standably in a foul mood. He and Joe had been parsing pints in Neary's and Harry was only at the midpoint of his roster of complaints. "What do I have to do to be treated fairly?" he asked. "Do I have to change my name to Smith?"

"You could change it to Dooley," Joe said, trying to lighten the mood. "It's a name that will serve. Anyway, even the royal family has a German name. It's not the name that's the problem. It's the fools who think there's something to it."

"Without papers, Joe, they'll never let me stay here."

"You could go back to America."

"Would you want me to do that?"

"Of course not, Harry."

"Then why did you suggest it?"

"Harry, I'm your friend. I'm trying to help you. Please don't be angry at me, too."

Harry drank up and ordered another round. "I'm sorry, Joe. It's just that—all my life, I've been told I was an outsider, different, not like everyone else—a German among Irishmen. An Evangelical among Catholics…"

"…a genius in a land of idiots," Joe added. Harry smiled. "Look, Ireland is an easy country to get lost in. While I'm overseas, you could go out west. I'm sure there are plenty of sympathetic farmers who could use someone to keep their horses and they won't be asking any questions."

"That's still a hiding life, Joe."

"Better than no life at all. It'll only be for a couple of months. You'll be safe there."

"I don't feel safe anywhere."

"Don't say that, Harry."

The barkeep handed them another pair of stouts.

"Well, that's scratched. I feel safe here."

"Here, in Dublin?"

"Here, in the sanctuary of the glass."

JOE AND HARRY SETTLED ON NO PLAN THAT NIGHT BUT EVENTS eventually overtook them. The following morning Germany issued an ultimatum to Serbia and the newspapers were full of war talk. Normal commerce was impossible and Sackville Street overflowed with listless spectators and newsboys hawking fifty-point headlines. Joe was certain that his mobilization orders would come down in a day or two and he and Harry were trying to make their way to the property offices on Tyrone Street to make sure his lease would stay in force.

Just then Joe recognized two soldiers from another section in his barracks walking toward him. They spotted Joe.

"Good morning, Corporal Dooley," the first one said.

"Good morning…excuse me, I can't remember your names."

"I'm Lieutenant Moore and this is Private Davies. Royal Irish Rifles… sir."

"It's a pleasure."

Joe was uncertain as to whether introducing Harry at this point was a good idea and his uncertainty was contagious. Harry took two steps back, climbing up on the curbstone so he could be a few inches taller than everyone else.

"Not in uniform, I see," said Davies.

"No. I'm only in for three shifts."

"Those days are done," Moore said, pointing to the masses in the street. "Look at 'em. There'll be a queue to enlist."

Davies swung around behind Harry and Harry took a few steps away from him. Joe's body tensed. There was something about the direction of the conversation that he didn't like.

"Are you a Dub, too?" Davies asked Harry.

"No, sir."

"Not in the army?"

"No."

"Not a volunteer?"

Joe interrupted. "I'm sorry, but we really must get to the estate office before it closes for lunch. Come on, Harry."

"They won't be opening their doors at all today, Dooley. What's your hurry?" Moore asked.

"Who's your friend?" chimed Davies, closing in on Harry.

"Joe…" Harry cried.

"Don't you have somewhere you need to get to?" Joe asked, crossing between them.

"What's up with you, Dooley?"

"All these questions. I'll see you around, boys," Joe said, putting his arm around Harry and turning away. Joe felt ashamed and afraid, both for himself and for Harry. It was the indirection of the threat that made him nervous. Something was going to happen and he didn't want to wait to find it out.

"We'll see you in France," Moore shouted after them.

As Joe and Harry retreated across Sackville Street, the crowd thickened around them. Beads of sweat were rolling down Harry's brow and a wide V of perspiration had soaked through his shirt. Behind his spectacles, Harry's eyes were red and clouded. They walked home swiftly and in silence and even there the struggle continued. The staircase at Talbot Street seemed steeper than it ever had before and the room was overheated from being closed up all morning. Harry tore off his shirt and collapsed on the couch.

"You're all right now, Harry. You're safe."

"No, I'm not."

"What are you talking about?"

"I can't stay here anymore."

"You have no money, Harry. Who else is going to take you in?"

"I mean I can't stay in Ireland anymore, Joe. I have to go to Germany."

"What? To fight for the Germans? That's madness."

"I have no papers. If I'm arrested here, I'll be detained for the duration."

"If you go to Berlin, they'll march you to Belgium."

"No one else will take me."

"You're scared, Harry. You're frightened. Let me talk some sense into you."

"If you really wanted to help me, you'd ask the union to smuggle me out of the country. What do you think your soldier friends would do to me if they had the chance?"

"They weren't my friends."

"Is this who you want to fight for?"

"I don't want to fight anyone."

"You don't have a choice anymore."

"No. I suppose I don't."

"Once I'm in Germany I can make my way to Leipzig. I know people there who will take care of me. They can help me and protect me. You'll see—I'll be back in Dublin in no time at all. We both will be."

"Harry, they're going to send me to fight."

"I know."

"I'd feel better if I knew you were safe."

"I will be."

"Why should I trust you, Harry?"

"Haven't I always trusted you, Joe?"

"Fair enough."

"All right then."

Joe got up and found Harry a clean shirt. He handed it to his friend and walked to the sink to pour them both glasses of cold water. Then he brought the two glasses back to the table and sat down. "What do you want me to do?"

"Tomorrow morning, as early as you can, go to Aungier Street and talk to a man named Colin. He's been helpful arranging ways to get men from Ireland to Scotland and then across the North Sea to Bremen."

"You've worked this all out, haven't you?"

"I saw it coming."

"And here it is."

THE NEXT DAY JOE WENT TO AUNGIER STREET AS HARRY ASKED AND got the papers from Colin and brought them back to Talbot Street. He helped Harry pack up as much as he could fit—two changes of clothes, a toothbrush and a bar of soap, and the sheet music to "*Für Elise*" that Harry had been carrying with him since America. They walked to Amiens Station where Harry would catch a train to the north. At the foot of the staircase, Harry turned around and grabbed Joe by the shoulders. "This is where we part, my friend. Where I am going is no place for a man in a British Army uniform."

Joe started to cry. Harry wrapped his arms tightly around him and held him close.

"I don't think I'll ever see you again," Joe said, rubbing the tears from his eyes,

"Don't say that, Joe. I'll find you, never fear."

"That's a hard promise you're making, Harry."

"Have you ever known me to make the easy ones?"

Joe tried to smile a little. "No."

"*Auf wiedersehn,* my friend."

"*Slan agat.*"

Harry climbed the steps to the platform. Joe turned away and walked down Talbot Street. He heard the whistle of the train as it approached and pulled into the station. He waited until he heard the gears shifting and the brakes whistling and the insistent and accelerating churning of the rods. As it slowly faded away, the sound jumbled his thoughts.

When Joe awoke the ferry was docking at Le Havre. It was a dream, after all.

# Chapter 8

◆ ◆ ◆

## *A Farmhouse in Neuve Eglise*

◆ ◆ ◆

JOE'S SECTION WAS MARCHING EAST TOWARD PLOEGSTEERT WOOD across open fields and dry ravines. The front line was ten miles away and the principal evidence of war other than themselves and their matériel was the scarcity of Belgians. From the stalls of the churches to the troughs in the barns the normal activities of civilization had been abandoned. Joe was struck by the poignancy of the grape vines with their deep purple fruit burgeoning on their shaded vines and no one to harvest them.

For their billets in Neuve Eglise the men found a friendly aubergiste who was willing to open his bar for the men and share a bottle of wine and a plat du jour. It was no more than a cellar and a table but for the Dubs it was Grafton Street. Billy and Mick had moved on from the wine and were passing around a tall bottle of ale that the proprietor had offered up as a bonus. Richard was carving a wheel of cheese on a wooden pallet. For one brief instant it was possible for Joe to imagine that this was all there was to war, as if it was no more complicated than arranging a picnic.

Tommy lifted the last of his burgundy and offered a toast. "To the Dubs in France!" he cheered, lifting his glass in the air.

"You can do better than that, Tom," Mick said.

"Wholly unimaginative," Billy added.

"I don't know what you mean, boys," said Tommy. "We're the Dubs. We're in France. I've a glass in my hand."

Mick stifled a laugh. Joe stood up. "We're in Belgium, Tommy."
Billy and Mick struck up a tune:

> I'm going to fight for Belgium, Ma.
> I'm going to win the war.
> I haven't a clue
> What to do
> Or what we're fighting for.

> I've dusted off my helmet.
> I've dusted off my pants.
> I'm going to fight for Belgium, Ma,
> But I'm doing it from France.

"That's enough," Joe said.

Tommy approached Billy with the look of murder in his eyes. "You tell me, Bill, if you're not grateful for a toast wherever it is."

"I am."

"Well, then."

"Sit down, Tommy," Mick said. "We were just having a joke is all."

"I'll stand when I want to."

"Don't cause a fuss, Tom," Joe said, finally. "We're all a bit fashed from marching. I think we should thank our host, pay up, and get some rest."

Mick stood up and hoisted what was left in his glass. "To the proprietor!"

Billy put four sous on the bar. "*Merci, monsieur.*"

"*Merci,*" the keeper replied agreeably. "*Bonne nuit.*"

"Ah, good night."

As the men climbed up the stairs Mick's uneven tenor filled the warm night air:

> I'm going to fight for Belgium, Ma.
> I'm going to win the war.
> I haven't a clue
> What to do
> Or what we're fighting for...

THE FOLLOWING DAY JOE RECEIVED A REPORT OF AN INFILTRATION of Prussians east of the village. Alongside the Dubs there were at least a dozen more sections attempting to establish a firm line from Lessines to Mons, a distance of nearly twenty miles. It was imperative for them to operate in tandem as quickly as possible. Joe thought it would be prudent for a scouting party to explore the woods and fields surrounding the village and determine the extent of the threat. He volunteered himself for the mission and asked Tommy to accompany him.

They set out around dusk, choosing a road that skirted the town. They passed an abandoned lunatic asylum, a glum brick building with barred windows. Fields of wildflowers lined the road with their yellow and orange heads bobbing in the breeze. At one point, Tommy spotted a man walking toward them across a cropped hillock and he pulled his rifle at the ready. It turned out to be the owner of the farm inspecting his till.

By nine o'clock, Joe and Tommy had advanced to the northeast perimeter of Neuve Eglise. They sat down on the side of the road and ate their rations—a tin of beef and a package of crackers—and shared a drink of water. Tommy took a nip from his rum. Just then they saw four torches in the distance. The torchbearers had split into pairs and fanned out, a certain sign that they were not farmers making a late-night inspection. Joe lifted his rifle and motioned Tommy to fall in behind him.

"Come with me," Joe whispered to Tommy as he slid off the road and took cover in a gully. "Lie as flat as you can and don't move until you see my signal."

Joe and Tommy pressed themselves down to the ground and waited. From his vantage point Joe could no longer see the torches but he watched their light touch the tips of the trees and gain in intensity as the glow advanced. There was no sound at all save the padding of the men's boots on the hard dirt. Finally, Joe heard their voices:

*"Ich hab' keine Zigarette an mir, Hans. Was sagst du?"*

*"Guch nicht so auf mich. Ich habe nichts."*

*"Gibt hier nichts mehr zu tun. Allons-y."*

That last blast of French got a rise out of the other fellow and he laughed. Joe could feel Tommy shaking beside him but it was too dangerous to say anything. He put his palm on the small of Tommy's back and held it there. The voices stopped. After a moment, Joe heard the footfalls resume. He waited until the sound had faded and the light from the torches was too diffuse to penetrate their position, then he climbed up on his knees and peered into the darkness.

"All clear."

Tommy stood up, a tragic look on his face.

"What's the matter, Tom? The Germans are gone."

"It's nothing."

"Tom?"

"I pissed myself, that's all."

"It happens to the best of us."

"It never happened to me."

"Welcome to the army, Tommy."

THE BOYS RETURNED TO THE ROAD BUT JOE DECIDED THEY HAD ventured too close to the houses where the Germans were most likely billeted. He told Tommy they were going to retrace their steps and spend the night in one of the barns they had passed a mile or so back. The first outbuilding they found had a rusty but still efficient padlock on the door; a second one two hundred yards farther up the road was green with mold and infested with mice. Joe was getting hungry again as well as tired from all the miles of marching but he thought of Tommy in his abjection and swallowed his complaints. Finally, they made out a little farmhouse set back about one hundred feet from the road. It was far enough away that another scouting party would most likely be incurious about it. Joe lit his torch and led the way along the gravel path.

The first thing Joe noticed as he approached the house was the smell of smoke in the air. It was too dark to see the chimney but the smell seemed to indicate that a fire was burning inside. The windows were covered with curtains and no light could be seen within. He knocked gently on the wooden door.

"*Excusez-moi?*" he whispered tentatively into the darkness. "*Est-ce que quelqu'un à la maison?*"

He waited patiently for a reply, then knocked again.

"Nobody's home, Joe."

"Wait."

Joe heard someone moving inside the house and saw a candle being lit by the window.

"*Quesque c'est?*" came a woman's voice from within.

"*Nous sommes les anglaises. Pouvons-nous entrer?*"

There was a moment's pause and then Joe heard the sound of the lock being turned. The door opened and a woman with long black hair greeted them.

"*Bonjour, madame. Parlez-vous anglais?*" Joe asked.

"Yes, a little."

"That's good. My friend and I are on a patrol and we would like to ask if you might be so kind as to allow us to stay with you until dawn."

"I am not sure."

"*Bien sur.* It is only with your indulgence that we would dare to come in. I promise we will not be a bother to you."

Just then, a young girl came up behind the woman and pulled on the sleeve of her chemise. "*Maman, ce qui est de ce?*"

"*Il n'y a rien,* Lisette."

"If it's too much of a bother, madame…"

The woman shook her head and pulled the door open all the way. "*Eh, bien…* You have already awakened the household and better you than the Germans. Come in."

The light from the single candle barely reached the corners of the room but Joe could see the woman ran a neat if not prosperous household. A shelf of white stoneware bowls over the stove gleamed in the dull glow and a simple but beautifully carved table and chairs were arranged in front of it. There was a framed photograph of the family hanging on the wall next to the door; the woman and her smiling daughter stared out from it, seated in front of a handsome young man in uniform.

"I am Giselle Picard, and this is my daughter, Lisette."

"I'm Corporal Joe Dooley, and this is Private Tommy Doyle."

Joe put out his hand but Giselle curtseyed instead and took a step back to put her arm around her daughter.

"Thank you, ma'am, for letting us in," Tommy said.

"Ah, you do speak," Giselle said, smiling. "For a moment I thought perhaps you were the corporal's…*comment dites-vous cela?*…dummy."

"Your English is quite good, madame," said Joe, surprised.

"I try not to let on, either to the English or the Germans. I find it is best to not understand what soldiers are trying to tell you."

"You have a lovely daughter, Madame Picard."

"*Merci.*" Giselle turned to her daughter. "*N'ayez pas peur des soldats, Lisette. Ils ne pourront pas te blesser.*"

Lisette took a step forward into the light and curtseyed.

"*Mon plaisance,*" Joe said.

"Your French is not so bad, either, Corporal Dooley."

"Thank you, madame. But we have taken up too much of your time as it is. Please tell us where we would be most out of your way and we will allow you and your daughter to return to your sleep."

"Take a look around you, sir. The only place where you would be most out of our way is in the potato patch. Would you like something to eat or drink before you try to become invisible?"

"That would be most kind, madame."

Tommy went to clean himself up. Giselle walked to the kitchen and brought back a bowl of apples and half a loaf of bread. Lisette carried a liter of wine and arranged the plates and glasses on the table.

"May I ask," Joe began, "Have the Germans come knocking?"

"Not since last week. I think they are all heading in the direction of Armentières."

"I don't want you to do or say anything for which you would feel uncomfortable, but it would be most valuable to me if you could be more precise about the number of men and their destination."

"If you mean do I know anything at all about the German troop movements, I would have to tell you in all honesty I do not."

"Thank you."

Tommy returned. Lisette stood behind her mother, silently refilling the glasses each time they were emptied.

"Your hospitality has exceeded our expectations, Madame Picard. But now I am certain we are overstaying our time in your company. I wish you both a good night."

"Good night, gentlemen," Giselle said.

"*Et bon nuit, Lisette,*" Joe whispered.

Lisette smiled. "*Bon nuit, monsieur.*"

BY SIX A.M. THE ROOM BEGAN TO FILL WITH LIGHT. JOE STAGGERED to his feet and put on his jacket and boots. The rest of the household slept peacefully around him. He went to the stove and lit the fire under the kettle. It would be kind to do something nice for Madame Picard and he thought to make some coffee for everyone before he and Tom crept back to the line. Joe was looking about the room for the tin of coffee grounds when he felt someone tap gently on his shoulder. Startled, he turned around to see Lisette standing beside him, holding out a folded newspaper.

"*Excusez-moi, monsieur,*" she began, whispering. "My mother tries very hard not to get involved but I think she likes me to be the brave one. I believe you would want this."

"What is it?" Joe asked.

"When the Germans came through, one of the soldiers had a newspaper with him. He left it behind."

"And…?"

"I do not speak any German so I thought nothing of it until two days ago when I went to put it in the fire. I opened it up and there was a paper inside of it—the paper that is there now. I know enough to know that this piece of paper should not have come to me so I am giving it to you."

"*Merci beaucoup, Lisette.*"

"*Que Dieu vous garde, monsieur.*"

Madame Picard began to stir so Joe took the newspaper from Lisette and tucked it into the pocket of his jacket. Just then, the water began to boil.

"Where is your coffee?" Joe asked.

"I know." Lisette turned to fetch it.

Giselle sat up. "Lisette, *ce que est passé?*"

"*Il n'y a rien, Maman.* I'm just helping the soldiers make some coffee."

Tommy sat up and stretched.

"Feeling better, Tom?" Joe asked.

"Ugh. Nightmares."

"And this from a peaceful billet in the Belgian countryside. I can't wait to see how you'll sleep through a battle."

"I'd rather have the nightmares here and the dreams on the battlefield."

"It's time. Let's drink up and get going before the Germans think twice about Neuve Eglise."

"Grand."

Tommy and Joe sat around the table with Mme. Picard and Lisette. The coffee was strong and sweet and there was a fresh loaf of bread and real butter on the table. Joe could imagine the scene repeating itself at Richard McCormack's home in Wicklow—Richard and Donal and the ma and da sipping from their Staffordshire as the butter melted and curled. It was a vision for him to sense this scene transposed to the front. He found himself thinking that if this was the beginning of his last day on earth he would not do better.

The boys repacked their kits and stowed their gear. The sun was just rising and if they walked quickly enough and did not lose their way they'd be back in the camp before a single Jerry could wipe the clouds from his eyes.

"I cannot thank you enough, Madame Picard, for your kindness and your hospitality."

"You are most welcome, Corporal Dooley."

"Goodbye, Lisette," Tommy cried as he headed out along the road.

"*Au revoir,* Lieutenant."

They waved from the road one last time before starting their walk.

"All clear, Joe?"

"All clear."

"I tell you, Joe. The next time we billet in a house with two women, could you arrange it so that at least one of them is between the ages of twenty and twenty-five?"

"I will do so, Tom, if next time you don't piss in your pants before we get there."

WHEN JOE AND TOMMY RETURNED TO THE LINE THE ONLY NEWS the Dubs wished to hear were the details of their adventure. They lost interest when it became apparent that the story lacked a romance. Joe took out the newspaper Lisette had given him and laid it down on the trestle table. There was a typed list of regiments in numerical order and penciled notes in German beside each entry. Joe thought it might prove valuable to someone with a larger scope of vision but when he sent it up he found out the intelligence it portrayed was old and discouraging. The news from the other sections was just as bad. German scouting parties had been spotted on every flank—to the west in Fletre, to the east coming out of Ploegsteert, and straight at them in even larger numbers from Messines. There was nowhere for the Dubs to go but south, crossing the border back into France and probing along the front until they found a hole.

For three days, Joe and his men traded places with the German infantry. In every town they entered, the other side had just pulled out. From Deulemont to St. Andre there wasn't a safe place to billet. Joe slept his men in the fields and marched them through the night. In Valenciennes they met up with a section from the Warwickshire Rifles. An ambush on the road to Mons had left a quarter of their men wounded and the church had been converted to a medical station. As Joe passed the row of beds he wondered how long it would be before one of his men was lying there.

BY THE LAST WEEK OF AUGUST JOE'S COMPANY HAD MADE IT TO Haucourt and well-deserved relief in the company of the 1st Warwickshires and the 2nd Lancashires. They were billeted in an old hotel and one of the rooms had a bathtub. It was a sight to see all those Tommies, black with grime and naked but for a scrap of a towel, queued up outside the door like a nervous swimming team before a meet. When it was Mick's turn he didn't stand on ceremony but dropped his towel right there in the hallway and nearly somersaulted into the tub.

"Jesus, the water's cold!" Mick shouted as the other Dubs angled in the doorway. "And who the hell used up all the soap?"

"There's a bar of soap above the sink, Mick," Joe called in, helpfully.

"I'm not getting out of the tub for a fecking bar of soap, M.T. Toss it to me or the hell with it."

"That's the attitude, Mick," said Billy.

Joe walked into the bathroom and handed Mick a bar of soap. "Here's your soap, Mick."

"And here's the water for it," Mick answered. He ladled his hands in the water and lifted huge plashes of it on Joe's head and chest. Joe wiped the suds and foam from his face. He approached the tub with a stern and serious expression on his face. "Private Kennedy."

Mick stood up. The water dripped from his chest and legs. "Yes, sir?"

"You know what that sort of behavior calls for, don't you?"

"Yes, sir."

At that, Joe crouched down and flung as much water as he could muster directly into Mick's astonished face. Mick let out a roar and grabbed Joe by the collar. Joe started to laugh and pushed back at Mick but he lost his balance and when Mick's arms came down he pulled Joe straight into the tub with him, uniform and all. This unleashed a general fracas. A naked Billy tried to wrestle the soap-soaked Mick out of the bathtub. Tommy was laughing uncontrollably, pointing at the waterlogged Joe who sat on the edge of the tub with a cockeyed smile upon his face.

"Come on in, Tom!" Joe shouted as Mick turned on the tap and flung the water in sheets in Doyle's direction.

Only Richard kept his dignity. "There's others waiting for the bath, Kennedy," he called out from the sidelines.

"I'm the commanding officer here, Richard, and I say there's enough water in France to wash the war off of every soldier from here to Calais."

"I've never received orders from a man in a bathtub before," Richard said.

"At least not while in uniform," Mick put in.

"Enough of that," Joe said. "Out you go, Mick. Who's next?"

"I believe I am," Billy said, standing in the center of the tub.

"So it appears," Mick answered, stepping into his towel.

Joe thought the moment had come to reassert control. "That's all right, but do it quickly, Bill. Tom, you go after Bill. I want you all the dining room in half an hour."

Joe's room was near the center staircase and as he padded down to it his soaked uniform left a trail of water along the parquet floor. He knew he had an extra shirt and pants but his mind went blank trying to recall what else was there. Luck, another pair of trousers, worn at the knee. 'Twill serve. And I'll wear a clean shirt to dinner. Why not? For the first time since landing in France, Joe felt himself in a merry mood.

When the men reassembled in the dining room, the sun had started to set and the shadowy light tinged everything with gold. The gas was working and one of the company cooks scraped together a potpie out of two tins of beef, a bunch of wilted carrots, three potatoes, and a pastry crust composed without a scrap of butter. The men served themselves with silver knives and forks on porcelain plates engraved with a decorated "H" in the center. It was a hearty meal for hungry soldiers.

After they had finished eating, Joe took his men aside and led them to the library. All the books were in French but Joe found a book of fairy tales that had the music to some old songs in it. This would do perfectly, he thought.

Mick, of course, was the first to sense the direction the evening was taking and the first by rights to criticize it. "Run for your lives," he began. "The M.T. has a book out."

"Just give me ten minutes, boys," Joe said. "There may not be many more chances for us to relax in this manner again for a long while."

"You never needed any sort of excuse to talk to us before," Billy chimed in.

"'Tis true."

"The clock is running. Eight more minutes and we walk out on you, Joe."

Joe picked up the book and opened it to a page of music. "I was a music teacher in Dublin…"

"We know all about the M.T., sir."

"…and I thought tonight instead of a prayer we could have a song as a benediction. I found one here. It's an old French folk tune called '*Au clair de la lune.*' French mothers have been singing it to their children for generations now."

"So now you're going to read us a bedtime story?" Tommy asked.

"It's not so much the meaning of the words but the sound of us all singing together that I think will lift our spirits. This is how it goes…"

Joe read through the music to himself, and then he put down the book and sang:

> *Au clair de la lune,*
> *Mon ami Pierrot.*
> *Prete-moi ta plume*
> *Pour écrire un mot.*
>
> *Ma chandelle est morte.*
> *Je n'ai plus de feu*
> *Ouvre-moi ta porte*
> *Pour l'amour de Dieu.*

"That's really lovely, Joe," Billy said. "But what does it mean?"

"It's all about hope. The singer is out in the dark and he comes to this house. He's asking for a light, so he can write a poem for his friend. Let's try it together."

Joe sang out the words slowly and carefully and the others joined in. Mick was tentative and off-key. Tommy was bold with a surprisingly assured baritone. Richard and Billy amused themselves by trying it in harmony and after the first few measures the sound was actually beautiful. The resonance of the overtones caught all of them, even Joe, by surprise and instead of petering out after the last line they struck up another verse:

> *Au clair de la lune*
> *Pierrot repondit*
> *Je n'ai pas de plume*
> *Je suis dans mon lit.*
>
> *Va chez la voisine*
> *Je crois qu'elle y est*

*Car dans sa cuisine*
*On bat le briquet.*

Richard walked over to Tommy and put his arm around him and they began to sway together to the rhythm of the music. The first verse came around again and Joe beamed as Mick and Billy marched around the library table with their candlesticks.

*Ma chandelle est morte.*
*Je n'ai plus de feu*
*Ouvre-moi ta porte*
*Pour l'amour de Dieu.*

When they reached the final "*pour l'amour de Dieu*" Joe slowed them down so that the full sound of their voices could be appreciated.

"'For the love of God,'" said Joe, "That's what the last line means."

"Amen," said Richard. And so said they all.

# Chapter 9

♦ ♦ ♦

## Doyle's Night Out

♦ ♦ ♦

At three a.m. five British soldiers came slouching up the road from Caudry. One of them had his right arm in a sling and another was hobbling on one leg, his weight borne by his buddy. Most of the Dubs were sleeping but Joe was sitting up against a poplar and reading a newspaper by torchlight. When the first of the Lancs approached, he stood up and saluted. "Good morning, men."

"We've lost the East Lancashires and we need medical attention," the one holding up his comrade began. "Do you know the best way back?"

With the sound of voices, Billy and Mick began to stir. In his fuddle Mick reached for his rifle too quickly and knocked over a stockpile of butter tins. The subsequent clatter succeeded in waking Tommy and Richard and the entire party assembled to hear the news.

"I think the road to Haucourt is clear," Joe answered. "We were billeted there yesterday and we've advanced this far without any trouble. You should find a decent dressing station there but if you need any bandages or iodine I'm certain we could spare some."

"Thanks, much," said the boy with the bad leg.

One of the healthier Lancs pulled out a cigarette and put a match to it. "Any takers?" he asked, offering up the box.

"Why not?" Mick asked, helping himself. "Now that I'm awake…"

"You'll be wanting to stay awake." The visitor regarded the Dubs critically. "There's an entire brigade of Jerries coming across the ravine from the northeast."

"Jesus," said Tommy.

"They cut us off while we were crossing from Fontaine to Caudry. We tried to call in our position but then the shells started to fly so we struck out to the southwest and hoped for the best."

"And the best is what you found, boys," Joe answered. "I'm Corporal Joe Dooley and these are the gleanings of the 2nd Royal Dublin Fusiliers."

"Pleased to meet you, corporal. And thanks."

There were introductions, and cigarettes and water bottles were passed around. Then the Lancs took a peek at Joe's maps. They were mostly of Belgium and of no use here but Joe found a crumpled fragment that represented a corner of France and proved an aid to reorientation. The Lancs repacked and heaved themselves into the center of the road, saluting and cheering until they fell out of sight. Billy swung around a tree trunk and whistled softly to himself. "Poor buggers," he began. "The Lancs must have been first in the line at Caudry."

"We've got to turn back, Joe," said Mick.

"No," Joe said. "It may be hard but we need to continue our advance. We've got to meet up with the King's Own and whatever Lancs made it through and cross that ravine. It's only a few miles and we'll have plenty of support. I know we can do it and we must do it."

"Yes, sir," Billy answered.

"I think we should keep sliding to the northwest," Richard suggested. "That way if there's a German advance we won't have our backs to it."

"That's a good idea." Joe checked his watch. "It's almost four now. The sun'll be up in two hours and it'll be a lot more difficult to find cover, so I suggest we move out."

"Yes, sir," said Mick.

"Why are you so quiet this morning, Tom?" Joe began. Tommy sat up and started putting his gear in his pack, busily arranging things as a substitute for the words that wouldn't come. "When I ask you something, Tommy, I would expect an answer."

"I was just thinking, Joe."

"You can think and talk at the same time, can't you, Tommy?"

"I was thinking about the day I joined up."

"And you never bargained for this, is that what you're saying?"

"No. I was recollecting our celebration that night."

"It all began in the Stag's Head, didn't it, Tom?" Billy asked.

"'Twas the Stag's Head, indeed."

⌢

THERE WAS A RACE AT FAIRYHOUSE THAT AFTERNOON AND A BAND of touts had settled along the perimeter of the bar blocking the normal access of the regulars. It took several minutes of jostling and a small amount of importuning before all four Dubs could be arrayed along the counter at the same time. (Richard, being the family man, had gone home). Once their territory had been annexed it took no time at all for the action to begin. Tom ordered up a quartet of stouts and the boys were busy clanking before their elbows hit the bar.

"To an army's worth of Doyles," Joe began.

"For what it's worth," Tommy said, smiling.

"I'm sure you have some value," Mick added. "I'd wager we would get at least two pounds for you on the open market."

"For me or for my uniform?"

"For the uniform, of course. If we stripped you naked you still wouldn't be worth a shilling."

"Not even science would be interested," Joe said.

"I've found I'm a very interesting medical curiosity," Tommy went on. "A Dublin man who manages to pay for his own drinks."

A roar of laughter erupted from the ranks as the boys showered the marble top with coins. The metal rang against the stone and two farthings landed on their edges and rolled into the sink. The barkeep fetched them out and sleighted them into his apron pocket. "That's two for the house, boys," he said as he pulled another round.

Joe enjoyed the milieu of the pub. It was liberating not being the center of attention for a change. Tommy Doyle was the new kid in town and Joe was merely a fellow soldier out for a grand night. It felt good for him to see Tommy so at ease. The Tommy Doyle Joe knew was the small and skinny ten year old he had left behind at St. Mary's. Now Tom was six feet tall and twenty-three years old and although he still looked like he only needed to shave once a week he had a smile that would slay the lassies if it were only to come out more often.

There were no orders to issue here and fewer than that to be obeyed. The sweet and sour of the beer on his tongue and the peripheral sounds of the conversations were a distraction. He found himself losing his focus on the persons and their words and instead watched the reflection of the tiny electric light bulbs over the bar as they shone in the dark mahogany panels and gold-painted ceiling.

"I'll stand the next round if you can balance a billiard ball on your nose for five seconds, Tom," Billy challenged.

"There's men using the table," Joe said, realizing at once that this merely served as a provocation.

"They can muster five minutes without one of their precious ivories," said Billy scornfully.

"You're on," Tom said.

Billy put his beer down on the counter and walked over to the snooker table. An old man with a gray beard was about to take a shot when Billy grabbed the no. 5 ball and carried it away in the palm of his hand like an egg.

"For shite's sake, boy, what are you doing with that ball?" the old man cried.

"Hold on to your stick, old man. It'll be back before you can count to ten."

The boys cleared out a space along the bar for Tommy to stand and Billy ceremoniously held the ball up in front of Tommy's face and rubbed it over and over again in his hands. "I'll put a little English on it to make the trick more difficult," he said.

"A little English makes everything more difficult," Mick confirmed.

Tommy planted his feet apart on the floor and raised his head to stare at the ceiling. Like a Greek statue he looked. Billy plucked the ball from his fist and planted it on the tip of Tommy's nose. It fell right off. A roar went up from the crowd as the ball bounced on the floor and rolled into a snug.

"Let's try it again; let's try it again," Tommy insisted as he fortified himself with another sip from his glass. The gentleman in the snug recalled the ball and delivered it to Billy.

"Maybe the problem isn't with the talent but with the set-up," Mick said. "Give me that ball." He grabbed the ball out of Billy's hand. "Enough of this nonsense. We've got to get back to drinking. Are ye ready, Tom?"

"Steady as she goes."

Mick laid the ball on Tommy's nose. This time, Tom shimmied like a variety dancer and the ball tipped a little left and right but stayed planted firmly on the tip of his nose as the parade along the bar counted it down.

"Five, four, three, two, one…"

At one, the ball rolled forward. Tom reached up and pushed it back into place.

"Zed!"

Cheers rang out. Billy launched a protest. "The ball fell off before the nought…"

"Put a cork in it, Macready, and order up."

"But…"

"The night is growing older, Charming Billy. Let it go."

THE DUBS HAD BEEN MARCHING FOR AN HOUR WHEN A SMALL RAIN began to fall. To cheer themselves up, they broke into a chorus of "Goodbye, Dolly Gray" and their notes resounded in the Picardy fields:

> *Goodbye Dolly I must leave you,*
> *Though it breaks my heart to go.*
> *Something tells me I am needed*
> *At the front to fight the foe…*

"Are we getting the words right, M.T.?" Mick shouted from the rear.

"Letter perfect, boys. Just don't let the Germans hear you."

"I hope they're listening. I can shoot better than I can sing."

"Doesn't take much."

"Shut up."

They continued:

> *See—the soldier boys are marching*
> *And I can no longer stay.*
> *Hark—I hear the bugle calling,*
> *Goodbye Dolly Gray.*

It was mid-morning before they reached the ravine. The far slope leading up from the basin was smooth and covered with vegetation and it offered ideal cover if less than ideal visibility. Joe called in and received favorable news: the Warwickshire's line held and the Dubs would be safe in this position for now. They clambered across the creek bed. Joe ordered a rest and the men rolled out their blankets on a dry stretch of ground under a spreading oak.

"We had a merry time on the town in our day, didn't we, Tom?" Mick began.

"With merrier days to come, God willing."

"God, luck, and superior munitions."

"If I recall, Tom, the Stag's Head was only the beginning of your adventure."

"You recall correctly. There's no limit to the trouble a Dublin lad can get himself into if given enough time. I'm the living proof of that."

⌒

THE CROWD AT THE STAG'S HEAD HAD GROWN THICK SO THE BOYS bailed out. They ambled up Grafton Street in the direction of Davy Byrne's. At Davy's they met a few stragglers from the Portobello barracks so the first round was taken care of. Mick and Billy were paying attention to a pair of young women who were sitting in a snug near the back.

"They're just now in the loo and they'll be right back, I assure you," one of the girls told Billy when he asked for the whereabouts of their escorts.

"And what are they doing in there together that caused them to so ungallantly abandon you?"

The other girl giggled and said, "I couldn't begin to imagine." She took a sip of her cider.

"Could you love a man in a uniform, darling?" Mick asked.

The first girl laughed. Just then, the two temporarily relocated young gentlemen returned. One of them was holding a bottle of Powers and two glasses. "What's this then, eh?" the first man asked.

"We were just making sure the woman remained unmolested while you were apart," Billy said. "It's all right now."

"I'll say it is," said the second man. "Scatter."

"If you put it that way," Billy answered.

Joe and Tommy nursed their Guinnesses at the end of the bar and watched the proceedings from a secure distance. When Mick and Billy returned, Tommy offered his condolences. "Nothing doing, eh, Mickey?"

"A pair of feckin' eejits is what I saw."

"We can't all be as perfect as Michael Kennedy now, can we?"

"Ask the girls yourself, Tom."

"Let go of the lasses and go back to your glasses, boys," said Joe.

"Cute, Joe."

One of the Portobello boys called for another round and the Dubs took it up. Joe was starting to feel a little a worse for wear and wondered when it was all going to end but he didn't want to be a poor sport and kept his mouth shut. It was Doyle's night out and if the boy wanted to end the evening on the floor of a bar in the City Centre who was Joe to disappoint him? Tommy was laughing hard at something Mick had shouted into his ear and then he draped his arm around Mick and said something back, causing Mick to roar in return. The crowd of soldiers, women, and businessmen continued to flow into the room and it soon became difficult to hear anything at all.

"One more round and then home for me," Joe said with the hope of inspiration.

"What's that?" Billy asked.

"I'm going to have one more glass and then I think I'd better cross the river, boys."

"We'll hear nothing of it, Corporal Dooley. It's a grand tradition in the Dubs to perform the last call at Neary's and you wouldn't be wanting your newest recruit to be denied the benefit of the ritual, would you now?"

"I suppose that's up to Tom now, isn't it?"

"I hear my name being called," Tommy cried out. "Is it for good news or bad that I'm hearing it?"

"Joe wants to head home and I want him to carry us all over to Neary's for last call," Mick said. "What do ye say to that?"

"I say last call at Neary's and I say Joe's buying."

"And what does Joe say to that?" Billy asked.

Joe pulled his pockets inside out and smiled a weak smile.

"I'm sold out, boys."

At that, Tommy reached over and plucked a five-pound note out of Joe's jacket pocket. "I planted this there at the top of the evening just in case such an eventuality overtook us," Tommy said, choosing his words in a manner that suggested that the moment had been well-rehearsed. "It's a magic trick I learned a long time ago."

Joe felt startled and delighted. He also felt very drunk. "You can hide your money on me anytime, Tom."

"'Round the corner, boys. It's almost time."

THE RAIN HAD GROWN STEADIER AND THE DAY WAS DYING COLD. JOE had received news that two sections of the King's Own had been cut off and captured in a field northeast of Haucourt. The bulk of the Dubs were going to be needed in reinforcement and his orders were to bring his men around to the road to Ligny and prepare to fight. Even the headquarters were in retreat, repositioning themselves to a field east of the village. This was two hours ago.

Gone was the joy present in the hotel less than a week before. Now Joe's blanket and uniform and pack were soggy and his skin was cold and his feet were sore from all the marching. Billy and Mick and Richard seemed all right; they were hard men and although he knew they were just as frightened as he was he wasn't fearful for them. Tommy was different. Tommy was looking at something no one else could see and Joe wished there was something he could say to help but all Tommy wanted to do was talk about the night the Dubs closed down Neary's.

⌒

IT WAS MIDNIGHT AND A CROWD WAS IN FROM THE GAIETY. THEY had just done *The Bohemian Girl* and three of the actors still swathed in their make-up had squeezed into the narrow end of the bar. One of the gentlemen was wearing a bright red wig and had rouged his cheeks. He was conducting a conversation with a man in a business suit standing beside him. To the Dubs, the incongruity of it seemed both rare and normal, a signifying detail destined to crown the evening.

Joe didn't particularly feel the need of a nightcap. He ordered a beer and prepared to develop an adversarial relationship with the glass. He felt bad about letting Tom do the buying but the boy seemed determined to spend his money and there was not a lot of opposition to the idea amongst his peers.

"That's a whole month's salary you're palming there, Tommy boy," Joe told him as they edged their way across the room and reassembled in a snug under a poor portrait of Robert Emmet. "Would you like me to break it for you and carve out a portion of it for posterity?"

"What's that?" Tommy looked puzzled, listening to Joe's words but clearly not grasping the meaning of them.

"The money," Joe said, helpfully but now cryptically.

"What of it, Joe? I've no need of money in the army, do I now? All it ever seems to do is get me into trouble."

That was Billy's cue. "What's that about trouble, Tom Doyle?"

"Nobody was talking about trouble."

"I heard…"

"What'ye having, Mick?"

"A measure of Jameson's if you will and a beer to chase it."

Tommy pounded on the bar. "Royal service, here. A bottle of whiskey and some glasses if you please."

The barkeep looked in Tommy's direction and returned to his taps.

"Well, then."

Joe noticed the mischievous glint in Mick's eye just seconds before the young man climbed over the counter and snared a bottle of whiskey from the top row. "Nothing like a fresh bottle," Mick cried as he swung around.

"Hey," the barkeep shouted. It proved an ineffectual command.

"Let's have the staff do the pouring, Mick," Joe said, putting his hand over the bottle.

"I was just trying to improve the service, Joe. No harm in trying, is there?"

The man tending the bar pushed a couple of small glasses along the wood and with an imploring look at Joe he ran his cloth along the top of the counter and turned his back on them.

"I tell you the service in Neary's has virtually collapsed since my glorified youth," Billy announced, helping himself to the whiskey. "Time was a man would look you in the eye when he served you."

"Time was a man wouldn't help himself to the stock," said Joe.

"'Twasn't me, Joe."

"I said I was just trying to improve the service," Mick cried out. "Mary and Joseph, could you just let a man drink in peace?"

Just then, two of the actors sitting at the end of the bar summoned their best Marie Lloyd. Their indeterminate baritones made the song even more ridiculous:

> When I take my morning promenade
> Quite a fashion card, on the promenade.
> Now I don' t mind nice boys staring hard
> If it satisfies their desire.
>
> Do you think my dress is a little bit,
> Just a little bit not too much of it?

*If it shows my shape just a little bit,*
*That's the little bit the boys admire.*

Joe looked at the time. Twenty minutes to last call. He left his beer on the counter untasted and walked around to where Tommy was standing. The rouge-cheeked actor was engaging Tommy in a lesson in the tricks of the trade.

"You've got to think of the effect it has in the back stalls, my boy. What ye're looking at here is all twisted out of perspective."

"Looks funny is all," Tom told him.

"It's a funny trade, I tell you. Have you ever acted on the stage?"

"Have I?" Tom laughed. "Not since Father O'Hanlan asked me to recite 'Dark Rosaleen' in the third form, no. I'd be scared to death to go up in front of a crowd."

"You don't seem to be afraid of a crowd of soldiers."

"What's this?" Tom pulled on his own shirt. "Do you see any enemies here?"

The actor looked slyly at the others and then put his arm closely around Tommy's neck. "You never can tell."

Tommy smiled but was too lost to care about the arm. Joe watched the drama unfold with a mixture of curiosity and benevolent interest.

"Ah," Tommy said. "We're all friends here."

"You look like a lad who could use a friend," the actor replied.

"Last call," the barkeep cried.

Joe walked up to Tom and his newfound actor friend and gently un-twined the arm from Tommy's shoulder. "It's time to go now, Tommy."

The actor turned to Joe with an exaggerated expression of pain on his face. "Now, sir. Your friend and I were just beginning to get acquainted."

"I'm his commanding officer and it's my responsibility to get him home safely," Joe answered.

"What's that, Joe?" Tommy asked, peeking out of his sleeve.

"It's nothing, Tommy. Let's go."

The men piled out onto Chatham Street.

"Welcome to the Dubs, Tommy!" Mick cried as he and Billy walked arm in arm toward Grafton Street.

Tommy whirled around at the sound of the voices but it was clear he wasn't sure where the noise came from. Tommy still lived with his family on the North Side and Joe concluded—actually, he had concluded about an hour before—that it would be his job to get Tom home. Now that the actual embarkation had begun, Joe could see that Tom was in no condition to face his kin. He would put him up at no. 10 and they could sort it out in the morning.

Although it was a very straight line indeed from Neary's to the College Green it seemed to take an age for Joe to move Tommy along it. Tommy collapsed in front of the bank but Joe was able to get him to his feet. They made it all the way to the quay together but then Tom took sick and Joe stood patiently on the sidewalk as his friend's moans and gasps echoed up and down the river. This revived Tommy's spirits enough to get him on his feet again and out onto the O'Connell Bridge.

Joe peeked into the murky water flowing below. Dark it was even on the brightest of days and tonight the color of the river struck him as deep beyond the usual inkiness. There was no moon and the Liffey flowed smoothly and evenly below him. The music that constantly sounded in Joe's head always struck him as having the characteristics of a tide, ebbing and flowing in and out of his consciousness like notes from a long-forgotten piece. In the soft and nearly silent burbling of the river he found its echo and its choir. An old song floated back into his memory and he sang it softly to himself:

> *Where the strawberry beds,*
> *Sweep down to the Liffey,*
> *You'll kiss away the troubles from my brow.*
> *I love you well today,*
> *And I'll love you more tomorrow,*
> *If you ever love me*
> *Molly, love me now!*

Joe wished he could perform for the world the symphony he was composing inside his head. In it he would express the affection he felt for his men and the fears he harbored for their future and for his own. It was both abstract and concrete to him just as the water flowing beneath his feet was both constant and constantly changing.

He looked up from his reverie to see Tommy climbing on to the stone balustrade on the northeast corner of the bridge. Tom stood straight up or at least as straight as his wavering and unbalanced frame could manage and waved at Joe from his imaginary parapet. "Look at me, Corporal Dooley!"

Joe rushed to Tommy's side but before he could reach him Tommy tripped over his own feet and started to tumble.

"Shite!" With that single oath Tommy slid off the siding and fell into the river. At that point of the crossing the fall was a distance of a mere half-dozen feet and the splash Tommy's body made was almost gentle. Still, it was nearly two o'clock in the morning and even in June the river was icy cold. Joe raced around to the side of the bridge and dove in to the water. Tommy was conscious and twisting about but his clothes were waterlogged and his body grew heavy. Joe tried to steer Tommy in the direction of the embankment but he ached and he was tired. Finally Joe managed to pull Tommy out of the murk. Tommy's trousers were torn and there was a small bruise on his forehead but he seemed otherwise unhurt. Tommy opened his eyes and smiled. "I'm not an Olympian yet, am I, Joe?"

It took half an hour but Joe managed to get Tommy all the way to Talbot Street and up the stairs to his apartment. He took off his own wet clothes and changed into a dry shirt and pants and then he helped Tommy undress and gave him a blanket. Tommy was already asleep when Joe rolled him up in the blanket and put a pillow under his head on the floor. He hung Tommy's wet clothes over the back of his chair and then he turned down the light and climbed into bed and tried to sleep. Tommy snored.

The engineers had constructed a road between Ligny and Clary where there was never supposed to be a road and the surface was pitted and uneven and made even more so by the transport crews who had run their trucks and the heavy artillery over it. About two miles outside of Clary, Joe instructed his section to fall out and try to get some rest. They had been marching for hours and it was apparent that they weren't going to make it to the village tonight.

Mick had been complaining of blisters all day and the first thing he did when they hit the side of the road was pull off his boots and socks and put his feet up on his kit. Billy and Richard were too wide awake to sleep so they decided to play a hand of cards by the light of a muffled torch. Joe settled in next to Tommy with an apple and a book.

"What'ya reading, Joe?"

"This? Housman. Helps me sleep."

"When I have a hard time, I count sheep."

"I've never met anyone who actually admitted to that, Tom. I'm impressed."

"It's not actually sheep. Or not always, like. Just counting."

"I understand."

"Sometimes it's flowers. Sometimes it's cats."

"Like a picture book."

"You're joshing me, Joe."

"Not at all, Tommy. Just trying to get my head around it is all."

"Sometimes it's blessings."

"A good Catholic boy is supposed to count his blessings."

"Do you believe in God, Joe?"

"Now where did that question come from?"

"I don't know. We were talking about counting blessings."

"I do, sure."

"So do I."

"Well, now that's settled. How's about you go back to counting whatever it is that you're counting and I go back to Shropshire?"

"All right, Joe."

Tommy tucked his head down and Joe picked up his book. The two of them sat together in silence for a few minutes. Then Tommy opened his eyes. "Tell me, Joe," he said. "How do you know you believe in God?"

"I don't know, Tommy. I don't really think of it that way or put it to myself as a question."

"I do."

"I guess you deserve an answer, then." Joe paused to measure his words. "I know I believe in God because I look at things. I listen to music. I have friends. All the things I see and hear and the people I see and hear them with, all of it is magical to me. It is a gift given in surprise and accepted always with gratitude and wonder. So you might as well ask me, do I believe in magic? And I say, I do. I believe in magic and I suppose the magic comes from God."

"You know, that's the best answer I think I've ever heard."

"What? Do you ask everyone this question? Are we doing 'The Man In The Street' now?"

"Don't be hard on me, Joe. I was just asking, is all."

"I didn't mean to sound hard, Tommy. It's just that when men usually ask me for something it's an extra ration or a pass they're after. I'm not used to discussing philosophy."

"It's not philosophy to me, Joe. It's what I think about."

"I never heard a better definition of philosophy, my friend. Now, how about you and I try to get some rest?"

"All right, Joe."

"Good night, Tommy."

"Good night."

For Billy and Richard their game of cards served admirably as a nepenthe and in the moments before Joe joined them he learned there is no better inspiration to sleep than philosophy. There would be dreams of heaven tonight.

# Chapter 10

◆ ◆ ◆

## Something Else Under the Sun

◆ ◆ ◆

JOE STUDIED THE LANDSCAPE AS IF IT WAS A PAINTING IN A GALLERY. Birch trees lay in the shadows to his left and to his right, their trunks darkened by the rain and their leaves once pale green now daubed with vermillion and umber. Nettles and ivies filled in the foreground. The clouds were the color of charcoal and slate, drizzled with white streaks of smoke from the sailing shells. In the distance Joe could just make out a stone fence trailing across a wheat field and open land all the way to the vanishing point.

Then all at once Joe's vision whirled into motion. First he noticed his feet—or more precisely, his boots—taking step upon deliberate step to avoid tripping over the exposed roots and waterlogged ditches in his path. Looking up he caught sight of another pair of boots similar to his own, and then another. Men rushed past. Now Joe saw streaks of light pass overhead. They were too low to be stars and moved too slowly to be bullets. It took him what seemed like a very long time to comprehend that the lights were shell fragments exploding in the air. Something that looked like a flock of starlings burst over his head.

Finally, Joe heard the sound. He thought it was strange that he of all people would leave this for last. Perhaps that was because it was so unmusical. There was nothing sweet or even controlled about it, like a factory whistle but oscillating and oh so loud. It was the sound a shell made as it flew in your direction and what Joe found most dismaying was that once you heard it coming it was too late to get out of the way. All you could do was shout out a warning—and an involuntary one at that—and dive for cover. As he did so, Joe allowed himself to make the ironic observation that although there was indeed nothing musical about the sound of the whirling shells you could make a case for the rat-a-tat of the rifle bullets as underscoring. All this while the precipitation of metal danced on his helmet.

The Dubs had been driven back across the Warnelle Ravine and were trying to make their way to Ligny but the left part of the line was not holding at all and now Joe's section was cut off from the larger part of the regiment. At dawn, Joe's orders had been to march southeast of the village and attach themselves to a band of Royal Irish and London Rifles but by midday every man was in retreat. The road was under heavy mortar fire so Joe had to take his men across the fields. The rain fell steadily and the topsoil turned to mud, creeping over the tops of the men's boots and soaking their feet. It was a miserable and unpromising day.

"Fifteen minutes rest," Joe ordered as the men heaped themselves under the eaves of a dying oak. "Eat something and then we'll try to press on."

"If I had something to eat, I'd eat it," said Billy mournfully. "I used up the last of my rations for breakfast."

"We can't always count on a cook on the line or a well-stocked kitchen in an abandoned farmhouse, you know."

"Don't give me grief, colonel."

"Well, don't complain to the air, Bill."

"I'm sorry, sir."

"Here. Take mine."

"But…"

"There isn't the time to argue. Take it."

Billy grabbed the tin out of Joe's hand and tore it open.

"Like a wild animal you are, Billy," Mick commented.

"That's what I feel like."

"Do you have something to eat, Tommy?" Joe asked.

"I do, sir."

"Why don't you eat it, then?"

"I'm not hungry, sir."

"Suit yourself."

Richard was carefully shaking the mud out of his boots. "When was the last time we saw any Dubs, Joe?"

"There was a section of 'em in Ligny. They've split off to the west and I'm not certain if we'll run into any of them again until we get to Selvigny."

"How far is that?" Tommy asked.

"I can't say for sure—four or five miles, I'd guess."

"In time for supper, I hope," said Mick.

"That would be a boon," Richard noted.

"A boon indeed," Joe said. "Let's move out."


Two more sections of Fusiliers materialized that afternoon. They reported ominous news. Their first two sorties had been blocked and now enemy infantry units were in pursuit. The headquarters in Haucourt had been abandoned. At one point it was nearly every man for himself. None of them had any rations to speak of and they were all hungry and dirty. There was no need for a mirror. All Joe's men had to do was look at their fellows and they saw a perfect likeness of their own misery.

Collectively, the Dubs now made up a party of thirteen. They found a makeshift road that was properly drained and followed it for approximately a half-mile, then realized they were marching in the wrong direction and turned about. To the left, a pasture rolled down to the southeast. Above them to the north the hills rose to a large stand of firs. The commanding officer of one of the other sections expressed his fears about the open field of fire and their own visibility. He suggested they avoid the road and try to make their way across the downward-sloping fields. Joe agreed.

The rain was not letting up and the ground that appeared well groomed from a distance was proving to be clogged with weeds and pitted with boulders. Peering through his glasses to the bottom of the last ridge before the road, Joe saw a party of German infantry soldiers marching straight toward them. He counted ten altogether, two full sections. There was no cover on either side and discovery was inevitable; they might as well use surprise as an ally. Joe ordered his men to ready their arms and lie down in the field and advance on their bellies. They slithered like snakes along the muddy grass. When they had reached a point approximately sixty feet from the road Joe ordered the attack. Half the men stood up and came around firing from the left and the other half did the same from the right. The Germans fanned out and the battle began.

In the middle of the firefight Joe found himself thinking: This is very familiar to me. What was well known wasn't so much the rush of adrenaline he felt as he placed his body in the path of the bullets but the play of the shadows of the men as they raced around him and the sound of their feet in the reeds and his own panting breath. This sense of aliveness filled him at the moment of peril and he embraced it the way one would embrace an old, once lost friend. This is why I joined the army, Joe felt. This is the reason for all the struggle—to have a purpose, to be with men who love you and depend upon you, to make a mark upon the surface of the world.

Joe tried to identify the fear he felt in the middle of the chaos that surrounded him but his mind kept short-circuiting at the approach of it. One small part of him was annoyed by this distraction, as if the perception of the terror of the situation was a requirement of the experience of it. He noticed that his vision was distorted and everything appeared to be mobile—his men, the opposition, bullets from both sides, and even the air—and in the midst of it he understood that it was not possible to tell them apart.

At one point, Joe thought he actually heard a bullet fly past his ear, a sharp intake of air like a human gasp and then gone. Colors went all out of whack; the grass looked red and the sky that had been filled with clouds turned a heavenly blue. Noises like the sounds of the men yelling and the guns repeating were mere undertones to the music flooding Joe's brain. It chimed like a symphony but was played by no instrument that Joe had ever heard. It was the harp of the wind and the drum of the earth and the voice of the heavenly spirit.

From the corner of his eye Joe could make out Mick and Billy in firing position. A body had fallen behind him but in the rush to get to cover and secure his position Joe couldn't turn around so he wasn't certain if the man was British or German. All his concentration was directed at one German soldier who was pulling his rifle over his shoulder and pointing it in Joe's direction. The soldier stood barely twenty-five yards away. He was swathed in a gray slicker and only half his face was visible in the shadow of it but in the one instant that Joe had to notice such a thing he did see something resembling fear in the boy's eyes. Joe fell to his knees aiming his rifle at the boy's legs. He pulled the trigger and the boy fell.

A voice behind him shouted something in German and Joe whirled around to see four soldiers running up the hill away from the road. He turned back again and saw Richard standing over the body of a soldier. Who had fallen? Where were the rest of the Germans? Where was Tommy? Then the picture in front of him began to resolve and like a person waking he heard voices and understood that the voices were real and no longer the voices of a dream.

"Joe! Joe! It's Tommy."

Tommy lay at Richard's feet. A bullet had hit Tommy on his side below his ribs and his uniform was soaked with fresh blood.

"I've bandages and iodine in my kit," Joe shouted.

Tommy moaned as Richard lifted him up and tore away his shirt. The wound was deep. Richard soaked the tip of a towel with iodine and spread it over the bullet hole. Tom roared but the roar proved he was still alive. They lifted him up and wrapped a bandage around his belly to stanch the bleeding. Joe reached into his kit and took out what was left of his ration of rum.

"Here, Tommy, drink this," he said, gently lifting Tommy's head to the bottle.

Tommy sipped at it and then closed his eyes. "Joe…"

"Don't worry, Tom. We'll have you as good as new in no time."

Mick came up with his rifle still smoking.

"Anyone still out there?" Joe asked.

"Only couple of Dubs. I think the Germans all ran away. How's Tom?"

"He's been hit. We have to get him to a dressing station as soon as possible."

"Is he going to live?" Billy asked.

"I don't know," Joe answered. "I don't know."

THEY FOUND TWO BLANKETS. JOE AND MICK WRAPPED TOMMY IN one of them and Billy and Richard used the other as a sling to carry him. It was hard work for any man and doubly so for men who had just come under fire and were now in their tenth hour with little food or sleep. From a roadside barn they took a cart that could hold Tommy and they put another blanket under him to help his circulation and pulled him along the road. The sun had set and still the rain fell. The road was flooded and the rows of retreating troops had to pull their equipment through several inches of mud. In their wisdom the British Army had left nearly all of their functioning transport vehicles in St. Quentin, eight miles away.

In Selvigny there were at least six other soldiers wounded as badly as Tommy and suffering equally from lack of medical attention. The wounded men were put by pairs into real beds where they would at least be dry and comfortable. Joe went out and found an *estimet* with a few edible sausages and a bunch of carrots and he shared them with his men and the dozen or so other soldiers who came straggling in from Haucourt and Ligny. Joe wanted to push on without any rest but all the roads were under fire. He helped to stabilize Tommy as best he could and then lay down to close his eyes for an hour or two.

It was a restless sleep. Joe dreamed of Tommy and of the German soldier he had shot in the leg and in his dream the two boys got mixed up and Joe awoke in a sweat thinking he had shot Tommy and rescued the German. As he awoke, Joe remembered that both boys had the same hazel-colored eyes.

As soon as the sun came up, the Dubs moved out. There were still no trucks to be had so they had to use the cart they had dragged through the mud. Tommy was having a hard time breathing and he was sweating. "Help me, Joe," he said. "I've a terrible pain in my side."

"You'll be fine, Tommy," Joe said, running his hand over Tommy's damp brow. "We're taking you to a hospital and you'll be properly cared for there."

"Thank you," Tommy whispered. "Is everyone else all right?"

"Yes."

"That's good."

"Ssh, Tom. Save your strength."

Tommy coughed and closed his eyes.

The entourage pressed on to Villers Outreaux, the last town before St. Quentin. In Villers they stopped to water the horses. They had traveled barely a mile when Tommy cried out and they stopped the cart.

"Joe, I'm dying."

Joe climbed around to the back of the cart and pressed his hand on Tommy's forehead. "It's just a bad fever, is all. You're not dying, Tom."

"No, Joe. I'm scared and I'm thinking things like saying my prayers and will I go to Heaven or Hell and…"

"You will kill yourself if you keep trying to talk."

Mick and Richard and Billy gathered around.

"What, is our little scaredy-cat afraid of a little pain?" Mick asked.

"Leave off, Mick," Joe answered. "He's frightened."

"It's just a scratch, Tom," Richard said.

"'Tis not," Tommy answered.

"'Tis," chimed Billy.

"Are you in want of anything, Tommy?" Joe asked. "We're near enough to a village. I can go back and find you something to eat or drink if you want."

"I'm grand, Joe. Thanks."

"If you say so."

Tommy closed his eyes. Mick walked up to the front of the cart.

"Jesus, Joe, Tom doesn't look well."

"It's only a few more miles to St. Quentin. Everyone's regrouped there. There's a hospital with lots of supplies and plenty of beds. He'll get good care."

"I hope so."

The other parties had already moved along so Joe and his men had to catch up. The cart that Tom was riding in jostled a bit and Tom cried out one more time. At one point, Billy needed to relieve himself so they pulled up as Billy marched out into the field. When he came back, he took a look in and noticed that Tommy had fallen asleep.

"Rest easy, there, Tommy boy."

But something didn't look right. He looked at Tommy more closely.

"Oh no."

"What is it, Billy?" Joe asked.

"It's Tommy. I don't think he's breathing."

"What?"

Joe raced around and put his hand on Tommy's neck. Then he pulled the blanket aside and laid his head down on Tommy's chest. Mick and Richard gathered around the cart but Joe kept his head down. Finally, Joe turned away. "Tommy's dead."

"The Lord have mercy on his soul," Richard said.

Mick pulled the blanket up to cover Tommy's face.

"God bless you, Tom," he said.

Joe took Tommy's identity tag from his neck and held it above the boy's body like a rosary. He felt the tears starting to run down his cheek. "Please, God," he said. "Let Tommy's spirit enter Heaven. He was a good soldier and he deserves to live by your right hand forever."

"Now at least we'll be able to give him a proper burial," Mick said.

"That's true," said Billy. "We've no reason to scurry to St. Quentin now."

They carried Tommy's body to the side of the road and laid him down there. Joe and Mick found a spot a few yards away which was smooth and level. They dug a hole deep enough and long enough to fit Tommy's body and then they wrapped his body in the blanket and placed it in the grave and covered it. Joe made a note of the location of the grave and then he and Mick improvised a cross out of two spare field staves. The Dubs gathered around the grave and said their prayers. Joe kissed his fingers and pressed them up against the cross. Then he said: "*Ave Maria, gratia plena, Dominus tecum. Benedicta tu in mulieribus, et benedictus fructus ventris tui, Iesus...*"

Softly, the others joined in. "*Sancta Maria, Mater Dei, ora pro nobis peccatoribus, nunc, et in hora mortis nostrae.* Amen."

"Amen," Joe said.

⌒

IN ST. QUENTIN, THE DUBS HAD THEIR FIRST CHANCE FOR A BATH and a cooked meal in a week but the city was overrun with retreating infantry, support troops, and refugees all clambering for space in the old rusted tubs and raiding fresh fruit and vegetables from the abandoned larders. The situation was chaotic. There were many casualties and sections were reforming almost as quickly as the names and identification cards of the dead could be collected. Four times in the first hour dazed soldiers came up to Joe to ask him for information and he was helpless to offer them anything.

Joe couldn't shake the feeling that there was something critical to the mission that he had forgotten or lost and he kept evaluating the contents of his kit in the vain hope that whatever it was he was looking for would surface there for him. Richard tried to act professionally indifferent and kept silent, whereas it seemed to Joe that Mick and Billy were behaving as if they were on a holiday and if only the water was a bit hotter and the service a little better there would be no reason to complain to the management. All these attempts at diversion were in vain for the thing they all held in common was that no one wanted to talk about Tommy and that everyone wished to talk about him.

On Sunday there was a memorial mass at the Basilica. The day was ironically one of the finest in a long while and it cheered Joe to see the warm sunlight streaming through the colored glass windows. The young girls of St. Quentin had established a flower market in the city square just outside the cathedral doors and the chapel was filled with British soldiers wearing daisies pinned to their jackets. What citizens remained squeezed into the remaining spaces in the aisles or in the back, their presence more a result of habit than from any sense of solidarity with their listless would-be conquerors.

The mass was in Latin and although Joe of course understood the language pretending it was in a foreign tongue provided him with another way to distance himself from his emotions. The crowd in the cheerful sunlight gave Joe a sense of public service which he felt was completely unconnected to the sorrowful feeling that flooded his soul. There would be a time to come, he knew, when attending to the bitterness and anger of experience would be a luxury but now it felt important to him to recognize it. More importantly, he felt it was his responsibility to give his men the same opportunity.

The mass concluded and the ranks flowed out into the street. Joe gave everyone six hours leave and asked them to report back to their billets at eighteen hundred. The first thing Joe did with his time was to find a table in the square and order a beer. The drink when it finally did arrive was watery and warm but the tang of it was enough to take him back to the snugs and parlors of Dame Street. Joe found that with the stress of the war he sometimes fragmented his experiences and he was both startled and fascinated to discover in repose how easily he was able to switch the command button when needed. Now that it was in the "off" position it no longer embarrassed him to think it.

It might have been leave for his men but the next thing Joe needed to do after calming himself with the beer was to uncover the location of his regimental command post and receive his orders. The communication lines had been laid down, lifted, and resettled so many times since Haucourt that it had become impossible for Joe to get any reliable messages in or out and if he could find his captain or anyone of suitable rank for that matter it would be a benefit. He asked the first soldier he passed if he had any information but that man was an engineer and didn't know any infantry sections at all. The next soldier he met was an officer in the London Rifles; he thought the whole division was being run out of the basement of a hotel on the western edge of the city. Finally, Joe found an intact regiment with a working telephone and in a matter of minutes had been connected with his command.

Joe was told that the entire expeditionary force had been pushed to the south and east and there was a great risk of getting split in half by the enemy's intermittent but ultimately successful plunge into Picardy. If the British were going to have any chance at all of defending the front, let alone challenging the German army in Belgium, they were going to have to establish a firm line all the way from the corner of France they currently occupied to the Belgian seacoast. In order to do this, the force had to regroup farther south and start a march to the sea. Joe's piece of this puzzle was to bring his men to Senlis; this maneuver would begin tomorrow morning. There was literally no rest for the weary.

ON HIS WAY BACK TO BILLETS, A TALL, FAIR-HAIRED MAN IN AN OFFIcer's uniform approached Joe. "Are ye Corporal Joe Dooley?" he asked.

Joe was startled at being recognized and unsure of the man's intentions but he could hardly deny his identity. "Yes, I am. How may I help you, Captain?"

"My name is William Collins. I am the captain of the 2nd Royal Munsters, out of Cork. I've been instructed to hand you this letter in person."

"This is all very cryptic."

"Please, sir, just take the letter." Collins held a small, soiled envelope in front of him.

Joe plucked it from the man's hand. "Thank you, Captain Collins." Joe saluted.

"As you were, Corporal."

Then he walked away.

Joe evaluated the envelope. It was addressed to him; that was true. The hand looked familiar, but there was no return on either the face or the recto. He slid his fingers along the seam and removed the paper, one folded sheet closely covered with an angular script.

AUGUST 1914

Dear Joe,

I have proof that the world is small, for I have found you. When you read this letter, you will understand why I had to have it delivered to you in person and with the utmost secrecy, for I am fighting for Ireland now and this makes me an enemy in the eyes of the Crown.

I am working with the Brotherhood smuggling guns and ammunition into Ireland. I have bought a boat—a small but powerful boat—that I employ between the Channel ports and Cork. Every week, I am placed in contact with men up and down the front who are with us and who help us. My job is to take the matériel out of France and get it into the hands of the Irish soldiers at home so we can defend ourselves when the English come calling and free ourselves at last from English tyranny. "England's danger is Ireland's opportunity." Although the work I do is perilous, I do not regret its undertaking for an instant.

I can picture you standing amazed with my letter dangling in your hand. I know you well enough to know you cannot think me a traitor. I know you will not betray me. I also know you secretly condemn me and must now harbor stern doubts about the future of our friendship. All I ask is that you remember our friendship and my love for you and trust me to believe that in doing what I do I mean no harm to any of your fellows and do not act in defense of your enemy. I am a patriot, no more and no less.

The purpose of this letter is twofold. The first is to let you know I am alive and well. This is true so far. The second is to reassure you of my love. I know why you are doing what you are doing as well—perhaps even better—than I understand myself. Because of our chosen paths we may not meet again, but I know that no matter what transpires we will always be together.

You must of course destroy this letter as soon as you read it. If you wish to respond, please do so immediately via your contact there. They will know how to find me. God bless you and Godspeed.

> *Rath Dé ort,*
> S.C.

JOE SLID SEVERIN'S LETTER BACK INTO ITS ENVELOPE AND LOOKED around. His first thought was to tear the paper apart right now, in the middle of the street. Then he thought of all the things he wanted to say to Severin—how foolish he was and how great a risk he was taking, how compromised he felt in being able to correspond with him and how important it was for him to be able to do so—and all his thoughts rushed together and overwhelmed him. But he must write something; it was a benefit too precious not to assay. Risking all, Joe walked back to billets with Severin's letter in his coat pocket and, borrowing a pen and some stationary from the first man he passed, he wrote out his reply.

SEPTEMBER 1914

Dear S.

I am amazed to hear from you and to hear your news. I am sworn to secrecy. Harm no one if you can and deliver yourself as safely as you deliver your goods. My hand cannot guide you but my heart can be at your side. My life is hard but I believe in what I am doing as I know you understand.

May this reach you in safety and may our connection across the land, across the sea, and across the years never be broken.

Take care.

Your friend,

J.D.

JOE RETURNED TO THE STREETS OF ST. QUENTIN AND ASKED AROUND until he uncovered the address where the Royal Munsters were billeted. There he found Captain Collins. "Take this from me and deliver it to Severin Coole."

"Who?"

"The man who wrote me."

"You must know I have no knowledge of the contents of the letter I gave you, nor do I know the identity of the author."

"Of course."

"Did you destroy the letter I gave you?"

"Then you did know…"

"Destroy it now."

Collins snatched Joe's letter out of his hand.

"Thank you, Captain," Joe cried.

Walking away, Collins muttered, "Do as I asked."

Joe asked the man standing in the doorway for a match.

"*D'accord,*" he said, offering a light.

Joe held Severin's letter up to the flame and watched as the fire consumed it and turned the whole of it to ash.

⌢

THE FINAL THING THAT JOE WISHED TO ACCOMPLISH BEFORE LEAVing St. Quentin was to arrange a memorial service for Tommy. The cathedral was very beautiful but Joe received no sense of Tommy's grace there. He needed to do more and he was certain that his men wanted more as well. They were billeted in an ordinary house in one of the busy quarters of the city but there was a parlor large enough for the four of them and a churchman. When he was on the phone to GHQ he asked if there was a chaplain attached to any of the units nearby and they helpfully found him Father Stephen. The father would be at their billets at six.

WHEN JOE RETURNED TO THE HOUSE AN UNEXPECTED VISITOR greeted him. That was Private Andrew Farris, the newest Dub. Andy was one of the survivors of Haucourt, a former Highlander who now found himself exiled from his Aberdonian roots and replanted in Irish turf. Joe took his hand after they had been introduced and welcomed him to the ranks.

"It's an honor and a pleasure to have you, Private Farris," Joe began. "I would introduce you to the rest of our section but of course they're late to report as usual."

"Discipline was never one of the Scots brigades' strong points either, sir." Andy grinned. "I'm certain in that regard we will be completely compatible."

"I am certain we will," Joe replied, smiling. "I'm waiting on a chaplain and the rest of the section for a memorial. You may join us if you wish."

"I do."

Joe and Andy sat together and reminisced about their respective provinces. Despite their ecumenical differences it was reassuring to Joe to hear of Andy's sense of exile from the central command. Aberdeen was farther from London than Dublin after all and Andy could even manage a phrase or two of Scots Gaelic for Joe's benefit and amusement. "*Sann à Aberdeen a tha mi,*" he began.

"*Is as Dublin dom,*" Joe answered. "And I guess we'll have to depend upon English from here on."

THE NEXT PERSON TO COME TO THE HOUSE WAS NOT UNEXPECTED by his presence but in his presentation. This was the cleric that headquarters had scrubbed up to help Joe with Tommy's service. After Joe had introduced himself to Private Farris, he went into the parlor where the service was to be held and saw Stephen. Joe's reaction was not new but it was recently vanquished: Stephen was handsome, startlingly so. The first thing Joe noticed was Stephen's eyes, which were ice blue and took Joe in with kindness and sympathy. Then there was the man's unmistakable charm, his poise in place that for reasons Joe could not immediately pinpoint reminded him of Donal McCormack. For Joe, it was an irresistible combination of physical beauty and spiritual confidence.

"Thank you for coming, Father," Joe said as he offered his hand.

"Please, call me Stephen."

"Of course."

"I'd like you to tell me a bit about Thomas Doyle."

Joe sat in the parlor with Stephen and told him about his childhood friendship with Tommy and how they reunited in the Dubs and how good a soldier he was turning out to be but all the while as the two young men were talking Joe was also remembering how it felt to fall in love. Not that he was falling in love with the priest, a thought that immediately brought an inner smile to his consciousness. But it had been a long time since Joe had allowed himself to think about beauty at all and the involuntariness of it all struck him as holy in a way. We cannot choose how and where we find beauty, in peace or in war, in men or in women. When your world is filled with terrible things, Joe thought, something as lovely as a man's eyes can be a blessing.

MICK AND BILLY STUMBLED IN AT HALF-PAST SIX, WITH RICHARD acting as their apparent chaperone. They had found a very friendly barkeep at a local *estimet* and she—they emphasized the word "she"—had been most happy to serve them despite their not having a sou.

"You're half an hour late," Joe reprimanded.

"Sorry, Joe."

"Did we miss the service?" Billy asked.

"Of course not," Joe answered. "It is for you as much as for anyone that we are having it. Why would you think…"

"That's all right, Joe. We're here now."

"I tried to keep my eye on the clock, Joe," Richard began.

"You've kept the Father waiting."

"It's my honor," Stephen said.

"Father?" Mick asked. "I didn't know we were to have a clergyman."

Andy stood in the doorway.

"Please, Private Farris, come join us," Joe said. "I would like you all to meet our new Dub, Andy Farris."

"From the 3rd Highlanders," Andy added.

"What's with the Highlanders?" asked Billy.

"We lost half of them and the rest of us have been dispersed, I'm afraid."

"That's awful news," Stephen said. "I'm sorry."

Mick started to sing:

> Oh, you take the high road
> And I'll take the low road...

Richard turned to him. "Hush, Mickey."

Joe turned to address the men. "I was looking for something to say about Tommy. All the simple and obvious things seemed insufficient, as I knew they would. Then I recalled a line from 'Romeo and Juliet.' Romeo's friend Benvolio says it about Mercutio. He says, 'That gallant spirit hath aspired the clouds, which too untimely here did scorn the earth.' I think that says it all."

"That's a lovely thought, sir," Richard said.

"Thank you. I'm going to write a letter to Mrs. Doyle and I'd like you all to sign it."

Most of the group muttered in assent but Mick stood apart, brooding in the corner of the room. Joe chose to ignore him. "Shall we begin, Stephen?"

"Of course." Stephen pulled out his little bible. "Joe told me a bit about Tommy. He seemed as if he was just coming into his own as a soldier."

"As are we all," Richard said.

"I'd like to read a passage from Ecclesiastes," Stephen said.

"I hope it's a brief one," said Mick, noisily pulling up a chair.

"Mick, shut up," Richard said.

Stephen overrode this interruption. "I think you will find it apt." He read:

*I have seen something else under the sun.*

*The race is not to the swift or the battle to the strong, nor does food come to the wise or wealth to the brilliant or favor to the learned; but time and chance happen to them all. More-over, no man knows when his hour will come: As fish are caught in a cruel net, or birds are taken in a snare, so men are trapped by evil times that fall unexpectedly among them.*

"That's a load of shite," Mick cried out.

Richard pulled Mick up from the chair and slugged him. Mick fell back against the chair and both the man and the furniture clattered to the floor. "I will not allow you to speak to a man of the church in that manner," Richard said.

Stephen took a step back as Joe pulled Richard away from Mick.

"And I…I will not allow a man of the church to preach to us with such hypocrisy. There's nothing about this that has anything to do with chance." Mick spat out the last word as if it was a curse.

"I am sorry if I offended anyone," Stephen said.

"Truly, Father, I am the one who should do the apologizing," Joe be-gan. "I am sorry for the condition of Private Kennedy and for the abuse which he has so improperly and inexcusably cast upon you."

"You sound like a goddamned officer now, Joe," Mick growled. "Ye're no different from the rest of 'em."

Joe turned on Mick, the look of violence spreading across his face. "If you don't stop talking this instant, I'll slug you myself, Mick."

"Go ahead."

Joe grabbed onto Mick's collar and pulled him up as straight as he could manage but instead of punching him he disdainfully and strongly turned out his elbow and cast Mick's body to the wall. Mick rolled up when he hit the wall and fell to the floor.

"It's Tommy's memory you're dishonoring," Joe shouted. "This has nothing to do with me, or the Church, or God. Now stand up and say you're sorry to Father Stephen and be done with it."

Mick stood up but he needed to hold on to the chair to keep from falling. He tried to speak but merely closed his eyes.

"There's courage for you," Joe said. Then he stormed out of the room.

Billy sat silently throughout the entire incident. Now he wrapped his arm around Andy and turned to him. "Welcome to the Dubs!"

# Chapter 11

◆ ◆ ◆

# The Truth in Her Eye

◆ ◆ ◆

THE LAST WEEK OF NOVEMBER JOE WAS OFFERED A SEVEN-DAY LEAVE. A car brought him from Armentières to St. Omer. From St. Omer Joe took a train to Calais, a ferry to Dover, and another train to a camp outside of London where he and a score of other soldiers passed the night. The next morning he was on another train, this time to Cardiff, followed by a ferry to Queenstown and home.

At first, Joe felt the sense of leisure that any man would feel when he is suddenly released from a constricted environment. The pure variety of the landscape was a novelty; it had been months since Joe had seen a cliff, a port, or the sea and the sounds and the smells of the life there enthralled him. In Cardiff there were straw baskets of fresh fruit heaped up in stalls along the harbor and women selling crawfish out of a barrel. Children ran up and down the narrow streets leading to the dock and Joe's instinct was to interrupt their games and warn them against dangers they were too young to know. By the time he crossed the Irish Sea he was in tears.

But then, as the spire of St. Colman's appeared on the western horizon and the painted eaves of the houses of Queenstown rose before him, Joe felt a touch of apprehension at the base of his spine. He could neither place the source of the anxiety nor comprehend the reason for it and in the manner with which he had always treated things he did not understand he postponed the consideration of it in the hope that when the time came to do so all will have been revealed. The ferry pulled up to the worn-out and familiar dock and its war-weary passengers disembarked.

Joe had sent a telegram to his ma announcing his leave. He wasn't sure if it had been delivered in time but there she was at the top of the hill, waving the telegram in her hand and running toward him, Kath in close step behind. "Joey, my Joey," she cried as she took her son in her arms, the tears beginning to choke her voice.

"Ah, Ma," was all Joe could manage before his own crying overtook him. Kathleen joined the embrace and there the three of them stood in the middle of the street, a huddled sketch of the Irish family.

"'Tis good to see you, Joe," Kathleen said. "Come up with us."

They climbed the small portion of the hill that remained before turning to the house. Kathleen took Joe's bag from him and Joe took his ma's hand and helped her up the walk. Joe saw a stoop in his mother's carriage and a hesitation to her step that he had never noticed before and he thought: Do I look older to her? Or in her mind's eye am I just home from my catechism and waiting for a cuppa and a clean shirt? The next thing Joe took in was the smell of the house. Joe had spent months in the company of men and before that he had his own home to keep and none of those places held the scent of lavender nor did they smell of the sea, the air moving in and out of the rooms like a ghost—clean, cold, and invisible.

"The house is yours outright now, isn't it, Ma?" Joe asked as he put up a kettle.

"Yes. After your poor aunt passed there was some legal folderol with her grandson but we were able to prove that we lived here for going on ten years and that was all it took to convince the magistrate. No worries there, son."

"And are there worries anywhere, Ma?"

"Only the ones that trail after you, Joe."

"Then you have none at all."

Kath returned holding a tree of Joe's old shirts. "I took these out and ironed them for you, Joe."

"That's quite kind of you, Kath," Joe laughed, "But you know I have to wear my uniform now."

"Don't they ever let you out of their clutches?"

"They do," Joe answered, "but when I'm off duty I still have to wear my dress uniform and a tie. That's the one thing the army is very good at providing."

"Are they taking care of you, Joe?" Ma asked.

"No better than I could take care of myself."

"That's what I worry about," Kath interjected. "In that case, we'd better send you back with a tailor and a chef."

"The army is my tailor and my chef now, Kathy."

It felt good to be treated with excess; Joe had forgotten what it was like to eat too much and lie down in a bed and not have to get up until one wanted to do it. Joe didn't even mind the cold in his room for it was not a damp cold and he had plenty of blankets to ward it off. The silence of the house in the dark scared him a bit; he was used to sudden, loud noises and waking at all hours of the night and it took him a while to literally let down his guard. Eventually, Joe drifted off to sleep.

Things began well enough at breakfast. The novelty of fresh baked bread and bacon with the fat dripping from it was a true diversion. He listened with amusement as his ma caught him up on the health trials and marriage scandals plaguing the neighbors. She rattled off names as if Joe knew them and Joe smiled and agreed with her because he knew that to do so would make her happy. Kath was quiet and diligent and Joe could sense that there was something that she wanted to talk to him about and so when the meal was finished and the ma was off at the sink cleaning up he took her aside and asked her about it.

"I think that having you in the war hurts her terribly, Joe," Kathleen began. "She prays for you night and day."

"I'll need all the prayers I can get, Kath," Joe began, "but none of them are going to get me home any sooner."

"It isn't sooner we're praying for Joe. 'Tis sound."

"I know it."

"It's a great strain upon her. I'd only wish you'd have chosen another path."

"Who's to say I did the choosing, Kathy?"

"What do you mean?"

"There's something about it which is my destiny, I tell you. I know that sounds like a strange word to be using for a lot of dirt and cold and killing. Fighting is a terrible thing. And don't think I'm easy about it, either. I've seen men die. I saw one of my men shot right next to me and die practically in my arms. But I believe God has a purpose for me and if I am to fulfill it I must follow my heart and do what it tells me to do. I love my men and they depend upon me. Their lives hang on my balance. So, I really have no choice. As hard as it is, with the way Ma feels and the way you feel and with all the love I have for the two of you, I ask you—can my path be any clearer?"

"No, Joe," Kath answered, uncertainty creeping into her voice. "I suppose not."

"It's settled then. Now let's go on and enjoy the time we have."

THE DAY TURNED COLD AND WET AND THE MA AND KATHLEEN thought to stay in and do some chores. Joe offered to help but they merely laughed him away and reminded him that this was his time to be free from cares of any sort. So Joe helped himself to an umbrella from the stand in the hall and decided to take a spin around the town.

Queenstown was an important port because of the war and the bustle of the waterfront seemed trebled to what Joe remembered of it. All the businesses of his youth had prospered and flourished. It was unusual for Irish men and women to move about as if they really did have something to do or somewhere to go but Joe had to admit they did all look as if they were going to give it a try. A smile crossed his face as he thought of Severin Coole and how entertained he would be to see this.

Joe settled in at a table in a café overlooking the harbor and sat there with a cup of tea and a biscuit. Joe was wearing his uniform and he felt conspicuous knowing that the townsfolk passing him would recognize him as a soldier. They might feel that I am a part of them, he thought, but I'm not. I am with you but not a part of you. I belong somewhere else. He thought about the ma's concern and their reunion. His family was like a faceted piece of glass that reflected the light differently with every turn. Just this morning, under the comfort of the coverlet or around the table with the crumbs and the grease, Joe had looked upon them like characters in a childhood storybook, full of clear intent and good will, permanent and eternal. They were not real people at all but mythic creatures whose power to influence his world was absolute.

But turn the glass again and another vision appears. Now Joe saw the house on the hill and the hill overlooking the sea and even the spire of St. Colman's as places on a penny postcard to be displayed, not touched or felt. As he walked along the quay with its singing gulls he could watch the girls and boys with their little black umbrellas and he could smell the salt of the sea in the breeze. But when he closed his eyes, he saw the dirt on the duckboards in the trench and the gray puffs of smoke from a shell and he heard the whistle of the bullets and the screams of men not hurt or hit but angry and terrified. There were Mick and Andy and Richard and Billy. And Tommy. Then Joe thought: I cannot abide here for seven days.

WHEN JOE CAME HOME HE DISCOVERED HIS MA HAD BEEN MENDA-cious about the chores. It had all been a ruse to arrange an impromptu tea party for his friends—which meant, in practical terms, her friends, since it was well-known that the Dooley boy was beloved by the older women in the neighborhood and wasn't it a shame that the lad had so few friends near his age to call his own? The assortment of McGillicuddies and O'Shaunesseys that were arrayed in a nearly complete circle around the sitting room cheered like boosters at a parochial school football game when Joe wandered into their ken. Joe smiled wanly and nodded to each as his mother called out their names. All the while Kathleen stood in the doorway to the kitchen stifling a laugh. Each and every time Joe managed to catch her eye he shot her a look of murder for her failure to give warning.

"I'm grand, Mrs. Kennedy, just grand," Joe announced as one of the ladies, not Mrs. Kennedy—he supposed it must have been Mary McGillicuddy but he couldn't be sure—pressed a madeleine into his hand and giggled for no known reason. Joe could hardly back out the door and claim he had entered the wrong house, although that explanation had crossed his mind. Short of that, there was little else Joe could do except wait a polite ten minutes, claim indigestion, and retreat to the sanctuary of what used to be and now could blessedly be claimed as his room.

THAT NIGHT AT THE DINNER TABLE, JOE EXPLAINED TO THE MA AND to Kath that although he was truly glad to see them and he appreciated how much they loved seeing him he had certain obligations he needed to meet during his time in Ireland and in order to fulfill them he would need to go to Dublin for the last few days of his leave.

"What is more important than your family, Joe Dooley?" Kathleen asked.

"Well, for one, I need to talk to the new recruits at my barracks. The command thought it might be invaluable."

"You might talk to us."

"You're being foolish, Kath. I am talking to you."

"I don't understand," Mrs. Dooley said. "What are you two arguing about?"

"We're not arguing, Ma."

"Not at all," said Joe.

"That's it?" Kathleen asked, resuming their nonexistent argument. "You have to give over half of your leave to talk to new recruits?"

"I also promised Richard McCormack that I'd visit his brother Donal in Dublin. Richard is my second in command and the two of us can't be out at the same time. This is the only chance either of us will have until well after Christmas so I thought it was the least I could do."

"How sweet."

"Don't be so sarcastic, dear sister. These things are important to a soldier. And then there's business to attend to—I need to check in at Talbot Street and make sure everything is on the up and up. And then...and then..."

Joe lost his concentration for a moment.

"What is the matter, Joe?" Mrs. Dooley asked.

"I should like to go and see Mrs. Doyle."

THE MORNING OF JOE'S FOURTH DAY OF LEAVE HE PUT ON HIS DRESS uniform and packed his bags. Kathleen had things to do in Cork so she was to accompany Joe on the first leg of his trip but the ma was staying put and so it was "The Leaving Of Liverpool" in the front parlor amidst a chorus of sighs.

"I'll write ye every chance I get, Ma, never doubt it."

"I've no doubts. But I've only one son."

"Have no fear, Ma. I'll be back in the spring—maybe for good."

"Good is all I want, Joe."

Joe embraced his ma and although it did not occur to him at first that this might be the last time he ever saw her he was certain this thought was foremost in her mind and he felt the pity of it. He kissed her once on the cheek and then again in the middle of her forehead.

"Farewell, Ma."

On the train to Cork Joe and Kath sat in silence. There wasn't much more to say and Joe felt that to provoke a discussion at this point would merely stir up more of the pain that neither one of them wished to bear. Although Joe understood that this last stretch of togetherness comforted his sister in some way he could not help but think that he would have been better off making a clean break of it back in Queenstown. The strands would have to be broken sooner or later so why make an endurance contest out of it? Joe found he was having less and less to do with old-fashioned sympathy. The interminability of it sat uncomfortably in contrast with the expedient attitude that pervaded the front lines. There, everyone was concentrating on the present; there was no time to dwell on the passage of time in either direction.

In Cork Joe needed to change trains; the one to Dublin was departing from the opposite platform in half an hour. Joe grabbed his bag from the overhead and went to find a W.C. where he could adjust his tie and wash up. When he came back, Kathleen was sitting on the bench on the platform. She was holding a handkerchief up to her face.

"Don't cry, Kath. I'll be grand."

"I'm not crying, you booby. I've got a cinder in my eye."

"Oh, that's all right then. I thought for one brief moment you were concerned about me."

"For one brief moment, I'll admit I was."

Joe smiled. But it was a real tear that he felt rising. "Dear Kathleen… I'm sorry I've gone missing so much from your life."

"I've grown used to it, Joe. It's the way you always were. I don't know why I should have thought the war would change you."

"But it has, Kath. I feel useful."

"Used would be a better word."

"Don't say that."

"You're right. I'm sorry. Really, I am."

"'S all right."

The whistle sounded.

"That's me."

"Oh, Joe…" Kathleen leaned over and kissed Joe.

"Take care o' the ma now."

"Now and always."

"Goodbye, Kathleen."

Joe slung his bag over his shoulder and climbed aboard. He walked halfway down the car and found a seat facing the window. He turned to wave to Kathleen but when he looked out she was already gone.

⌒

THE FIRST PLACE JOE VISITED WHEN HE ARRIVED IN DUBLIN WAS Talbot Street. Mr. O'Connor was in his shop to greet him. "Well now, Joe. This is a surprise."

"I'm sorry I didn't call, sir. I only planned the Dublin leg of my leave a few days ago and there wasn't the time."

"It's just that—I'm embarrassed to say so but my niece and two of her friends from Roscommon are in town for the week and I've given them the run of the flat. I'm certain..."

"Now don't you bother them about it, Mr. O'Connor. I was wrong not to inform you of my visit. I can bunk at the barracks. Not to worry. How are things with you?"

"Oh, I'm grand, as always. Can't complain." Mr. O'Connor searched for a thought that lay just outside of his reach. Then it came to him: "Ah, I knew there was something in the seeing of you. I've a stack of your letters. You never said what I was to do about it so I've been collecting them. Let me fetch them."

"Letters?"

"They put everything in the post these days—solicitations, testimonials, announcements of all sorts. Nothing terribly important, I'm sure— you're doing all the important work, after all. Still..."

Mr. O'Connor excused himself and came back into the room carrying a large envelope. He handed it over to Joe.

"Thank you, sir," Joe said, putting the package in the outer compartment of his bag.

"You are most welcome, Joe," O'Connor answered. "And thank you for your understanding regarding my grave social error. If you write me the next time you wish to visit, I'll arrange for my out-of-town relations to remain out of town."

Joe laughed and shook Mr. O'Connor's hand. "I'll do that, sir. Thanks!"

Joe sat down on the nearest bench to review the package Mr. O'Connor had handed him. He had to admit he was surprised to see it; he received so little mail under ordinary circumstances that it had never occurred to him to provide for the duration. He opened the envelope and spread the contents out on the seat. There was a circular from the Dublin Corporation informing residents in the neighborhood of street construction and a letter from the alumni association of the University College. Parts of two pieces were spoiled from damp. The ink had run and the papers were stuck together. Joe tried to pry them apart and when he succeeded in separating them one of the letters that fell out held a Swiss postmark.

The envelope was addressed to Joe and there was no return given. Joe ran his finger carefully along the seal and slid out the single piece of paper inside. Then he read the letter:

GENEVA, OCT.30, 1914

Dear Joe,

If you are reading this letter, it means I have succeeded in evading the eye of the censors. I am writing to you from Switzerland, where I have temporarily sought relief. I say temporarily, for as you will learn if you read the rest of my letter I have no intention of *'requiescat in pace,'* to coin a phrase.

I suppose I'd better catch you up. When I left you at Amiens Street that night in August, you knew I was headed north to catch a boat that was to smuggle me to Germany. With that I was a startling success. I met many like-minded men who held no animosity toward my native land and many natives who treated me as Irish and proved equally kind. Within a week I was in Saxony. As I'm sure you might imagine war hysteria was sweeping Kaiserdom and in order to avoid suspicion I had to play along. My German was rusty but I am a better actor than you ever imagined and my perfect grasp of English opened doors. In short, I entered the German army.

When the war began I found that learning information about underground activities in Germany and all along the line was tremendously simpler if you were actually in the army and not one of those poor, pathetic pacifists who drew meager crowds only to find themselves dragged off to jail. Anyone with a bit of intelligence and the ability to shout in complete sentences would be handed a commission and I received mine straight into the Royal Saxons. A fortnight after my stormy sailing across the Irish Sea I was on my way to the front.

In two months of fighting I have managed to avoid killing any soldiers, although the odds are good that if I stay in such a vulnerable position for much longer one of us will pay the ultimate price. All the while I counsel men to lessen their animosity toward their enemy. I try to keep in touch with the medical volunteers and neutral observers who will be useful when the right moment comes. It is taxing work—and dangerous, too—but I vastly prefer it to the alternative, which would be to cower or to escape and avoid it. I am certain you recall our conversation all those months ago about how much I wished to avoid a hiding life and I have not changed my opinion one dram since then.

Dear Joe, I know how you will react to this letter if and when you see it. You must think me doubly a traitor, to profess my love for you and for your countrymen and then to hear of me putting on the uniform of your enemy. Please know I do this with the full knowledge of the consequences of my actions and only with the hope that these actions will do some small good in bringing this terrible war to a swift conclusion. I cannot hope to change the direction of the combatant armies but I do hope and must hope that I can change every soldier I engage and that, soldier by soldier, arms will be cast away and friendship will be restored.

I write to you from my leave. Tomorrow, I return to France and my post. If this letter reaches you, I advise you to commit it to memory and burn it at once. If I were caught mailing it I would be hanged. I wish there was some way I could speak these lines to you in person and perhaps, if God is willing, someday this may be true but until then please know that you are in my heart and in my thoughts. May He protect you as he has protected me. Take care.

Your pal, *Harry Vogeler.*

JOE'S HEAD ACHED FROM THE JOLT HARRY'S LETTER LENT TO HIS imagination. His mind was swirling with questions—where was Harry's section? What did he mean by his "actions" and what was he doing? If he cared so much about ending the war how did he propose to do it while wearing a German uniform? Joe grew angry at the thought of it and it commingled in his memory with his last conversation with Donal and the letter he had received from Severin. Did his friends think he was committed to killing? Did they think all problems could be solved by a simple abdication? It was all Joe could do to resist the temptation to tear Harry's letter into a hundred pieces and send them fluttering into the sky.

Instead, Joe folded the letter and put it in the battered envelope Mr. O'Connor had given him and put the whole of it back in his bag. He looked up from the bench. The sun was out and the roads and walkways were filled with people. How calmly and innocently did they go about their work! —shopping for trinkets and balancing their ledgers while all around them unnoticed the world was struggling to exist. For the first time since the war began Joe felt a deep sense of the moral fight he was engaged in. In retrospect, the physical battle—the loading of the guns and the digging of the trenches and the maps and charts and rations—all of this was the simple part. Anyone could follow orders. Much more difficult and, after reading Harry's letter, apparently much more pervasive, was the battle that was conducted inside a man's soul.

WITH ALL THESE THOUGHTS IN HIS HEAD JOE WONDERED IF HE WAS truly prepared to speak to Mrs. Doyle. Yet here he was on Talbot Street and the Doyles lived on Tyrone, one block to the north. I must steel myself to the task, Joe thought. It is what is expected of me. Harry might have his duplicity to pull him through but I believe in what I am doing and I owe this to my men and to their families. Joe felt he was not convincing himself of this but it seemed silly to keep walking around the block until he did, so he knocked on the door at no. 21 Tyrone and prayed to God that no one would be at home. The door was answered and his prayers were not. An elderly woman greeted him. "Good afternoon, young man. How may I help you?"

"Mrs. Doyle?"

"Yes, I'm she."

"I'm Corporal Joseph Dooley. Your son Tommy was my friend."

"Please, corporal, come in."

The Doyle sitting room was small and furnished in the old-fashioned way. It had the look of a room that had not changed in a score of years.

"Please, have a seat," Mrs. Doyle said. "Would you like some tea?"

"No, thank you, ma'am."

"I remember you, Joe. You and Tommy went to St. Mary's together."

"That we did, Mrs. Doyle. We were close friends for many years."

"It's nice of you to come and visit. How did you hear about Tommy?"

At that moment, Joe understood that Mrs. Doyle did not truly remember who he was. Or rather, she remembered the boy he had been but not who he was now.

"I served with him, ma'am. I was with him in France. The letter…"

"Yes."

"I was the man who wrote it, Mrs. Doyle."

"That was very kind of you, Joe." Mrs. Doyle looked down the hall. "Are you certain I can't get you anything at all?"

Joe felt the tension rising in his throat. "To tell the truth, Mrs. Doyle, I could do with a drop of water."

"Of course."

Mrs. Doyle got up and walked into the kitchen and returned with a tall glass of water. Joe took a few sips and put the glass down on the table.

"You have a lovely home, Mrs. Doyle."

"Thank you, Joe," Mrs. Doyle answered. "It's only me now. My husband passed away years ago and all of Tommy's brothers and sisters have families of their own."

"I'm glad I could come and see you."

"When do you go back to France, Joe?"

"I'll be in Belgium, ma'am. The day after tomorrow."

"You poor boy."

"I don't mind."

"Tommy spoke well of you, and often."

"Did he, ma'am? That's good to hear."

"He said you were his best friend in school."

"Thank you, ma'am."

Joe started to cry. Mrs. Doyle got up and put her arm around him. "Now let's not start in with that. I have some biscuits in the kitchen and I'll be right back."


At Beggars Bush Corporal Joe Dooley was greeted as a hero. He had only been gone for three months but already the new recruits struck Joe as being a generation younger than he. Most heartbreaking of all was the boy—and no matter what his age, he was certainly no more than a boy—who had inherited Joe's locker. He was tall with short black hair and dark eyebrows that met in the middle of his forehead and gave him an incongruously scholarly appearance. He was changing when Joe walked in and he was wearing the bottom half of his uniform. As a new recruit the boy hadn't had the opportunity to work on his build yet and his lack of musculature reminded Joe of his own underwhelming physique.

"This was my locker before the war," Joe said, coming up to the boy. "I'm Corporal Joseph Dooley."

"Private Michael Shanley, sir." The boy offered his hand.

"A pleasure, Private Shanley."

"How's the game, sir?"

"We're holding our own. Winter's coming and that will quiet things down."

"I'm glad to hear it."

"Where are you from, Michael?"

"I'm a Dalkey man, sir."

"Glad to hear Dalkey is doing their part."

"What's it like, sir?"

"What's what like?"

"The war."

Joe felt like he was seventy years old and he was talking to his grandchildren. And yet only four or five years at the most separated them. "If you're lucky, Michael, you won't need to know."

The barracks commander took Joe aside at one point and told him that he was welcome to spend the night here if he didn't mind a cot on the floor as recruits had taken all the beds. Joe measured in his mind a comparison between a cot on the plank floor of Beggars Bush and a plush mattress in Donal McCormack's flat in Ely Place and decided that in this case the comforts of leave overrode the propriety of asking your ex-lover for a spare bed and he bade farewell.

On the way out, Joe passed Shanley. The private had put together a group of new Dubs for Joe's inspection. They stood in a row in front of the barracks doorway wearing their fresh uniforms with their cap badges carefully pinned in place and their rifles held at the ready.

"Begging your pardon, Corporal Dooley. Thank you for visiting us, sir."

"At ease, men. You're welcome. Good luck."

"Will that be all, sir?"

Joe thought about Harry's letter. Intimacy arrives from strange directions and Joe wanted with all his heart to reach out to Michael Shanley and all of the proud and handsome young men with him and take them under his arm and touch them, to reassure them that what they were doing was right and true and to tell them all about how dedication to their work and love of their fellow man could carry the day. But then he thought about Mrs. Doyle and that heavenly place beyond caring where she seemed to be. Better to split the difference and do nothing.

"Yes, that will be all."

DONAL MCCORMACK HAD COME UP IN THE WORLD OR, MORE PRE-cisely, moved to a new level of prosperity in respect to his wealth and class. Heidelberg was far behind him, and so was his anatomy. He had thrown over medicine for the law and at the budding age of twenty-three Donal was at home on Ely Place, cheek-to-jowl with the ambassadors and clubs of the ancient Protestant orders. When Joe arrived at the flat, a butler took his bag, coat, and cap and led him to a sitting room domi-nated by a Watteau.

"Mr. McCormack will be down presently," the man said, and then disappeared.

Joe was used to Donal's playful attitude toward his family's position but this seemed to be carrying the joke a little too far. If the people who bowed to the McCormack family whims, who polished the banisters and baked the scones or prepared the papers and protected the invest-ments suspected anything of Donal's specific interests in young men or his republican sympathies it was not in evidence. Apparently, there was considerable charm to be garnered by playing the Lord.

When Donal come in, he embraced Joe and then framed him at arms' length as if inspecting a picture. "Look at you, Joe. Flawless. You'd hardly think there's a war on."

"I might say the same of you, Donal."

Donal twirled around and held out the tails of his suit. "I'm not so much of a patriot as to eschew Savile Row."

"You do look grand."

"I find it's much easier to get people to do what you want when you smile at them while wearing an expensive suit of clothes. And since it's a good part of a solicitor's business to get people to do what I want them to do, it's practically a requirement. But you didn't come to hear me sing my praises—or did you?"

"I did not."

"Then, let's begin. Can I get you anything?"

"No, Donal, not at all."

"Then you must allow me to treat you to supper."

"That would be grand."

"It's settled, then."

THEY HAD DINNER AT A CLUB ON LEINSTER STREET. JOE ALLOWED Donal to order the twin lobster thermidor ("You won't see anything like this on a plate in Brussels") and a bottle of Veuve Clicquot ("Not one of the better years, but we have to make some concessions to the war, don't we?"). The crustaceans were delicious and the wine spectacular and Joe wondered as he was being pampered if this was a plot to drug him into equanimity and sequester him away from the army. Joe arrived at Ely Place armed to the teeth with his defenses: the war had taken a serious turn, he had lost a good friend and fellow soldier, home life with its petty inconveniences and lack of any sense of purpose was intolerable. But Donal was expert at wearing him down.

"Now, Joe, I do not doubt that there is no comparison in our experiences. I'm sure nothing that I could imagine about your time at the front would equal what you yourself have seen and done. But my point is: that doesn't mean I can't enjoy myself or do my work. And even though I honor what you are doing, surely you understand how I still need to do everything in my power to dissuade you from doing it."

Joe drained his glass and sat back at the table. The wine, as usual, had gone to his head and it made all the thoughts which had been swirling around in it since reading Harry's letter begin to settle and if not clarify at least gather in strength.

"It is very curious to me," said Joe, "that all your talk of stopping the war takes place as far away from the actual fighting as possible. Don't you agree with me that it is entirely facile to make such an argument from the dining room of a Dublin club? Do you honestly think such a consideration could be entertained in a dugout? I'm all for intellectual exercises but when you point a gun at my head I'm not going to issue a petition."

"Now you're being silly. I haven't said a word about not fighting. I'm only saying you might be fighting the wrong enemy. Why are you working so hard to defend the British Empire?"

"We're both wearing uniforms, Donal. As far as defending the British Empire, what difference does it make whether one is wearing khaki or Henry Poole?"

"The difference," muttered Donal, lighting a cigarette, "is that everyone can see what you are doing and no one can see what I am doing."

"That doesn't make you a patriot. It makes you a hypocrite."

The room began to fill with smoke. Joe expected to be pulled into an argument with his friend and it seemed in retrospect that Donal was baiting him. It was too much to resist. Now he regretted his tone and the direction of their conversation and wished he had stayed at the barracks.

"Maybe I should go, Donal."

"I wouldn't allow it. We were pals once, Joe, and I'd like to be your pal again. Can't you understand at least that much?"

"I got a letter this morning from my old friend Harry Vogeler. He fled to Germany when the war began and now he's serving in the German army, trying to do the same thing you are."

"How do you mean?"

"I think he believes he can end the war one soldier at a time."

"There doesn't seem to be any other way."

"One can win."

"Do you really believe that?"

"I have to, Donal."

Donal lowered his voice. "I remember you used to love me, Joe."

"I did. But there's all kinds of love, you know. Love can be selfish, and an unselfish love is much harder to effect and much more rewarding. When I joined the British Army I did so because it gave me a chance to show my love to more people in a better way and all that I have learned and seen since then has only reinforced this. That doesn't mean I must needlessly cause hurt, although I do have to defend myself. And it doesn't mean that I can dismiss the feelings of friends like you and Harry, people I love and trust. But it does mean that I cannot betray my fellow soldiers and I cannot hide who I am."

Donal took a thought-filled draught on his cigarette. Then he said, "Do you mean to tell me that in order to save the lives of the three or four or five men in your section you would return to the front and take up arms and support the actions of an army that will kill hundreds and thousands of others? Whereas if you sacrificed yourself to the cause of ending the war and making Ireland free you might lose the companionship of your small circle of friends but gain the freedom and possibly save the lives of so many of those hundred and thousands?"

"You may believe that you can end the war one soldier at a time," Joe said. "I believe that is also the only way to win it."

AFTER DINNER, JOE AND DONAL WALKED DOWN LEINSTER STREET past Trinity College and along Dame Street. The night was cold and the air was helping Joe to clear his mind. It was true that he had once loved Donal and he could still see what it was about him that he loved. There was never any ambiguity about what Donal was after and Joe admired that quality in him. That was what had made their intimate life together so exciting. But when challenged Joe was beginning to believe that he was capable of giving as good as he got and now Donal McCormack was an obstacle.

At the corner of Lower George's Street, Joe stopped. "If we have a little more time, Donal, I'd like to show you something."

"I have all the time in the world for you, Joe. You know that's true."

"Then follow me."

Joe took Donal's hand and they walked up the street to the Long Hall. It was nine o'clock now and the room was filled with women and men and the sound of glasses clanking and laughing voices. There was a *sessun* going on at the back of the bar and two fiddlers, a girl with a flute, and a young boy with a bodhran were banging away at a rough and ready version of "The Rose of Tralee." The notes filtered into the room and seemed the logical accompaniment to the rest of the noise.

"Let me treat you," Joe said to Donal as they shifted to a corner near a snug. "What would you like?"

"A measure of whiskey, if you please."

Joe turned to the barkeep. "Two measures of Jameson and two stouts."

"Yes, sir."

Joe gathered their drinks and the two men settled in to listen to the rest of the song. The bodhran player in particular had a lovely voice, sweet and high like a girl's but with a man's assertiveness. As Joe listened he remembered the ache that he felt when he thought about Tommy and the fears he held for Harry. Then he looked at Donal and remembered his love and he wished he could unite them all and not have the world crumble in his hands. And as the boy sang it seemed to Joe in this one brief moment that music itself might be the way to effect his wish:

> *Though lovely and fair as the rose of the summer*
> *Yet, 'twas not her beauty alone that won me*
> *Oh no! 'Twas the truth in her eye ever beaming*
> *That made me love Mary, the Rose of Tralee.*

"There's all that we're fighting for, Donal," Joe said.

"What's that?"

"The truth."

"Be it ever so elusive."

"Indeed. Do you think we can ever know it?"

"If anyone can, Joe, it would be you. I do believe you are positively running in a straight line for it."

"Thanks for putting me up, Donal."

"Putting up with you, you mean."

"That, too."

The music faded and the crowd noise expanded but Joe still heard the notes ringing in his head. It was not enough just to know the truth, he thought. It must be acted upon as well as known and done in equal portions like the beer and the whiskey before him. One without the other wouldn't do. These were the promises he had made to himself that still needed to be redeemed.

"How's my brother doing, Joe?"

"I was wondering when you were going to ask about Richard."

"Is he all right? I mean, I've been to visit Mary several times and she shows me his letters but that's not the same thing at all."

Joe reached over and put his arm around Donal. "Your brother is the steadiest man I know."

"Is that saying much?"

Joe laughed.

"You need to join the army to find out, my friend."

"I'd rather find out from you."

"It is saying much, indeed."

"Thanks, Joe. I love my brother."

"And I love his."

"You don't need say that, Joe."

"No, Donal. I do. I mustn't let you think that the war has come between us."

"But it has."

"Yes, it has. But our bond will last."

"I hope so."

"Drink up. We've time for another round."

AT ELY PLACE THEY STUMBLED INTO THE HOUSE IN THE DARK. "I don't want to wake anyone up," Donal said. He then proceeded to kick over the umbrella stand and send the contents clattering to the floor.

"Oh, well," Joe laughed.

Donal laughed with him. "Your room is on the second floor, immediately to the right. Unless…"

"No, Donal. It's best this way. Let's leave things as they were. It's the one thing I can hold on to."

They parted at the landing.

"Good night."

Joe leaned over and gave Donal a kiss.

"Good night."

As Joe turned down the lamp by his bed he remembered what it was like to feel Donal beside him and he thought of Tommy in his suffering and at that moment he understood how the embers of a memory can truly be bellowed into a flame and turn love into a kind of resurrection.

# Chapter 12

◆ ◆ ◆

## Silence

◆ ◆ ◆

JOE LAID HIS DANTE DOWN ON THE FIRE STEP. IT WAS THE ONLY dry spot available. *Nel mezzo del cammin di nostra vita mi ritrovai per una selva oscura,* indeed, although under the circumstances Joe felt he would be lucky to be in the middle of the road of his life. Ploegsteert certainly fit the bill as a dark wood although the irony of it was that Virgil had not yet even approached the Gates of Hell whereas Joe found himself in the thick of it. This week, his *Divina Commedia* held pride of place in his dugout, more prominent than his toothbrush, toolkit, or razor. Last week, it had been Keats and a week's worth of the *Irish Times*. If the action wasn't too hot Joe hoped by next week he could exchange the Dante for some Rabelais.

Such was existence in Joe's section. The soggy days of November had led inexorably to the frosts and flurries of December and the only boon to the baleful weather had been that it distracted both sides from fighting. Evenings were spent with the pick shovel, the wire cutters, and scraps of duckboard as the men dug deeper into the Belgian mud or scouted and barbed the perimeters. The earth was cold and the work was hard. The snow built up and then melted and sluiced into the trench and the sandbags shifted and slid, making a simple walk from one end of the camp to the other a messy adventure. Even the communication trenches, designed for speed, quickly became filled with wind-blown brush, metal fragments, and slush.

Joe was frustrated by this stagnation. Ever since he had returned from his leave he had been filled with the desire to rededicate himself to his work and to his men. All the way from Dublin to Gravesend and from Calais to St. Omer Joe dreamed of a sweeping campaign across the fields of Flanders, a heroic charge crowned by a decisive maneuver. Even as the snows began to fall and the roads grew thick with stalled motorcars and rank upon rank of pashed soldiers Joe refused to give up his self-image of strength and mobility. When he was finally reunited with his men and saw that what they needed most from him was any activity leading to a small sense of purpose he lowered his expectations but still refused to abandon them.

One night in early December Joe arranged a scouting party with Richard and Andy. They were to clear the communication trenches running to the northeast from their section in the hope of establishing an open path to St. Ives and the Warwickshires who had dug in there. Time upon time one regiment or another had made the attempt and each time they had come up short or retreated under fire from the flanking Germans. If one man could serve as a sort of router the entire thread would suddenly become passable and a valuable supply route would be opened.

The men moved out around midnight. A gray moon had risen over the ruins of the wood and the scarred trunks iridized in the dim light. There was a frost but because of all the activity it didn't seem terribly cold and in fact Joe felt a little overheated due to his nerves. Richard was sweeping along in front of him and Andy was coming up behind. As they marched farther and farther away from the line the darkness grew deeper and the elongated moon shadows made fantastic shapes along the trench walls and floors. At one point, Richard couldn't see where he was going and with a muttered curse he fell into a foot-deep pool of water. Just beyond this point they ran into a sentry at a crossroads.

"Royal Dubs, sir. Requesting permission to advance."

"First Warwickshires. Approach."

"All clear?"

"Quiet all night."

"Thanks."

"We've a dugout fifty yards ahead. Will you call in?"

"We're grand."

"Then follow Fleet Street to the right."

"What's at the end of it?"

"That's the question, mates."

"All right, then."

"Carry on, and mind the wire."

"Thanks, much."

The Warwick saluted and Joe saluted back and then he took the lead and Andy and Richard followed him. They scrambled into the communication trench and started to beat a path forward. The way had not been cleared in a while. Whole portions of blasted trees had fallen across the trenches, blocking and sometimes collapsing them, and the three of them had to stop completely every twenty yards or so to dig themselves out. It was clear to Joe that this was an important piece of the puzzle and he felt the imperative to complete it. The level of struggle merely underscored this for him; this was just the kind of forceful gesture he had sought to make.

As Andy and Richard worked behind him Joe could feel their shovels digging and hear the grunts and grappling sounds and the thump of their anchored footfalls. Joe liked to lead by deeds and not by words and he was not the type to offer empty praise anyway so he put his back into his work and redoubled his efforts to be the first through every obstacle of wood, soil, or stone. At times it felt as if they were constructing the trench anew. There was no cover to speak of and the amount of risk they were taking was greater than that with which Joe was comfortable but there was some solace in the company and the bracing air.

After an hour of hard work the three men had advanced about a quarter mile along the perimeter of the wood. The moon was setting and it was too dangerous to light any torches so the men stopped to consider their position. Joe calculated they were now about a half mile farther east of the Warwickshire camp, very close to No Man's Land. The German trenches could be three hundred yards away. Very slowly, Joe crept up over the top of the escarpment and took out his field glasses, peering into the black for any sight of movement. There was nothing there. Just then, one of the logs that they had rolled up against the top of the trench wall slid off and tumbled over with a loud crash. The sudden sound and movement startled Andy and he shouted at Joe. That noise was all it took to provide their location. A pair of Very lights arched over the middle distance and the sky filled with the sound of rushing air.

"Shell!" Joe yelled as he tried to retreat along the path of the half-dug trench. His foot got caught on a piece of a branch and he fell into the mud. As he did so, he saw Richard jump over him and Andy follow right behind. "Take cover!"

Machine-gun fire opened up from behind them. Joe saw Richard turn and head in the direction of the fire. Andy rolled over and came back.

"McCormack… McCormack…" Joe shouted. Then the shell exploded.

Joe closed his eyes as the metal fragments sprayed his helmet and his first thought was that if he was feeling the metal he must still be alive. Then he noticed that he only felt the metal. He didn't hear it. There was no noise, no sound of the fire bursting over his head, nothing at all. It was fantastic, lying there in the mud with so many pounds of metal torn into tiny pieces flying through the air and racing toward your head but not making any sound at all. Not a word from Andy, although Joe saw his mouth moving. No cries from Richard, although he still must have been less than fifty feet away and under fire. No thunder from the explosion of the metal. Not even the warning song of a bird from a blasted tree. Only silence.

Until this moment in his life Joe had never noticed the sound the air makes. One would think that air is silent but in fact this is never the case. It whispers when it passes you in the breeze. It calls to you when you stand on a hilltop and watch the clouds sail across the sky. Air sings when it moves and sighs when it waits and it was completely uncanny how in the wake of the shell Joe felt as if he was suffocating. The air was gone. And, of course, one hears music in the air. Without air, there can be no music. As he watched the metal dust settle silently around him, Joe thought of what his life would be like if there was no music, if suddenly and for no true reason at all he was no longer able to hear a Brahms piano sonata or the reedy cry of a pipe or a tenor's solo. That would truly be asphyxiation.

For what seemed like an eternity but was in actuality no longer than ten seconds, Joe lay supine on the floor of the trench, soaking in the mud and trying to understand if there was any air or any music left in the world. The lack of sound was terrifying to him, far more terrifying than any rifle pointed at his chest or even the blackest darkness of death. Joe prayed to God to take him now if he was to endure even as much as a minute of this noiseless universe. To not hear the cry of a baby or the soft words of a friend, to be kept apart from the din of a crowd in the street or the oratory of a man of the people, this was enough of a death, but to go further than this and deprive him of the only harmony he had ever heard was to negate his life. For Joe the opposite of harmony was not disharmony but nonexistence.

Then the roar of the world rose and blew apart before him. Like the last crescendo of Beethoven's Sixth Symphony and just as beautiful Joe heard the pulsating reverberation of a shell exploding to his right. Although he knew he was in danger and the good part of him that was running on instinct knew to lay low and crawl away from the direction of the fire still he felt a small bit of a smile creep across his face at the lovely sound of it. Joe thought: I'm alive. He tried to move but found that his leg was heavy. Was he hit? There was no blood. Probably just a form of shock. Then Andy came up beside him.

"We've exposed the German flank and they're firing on us to cover it," Andy shouted. "We've got to go back before one of those shells gets lucky. Can you walk?"

"I'm not certain," Joe answered. "Help me up."

Andy helped Joe hobble to his feet.

"How's that?" Andy asked.

"There's no time for consideration. Where's Richard?"

"I lost him."

"Hand me my glasses."

Andy handed them to Joe and Joe peered out into the darkness. There was Richard, about two hundred yards away. His rifle was at his feet and he was holding his arms folded behind his head: prisoner.

"They got him," Joe said.

"Shite."

"We dug straight into their exposed side," Joe continued. "It's important that we return with this information. It will take them about an hour to close the gap and find us and we can be back in our trench by then if we move quickly enough. But it's hard for me to walk. Can you help me?"

"I used to carry a four-stone barley sack for my father and I wasn't more than ten years old."

"Well, if you can still do so, Andy, this old barley sack would be right glad of it."

Andy pulled his rifle around by the straps so it hung over his back and he helped Joe to his feet and levered him up so that his injured leg wasn't touching the ground. Together they bent low to the earth and pulled and heaved their way backwards along the now cleared communicating trench. As they retraced their steps, another shell landed nearby but the trench was deeper now and the metal flew over their heads. Joe calculated—correctly, as it turned out—that the Germans would not risk an infantry pursuit if they could not gauge the enemy's strength. On the other hand, Joe had failed to make a proper gauge in return and his error had cost Richard McCormack his freedom.

Joe wondered who was opposite them on the line. If their nemesis were Hessians, Richard would likely be beaten and deported. If on the other hand they were Saxons there would be nothing to fear. Joe remembered that Harry was a Saxon and he liked to imagine that the whole of the rank and file of that regiment of the German Army was as humane as he.

Andy rolled Joe back into the Dubs' trench and tumbled in behind him. It was now nearly three in the morning and the noise woke up Mick and Billy.

"They got Richard," Joe said.

"Jesus, Joe," Mick cried. "What happened?"

"We were shelled. I got knocked out and Richard ran around me. It was my fault."

"It was nothing of the kind," Andy answered. "Richard was trying to protect us."

"Are you hurt?" Billy asked Joe.

"I twisted my knee is all. Andy practically carried me back."

"I'm nothing if not practical," Andy said.

"That's a miserable bit of news about Richard," Mick said. "We should try to save him."

"I have no idea how many men are holding him," Joe began. "We could easily be killed trying and what good would that do? Richard's a smart soldier. He'll live to play another round."

"That he will," said Andy.

"So we won't even try to save Richard?" Mick asked.

"We can't afford it and you know that's true," said Joe. "You should thank Andy for having the wherewithal to save me."

"Thank ye, Andy," Billy said.

"You were a mighty good thing for me," Joe added.

"Mighty is as mighty was, sir. You'll save me next time."

"Next time," Joe answered, "I will."

Mick said nothing.

⌢

THE WEEK BEFORE CHRISTMAS JOE'S SECTION WAS ORDERED IN RE-lief. They billeted in an abandoned chateau that lay just off the Armentières-Neuve Chapelle road. The entire building had been shelled early in the war and the roof was gone and let in the sleet and the cold. The front-line trenches lay a mere quarter of a mile to the northeast and had he been asked Joe might have preferred the camaraderie of the mud to the ghosts of the rotted chateau. Still, it was quiet and in war quiet has its boosters.

What remained of the floor of the house had been converted into a first-aid post and three wounded soldiers had been carried in and laid down on cots. Joe passed them on his way to the kitchen and they seemed cheered by the fact that their wounds might be good enough for a blighty. One man, his arm wrapped in a sling, was cheerily singing:

> *For thy parting neither say nor sing,*
> *By, by lully, lullay. Lully, lullay,*
> *Thou tiny child, by, by, lully lullay.*

"You must be a Coventry man," Joe said as he approached him. He offered his hand. "I'm Corporal Joseph Dooley."

"Lieutenant Corporal Francis Atkins, sir. You recognized the carol."

"That I did. You have a lovely voice."

"Thanks, much. 'Tis a fine day when a wounded man can be complemented on his tenor."

"What happened to you?"

"The 'shires were up along the Warnelle ridge, digging in. We had hardly made a go of it when a brigade's worth of Jerries stormed our parapets. In a shooting war you don't want to be the one being shot at so we dashed for the wood—or what was left of it—and what you see here is pretty much all that is left of my section."

"I am sorry to hear it."

"Now they tell me I am to be carried back through the line to recuperate in Dover. So it's a Merry Christmas to me after all and a carol for my send-off. What's your story?"

"2nd R.D.F. We're your relief."

"And a relief it is to have you."

"Good luck, Lieutenant."

"And the same to you, Corporal Dooley. Merry Christmas."

"Merry Christmas."

THAT NIGHT JOE HAD A FITFUL SLEEP. HE TRIED VERY HARD NOT TO succumb to war-weariness but the evidence of it was trailing after him and it was hard to ignore. A man is a resilient thing but you can wear him down in much the same way that the smallest rivulet can wear away a hard stone. Joe was not one to pay much attention to dreams but this night it was Tommy and Richard and even Francis Atkins who passed by like figures called to a processional and although they were marching somewhere it was not a battlefield but a flower bed that they crossed and it was not to war but to some permanent conclusion that they were directed.

The next day Joe and his men went up the line toward La Hutte, skirting the edge of the wood over frost-covered hillocks and muddy ravines now frozen like lava. Their destination was the trench currently occupied by the decimated Warwickshires. Joe expected to find the usual accoutrements of half-torn sandbags and unevenly laid wire; upon his arrival and to his amazement he found a small independency. The trench walls were constructed of rusted but still sound corrugated iron, bucked up by hacked pine boards and raised out of the mire by an architectural fantasy of duckboards and canvas tacks. The men who had passed in and out of here built real dugouts where you could sleep and tiered shelves lined with wood scraps where you could stash a candle or a bottle and reasonably expect it to stay put. Even the telephone and electric wires looked subject to deliberation.

"My heartiest welcome, Colonel Dooley," said a mustachioed officer in greeting. "I'm Captain William Hartley."

"Thanks, Captain." Joe saluted. "I'm glad we can help you."

There were three other Warwicks lying about and introductions were made all around. Joe learned that the sections had been trading places for a week without any support and with their ranks depleted there was the danger of an indefensible attack. All the regiments were facing the same shortage and filling in with relief, the Highlanders to their left and the Royal Irish to their right.

"Royal Irish?" Billy asked. "Have you met any of their men?"

"Only across the telephone lines, I'm afraid."

Billy said, "I trained with a pack o' them in Dublin a year ago."

"None finer for a bottle," said Mick.

"Here's to the hope that you're back at it again and soon," Hartley replied.

"Not soon enough, mate." Mick shook his head. "Not soon enough."

"To that end, let's stow your gear and get you acquainted with the fire step."

Hartley moved out and gathered Billy and Mick with him. In Richard's absence Andy had turned into a bit of an adjutant and so he remained by Joe's side awaiting further orders but Joe was still looking at the fairyland trench.

"Nice setup, eh, Joe?" Andy said.

"I wouldn't call it cushy but it beats the funhouse we lay in last night."

"You didn't care for the old chateau?"

"Give me a blanket under the stars anytime."

"Are those stars or flares?"

"Get going, Andy."

THE NEXT MORNING IT STARTED TO SNOW. IF THE ENEMY WAS OUT there at all, they were busy twisting wires and stacking sandbags and couldn't be bothered to take potshots at anyone. It was never complacency but at times it could look like a kind of game. At one point in the early afternoon during the shifting of the guard someone shouted out a warning and every man ran for his helmet and rifle but it turned out to be two lost sheep literally and not in the Christian sense and had the men not feared too greatly rousing German attention there might have been a feast of lamb for dinner.

With sunset it was Joe's turn at sentry duty. Behind and beneath him in the safety of the trench Joe saw Billy and Andy sleeping and Mick in the next bay down talking to one of the Warwicks. When Mick caught Joe looking at him, he waved and Joe waved back, like two schoolmates in the grandstand at a football match. Before him was a landscape after Brueghel: the top of the trench looked out over a snow-covered field that sloped steeply down to La Hutte. What trees and shrubs survived were laid out in neat array. One family must have remained in their home for a tiny piping of smoke rose from a distant chimney and it was cheering to see the fog of domesticity hovering over the dying earth. The weather had not completely cleared but the tangerine glow of the setting sun edged the clouds and the trunks of the stunted trees threw purple shadows in his direction.

Joe slung his rifle over his back and picked up his glasses, searching the horizon for a sign of life or death or anything. The stillness was not natural and he felt slightly unnerved by it. Then for an instant the clouds parted and the rays of the sun seared directly into the lenses and blinded him, bursting white upon his eyes. Joe saw a flash of fire and wondered how the sun could be so bright in the middle of December. Then he looked down at his chest and saw the blood soaking his uniform.

JOE WAS CERTAIN HE WAS IN A CLASSROOM; THERE WAS AN ARRANGE-ment of wooden desks in a neat semicircle and he was standing in front of them as if he was giving a lesson. Strange it was, though, that he had no sense of how many desks were in the room or even where the room started and ended for it seemed to him that the rows went on beyond his field of vision. Nor did he receive any sense of a chalkboard or even a wall behind him; it might have been an open-air lesson for all that, although he had never known of an open-air lesson where they dragged the desks into the field.

His perception of the situation came from the furnishings but in truth that was not what held Joe's interest. All his sense of the space was merely the setting for the drama that lay on the faces of his charges, the young men who were sitting in front of him and watching him with almost reverential attention. In front to his left, there was a boy who looked to be seventeen or eighteen years of age. His hair hung in black waves across his forehead and his steel-gray eyes stared directly at Joe. The boy's mouth was open and he seemed to be singing. There was another boy beside him, even younger in appearance, fair-haired, blue eyed, and smiling. He, too, was at song.

There must have been singing; that was why the boy's mouths were rounded O's and although Joe could see the boys' faces he couldn't hear any music. It was if he had plugs in his ears. Something small was audible but it did not have the clear, harmonic fullness of a song. Certainly there was not enough of the sound to give it a name. Still, it was a pleasant sight for Joe to behold and he continued to enjoy his conducting of it despite the confusion as to the circumstances. Then, slowly but with gently increasing volume, the music began to grow louder—a hymn of sorts, ranging high like a boy's choir. It was Darby's "Ten Thousand Voices," a memory from Joe's childhood:

> Hark! ten thousand voices crying
> "Lamb of God!" with one accord.

*Thousand, thousand saints replying*
*Wake at once the echoing chord.*

One by one, the boys stood and as they stood, he saw that they were naked. As the crescendo of joyful boyish voices soared, the fair-haired lad moved away from his seat and walked up to Joe and caressed him. He put his arms around Joe's neck and pressed him close to his chest and then he put his lips on Joe's mouth and kissed him. Joe returned the kiss and wondered how the kiss could be made and yet his singing continued. The boy's voice was as beautiful as any Joe had ever heard. Joe closed his eyes and disappeared into the boy's embrace, the music enveloping him and his chest swelling and his heart bursting with the boy's touch.

*"Praise the Lamb," the chorus waking*
*All in heaven together throng.*
*Loud and far each tongue partaking*
*Rolls around the endless song.*

In a small corner of his mind, Joe wondered what the other singing students would think of this quite natural but entirely inappropriate love of his student but when he opened his eyes the fair-haired student was no longer there. His place had been taken by another boy, the dark-haired lad Joe had first noticed sitting in the front row. By now their embrace was no longer chaste but sexual, their bodies tightly drawn together. Joe, too, had removed his clothes. He and the young man writhed together as the choir continued to sing their joyous song. In the moment when he separated from the boy to catch his breath, Joe looked down at his own body and noticed that his chest and belly were covered in blood.

"YOU'RE ALL RIGHT, COLONEL DOOLEY. YOU'RE GOING TO LIVE."

Joe opened his eyes and tried to see where he was, but the pain was too intense.

"Don't try to talk. I'll give you some morphine."

"What…what happened to me?"

"You are a very lucky man, Joe Dooley. A sniper found you but the bullet went straight through. You didn't even break a rib. I've bandaged you up right well and discounting the pain in your side you should be back with your men by Christmas."

"I…I…thank you, sir…mister…"

"My name is Davy Rose. I'm a medical volunteer."

"Thank you, Mr. Rose."

"I'm Davy to everyone."

"Thank you, Davy. Do you know…can you tell me—are my men all right?"

"I'll find out for you."

"Thank you."

"You should stop thanking me and try to sleep. That's what you need the most."

Joe tried to fight through the pain and take in his surroundings. The dressing station was a tent pitched on the side of a dilapidated townhouse. From his cot, Joe could see a row of men in bandages, casts, and slings.

"Tomorrow, you and I are going down the line to the clearing hospital in St. Omer," Davy said. "As you can no doubt see, this is no place to recover from a bullet wound."

"Can you get word to my men?"

"If you continue to insist on trying to hold a conversation, Joe, I'm afraid I'll have no choice but to smother you with a pillow."

This raised a smile on Joe's face.

"Good. Message received," Davy said. "See you tomorrow."

Just before he fell asleep Joe recalled the choir of students who serenaded him. They were beautiful, but in the end he was glad it was only a dream. If that's what Heaven is like, I can stand to wait, Joe thought, for death hath no dominion and despite the pain and all the mire around me I would still much rather be here.

# Chapter 13

◆ ◆ ◆

## From Hospitalis

◆ ◆ ◆

JOE LOOKED AT HIS WOUND IN THE SHAVING MIRROR. ONLY TWO days had passed since they sewed him up and it looked as if a battle had been fought upon the surface of his body. An uneven line of black thread zigzagged from a point just below his lowest rib to conclude in a bruised knot near the small of his back, tracing the path of the bullet. The pain had abated to the point of a constant dull ache but he still had the sense of heat coursing through his side. It was as if through its own efficiency his flesh had developed a fever independent of the rest of him.

He recalled the moment he was shot. It was not the physical sensation of the bullet entering his body but the emotional states that he passed through that gave the experience its true expression. First there was his lack of fear. Joe understood that the terror of the possibility of being shot was what held back his courage and that once the event had transpired he was no longer afraid of it. After that came the sense of pain, a pain unequal to the adjectives he had heard others use to describe it—searing, burning—metaphors for fire that really had no correlative to the fact. It wasn't fire he felt but annihilation. This was a pain that delineated the borders of his sense of self and for one brief instant converted his soul into a pure wraith. And in the end there was self-preservation, the in-stinct that armies since Hannibal have depended upon for survival. The only thing Joe felt after the bullet passed through him was his need to live one minute longer.

THIS MORNING JOE TRIED TO WALK ON HIS OWN, ALL THE WAY TO the latrine and the mess table and back again to his bunk. The west wing of the hospital at St. Omer held approximately two hundred cots and almost all of them were occupied. As Joe made his way past the rows of turned-back bedcovers, he smiled at the soldiers and took in their faces. Some had their arms in slings; others were bandaged below the knees. Joe felt it was all part of a God-induced equilibrium. There were two push-weights to the scales: the men who were only mildly damaged like himself, who were treated like tourists, greeted with a uniform cheerfulness, and then politely forgotten, and those who were about to die. The latter were allowed their reverent few hours in the bed and then literally disappeared. Even the blood they left behind on the sheets was eradicated.

When Joe got back to his cot his neighbor, a boy from Kent named Larkin, was breaking out a deck of cards. "Will you partner me in a round of whist, Dooley?" he asked as he dealt. "McGowan and Watts here have formed a coalition against me and I need to win back a ration's worth of Black Cats."

Joe eased himself down on the bed. "Sure thing."

"How's the stitches, Joe?" asked Watts.

"The stitches itches."

"Deal."

Just then one of the V.A.D. nurses entered the wing. Her name was Sharon and she was a very pretty girl, barely eighteen years of age and cheerful as most volunteers were but as inexperienced at war as any of the soldiers she was treating—possibly even more so. Still it was novel to have women in your field of vision for any reason at all and for this the men were exceedingly grateful.

"Anything from the canteen?" Sharon asked to no one in particular.

"Aye, a bottle of whisky and a dozen glasses," came a shout from the corner.

"If I had a bottle, sir, I wouldn't share it with you!"

The men laughed.

"With me, then, Sharon?"

"With you, Bobby—maybe."

A roar rose up from Bobby's vicinity.

"I'll be back for lunch, then."

"Too much a wait to bear," Bobby shouted.

Watts groaned and led with spades.

"I've had my share of pretty nurses before but I must confess Sharon heads the pack," Larkin said. He threw down a seven.

"I didn't know you could have a share of a nurse," Watts commented. "I was pretty much convinced that the deal was all or nothing."

"If I had something to throw at you, Watts, you'd be showered."

"You can barely throw your cards down. I'd hold off with your threats."

"Ten," Joe announced.

"Trump."

"Shite."

"In my day, Billy boy, I had nurses, waitresses, and even a college girl."

"A college girl?" McGowan asked. "Did you do formulas together?"

"We were explosive."

"I bet I know where the explosion occurred."

"Daily, I tell you."

"Hearts," Joe pleaded, tossing his eight.

"Fecking hell, Dooley. You and your hearts."

"I don't see how that's my fault."

"You're the N.C.O. in this party. Everything's your fault."

"So I've learned."

"A queen," said McGowan.

"A king," chimed Watts.

"Your hand."

"Give me two hands and a queen and I could go far, boys."

"For what you'll be doing, you only need one hand."

"You're a rough one, McGowan."

Joe thought of stepping into the ribaldry but just then Davy Rose came in. "Morning, boys."

"If it isn't the Rose of England," Watts exclaimed.

Davy walked up to Joe's cot and put his arm around him. "How'ye feeling today, Joe?"

"Much better, thanks. I walked all the way to the latrine."

"Thank God for that," McGowan said.

"We're trying to play here, Rose," Watts said. 'D'ye mind?"

"Speaking of which," Larkin interjected. "I've got to go. Why don't you stand my hand, Rose, while I'm abroad?"

Davy picked up Larkin's hand and settled in next to Joe.

"Your lead."

Davy threw down the ten of hearts.

"Hearts again!" McGowan exploded. "Mary and Joseph, what's with these hearts?"

⌒

IT WAS DAVY ROSE WHO RESCUED JOE. BY SOME LUCK OF THE DRAW his transport vehicle was crossing the line when the sniper hit. Joe was given morphine and put in the van straight away. Then he passed out. It was only when he awoke with his chest wrapped in gauze that he was able to speak.

"What happened to me? Where am I going?"

Davy took Joe's hand in his own and bent down to whisper in his ear. "You were shot in the chest, Joe. We're moving you to St. Omer where there are better medical facilities."

"Who are you?"

"You don't remember this face? I was with you at La Hutte, when you were shot. My name is David Rose. But all my friends call me Davy."

"Then I must call you Davy, too."

"That's a smile I see."

"I suppose."

"Good."

The van dove into a ditch and Joe's cot tumbled to the floor. "Christ almighty," Joe yelled. "The pain's something awful."

"Just another few minutes and we'll have you in a real bed."

"You're not in uniform. Are you Medical Corps?"

"I'm a volunteer."

"For who?"

"You really should be resting and not asking all these questions."

"If the driver had any sense of the road and the man with the morphine had been in a more generous mood, I would be resting," Joe said, the anger rising in his voice, "but he doesn't and he didn't and I'm not and I really just want to get out of this van and back to my men as soon as possible."

"Hold up, Joe," Davy said. "That's too many words at once." He leaned in and put his hand on Joe's shoulder.

"And stop touching me," said Joe.

"Why?" Davy asked.

"It hurts."

"It's not my touching you that caused the hurting. Let me help you." Davy reached out and laid his palm against Joe's neck. "Is this better?"

"Yes."

"Now close your eyes. We'll be in St. Omer in no time."

ON THE THIRD DAY, DAVY ASKED JOE IF HE WOULD LIKE TO GO FOR a walk and Joe received permission to leave the grounds. The morning was cold but fine and Joe felt inspired. He had survived his first real test of combat and he had grown stronger for it. All that was needed for him to complete his recovery was be reunited with his men and this would be happening soon enough.

The road they chose threaded up the hill behind the hospital and narrowed into a lane lined with bare brush and leafless trees. He and Davy walked together in silence past the ruined remnants of a forest and across an ice-limned field until they came to a hollow where a stand of fallen trees made a natural bench.

"I need to sit for a moment," Joe said.

"I'm sorry. I should have suggested a resting place sooner."

"'S all right."

"It is an honor and a pleasure to know you, Joseph Dooley."

"I might say the same, David Rose."

"You seem like a kind and intelligent young man."

"Now you sound like one of my teachers."

Davy picked up a stick and idly drew a pattern in the dirt.

"Did you ever learn any Latin?" he asked.

"I'm a Catholic boy living in Ireland," Joe answered. "What do you think?"

"I don't know. You might have forgotten it."

"Not possible with the sisters I had. Why do you ask?"

"Latin was about as far from my experience as one could go—a Jewish boy from Stepney. Latin was something I saw carved in stone over the doors of buildings. So I saw it as a challenge."

"I'm beginning to believe that you see just about everything as a bit of a challenge."

"I do. I got hold of a volume of Catullus and a really good grammar and I taught myself how to recite a couple of verses. The fun I had cracking it open in front of the crusties in my plummy accent..."

> *Cui dono lepidum novum libellum*
> *arida modo pumice expolitum?*

"'To whom do I dedicate this charming book, freshly polished with pumice?'"

"Very good."

"Why are you telling me this?"

"Oh, my mind circles around things that way. I was thinking of the root of the word for 'hospital.' It comes from '*hospitalis*' and ties in with all these other really oblique English words like 'hospice' and 'hospitality' which mean friendship, openness, and caring."

"So?"

"Joe, you're not nearly as much of a dummy as you pretend to be. Stop trying to be a soldier and every now and then remember what you were like before you entered the army."

"Why should I?"

"Once upon a time you had a whole lot of things you'd rather be doing than fighting a war."

"Isn't that so for everyone?"

"Yes, but we're not all from the same cutter. We all have different dreams, different hopes, and different reasons for everything. I singled you out because I hoped you might find my point of view interesting and you might think the same of me."

"You're not an ordinary volunteer, are you, Mr. Rose?"

"How d'ye mean?"

"I've been at this game for four months now and every volunteer I've met is so overwhelmed with minding their scrap of business and serving King and Crown that they've hardly the time for a cup of tea let alone Latin verse."

"I refuse to act inhuman in an inhumane situation."

"Admirable, but will it get you to tomorrow?"

"I think you know it will."

"What makes you so certain?"

"Something."

"That's precise."

"Poetry is never precise."

"This is poetry?"

"No, you are."

Joe watched his breath cloud the winter air. Their stopping place was very near to the apex of the hill. It seemed strange to Joe to be so exposed; he was unused to both the literal and the figurative expansiveness that Davy represented. Davy's talk was queer and his indirection had a purpose to it; for a small man he evinced an awful lot of power. Now that Joe had a closer look at him in the bright light of day, he thought Davy could easily pass for the army type. Although he was shorter than Joe—barely five foot six—he had a muscular build and strong arms. His hair and his eyes were black and they set off features that were almost aristocratic in their exuberance. You would hardly call him handsome and yet the sum of him in many ways was beautiful.

"I'm glad you're taking the measure of me," Davy said, as if he had been reading Joe's mind. "You trusted me with your life."

"You might recall I really didn't have any choice."

"You'd be surprised how much of what happens to you is fated."

"I was wondering how you ended up in such brilliant physical shape."

"I was a boxer in London before the war."

"A boxer?"

"Fight clubs. Brady Street, Saint George –there're dozens of 'em."

"Who do you fight?"

"Other boys in the neighborhood—lads from Whitechapel, mostly. They're Jewish boxing clubs."

"We don't have anything like that in Dublin."

"London is a big city."

"Did you ever win?"

"I lost a championship fight once. You have to win every now and then in order to get to a championship fight."

"Why with all your boxing didn't you enlist?"

"I'll fight one man at a time when I know his name and I'll use my fists. I won't fight thousands and I won't fire a gun.

"A conshie, eh? But you strapped on the Red Cross."

"When I take the measure of a man, Joe, I include myself in the fitting. I want to be certain that every thought I have and every action I take is meaningful to me and helpful to my friends. I couldn't just hang a signboard around my neck and say 'to hell with this war.' I had to act on my feelings."

Joe thought of Harry. "I had a friend back in Dublin who felt the same way," he said. "I seem to attract the idealistic type. It will all make for a lovely newspaper article after the war but for the duration it does seem a little bit impractical to me."

"If it's practicality you're after you should be a general. Down amongst the ranks everything's impractical. So I thought I might as well aim for the truth."

"Ah, the truth. Now we're not only being impractical but also indefinite. No wonder we're stuck in No Man's Land."

"Oh no, my chum—it is I who am stuck in No Man's Land. You're stuck in the British Army."

"So it seems."

"So tell me—what were you once upon a time?"

"I was a music teacher."

"Ah—perfect training for the military. All that precision, all that harmony."

"They say it's all mathematical but I don't think of it that way. You might say music is how I take the measure of a man. When I listen to Schubert…"

"*Achtung!* No German music allowed."

"Bad example."

"No—perfect, in my book. I adore German music."

"So do I. When I'm listening to Schubert, I like to imagine I can do anything." Joe paused and watched the cold mist of the morning melt into the hillside. "Have you ever seen a Jerry?" he asked.

"I've treated them."

"Is that allowed?"

"Kindness? Did Haldane issue an edict against it? I wouldn't be surprised. He's tried to skedaddle every other type of human behavior."

"You know what I mean."

"Unfortunately, I do. And yes, I am allowed to treat anyone in need of medical attention. The only difference is the Germans end up in prison."

"I could start in with Hamlet and how the world is a prison but I don't wish you to think I'm any brighter than you already do."

"Too late. I've found myself a genius."

"I thought you said I was a poet."

Davy wrapped his arm around Joe and pulled him to his side. "Not a poet, Joe. Poetry."

⌒

JOE WAS RELEASED FROM THE HOSPITAL TWO DAYS BEFORE CHRISTmas. That morning, he woke up and discovered that overnight Watts had developed an infection and had been shipped back to England. Another man already occupied his cot. It was as if they were at a picture show; people came and went in the dark and if you sat through enough shows the entire audience would be replaced over time. Joe was perturbed to discover just how easily he had slipped into this view of things and he wondered to himself if his own disappearance would have been greeted by a similar acceptance. Then he understood that the tragedy of the situation was the simple fact that it was not a case of indifference that led the men to such acquiescence but pure numbness.

As Joe packed his bag and changed out of his blues, he looked around and wondered how many more men would be exchanged in the coming days and months. Not that the men themselves seemed to have any sense of this. Advent had cheered the ranks. There were tinsel twists hanging from the lanterns and packages wrapped in colored paper heaped upon the floor. It seemed to Joe that a hard layer of irony had been spread upon the already existing stratum of courage and humor that was the soldiers' bedrock and he sighed to realize that with any luck at all it would still take a lifetime of excavation for a man to dig down to his own loamy heart.

When the V.A.D. contingent arrived to help him back up the line it made Joe exceedingly happy to see Billy Macready accompanying them.

"Greetings of the season, old pal of my heart,' Billy said as he rushed forward to greet Joe and embrace him.

"'Tis good to see you, Billy."

"The Dubs are lost without you, Joe," Billy said. 'You should have seen Mick trying to stir the pot and no pot to stir. 'Twas a sight to behold."

Sharon took Joe's bag and carried it over to the transport. "Joe never gave us any trouble," she said, although no one had posed the question.

"It's the trouble he gets not the trouble he gives that's the real story, Miss…Miss…"

"I'm Nurse O'Connor."

"Surely ye must have a Christian name, Miss O'Connor?"

"It's Sharon."

"A rose of the old sod."

"County Antrim."

"Sometimes I think the whole of Ireland has moved to Flanders."

"It seems that way, so."

Joe coughed. "If I may interrupt your little confraternity," he said. "I'd like to go inside and say Merry Christmas."

"It's now or never," Billy said. "You've got twenty minutes."

"Who's the commanding officer here?" Joe asked.

"She is!" Billy exclaimed, squeezing Sharon and setting her off upon a whoop of laughter.

Joe ducked through the door to the hospital wing and walked down the aisle of cots until he came to the entranceway. There were Larkin and McGowan, at cards again.

"I'm off to paradise, boys," he began.

McGowan lifted a distracted finger. "Then you won't need our prayers."

Joe peeked at Larkin's hand. "Are you going to keep throwing away your aces until you haven't a fag to your name?"

Larkin laughed. "Are ye betting on it, Joe?"

"Good luck," McGowan said, offering his hand.

"Much thanks and a Merry Christmas to you."

"Merry Christmas, Joe."

Joe found himself wishing he had the chance to say goodbye to Davy Rose and as if every wish came true at the moment of the wishing of it there he was, entering from the opposite door. He was pulling a small trolley laden with boxes that he was distributing ad hoc to the injured men.

"Here's a pudding for you, Stoddard—don't aim it at anyone's head or you're liable to knock them senseless. And what have we here?" Davy grabbed another package from the cart and shook it violently. "Sounds like a quart of decent whiskey. Must be for you, Smith."

The men roared as Davy played Father Christmas. Joe ambled down the aisle and the two of them met in the middle.

"I'm glad I caught you, Davy," Joe began. "I wanted to thank you again and wish you...oh, wait..."

"It's all right to wish a Jewish boy a Merry Christmas, Joe. It's even acceptable to offer me a gift."

"I don't have anything for you, Davy."

"Ah—but I do have something for you. My original plan was to leave it on the van with a note but this is much better." Davy went behind the trolley and came up with a squeezebox. "It was too large to wrap but I hope you'll accept it all the same."

Joe looked at the musical instrument with a boy's own wonder. He'd seen all forms of accordions before but this was a model beyond his experience. It was the approximate size of a typewriter: two wooden boxes and the black leather bellows between. The decorations on the boxes had faded but had once depicted a traveling circus. Bits of red and yellow paint still hung forlornly from the central sections farthest away from the buttons, two of which were completely missing. The bellows had been repaired with ill-matching cloth enough times to make the surface resemble a quilt.

"I rescued it from a burned-out building," Davy said. "It's as battle-scarred as the rest of us but I do believe it still can make music. The instant I spotted it I thought of you."

"Thank you, Davy." Joe felt truly overwhelmed with gratitude.

"Well, don't just stand there like a eejit. Play something."

Joe cradled the instrument in his arms.

"It's not a baby, Dooley," one of the men shouted at him.

"There's no strap."

The man sitting in the bed beside Joe reached into his bag and handed Joe a pair of braces. "These are of no use to me here," he said. "Try them."

Joe took one of the cloth strips from the man and attached the clips to the metal handles on the squeezebox and then he swung it around so that he could get at the keys. "What shall we have?"

All at once this room in a hospital in France turned into a variety hall. Men who were capable of it leaped from their cots and gathered in the wings while those with more debilitating injuries shouted their requests from the footlights.

"'Where Did You Get That Hat?'" one shouted.

"'Silver Threads Among The Gold.'"

That got the hook.

"'Down At The Old Bull & Bush.'"

"Don't know it," Joe laughed.

Just then Billy and Sharon came in from the cold. "We was wondering what happened to ye," Sharon cried.

"Looks like the old M.T. is at it again," Billy announced.

"M.T.?" Sharon asked.

"Music Teacher. Joe was a music teacher in Dublin."

"It looks to me like he's a music teacher in St. Omer just as well."

Joe continued to entertain requests.

"'Mademoiselle.'"

"Sick of it."

"'Far, Far From Ypres.'"

That gained a unanimous cheer. Joe smiled and tested a note. It was sour and quavered like a duck.

"N.B.G., M.T.," Billy said.

"Hold on, hold on." Joe twiddled with a couple of the knobs on the board. One fell off. "Uh, oh." He sorted through the keys and was able to produce a reasonably complete scale. "Here we go."

The notes came out unevenly at first and then with more confidence of tone as Joe gained a better sense of the give and take of the bellows and the idiosyncrasies of the keyboard. After demonstrating the melody (as if this was at all necessary), Joe lifted his head as a signal to begin the singing:

> Far, far from Ypres I long to be,
> Where the German snipers can't snipe at me.
> Damp is my dugout,
> Cold are my feet,
> Waiting for whiz-bangs
> To send me to sleep.

The sound of the soldiers' singing brought tears to Joe's eyes not for the words but because of the earnest conviction of their voices, so untrained and so full of enthusiasm. At that moment Joe felt it was really true, that the sounds of human voices singing together had greater healing power than all the Dakin's solution in the universe. As they were singing Joe looked at Davy. The image of the young man—his eyes bright with excitement, his face flushed from exertion, and his mouth open in song—filled Joe's heart with hope.

"I really need to be going," Joe announced after the applause died down.

"One last song for the season," Davy cried.

"Yes," Sharon chimed. "One last song for the season."

Joe thought. "Don't bother shouting your requests," he said. "I know what I want to play." He sorted out a few tentative notes and then broke into "Good King Wenceslas." It was a melody that everyone knew and the intervals and harmonies were composed to increase happiness, something of which there could be no surfeit of this day. Joe was particularly touched by the fact that nearly all of the soldiers knew the words deep into the penultimate verse, for it was this verse that most impressed itself in his memory and was the wellspring to his choice:

> Sire, the night is darker now,
> And the wind blows stronger.

*Fails my heart, I know not how*
*I can go no longer.*

*Mark my footsteps, my good page*
*Tread thou in them boldly*
*Thou shalt find the winter's rage*
*Freeze thy blood less coldly.*

The assembly completed the song and applauded themselves for it. Joe beamed with joy and made a circuit of the room shaking hands and exchanging the sign of peace. Billy stood at the end of the line. "We should be going now, Corporal."

"Wait for me in the car, Billy."

"Yes, sir."

Joe craned his neck to look about the room, trying to pick Davy out from the crowd. There he was in the corner, lounging against the canteen, raising a cup of cheer to his benefactors. He looked quite handsome in his blue uniform and white shirt, a broad smile spreading across his face. Joe made his way to the alcove and offered Davy his hand. "Davy…" Joe began.

"I know, you can't thank me enough."

"Well, yes."

"Actually, you can."

"Tell me how."

"Remember what we talked about yesterday. Remember what you saw here today. Remember the look on everyone's faces when the music brought them peace."

"I shan't forget."

"It'll be difficult."

"Ever and always."

"Words come easy. Actions are harder."

"We'll see."

Davy took a step closer in to Joe. Joe felt the increase in the intimacy. Somehow Davy had this ability to make the world go away.

"How are you healing?"

"It hurts every now and then."

"Let me see."

"Now?"

"Let me see."

Joe opened his coat and pulled up his shirt. Davy slowly ran his hand across the scar. This soothed Joe in a way that struck him as both medically justified and then just a little bit more. It felt to Joe as if in some way meaningful to the both of them Davy was tracing the path of the bullet like a shaman exorcising an evil spirit. Davy's hand pressed into Joe's flesh and the warmth of his hand against his body contrasted with the cold air of the hospital vestibule and emanated outwards from the spot that he touched to encompass all of Joe's body. When Davy was done, he pulled his hand away and tucked Joe's shirt for him.

"Good luck, Joe," he said.

"Thanks," Joe whispered.

"And Merry Christmas."

"Will I see you on the line?" Joe asked.

"I'll be up there somewhere. You don't necessarily want to see me, you know. That usually means someone needs my help."

"I know. But maybe, for Christmas…"

"Maybe."

"Cheerio."

Joe walked out along the gravel path and climbed into the car. It had started to snow and the flakes were big and geometric and they obscured the view, forming a deep and natural curtain around the landscape. As the car drove down the hill, Joe tried to imagine how the scene must have looked on such a Christmas Eve a very long time ago, when men and women were gathering wood in the fields and the smoke of the home fires rose from every chimney. It must have been easier then for men to lead and for their followers to turn to them for comfort. Tell me, Wenceslas, Joe thought: was it ever so?

# Chapter 14

◆ ◆ ◆

## At Ten Stone Two

◆ ◆ ◆

WHEN JOE AWOKE HE DID NOT KNOW WHERE HE WAS. THERE IS always a bit of disorientation on the part of the dreamer in that moment between sleep and waking but today that feeling extended beyond Joe's fuddled mind, surpassing the trench walls and reaching all the way to the tops of the trees. Although he could give a name to everything he could see, Joe was unable to place them.

The men had slept through their call. Under ordinary circumstances, such an error in discipline could have been fatal. A raiding party might have found them, for there was no one at sentry. A shell could have obliterated the trench; no listening post was manned. But there were no raiding parties this morning and no screaming shell filled the air with its inhuman cry. Other than the sound of the birds, the wood was completely silent. Joe wiped the grime from his eyes and sat up. It was Christmas morning.

Joe grabbed his rifle and bolted to a standing position, instinctively countering the lapse in his responsibility with an overly martial gesture. At once he saw the ridiculousness of his action. The men remained fast asleep at his feet. Mick was curled up against a rotted log with only a scrap of a blanket covering his body, his cap pulled all the down across his face. Billy and Andy had collapsed on the opposite side of the trench in their own little dugout, back to back like brothers. Suddenly Joe felt terribly hungry. He fished a biscuit out of his pack and ate it.

When Joe climbed up onto the fire step and cautiously looked out across No Man's Land, he saw that the German section opposite had already lit a fire. The men were out on top cooking bacon. One of them saw Joe and waved wildly. "Merry Christmas, English!"

Joe saluted and waved and then felt very foolish. What if it was a trick? What if it was a ploy to get us to abandon our caution only to be slaughtered in our sleep or at our prayers? The thought of prayer reminded him: there would need to be some sort of service. Perhaps we could have a reading from the Bible or a hymn? Joe shook a little more of the sleep from his head. I'm getting ahead of myself, he thought. I must consider that the enemy is sitting plainly within my sight cooking breakfast and wishing me merry.

Not wanting to be rude, Joe finally yelled, "Merry Christmas, Germans."

A cheer went up from their trench.

"Have you forgotten we are Saxons?" the man called out.

"Have you forgotten we are Irish?" Joe shot back.

"Then we are not at war," the other soldier said. "For I do believe the argument is between the English and the Germans and as we are all from auxiliary tribes…"

"Your English is quite good."

"It should be. I was a butcher in Manchester before the war."

Joe thought of Harry and wished he could be here to see this. "No wonder the bacon smells so good."

"Come, wake up your friends. There's to be no fighting today. We shall celebrate Christmas together."

By the time Billy, Mick, and Andy were dressed Joe had helped the German soldiers drag a table into No Man's Land. They filled a plate with the shiny strips of bacon and some biscuits and poured cups of ale for everyone. It was hardly a Christmas goose and a plum pudding but what it lacked as provender was compensated by good will: Richard was allowed to climb back into the Dubs' trench.

"How are they treating ye, Richard?" Mick asked.

"I'm well," Richard replied with his usual stoicism. "I think they intended to send me to Berlin with the other prisoners but their communication lines broke down and I've been relegated to hiding in the back of the line for three weeks."

"Three weeks?"

"I know it's crazy. But at least they haven't asked me to dig trenches or carry packs. All I have to do is pull my own weight. They even feed me out of their rations."

"Sounds like you have it easier than we do."

"If easier was what I was after, I would agree. But it's awful being away from all of you. As it is, if they thought I was breathing a word about their fortifications or strength they'd have me shot in an instant. Their forbearance could wear thin and this truce could end at any moment."

Just then Davy Rose drove up with a truck full of gifts. There were tins of tobacco for anyone who smoked and boxes of sweets tied with red and green ribbons. These were the official presents; beyond that, Davy had ransacked whatever surpluses he could find and arranged rough baskets of games, old magazines, jars of plum jam, and books with their covers torn away. The Germans went straight for the dominoes and anything with pictures of women on it; they all spoke English well-enough but the dots and the tarts required no translation. The Irishmen were content with their extra plugs and their gibraltars.

Introductions were made all around. Lukas was the older man who had been a butcher in Manchester; he was the others' commanding officer. The first in on the fancy magazines was a young man named Adam; in turn, he dragged the shy soldier hanging back and forced him to choose something from the bounty.

"Go ahead, Friedrich," Adam began. "No one will report you for accepting a gift from an Englishman."

Friedrich tentatively choose a ransacked copy of *David Copperfield*.

"Dickens?" Billy cried.

"Friedrich needs to improve his English," Lukas said. "So as to fit in when we arrive in London."

"Better he blend in to the crowd when we march on Berlin."

Davy interrupted their banter. "There's a truce all up and down the line. I heard it from Warwick this very morning and they got it from Wiltshire by telephone. Everywhere from St. Eloi to La Bassée."

"Amazing," said Adam.

"Once the news hits the G.H.Q. we'll be countermanded," Mick predicted.

"We'll surely be fighting again by then."

"Way of the world," said Richard.

"And you'll be a prisoner again."

"I'm a prisoner now," Richard answered. "Only there's no prison."

"Any more to eat?" Lukas asked.

"I've got some cheddar here."

"Maybe the generals will let us have the day off."

"Maybe the generals will let us have two."

"Pass the bottle, please."

"Now if only we were on the Unter der Linden instead of in this damned forest."

"Did anyone say grace?"

"No, we forgot."

"Never too late."

The men stopped eating. They folded their hands in their laps and bowed their heads. Richard spoke first: "Bless us, O Lord, and these Thy gifts, which of Thy bounty we are about to receive. Through Christ, our Lord. Amen".

Then Adam followed: "*Alles das wir haben, Alles ist gegaben. Es kommt, O Gott, von dir. Wir danken dir dafuer! Amen.*"

All murmured "Amen."

⌒

DAVY LEAPT UP FROM BEHIND JOE AND WRAPPED HIM IN A BEAR hug. "Care for a walk?"

"We're not on holiday, Rose. I have work to do."

"Where? I see Mick and Adam playing cards. I see Richard writing a letter. I see Billy taking up Andy, Friedrich, and Lukas for a kick-about. What I don't see is any work."

"What if something were to happen?"

"I would hope something would happen. I think it's happening."

"You know what I mean."

"And you know what I mean."

"I'm in command here."

"Don't give me that excuse, Joe. You like to be in command of everything but yourself."

"I suppose it will be all right. It's Christmas."

"Yes, it's Christmas. Why not keep the Jewish boy company?"

At that, Joe laughed. "I could leave Andy in charge for an hour or so."

"There you have it."

"Give me a minute."

"I'll be a sport. Ninety seconds."

"Thanks."

DAVY TOOK JOE AWAY FROM NO MAN'S LAND, DOWN A HILL THAT led to a stream. They followed the path of the stream for about a quarter of a mile, then crossed over and walked up the opposite hill before turning back to the east. The sun had come out and as they climbed the melting snow was trickling under their feet.

"I've never seen a natural wilderness before," Davy began. "It's such a shame that when I do get to see one, all that's left of it is charcoal and dirt."

"Didn't you ever get out of London?" Joe asked.

"How could I? Stepney isn't Dublin, Joe. Dublin's just a little old town. In London the whole of the world was in my way. Here's a story: try to imagine Mile End Road. It's fifty feet wide. There's carts that line up on both sides of the road filled with leather straps, cantaloupes, gold brooches, duck's eggs, old books, tin toys, prayer shawls—five feet deep and ragged as all Hell with customers crowded alongside in thick threes and fours. Now look up from the carts to the buildings on either side of the road, five stories tall—rotting wood where families of seven or eight fit into each room.

"Follow me as I walk past the rows of carts and crowds of people into the entranceway to one of the buildings and climb the steps to the top floor. That's home for me and for my mother and father and my two brothers and my three sisters. My dad bakes bread. His shop is around the corner and he's there from five in the morning to five in the evening every day except Shabbat. That leaves my mom to raise us and feed us and keep us out of trouble. And trouble wasn't far away."

"I'm sorry for your hard life, Davy," Joe said.

"I'm not. I knew from the time I was six that I had to fight to get what I wanted and I fought and I got it."

"What was it that you wanted?"

"It wasn't so much what I wanted but what I didn't want that I grew certain of. I didn't want to stand next to my Dad punching out the challah every dawn. I didn't want to be one of those poor guys in the stalls bartering in Yiddish and hoping to take home tuppence. And I certainly didn't aspire to end up on the other end of the equation, living in a flat overlooking the Stepney Green and paying everyone to do my bidding. I wanted my life in front of me, in my own two hands. So when I was twelve years old I started in with the boxing clubs. My dad was furious. The first few times he came in and literally pulled me out of the ring. He was bigger than me then and I couldn't do anything about it. He wanted me to stay in the kitchen covered with flour and find some nice Jewish girl who would raise a half dozen starving Jewish children like he did. And I wouldn't have any of it.

"Finally—I think it was the summer of 1910—I was big enough and strong enough to beat my father in a fair fight. I knocked him down, I did, and there wasn't anything he could do to stop me anymore. I was seventeen years old and I was free. There were clubs all over the East End. I joined Brady Street because that was where the Stepney boys fought and you had to be with your own boys but there was the St. George and the Oxford and all those other places with Regency names in case you needed to feel like you were actually British. I wanted none of that sludge. Did you ever hear of Kid Lewis? I didn't think so. He was the best Jewish boxer in London when I was growing up and I saw him fight a half-dozen times. He was the best.

"I trained at Brady and I lived in a room above the club with three other lads. At first it was manna to me, I tell you. Three square and an extra pair of gloves, what more could a boy want from life? But I saw what was happening to my friends as they grew up. I saw them sink back into the streets and end up fighting for the pennies that could buy them a beer. It wasn't until I had climbed those stairs a hundred times and won and lost a score of fights that I finally figured out that boxing wasn't everything. That I wasn't going to be able to fight my way through life. And that's when I started going down to the Carnegie library in Shoreditch, every afternoon after practice. All I ever wanted to know about the world, and free! I read about Nelson one week, Hannibal the next…a little French grammar, a little Latin. Aeschylus. The Brontës. Darwin. Everything. I got an education and no one could take advantage of me anymore. Not my father. Not my manager. No one."

Davy paused. "Which way?"

The two men had reached a crossing. One road led up the hill and back toward camp; the other ran deeper into an undestroyed part of the forest. The canopy of pines was tempting with their purple and green needles limned with gleaming frost and their heavy boughs pushed down by the weight of the water to nuzzle the needle-lined dirt. Joe checked his watch; they had only been gone for twenty minutes. It felt much longer. He looked at Davy, and he saw a Davy he had never seen before. In the act of telling his tale, Davy seemed to be transformed. The level, carefree surface that Davy presented to the world lay on top of deeper, needier, and prouder soil. Joe felt honored to be given a glimpse of what lies beneath and it inspired his trust. He pointed down into the forest.

"That way."

The road through the forest dipped down once more to run parallel to the stream. More of the frost and snow was melting and the cold water was running clearer and faster now. Davy spotted a rise with a view and they rested there.

"Look at that," Davy said, pointing to the valley below. "All that beauty destroyed by madness." He paused as if literally lost in thought. Then he went on with his story. "That fall, I got my chance. My record was twenty-three and that qualified me for a championship fight. I was a welterweight and the welterweight champion at the time was Anschel Joseph. Did you ever hear of him? I didn't think so. He called himself 'Young Joseph' and I guess that was because he figured if he lost the Jewish name he might someday be able to make some real money. He was a very good boxer, taller and a little heavier than me.

"The day of the match I come downstairs to the club like I always do and this time there's a guy there—a kid, really—maybe eighteen years old, and he says to me 'I really like the way you fight, Rose. You need a new manager.' I looked him over and as I said he looked like he was up past his bedtime but there's a real sweet gleam in his eye and I liked the cut of his jib so I say to him prove it and I say to myself why not? He tells me his name is Bobby. And Bobby immediately starts to prep me for the fight. He gets my water. He rubs me down. He's good. And I'm not stupid. I can tell what he wants. He wants me. And Joe, you know what? I wanted him.

"So I climb into the ring with my friend Anschel. Nothing in my life has ever matched that moment when the referee called us out. The pride I felt when I heard my name was immeasurable: 'Ladies and gentlemen, in the far corner, at ten stone two, the challenger, David Rose.' I should have quit the fight then and there. But I didn't, and you know, I didn't do too badly. I lasted five rounds and lost on a long count. I was beat up pretty well so Bobby collected me afterwards and he rubs me down again and he touches me in places where a manager isn't supposed to touch a fighter and I let him. He tells me he has a place and it ends up being a room behind a tavern on Whitechapel Road and we go there and we messed about. And I liked it."

Davy paused to see how his story was going over. At first Joe said nothing and Davy interpreted this to mean disgust or at least approbation so he got up and started to walk away.

"Where are you going?" Joe asked.

"I figured…"

"You figured wrong."

"I thought you should know…"

"Know what?"

"Nothing."

The two of them sat there in silence for a minute or so. Then Davy went on. "I built a shell around myself. This shell that I thought I had so cleverly constructed to keep the world out ended up keeping me in. I thought I had to protect myself and defend myself—from my father, from the bullies and the anti-Semites, from the other boxers who tried to cut me down and from anyone who tried to touch me in any way other than to hurt me. I thought that my education would protect me—that once I learned everything there was to learn about the world from books I would be completely self-sufficient. I had all the nouns down flat but I had no adjectives to call upon. I felt nothing. And then Bobby touched me.

"It was almost like a religious experience. Think it blasphemous if you want, but there's no other way I can explain it. I thought my God was all about being different and here I was learning that God is truly all about love. There's a biblical passage that almost directly managed to express how I was feeling. It's from Job. He appeals for pity, or rather, he denies pity's appeal. He asks, 'Did I say "Bring unto me? Or give a reward for me of your substance? Or, deliver me from the enemy's hand or redeem me from the hand of the mighty?" Teach me and I will hold my tongue and cause me to understand wherein I have erred.' I was wrong. It wasn't victory I sought in all I did; it was redemption. In my loss, I was challenged but in my love for Bobby I was redeemed."

"What happened to him?" Joe asked.

"We met at Whitechapel Road a few more times after that. But I think the revelation that swept over me left him unmoved. I learned a lot about love from Bobby, even if in the end he didn't love me, because I learned how to crack open my shell and feel something. Before I knew him, friendship was a wary coexistence and a relationship built upon fear. Now, it is an offering I can freely bestow. If I survive the war, I'll still box, but I won't be fighting out of fear anymore. It'll be for love."

"Why are you telling me this?" 204

"I don't know," Davy answered.

"I think you do," said Joe.

He reached out and put his hand on Davy's cheek. Then he pulled Davy's face toward his own and leaned over and kissed him. Davy held the kiss for an instant and then returned it.

"Joe…"

"There's no need to explain."

"Kiss me again."

The two men kissed. Joe pulled Davy's body close to his and ran his hands along Davy's back. Davy absorbed the embrace and returned it by gently pushing Joe's body to the ground and cradling it in his arms. Davy's body was heavy but to Joe it felt exactly like the opposite, as if a huge weight was being pulled away from him and scattered in pieces across the sky. As Joe lay there he felt the contrast between the world that filled his field of vision when his eyes were open—a world of unrepentant darkness and colorless vistas—and the world with his eyes closed, the inner light, that bright kaleidoscope. And he saw that the light was good.

"YOU SHOULD CLIMB INTO THE RING WITH ME SOMEDAY," DAVY SAID as they separated. "You've already got a pretty good build."

"You'd knock me out in ten seconds."

"I could if I wanted to. But why would I want to? Just to see you sweat and dance for a few rounds would be bon."

"Thanks for the vote of confidence."

Davy laughed.

"I should get back," Joe said.

"One more kiss. Who knows when we'll have this chance again?"

"That's true. Christmas doesn't last forever."

Davy kissed Joe once on his forehead, then again on his lips. "Christmas is just a day like any other to me," he said, pulling Joe into his arms. "No different from any other day at all."

⌒

WHEN JOE RETURNED TO THE LINE HE DISCOVERED THAT RICHARD had arranged an impromptu Christmas service in No Man's Land. In melding together the two different liturgies Richard had come up with a series of prayers and songs that he thought might increase the sanctity of the day. The German side suggested the opportunity might be taken to bury two of their companions. It was agreed to do so and to add to the ceremony two British soldiers also recently fallen. With the four bodies on stretchers and covered with cloth and nine men all around standing at attention it was a sight to behold. Prayers in two languages were exchanged and all the men took turns digging into the hard earth until all that remained of their comrades had been commended to their maker.

After the burials, Richard strode to the front of the assembly with a Bible and asked for volunteer readers. The first man up was Friedrich, who in lightly accented English recounted the tale of the birth of Jesus. After him, Andy read a passage from Isaiah:

> *Thus sayeth the Lord thy Redeemer,*
> *The Holy One of Israel:*
> *I am the Lord, thy God*
> *Which teacheth thee to profit and*
> *Which leadeth thee by the way to go.*
>
> *O, that thou had hearkened to my commandments!*
> *Then had thy peace been as a river*
> *And thy righteousness as the waves of the sea.*

It came upon Adam and Lukas to lead their little group in a German prayer, after which it was felt appropriate that the Dubs should say something in Irish. The enterprise was concluded by the M.T. leading an international chorale in a performance of "Silent Night." Here on this Day of Days beside the fresh graves of their fellows the music flowed together like two joining streams.

> Stille Nacht, heilige Nacht,
> *Silent night, holy night.*
> Hirten erst kundgemacht
> *Shepherds quake at the sight.*
> Durch der Engel Hallelujah,
> *Glories stream from heaven afar,*
> Tönt es laut von fern und nah!
> *Heavenly hosts sing Alleluia!*
> Christ, der Retter ist da!
> *Christ, the Savior is born*
> Christ, der Retter ist da!
> *Christ, the Savior is born!*

As the final chorus swelled Joe felt a tear catch in his voice and he uttered a silent prayer for his mother and Kathleen and especially for his friends Severin and Harry, whom he knew to be wandering in unknowable places and on an unknowable journey.

AFTER THE SERVICE, JOE ASKED DAVY TO JOIN THEM FOR THEIR Christmas dinner. There was tinned beef and mashed potatoes, ginger biscuits and a barrel of good German beer. Then the cameras came out and everyone started snapping photographs of each other. Lukas was particularly interested in hearing about Davy's status as a conscientious objector; the German army had their counterparts, of course, but they would not end up in the front lines. Davy felt obliged to point out that his situation was exceptional and that he chose to be where the battles raged as a constant reminder to the combatants that mercy can be as much a consequence of war as victory or defeat.

By late afternoon everyone was sated by the food, drink, and festivities. Davy returned to the van and headed out to advance his brand of seasonal joy to the Lancs while the men returned to their respective trenches. Mick, always the skeptic, openly speculated about the truce's prognosis.

"I'd keep one eye open for the Jerries," he began. "You settle in with a cigar and the next thing you know you're under a shell."

"I'm sure they are saying the same things about us," Andy noted. "But we've grown fond of their beer and they've become attached to our chocolate. As long as the liquor and the sweets don't run out I don't think anyone will be doing any shelling."

"I hope it lasts through Boxing Day," Billy said. "It would be nice to gain another day for Richard. Where is he, by the way?"

"He's back in the German trenches, under obligation," Joe explained. "I suppose he'll be allowed to pop in again if we have another round of caroling."

"What do ye make of our conshie?" Mick asked of no one in particular.

"Who's that?" Andy chimed in.

"That fireplug of an Englishman who won't pick up a bloody gun but goes around spouting out pacifist shite to anyone who will listen."

"He's all right," Billy said, noncommittally.

"Is he even allowed up here?" Mick asked.

"Davy Rose is a volunteer, and a valuable one at that," said Joe. "He saved my life when I was shot. He risked being shot himself."

"Bloody fool who risks being shot and won't carry a gun."

"To each," Billy said.

"I don't know about that," Mick wondered. "There's something I don't like about him. I can't put my finger on it. It's as if he's doing one thing and thinking something else."

"Something you've never done, of course," Joe said.

"I'm not talking about daydreaming. Any man can do that. It's that sweet talk and plying us with gifts all the time."

"I guess you can't stand the idea of someone being nice for the hell of it, can you, Mickey?"

"You tell me."

"Not even on Christmas."

"Especially on Christmas, especially since he isn't even a Christian."

"Now what does that have to do with it?"

"Nothing."

"Then why did you bring it up?"

"I'm just saying."

Joe took one last swig from his glass of beer and stood up. "I don't know about the rest of you but I'm not going to waste what might turn out to be my last hours of peace arguing with you fellows about a man's faith."

"No one was doing any arguing, Joe," Mick pleaded.

"No, I guess not."

"Still, you've got to admit, the man's a queer fellow."

"I'd say he's the sanest one of our bunch, and I'll include myself in it."

"Conshies don't bother you, Joe?"

"Right now, I'd have to say he doesn't bother me nearly as much as you do."

"Oh boy," Billy exclaimed. "Oh boy."

Mick stood up.

"Sit down, Mickey," Andy said.

"I will not."

"I'm sorry, Mick," Joe began. "Let's forget it."

"I will if you will."

"Yes, of course."

"Then I apologize, sir."

"Apology accepted."

Billy climbed down into the dugout. "I think I need a nap."

"I think we all do," Andy answered.

"I'll stand watch for an hour," Joe volunteered. "Andy, could you pick up at 15:00?"

"Do you really think that Fritz…?"

"It was all *laissez-faire* this morning but that was a mistake I do not care to make again."

"Yes, sir."

Andy and Mick went down to the dugout. Joe grabbed his rifle and climbed up on to the fire step. Out in No Man's Land, a German officer from another section was engaged in earnest conversation with two English soldiers. Joe peered at them through his field glasses. One of the English soldiers was a Lanc but the other was a Highlander. The Highlander was showing the others something small he held in his hand—a photograph or a medal. On their left a posse of soldiers from both armies were passing around a bottle of wine. The mist had burned away and a cold sun shined its clarifying light on every surface.

Joe had forgotten his duty and this bothered him. He was torn between the oath he had sworn to protect his men and the unsettled feeling he felt in his stomach whenever he thought about Davy and what he and Davy had done or would care to do. He thought of the men trying to sleep at his feet. He thought of the responsibility he felt toward them. Then he remembered Davy's kiss and the warmth of his body pressed against his own and he wished for an army of lovers, some institution that could bind his split affections together in his own heart. If such a thing could be found, Joe thought, I would join it and everyone would receive the benefit of my intentions.

This was easy enough to make apparent in the ring. No wonder Davy felt at home there. At ten stone two, he could afford to make the fight. But Joe was different. Joe didn't have a pair of gloves to hide behind or the ability to make a man bend to his will with a fist. The problem was he never wanted to inflict his will at all. All his life things came crashing into him and it was all he could do to withstand the blows and stay on his feet. Davy was a man who turned all of that around, who used his strength to shower love and praise upon his fellow man and in a world already upside down he was starting to make sense.

# Chapter 15

◆ ◆ ◆

## A Plate of Eggs

◆ ◆ ◆

On Christmas night all of Ploegsteert Wood resembled the Sacred Grove of Nemi. Small roving bands of troops from both sides passed between the bare trees and settled into the hollows, their torches marking the landscape like fairy lights at a garden party. In the shadows some of the men played drums or flutes and softly lifted their voices in song while other men drank and laughed as if their cares had evaporated with the daylight. Joe played a soft tarantella on his accordion while Mick and Andy sang and danced around him:

> Mamma mia, mamma mia,
> Gia la luna e in mezzo al mare,
> Mamma mia, mamma mia, mamma mia,
> Si saltera—frinche, frinche, frinche...

It had been over twenty-four hours since anyone on the line had heard a gunshot or seen the flare of a shell and in the horology of war this amounted to a lifetime.

During the course of the day Joe telephoned the other sections and tried to uncover the extent of the truce but the commanding officers he spoke with were hesitant to put what they saw into words. It seemed that each one of them rightfully feared the judgment of their superiors, and caught between the censure that was certain to fall upon them from above and the evident and open fraternization that was happening right in front of them they chose to say nothing. This had the unenviable result of giving the truce an even wider berth of acceptance while leaving the bed of support it stood upon thin enough to collapse with a single wayward bullet.

The only reality left to the Dubs was that which they could see with their own eyes. To this end, Joe organized a scouting party. His idea was that in the course of two or three hours they could circle the northeast corner of the wood and sweep down across the edge of the village. If there was any action at all they would hear it and be able to report it back; if not, it would be a useful exercise in evaluating the strength of their position and indirectly that of their once and future enemy as well.

Joe asked Mick to accompany him. The ebb and flow of their communication was never more than adequate and although Joe knew he had earned Mick's respect there was a part of him that felt that without a genuine friendship something was lacking in his command. The truce provided an opportunity for just this kind of experiment. The Saxons were apparently sleeping off their Christmas feast; there was no interest from their camp in the activities going on across the wire and Joe supposed in the end that was preferable to scrutiny no matter how peaceful things appeared to be. As Joe refilled his water jar he was certain he saw Mick draining a little rum into his own but he decided not to mention it. They loaded up their packs and walked out into the night.

UNDER COMBAT CONDITIONS JOE AND MICK WOULD HAVE EXTINguished their torches for the length of the march but the midwinter dark was too thick and the general knowledge of the truce so great Joe felt confident in ordering light. The ground was uneven and littered with dead branches. One hundred yards out from the trench the path suddenly dipped down into a ravine and Mick nearly lost his balance. Joe was already halfway up the next incline.

"How're you doing back there, Mick?"

"I'm grand, Joe. Bugger the weeds. They never die."

"Don't get too far behind me," Joe called back to Mick, who was now untangling himself from a fret of vines around his feet.

"I'm doing my damnedest, sir," Mick complained. "There's not much I can see, even with my light."

"If my map is correct, we should hit a flat stretch right after this hill," Joe said.

"I'm not overly fond of the word 'if,'" Mick answered.

"Stand by me and you'll be fine."

Joe was right to be confident; at the top of the next rise nearly the whole of Ploegsteert lay at their feet. The weave of the woods fell gently into the darkness and the cold air was infused with silence. The glory of the world in winter was on display before them with the gray stars dim in the quarter-mooned sky and the icing on the tree limbs giving off a low shine. For one brief moment both Mick and Joe had forgotten it was Christmas Day and God in his arrangement had chosen this time and this view to remind them.

"You'd almost say it was beautiful," Joe cried.

"'Tis," said Mick.

"Well, we must keep going."

"This is a crazy war, Joe."

"That it is."

"But we've got to do our duty."

"Yes."

"The view was nice, though."

"Yes." Joe didn't need to wonder what inspired this reverie—it was all around them. There was something about the mood of Christmas that instantly turned all grown men into fun-seeking boys. If there had been enough snow on the ground the two of them might have fallen down laughing and carved angels' wings with their arms.

They zigzagged down the hill and followed the path to the right as it swept around a large stand of trees. Their walk continued uneventfully for another half mile or so. Once Joe shone his light into a dark corner and sorted a startled rabbit. The rabbit froze in the beam and then shot off into cover. The quiet was so profound that they could hear the tumble of the stones they loosened with their boots. Finally signs of civilization returned: at one point a rusted McCormick blocked their path, and a hundred yards farther along they ran up against a fence that continued with a few splintered interruptions as far as they could measure. They were evidently crossing a farmstead; as they moved farther along the men could just discern the outline of a stone cottage in the distance. Just then, Mick noticed the light from a single torch moving parallel to them from a spot next to the cottage.

"Joe," Mick whispered. "Look!"

Joe pulled his rifle and signaled to Mick to turn out his torch. In the darkness there was no way to tell who was there. If Joe called out in English, there was a fifty-fifty chance he would be challenged. But if he crept up unannounced the gulf of misinterpretation could only grow wider and even more dangerous. Joe's debate with himself might have gone on for some time had it not been interrupted by a shout from their interloper. "*Bitte, nicht schiessen! Ich bin unbewaffnet.*"

"What's he saying, Joe?" Mick whispered.

"He says he's unarmed."

"Do you believe him?"

"Not yet."

Joe took two small steps forward into the darkness in the direction of the voice. Then he said: "*Sie beweisen, wenden sie sich bitte.*"

The German soldier walked out with his hands above his head. Joe held his gun pointed at the man's chest.

"Are you alone?" Joe asked him.

"*Nein.*"

"Is your friend armed?"

"Yes, our guns are in the house. I was looking for wood."

"If I hear any movement at all from the house I will shoot you. Do you understand?"

"Yes."

"So you speak English?"

"A little."

"Tell your friend we are going to the house and to come out with his hands up."

"He speaks English."

"Call him out anyway."

"*Leutnant, es gibt hier britischer. Aus mit den Händen bis.*"

Joe marched the man toward the cottage. A face appeared in the doorway and Mick raised his rifle.

"Don't shoot," came the voice from the doorway. "We are obeying the truce."

"Let's be sure of that," Joe commanded. "Come all the way out."

At first, Joe was confused. He recognized the red hair and the gold-rimmed spectacles. There was something familiar about the man's features and his build. His mind swirled around every possibility—someone from the line, a face from a distant battle, a briefly glimpsed prisoner—until the picture before him snapped into focus.

It was Harry Vogeler.

"Christ Almighty!" Joe cried.

"You have the right day, Joe Dooley."

"You know each other?" Mick asked.

"Heinrich, *was ist das?*"

A big smile crept upon Harry's face. "We were best friends in Dublin."

"Dublin?" Mick asked. "I don't understand…what are you…?"

"We're all cousins here, are we not?" Harry began. "You look stupefied, Dooley. Come here and let me give an old friend a real hug."

Harry stepped forward and held Joe.

"Harry. Harry Vogeler. Harry," Joe muttered, as if there was nothing else he could say that would ever make sense.

"I REMEMBER YOU NOW." MICK ADDRESSED ADAM AS THE FOUR soldiers sat down around the fireplace. "You're the eejit who insisted that your watered-down lager was superior to Irish stout."

"Yes, but that was yesterday. Today I have forgiven you," said Adam with a grin.

"Forgiven me? I would think…"

"Okay, boys—if it's going to be war one way or another, at least fight over something worth fighting for," Harry interjected.

"A good beer is worth fighting for," Mick insisted.

"At last, something we can agree upon," came Adam's response.

"A truce within the truce," Joe added. "Are we going to need a recording secretary?"

"A handshake will do."

Adam stood up and offered Mick his hand. "Until we meet on the battlefield."

They shook hands. Harry and Joe beamed.

"The two of you look like a pair of truant schoolboys," Mick said. "What's the story here?"

Harry opened his pack and took out a pipe. He banged it clean on the table and refilled it with a plug before continuing. "I'm afraid there's shenanigans on my part going in both directions. And I'm going to have to make a bit of an explanation in order to complete the picture. Adam, you're up first. Before the war I was living in Ireland. It's true I am a Saxon—I was born in Redemitz—but I haven't lived there since I was ten.

I never took out papers, which is why when August came around I ske-daddled out of the British Isles and volunteered for the Germany Army.

"This much, Joe, you knew. And I believe you also knew—because of the one time I was on leave in Switzerland and I managed to get a letter out of the country—is that I have been quite successfully playing the part of an officer in the Kaiser's service. It's a very interesting position to be in if, like me, you are opposed to this war. It's actually easy to be a pacifist if you are a good sharpshooter and a better dancer. How else do you think I have avoided killing any one and getting shot myself?"

"So if tried to shoot you right now you wouldn't defend yourself?" Mick asked.

Harry laughed. "I didn't say I wouldn't fight the war. I only said I objected to it. This truce has given me the opportunity to articulate a philosophy that up until today I only understand in the execution."

"And what is this philosophy?" Adam asked.

"That the only way to fight this war is also the best way to end it, one soldier at a time. In every engagement, in every battle, I try to balance self-preservation with honest respect for my fellow, be he colleague or enemy. I try not to kill but to dissuade…that's the wrong word…to dis-engage my opponent so he no longer feels the need to kill me. My goal is to meld our separate destinies so that one can not go forward without the other."

"Harry, will it work?" Joe asked.

"In theory, Joe, it can't. You know the truth of that as plainly as I do—especially you, who are in command. In sheer numbers, the amount of men with guns trying to kill each other overwhelms the number of men who might think as I do and wish to sue for peace at the lowest cost possible. I am certain it is only a matter of time before I am forced to kill my enemy or he is forced to kill me. I have no control over what is happening around me. But what I do have control over is how I live until I die, and I refuse to brutalize myself by being a brute to humanity.

"I see that the Dubs have already met Jaeger Behr. You may wonder why I was not with him on Christmas Eve or any part of this day. That is because I have come from a different section. One of the unintended consequences of this awful war is that in the confusion whole sections are being uprooted, reconstituted, and reassigned. For a soldier in my position—always willing, deviously sowing doubts, and constantly under pressure from my commanding officers to shut up or be shot for disloy-alty—it is a great boon to spend no more than a week or two in any unit.

*Hallo, hier bin ich*—and then off I go...the 106th, the 104th... by the time the authorities catch up with me I'm gone.

"On Christmas Eve, I saw what was happening and concluded I had an unprecedented opportunity to see what was up with the British. Obviously, no one would wonder about my English and under the circumstances no one was going to shoot me merely for wearing my *feldgrau* so I set out on a little scouting party of my own construction. I met many men along the way and you'd be amazed to discover how friendly a man can be the instant he no longer needs to judge you. The sun went down and I was just settling in to this lovely little farmstead when Herr Behr came wandering by. Fast friends and good times—especially when we discovered two barrels of beer in the coal cellar."

At this, Mick started to pay attention.

"Yes, we have two barrels downstairs, and the hens who haven't perished of the cold have left us with a dozen really fresh eggs. But you must be tired of listening to me talk. I think we should conclude the lecture portion of our class. I suppose all that is left us is the fieldwork. There's nearly an entire wheel of Gruyere sitting on top of one of the barrels and only about a third of it has turned green. For your final examination, can any of you calculate the effect of a plate of eggs and a glass of beer on a soldier's constitution?"

"Now if we only had a pickle jar our ploughman's luncheon would be complete," Adam said. The joint committee formed by this unlikely band of allies produced a half-dozen eggs and enough palatable shards of cheese to melt inside them. There were no napkins to be had and a thorough search of the kitchen produced only one spoon and one fork. Harry manned the stove. A wiped-down rusted garden knife did the carving and a half-tin of bully beef provided the grease.

"Where did you learn to cook like this, Harry?" Joe asked as he cleaned his fork and passed it to Mick. "I always thought if it wasn't on the menu at Bewley's you wouldn't know how to eat it."

Harry looked up. "Vagabond dogs are required to learn new tricks."

"Draw me another glass, ye hound," Mick said.

Harry lifted Mick's glass and held it under the tap while he tipped the barrel. The beer was cold but sour. It might have lasted the winter under current conditions but the men were in no hurry to draw out the experiment.

"Do you think we could roll one of these barrels back to the line?" Adam asked.

"I don't know." Mick squinted as if with enough concentration he could produce an estimate of the distance. "It must be at least two miles."

"The drink is making you stupid, Mick," Joe began. "You've forgotten what a wilderness we crossed."

"True enough, Joe. I suppose we could empty it here and carry it back but that would dull the purpose, don't you think?"

A sly smile stole across Mick's face. Joe hoisted one of the barrels up off the floor. "I think you're more than halfway to empty already, mate."

Adam banged his glass on the trestle and Joe refilled it.

"This will be one Christmas for the memory books," he began. "One is always ahead of the game when a barrel of the beer is more familiar than a barrel of a gun."

"Well thought through, Professor Behr," Joe remarked.

"I was just starting to uncover the professor's curriculum vitae when your brigade interrupted my interview," Harry announced. "So, Adam: what brought you to this pretty pass?"

Adam drained his cup and wiped his mouth on his sleeve. "I never thought of myself as particularly patriotic but when war came I immediately felt myself to be a Saxon," he said. "It is true that in many ways Germany is a very young country. We are all just starting to sort our way through what it means to be a part of a nation. I think this may be one thing that the Germans and the Irish have in common and I have always wondered as I faced the British across the line how all those little pieces of empire fit together. But there is yet one more thing that you and I share. That is our love of family.

"My family lives in Leipzig and I think of them often. It is an hour earlier there, so right now they are finishing up their Christmas dinner. I'm sure my Papa has his usual glass of cherry wine by his hand and my dear sister is chiding him for scattering breadcrumbs across the tablecloth. If I had been there, I would be helping to clear the table. Then everyone would be getting ready to go to sleep or sing carols but I would be on fire to see my girl. Her name is Greta. I have a photograph of her in my dugout. She is a year older than me, it is true, but we are very well matched and she will make a fine wife if she can wait for me and I survive."

The candlelight closed in around the soldiers in the room and everyone became a willing participant to Adam Behr's imagination. The walls collapsed and disappeared; the stifling air of the cottage was replaced by something biting and free. The men closed their eyes.

"Follow me now as Greta and I walk hand in hand. I am walking her home. A foot of snow fell last night. There is a hush in the air because of this and the people seem to slow down and even whisper to each other. Greta and I stop to admire a tray of chocolates in a window and I know she is secretly picking out her selection for tomorrow. My happiness is endless. I feel enchanted.

"Now, as we head up the walkway which leads to her building, I take her aside and there under the last flicker of the streetlamp I kiss her and hold her close by my side. Then just at the very moment when my kiss is about to be returned and the warmth of her body floods my mind I open my eyes and look around me. I am in the depths of my trench. The walls are made of mud and the floors are wooden planks. There is no gaslight and there is no snow. There are no chocolates in the window of the shop—in fact, there is no shop at all. And of course, there is no Greta."

At this, the taleteller paused to shake off his pang of regret.

"But there is you—and you, and you—and a good dinner and a barrel of beer and I am alive and it is Christmas and from now on there can be nothing wrong with the world."

Joe listened with great intent to Adam's story and found himself amazed at the depth of his sympathy. He heard the music in the air when he thought of Adam and Greta's enchantment and his heart rang when he imagined the warmth of their kiss. That this was so was a revelation to him. I now know what I had never dreamed of being true, he thought. I am not that much different from everybody else.

AROUND MIDNIGHT THE MEN DECIDED THAT THEY HAD BEST RE port back to their sections before their seconds-in-command filed a re-port. Harry announced he was now one of the 134th and would return with Adam, although it was obvious to all that the only reason for this was so that he and Joe could continue their reunion for as long as the truce held. This last was a variable that of course could not be predicted and was a great source of consternation on Joe's part but Harry wouldn't hear of exile and Joe couldn't bear to spoil the mood by standing on the rule book. So the scouts that started the night as a party of two and two were now a party of four, equipped with a goodly store of stale Swiss cheese, a newly serviceable knife, and water bottles filled to the brim with beer.

The moon had completed its rise and the mist had lifted, tingeing the tops of the firs with silver aureoles. For the first half-mile or so the men moved along the road at a jaunty pace without the benefit of torches at all. Then the ground grew rough and the clear passage narrowed. They needed to light the way and advance in pairs. Mick and Adam had become fast friends and all memory of their earlier altercation had faded upon the bonhomie provided by the cottage provisions. They led the parade and Joe and Harry followed a hundred paces behind.

At first, Harry merely grinned at Joe, not really knowing how to begin the conversation. For this Joe was initially grateful. In fact his mind was brimming with thoughts, some kindly, some curious, and some confused, and he held the fear that if he started to speak his mind right away all these thoughts would come out unmeasured and possibly insensibly. But this could hardly last for two hours of marching and it was Harry who first breached the silence.

"D'you know what I was thinking just now, Joe?"

"I can't begin to guess."

"I was thinking of that ice cream parlor on Sackville Street."

"Rabiaotti's. We were ten years old. I'm amazed that you remember."

"Rabiaotti's. That was the place. My God—a cup of vanilla ice cream in the dead of winter. How did we ever do it?"

"If I recall correctly, you didn't do it. That was my vanilla ice cream you got your tongue all over. The penny your Papa gave you was barely enough for you to walk off with a gob-stopper."

"Still, I remember standing on the line with you all the same. Didn't we ever go there in the summertime? Funny, I have no memories of it at all in the sunshine."

"When it was hot, we'd walk to Drumconda and dip our toes in the stream. There was always a vendor there with ices. You don't remember that?"

"No."

"Wait—of course. That was Tommy Doyle. I hadn't met you yet."

"I'm glad to see your memory is improving with age."

Suddenly Joe felt a cloud of sorrow darken his mood. It must have spread to his face, for Harry noticed it.

"What's wrong, Joe?"

Although Mick and Adam were far ahead of them, Joe lowered his voice. "You came and went so fast, Harry."

"I came. You went."

"I suppose. Then you went."

"That was different. The war was coming. I would be in jail now if I stayed."

"Water under, Harry."

Harry stumbled over an unseen branch that had fallen across the road and stubbed his ankle against it. "*Schiesse!*"

"I see your native instincts are coming back to you."

"You know if I had my way we'd be back in Dublin and you'd be teaching music and I'd be a barber and we'd close down Neary's every night."

"That's a very romantic view of the situation. Even if there wasn't a war, I could hardly make a living by teaching. As for you, when did you ever get it into your head that you could be a barber?"

"My papa was a barber."

"Last I looked, a talent for shaving was not determined by progeniture."

"I am capable of learning a trade, you know."

"Yes, that's true. I suppose if we want to fantasize ourselves out of our current abhorrent predicament that is one of the more logical solutions."

"I don't see anything particularly abhorrent about our current predicament."

"Harry, how much longer do you think this truce is going to last—one day, maybe two? My captain is going to ask me about our strategy and when I tell him that I am hoping that the Germans and the Irish would make some sort of accommodation and we can all settle in to our trenches with a good book and perhaps put in an order for some nice steaks I don't think my request will be granted."

"Why not, Joe? From my vantage point it doesn't sound a hell of a lot different from what we've been doing since October. I dig a trench, you dig a trench. I fire a shell into your trench. Someone dies. You fire a shell into my trench. Someone else dies. We run across the field and dig another trench…"

"You can stop there. I get the point and I agree with you. The crucible comes when one of those shells is aimed at my men. That's when I change my tune. Their lives are in my hands and I have to do whatever I need to do to protect them. And sometimes that means defending them to the death."

"I don't deny you your glory or your honor, Joe. Let's not argue about that. But soon it will be midnight. Christmas will be over. Your captain will get wind of the truce and end it. My captain will want me back in his section. Tomorrow you'll put away the cigars and the buttons and the extra bottles of champagne and begin fortifying your trench. Tomorrow I will leave you again. The question is: What can we do about it?"

Just then, Adam called out. "*Lichter, geradeaus!*"

At a turn in the lane, Mick and Adam had come upon an open field dotted with small circles of light. It could have been cars on a roadway had there been a roadway but there was none nearby. Joe and Harry pulled up and Adam grabbed his rifle.

"Who do you think it can be?" he asked.

"Can we get a closer look?"

"Follow me."

The four of them veered off the path and crept low through the underbrush until they were fifty yards away and parallel to the field. The answer to Adam's initial question came a moment thereafter when a football rolled in their direction, followed by the furious stampede of a charging soldiers.

"*Dort aus geht es!*" one shouted.

"Move it, McCormack!" came the reply from the other quarter.

Adam tried to unhook his pack and Mick dove out of the way but the ball kept careening toward them, leaving Joe and Harry directly in its path. They had an instant to respond and then Lukas, Richard, Friedrich, Andy, and Billy rolled into them and sent everyone scattering like ninepins.

"Mary and Joseph," Billy cried as he righted himself and snagged the ball out of Joe's startled hands. "If you're not going to play will you get off the pitch, man?"

Joe's accordion was one of the goalposts.

# Chapter 16

◆ ◆ ◆

## Hunting the Wren

◆ ◆ ◆

Sᴛ. Sᴛᴇᴘʜᴇɴ's ᴍᴏʀɴɪɴɢ ᴀɴᴅ Jᴏᴇ ʜᴀᴅ ᴛʜᴇ ꜰɪʀsᴛ sᴇɴᴛʀʏ ᴘᴏsᴛ. Iᴛ was not yet seven and the roseate light was tracing the bare treetops but the birds were already at their calling, chirruping each to the other as if the news couldn't wait. For Joe the sound was musical, high A's and C's in staccato triplets and incomplete scales of uncertain melodic intent. Joe recalled the cadenza from the second movement of Beethoven's Sixth where the composer marked the woodwind voices as nightingale, quail, and cuckoo and he thought what a sweet accompaniment his Plug Street birds were providing. As the sun rose with the songs Joe could almost imagine it was God's blessing upon the peace.

In his quietude, Joe remembered an earlier St. Stephen's Day. He was a second-year student at the college and new to the choral union. It was expected of all the choristers that they would gather in the anteroom of the concert hall at some point in the evening and go hunting the wren. Not knowing what to expect Joe anticipated netting and archers. He was relieved to discover that the bird was a model and the ritual was a residual of some ancient Manx cult that had evolved over the years into mummery.

When Joe walked into the room he was greeted with a huzzah. There was Donal McCormack with a week's worth of straw fruit baskets tied around his arms and legs. His job was to lead the masked paraders and he held a stick in his hand with a poor imitation of a stuffed bird dangling from the stick by a string. Hugh Macauley trailed behind him with a hornpipe and the rest of the clan followed thereafter, beating on their bodhrans and cans and anything else that would care to make a noise.

"C'mon, Dooley. There's still seven houses to hit and I'm getting thirsty," Hugh roared as the procession moved out from the hall and began their slow passage along the gaslit alley that led to the green. With their straw man at the helm the band of men set sail with their noisemakers, all the while singing lustily to the purpose of their foray:

> The wren oh the wren he's the king of all birds,
> On St. Stephens day he got caught in the furze,
> So it's up with the kettle and its down with the pan.
> Won't you give me a penny for to bury the wren?

When they arrived at the portico of no. 78 the musicians stopped playing and everyone started beating out a rhythm, clapping or stamping their feet or knocking the cans together until the denizens of the house slid open the windows and one by one tossed pieces of candy. Donal took off his hat and collected what he could, and then he looked up at the highest window and shouted his revenge. "Gibraltars and toffees are fine and dandy but where are the ha'pennies I so richly deserve?"

"You'll get your ha'pennies when you pass your Latin requirements, McCormack," was his answer. Another good-natured roar went up from the crowd as the wren boys recommenced their wailing and banging in front of the next address.

> Oh please give us something for the little bird's wake.
> A big lump of pudding or some Christmas cake.
> A fist full o' goose and a hot cup o' tay,
> And then we'll be going soon on our way.

As they rounded the corner Donal's suit of armor began to collapse and two of the boys grabbed what pieces they could salvage and poked them into their pockets. The drums went out of tune and the singing soon followed and the flasks came out to satiate the disappointment. One of the bigger boys collared Joe—he thought it was Michael O'Connor but he couldn't be certain of it—and pulled him under his arm.

"How d'ye like our straw man, Joe?" he asked, his roughhousing causing Joe to stumble a step.

"I like him very well, sir."

"Good. There's a pudding in the pot for every one of us back at the Union, you know."

"I didn't know."

"Well, now you do."

At that, O'Connor ran off and left Joe mildly bruised and warm and happy. Joe was still amazed to discover how easily he could be accepted and how readily his disguise was believed, for he was convinced if any one of his fellows knew how much he really enjoyed the fustiness of their embrace and the easy physicality of their affection they would cast him to the walk like the discarded straw of the mummer. Joe knew if he was patient enough and pliant enough he would get what he wanted. It only took a few rounds of malt later that evening and a deliberate wrong turn down the servant's alley for him to have the opportunity to satisfy Donal McCormack's curiosity and at the same time gain an even greater understanding of his own fluctuating passions.

JOE'S SWEET REVERIE WAS INTERRUPTED BY THE SOUND OF GUNFIRE. Three shots rang out. The sound was so close and so unexpected that at first Joe thought he was imagining it. Then when he realized it was nothing like his imagination he reached for his rifle. He did this too quickly and fell backwards into the trench, landing on Andy's back and waking him as rudely as possible. This in turn lead Andy to grab his gun and the whole thing might have ended in epic disaster had it not turned out to be a British gun fired in salute.

A lance-jack from the Irish Rifles stood atop the trench wall.

"Wake up! Wake up, ye toddy-heads. Which one of you gobeens is Corporal Joe Dooley?"

"For shite's sake, man, could you announce yourself a little less dramatically?" Joe asked, wiping the mud off his face. "You're looking at him."

"Bleedin' Rifles" was all Andy could muster before he turned around and tried to go back to sleep.

"I'm sorry, mate. I just walked straight through the German line to get here so I assumed no one would pay any attention to how I saluted you."

"You made an incorrect assumption."

"I have strict instructions to deliver a letter to you in person."

"Well, here I am."

The man handed Joe an envelope. "Merry Christmas, Corporal."

He clicked his heels and departed. Joe looked at what he was handed. It was another letter from Severin Coole. How does he keep finding me? Joe wondered. The depth of the republican network amazed him although in the consideration of it he should not have been surprised. All Joe had to do was remember his friend's determination and perseverance and know that if a deed were possible Severin would accomplish it. He opened the letter.

DECEMBER, 1914.

Dear Joe,

Christmas greetings from somewhere in Holland! I hope this letter finds you and I hope you are well and enjoying your pudding. I have urgent need to try to get in touch with you. My operation has grown apace. I have teamed up with other men who share my sympathies and we have brought three more boats into contention and expanded our cargo to include livestock of the human variety.

It seems as if with every day more and more patriots are leaving this continental war to the continentals and choosing to join us in our fight for freedom. I know I cannot ask you to do the same but if any of your men or any men you come across wish to join us, you must tell them to get in touch with us. Just call at any Irish regiment. The password is a question and it will certainly amuse you. You ask: "Do you like John McCormack?" and if the answer is "Yes, and 'The Minstrel Boy' most of all" you'll know he's one of us.

Funny, isn't it? I heard that plaintive song in my head and I thought of you at once and all those days so many years ago when we sat together and listened to dear old John on Mr. Murphy's Victrola. "Oh, what a tangled web we weave," to coin a phrase. My little endeavor has turned out to be more than efficient and as long as I am careful and not betrayed I think I will continue to be successful.

Do this for me, Joe, if you do nothing else. You know I trust you. You must trust me as well. Now burn me.

Your friend,

S.

Joe considered just how far he could go along with Severin's plot. Knowing of a friend who was helping the Irish to work against the English was hardly prejudicial, but actively aiding men who wanted to work with him was another matter entirely. If he knew of a man who wanted to do such a thing, was it required of him to try to dissuade him? Did it make any difference if the man was under his command or another's?

For one brief instant, Joe felt as if this damned truce was causing more trouble than it was worth. How much easier everything was when it was war! There was no ambiguity to the orders, no entanglement with the enemy, no causes to discuss, and no choices to make. It was a battlefield that fronted upon an impregnable fortress but now the walls to the castle had been freely opened and it might not be so easy to lay the barricades again. In consideration of Severin's request Joe dearly hoped that no one would ask him about John McCormack, for if the question was never posed then no answer would ever need to be given.

He thought this as he set fire to the letter.

⌒

THE MORNING PASSED AND JOE WONDERED: WHAT WAS THE PURPOSE of his standing at the sentry post when soldiers from both sides mingled in front of him like picnickers at a feis? It was as if they were neighbors instead of enemies. When Joe climbed down from the fire step, he found Lukas in the trench asking Mick if he could borrow a couple of strips of bacon.

"I guess the truce is holding," Joe exclaimed as Mick put a ration of meat on a plate for Lukas to carry back to his line.

"Guess so, Joe," said Mick nonchalantly.

"I mean, I would think you should have checked with me before inviting the Germans over for some egg and chips."

"You were staring out over the parapet. You could see as plain as day that the only firing going on was at the stove." Mick stuck his fork into a piece of bread and warmed it over the fire. "By the way, Richard came over and telephoned the Lancs. Some eejit started a gun battle in Houplines, but that's a mile to the south. None of those bullets came close."

"You didn't mention that," Andy said as he helped himself to another piece of toast.

"What care I who's shooting who in Hou...Hou...Houplines?" Mick asked, making a clever song of it.

"I do, for one," Joe answered. "Don't you think we ought to find out if there's a shooting war headed in our direction before we start planning a luncheon?"

"Now you're being quarrelsome, Joe. Being quarrelsome doesn't become you."

Lukas stopped at the top of the trench and held the plate with his proffered rations over his head. "You can have it back if it's causing such a difficulty."

Joe sent him along with a wave of his hand. Then he turned to Mick and Billy. "Where's Richard now?"

"I think he's eating with the Saxons."

Joe sighed in exasperation. "Sometimes I think I'm running a restaurant instead of an army section. Let me go see if I can solve this."

"I didn't know there was anything to be solved," said Mick, but Joe was already out of the trench and headed over to the German line. Adam and Lukas greeted him and Joe grudgingly smiled and wished them a good morning.

"I'm sorry if I created any problems by coming over," Lukas said. "My commanding officer reprimanded me as soon as I returned. And ate half of my bacon."

Adam corrected him. "Our bacon." He took Joe's hand. "I think we can afford to be friends for one more day, don't you, Colonel Dooley?"

"I heard a report of a gun fight in Houplines."

"Just a misunderstanding, so I've been told. Our captain said the truce will end at midnight tonight."

"Where did he hear this?"

"He told us he heard it from our infantry brigade in Frelinghien."

"How far is that from here?"

"Approximately three and a half miles to our west."

"It sounds a little tentative and unofficial to me."

"Pardon me, Colonel Dooley, but hasn't the entire truce been tentative and unofficial?"

"True enough. I suppose I must rely on your intelligence for now. I'm going to place another call to the British HQ."

Joe started to climb out of the trench.

"I would like to offer you something of our hospitality in return for yours," Adam said. "Why don't you take this box of cigars? The Kronprinz sent one to every unit and we don't have any smokers here."

"Thank you." Joe palmed the box.

"*Guten Morgen.*"

"Good morning."

When Joe returned to the Dubs he found Davy Rose planted next to Mick Kennedy. They were not exchanging pleasantries.

"Isn't there some other section you could bother?" Mick was asking. "I'm tiring of seeing you around here."

"I'm not sure what I've done to cause you to feel this way, Private Kennedy."

"You should let the soldiers who are doing the fighting enjoy themselves. We don't need a conshie to show us how to do it."

"Is that it?" Davy asked.

"I don't trust you as far as I can throw you," said Mick.

Joe kept walking until he was straight between the two of them.

"Get out of my way, Joe," Mick began. "I can take care of myself."

"You shouldn't speak that way to me, Mick."

"Then ask Rose to skedaddle."

Joe turned to Davy. "What's this all about then?"

"I'm sorry, Joe. I thought it was my job to go from section to section and see what is needed."

"What is needed," Mick said, "is for you to leave."

"I will if I'm ordered to."

"You're a volunteer, Davy," said Joe. "You're not under anyone's orders."

"Then I will if I'm asked."

"Here's me asking," Mick said.

Mick ran around Joe and landed a hard punch on Davy's shoulder. Davy fell back a step in surprise but when Mick tried to come around with his left Davy blocked him and countered with a blow straight to Mick's neck. Mick was staggered, stunned by the ferocity of the hit. As he righted himself he bowed his head and ran as hard as he could into Davy's chest. Davy let out a full breath from the impact of it but then turned and punched Mick in his stomach. With that Mick wrapped his arms tightly around his middle and collapsed to the ground.

"You're not used to a conshie who was a welterweight champion, are you, Private Kennedy?" Davy cried. "And I'm not used to being beaten up for trying to help people. So let's call it even."

Davy put his hands down at his side. Then he climbed out of the trench.

"Davy, wait…" Joe called. But he was already over the top.

Mick had crawled up into a sitting position, his hands tightly wrapped around his knees.

"Joe…" Mick implored.

"No man should hit a Dub," Joe said. "I'll back you up."

"Thank you, Joe," Mick said as Joe followed Davy. When Joe got out to No Man's Land he saw Davy climbing into his truck.

"Rose, slow down"

Davy started the engine and pulled away. Joe put his feet on the step and jumped up. The car moved forward with Joe hanging on to the side. Davy plunged on the brake. "What the hell are you doing, Joe?"

"Talking to you."

"You'll be talking to me with tire tracks running down your back. Get in."

Joe swung around and took a seat. Davy found the road and started driving away.

"What was that about?" Joe asked. "I want to know why you hit one of my men."

"I may not be a soldier, Joe, but don't I have the right to defend myself when I am hit?"

"I expected a little more self-restraint from you, that's all."

"I don't know why you expected such a thing. Have you seen me express it anywhere else? I do what I think is right and I say what I think is true. That's part of the deal I made with myself when I volunteered to do this job."

"I should report you."

"Go ahead. How far up would that report go? Honestly, Joe, don't you have more important things to do?"

Joe's voice tightened with anger. "You may choose to obey the rules or not but I've got to do better than that."

"Your officious threats are empty, Joe—and you know it."

"Are you mocking my command?"

"No. I'm saying you don't want to report me so why do it?"

"And Mick hit you first."

"And Mick hit me first."

Joe shook his head in exasperation. "God help me, sometimes I can't tell the difference between running an army section and keeping unruly first formers in line."

"Maybe that's because there isn't any difference."

"Maybe you're right."

Joe had nothing more to say to Davy. He sat silently as the truck rolled over a hill and rattled down an embankment.

"Where are we going?" Joe finally asked.

"I was scheduled to skip through the Lancashires this morning but I didn't expect I'd be fighting a match. I don't know where I'm going, to tell you the truth."

"So stop."

Davy pulled the truck over to the side of the road and turned off the engine. The dirt lane was surrounded by an undamaged grove thick with underbrush and the winter sun threw long shadows over it. Joe sat there next to Davy without saying anything. Then, finally, he asked, "Is it true, the truce will end at midnight?"

"I heard that. I also heard that two Germans were shot last night in Armentières. Warwick tells me the Germans don't want to start fighting again until after the New Year. Believe what you wish."

Joe noticed the sound of anger and frustration in Davy's voice.

"What's wrong, Davy?"

"I'm sorry, Joe." Davy shook his head. "I should never have allowed a confrontation with a soldier to affect me in such a way and I never should have retaliated as I did."

Joe smiled. "I guess you turned out to be a human being like the rest of us," he said.

"I'm a human being. I'll grant you that. But like the rest of you…?" Davy returned the smile. "I don't know about that. If you said 'like me,' that I could understand. I wish I could be more like you."

"That's just silly, Davy."

"Listen, Joe. I have a confession to make to you."

"Your name is really Michael O'Malley. You're a Jesuit priest."

Davy laughed. "I wish it was something whimsical. Unfortunately, it is a serious business."

"Serious how?"

"I'm working with someone in St. Omer. We're smugglers of a sort. We bring men across the border into Holland."

"I knew something was up. I'm not stupid, Davy."

"We have false papers and I.D. cards. We match men up with others who can get them off the continent."

"And when—if ever—were you going to tell me about all this?"

"I'm telling you now. Isn't that enough? The time is right. I want you to join us."

"So Mick was on to you, after all."

"Insofar as I was doing one thing and saying another, yes."

"You know how I feel about my responsibilities. How could you expect me to come with you?"

"I don't expect you to come with me. I said I want you to come with me."

"Davy…"

"I fell for you from the start and I kept on falling long after I knew you meant what you said about your commitment. But that's all right, Joe. I know this is where you belong."

"I'm glad you do. I would have been hurt to think you misunderstood me."

"I do love you, Joe."

"I bet you say that to everyone you rescue from rifle fire."

Davy smiled. "I might. But you're the first one who's ever loved me in return."

☉

By the time Davy dropped Joe off the sun was starting to set and both sides were returning to their dugouts to warily wait out the truce. It was strange that despite all the evidence and assurances no one knew if the truce would hold. As the clock ran down the Dubs grew quiet and finally took to doing nothing but sitting still in silence or reading by candlelight. Mick was still quietly nursing his resentment and Joe spent some time with him reassuring him of his standing. Andy and Billy picked up a hand of cards but they had a difficult time concentrating on the game. The waiting was unnerving to Billy in particular so he volunteered for extra sentry duty in the hope that it might cut the tension and the boredom.

Midnight came and went and no shots were fired. At one point, Lukas stood on his firing step and with an imploring look on his face tried to see if he could get the Dubs to respond to his inquiries but all he got was a "Nothing doing" from Billy. At around one a.m. someone in the German line rolled a ball across No Man's Land but it bounced into a tree stump and rolled to a spot near where one of the English soldiers had been buried and no one had the nerve to retrieve it. Considering what both sides had been through in the previous forty-eight hours it was hard to believe that anyone could get shot for chasing a football but not a man was willing to put his faith in so weak a credo.

It was Joe who volunteered to take the midnight shift. He thought he might as well be the one to report any gunfire. But other than the wayward ball nothing stirred. Then, around two, a bird started to sing. It was uncanny and improbable, but it was a bird nonetheless—most likely an owl. Its long, drawn-out cry repeated itself over and over again...*too-wit, too-wit, too-wit* and for Joe the rhythm and rising cadence had some aspect of an augury about it. Without any visual correlative, Joe was left to imagine the solemn bird sitting on a blasted limb, surveying the world's folly from the darkness and commenting upon it with its own very simple and heartfelt carol.

There was a rustle in the vegetation about fifty yards to Joe's right. Joe pulled his rifle. "Who goes there?" he asked.

"Joe, it's me," a voice whispered.

Harry emerged from the wood. Joe imitated Harry's whisper. "What are you doing out here?"

"I snuck away."

"Why?"

"Listen, Joe. I don't know how much longer the truce will last. I wanted to ask you yesterday, but..."

"Ask me what."

"I want you to come away with me."

"What?"

"Come away. We can get out together before the fighting starts again. I know people who can get us false papers and bring us into Holland and then back to Ireland."

Joe thought of Davy and shook his head. "I swear this truce has made the entire army on both sides go stark, raving mad. Why would you think for even one moment I would choose to leave my men and do such a thing?"

"I thought you wanted to end the war."

"We all want to end the war. But walking away from it isn't going to end it."

"Neither is dying for it."

"I am not a deserter."

"No, Joe. You are a hero. And a true hero sacrifices himself to help others."

"What would your fellows think of this?"

"They'd think I'd been reassigned, just like my section before and the one before that."

"Don't you think you'd better get back behind your line before you get reassigned to Heaven?"

"Listen to me. We don't have much time. I know a man in the section opposite us. If we go to him he'll get us in touch with someone who can get us a suit of clothes and two sets of papers. We'll be Dutch citizens in neutral territory. We'd be free."

"You'd better go yourself, Harry. I'm staying here."

"Aren't you my friend, Joe?"

Joe took a step back. "Harry, we were friends once and maybe some-day we'll be friends again. But I won't subject myself to such a betrayal. You hold to your principles. I'll hold to mine. I'm afraid they are irrec-oncilable."

"This is not the Joe Dooley I know."

"You don't know Joe Dooley, Harry. You only remember him."

"Ah, Joe…"

"The Harry Vogeler I knew respected me. I even thought he loved me."

"You're not making sense, Joe. You're blinded by your crazy sense of honor."

"I hate what you are telling me."

"It's the truth."

"Then I hate you for believing it. It's not the truth for me. You should get the hell away from me."

"What?"

"Go on. Get the hell away."

Harry turned around. "Goodbye then, Joe."

And he was gone.

Joe wondered what he had done to end up so at odds with the men he most loved. All of them—Severin, Davy, and Harry—chose to walk into this war only to try to lead men out of it. I came to this place against my will and I chose to make my stand here. What do they know of my sacrifice? How can they know the truth? They know nothing of what I know and no part of it can ever be their own.

Joe was curious to hear what his heart was saying and he strained to listen to it. But all he heard was the owl singing once more, *too-wit, too-wit, too-wit* to the moon and the stars. Soon the sun will rise and the lark and the wren will be singing as well. Even through the sounds of the shells exploding, Joe thought, they will sing.

# Chapter 17

✦ ✦ ✦

# The Fall from the Garden

✦ ✦ ✦

SOMETHING HAD GONE WRONG. JOE THOUGHT HE WAS FACING north and the hill that was supposed to provide their cover would be directly in front of him but he was already on an incline and the loose brush and stones were tumbling down to his left. From his position he couldn't see where the others had ended up. He listened for their voices but even his sense of hearing was distorted; his own footfalls seemed amplified and beyond that no other sound could be heard. What began as a cool, moonlit evening had suddenly turned squally and black. When the men first ran into the wood, Joe was on the left and Mick was on the right and Billy and Andy were supposed to hold the middle but the night seemed to eat them up.

The maneuver wasn't supposed to end up this way. When he and Adam Behr formulated their plan on paper everything about it had seemed exemplary. The days beyond Christmas and drifting into January had passed as well as could be expected. Although both sides received daily reminders via message and telephone that the truce that had never been officially declared was now over, neither the Irishmen nor the Germans felt particularly inclined to raise their weapons. It seemed ungentlemanly to simply start shooting so Joe and Adam devised a plan to mimic the activity of war without actually inflicting it with the hope that by the time their sense memories for battle had returned sufficient distance would have been created between the lines to keep them apart from danger. The men would be ready to shoot again but there would be no one to shoot at.

The idea was this: the Saxons would perform a flanking maneuver out of their trench trending up the hill toward a spot equidistant from their lines and the enemy's. At the same time but trailing, the Dubs were to move out from their position downhill. Both sides were to be nearly in full view of each other but far enough apart to be justified in withholding their fire. At the conclusion of the action everyone would file back into the trenches and the recipients of their reports would be none the wiser. Joe introduced the plan to his men and Adam did the same on his part and everyone acquiesced. At the appointed hour they marched out into No Man's Land. Then the moon dove under a cloud and the sleet began to fall.

"BILLY! BILLY!" JOE SCREAMED AS A SHELL EXPLODED BEHIND HIM.

"I'm right next to you, Joe," Billy cried but Joe could not see him. "There's a hole. I'm in the hole."

"Joe, where'd that shell come from?"

Joe heard Mick's voice barreling out of the darkness. "I don't know."

"Well for feck's sake, we'd better find out before the next one lands."

"Can ye retreat?"

"Retreat to where? Which way's the trench?"

"I think it's a hundred yards behind us to the left."

"Which way is left, Joe? Which way is left?"

That was Mick and although out of context one might imagine his question was a mild attempt at humor in fact it was unclear where left began and right left off. In their initial fuddle they had been turned around.

"Can you hear me, Andy?" Joe shouted to the black.

"Aye, Joe. I'm on your right."

"Good."

Just then a flare lit up the sky, its coppery trails sparking the tops of the trees and drizzling to the ground like falling stars.

"Shite!"

The mortar came down less than thirty yards to Joe's right, more or less where Joe supposed Andy to be. The gust from the explosion blew up the dirt at Joe's feet and knocked him backwards to the ground and suddenly in the incongruousness of the cold and the ice the branches all around him were burning with fire.

"Andy? Andy?"

Joe screamed into the night. The only sound was the distant rumble of another shell landing. Then, finally: "I'm all right, Joe. Just nicked by shrapnel."

"Can you move forward?"

"Will do."

"Billy, where are you?"

"I'm still here, Joe."

His voice was startlingly close. Billy lay curled up in a ball in a hole no more than ten feet away from Joe's position.

"Are ye hurt?"

"No. I'm grand."

"We've got to get out of here."

"You're telling me."

"Joe? Joe?" Mick's voice came from a place far out in the dark.

"Mick?"

"Who the feck is shelling us?" he cried. "Where in hell are they coming from?"

"I don't know, Mick."

"Are they German shells or English shells?"

"Didn't you get their fecking address, Mick?" was Andy's riposte.

"Shut yer trap, Andy."

"Fellas?" Joe cried, hopelessly.

"I think there's a gun nest on my right," Mick shouted.

"Anyone want to try saying 'don't shoot' in German?" Andy cried.

"I don't understand," Joe said, to no one in particular.

"Understand what?" Billy said. "They're trying to kill us, is all. What more is there to understand?"

When Joe stood up and tried to run to the curve in the earth where Billy had pressed his body a round of rifle fire opened up around him. Joe could see the bullets hitting the ground beneath him, tearing it into muddy clots. He dove on top of Billy and threw his body over him.

"Who's shooting at us, Joe?" Billy cried. "Why are they shooting at us?"

"Someone must have seen us moving out," Joe told him. "Someone who was not in on it."

Just then Joe heard Andy shouting. "Mick, Mick, can ye flow this way?"

Mick did not answer.

"Mick!" Joe screamed.

"Shite," groaned Billy.

Joe's back was being pelted by hail. It was hard and it hurt and he thought: This must be God's punishment. This must be the message he has for us, that the misery of hurt, death, and destruction is not enough. We must also be shelled by ice.

"I can't get to my glasses," Joe said to Billy.

"And what would you see if you had them?" Billy asked.

"Andy?" Joe yelled.

"I'm down here Joe." The voice came from behind a tree.

"Where's Mick?"

"I don't know."

A half-dozen rifle shots rang out, the bullets dinging the trees and echoing dully in the thick air.

"What should I shoot at, Joe?" Andy asked.

"I don't know."

"Will somebody give me something to shoot at?"

Joe felt himself on the edge of tears. He fought back the urge to cry and tried very hard not to think about the danger of the situation but only to evaluate what he needed to do to extricate himself and his men from it. The first thing to do, Joe thought, was locate Mick. Everything depended on that. From there, we can make out the proper direction to the trench and evaluate what we need to do to get there. Joe was glad that he was able to form a rational plan of action in his mind and it comforted him that he was still able to think this way. This comfort in turn increased his confidence and allowed him to remember that it was he, after all, who was supposed to give the orders.

Joe turned to Billy. "Follow me."

Joe put his arm around Billy and gently pushed him out on to the path. Together they raced—almost rolled, really—down the incline until they barreled into Andy's tree. Billy hit the tree hard and grabbed his arm and cried out as rifle fire broke out over their heads. One of the bullets grazed Billy's cap and knocked it off and as he righted himself and went to replace it he felt blood running down his chin. He wiped the blood away and it flowed and he knew he had either been hit or cut.

"Are ye all right, Bill?"

"'Tis a slash is all."

Joe spotted himself behind Billy, crouching in the dirt. He had his glasses out now and he was peering out into the dark. He scanned the horizon left and right. Then he put the glasses down.

"I see Mick," he said. "I'm going."

"Joe!"

Billy tried to stop him but it was too late. Joe ran out into the field of fire. He dove at the spot where Mick was lying. Mick's body was splayed across the dirt. His shirt was torn open as if he had been trying to get rid of it and his chest and belly were covered with muddy blood. Some sort of struggle had occurred between Mick Kennedy and nature and the evidence of it was that nature had persevered. Joe flattened his body as well as he could and let a flow of bullets ride over him, then he pushed his head down hard on Mick's greasy chest and listened. There was no heartbeat.

While he was alive Mick certainly weighed well over a dozen stone but Joe knew that there is no amount of heaviness to a body that cannot be moved once its spirit has been safely commended to God. Joe said a little prayer. Then trying not to be blinded by the hail or to be punctured by a whistling bullet, Joe slid down and took hold of Mick's feet and started to pull him back to the safety of the tree. Another rain of bullets rang out and Joe saw one of them find Mick's leg.

He's already dead, you bloody eejits, Joe thought, realizing at once that of course bullets were never meant for the dead but for the living, a club to which at least for the moment he still held membership. Another bullet reached Joe but, finding him in noncompliance, innocently bounced off his cap badge and fell to the earth.

Joe heaved Mick's body through the mud. An unnerving quantity of distance separated him from the safety of the tree. Andy spotted Joe and burst out of hiding. Taking Mick by the arms and legs the two of them succeeded in carrying Mick to their side. They laid him down on the lee of the hill. They took off his cap and crossed his hands over his chest. Joe turned to ask Billy if he wanted to say anything but Billy had passed out.

"It's just you and me, Joe," Andy began.

"Bill'll be all right."

"We can't carry the two of them."

"Here."

Joe sat down next to Billy and passed his arm behind his head. The blood on Billy's face was beginning to dry now and the cut didn't seem too deep. Joe wished at that moment that Davy were here. Davy would know what to do. And then Joe thought: If I were Davy, what would I do? And he opened up his water can and splashed a little of the water across Billy's face like a blessing. Then he held the can up to Billy's lips and thought for one brief instant that Billy was actually drinking some of it. He kept his arm in place to hold Billy's head and then he took his other arm and turned Billy around toward him and embraced him.

"C'mon, Billy. I need you now," he whispered, knowing Billy heard him. Billy opened his eyes. At first he was startled to find himself in Joe's arms. Then he smiled.

"Darlin'," Billy said.

"Billy, it's Mick."

"What?"

"He was shot."

"I…"

"He's dead, Billy. He's here. Andy and I pulled him in, but he's dead."

"Aw, Joe."

"How are ye, Billy?" Andy asked.

"I got knocked. I guess I'm all right now."

"We need your help, Bill," Joe said.

"That you do."

"We need to get away from these shooters before a shell finds us. Can you walk?"

"I can."

"Now."

Billy hobbled to his feet and covered Joe and Andy as they lifted and carried Mick's body back up the hill in the direction of the trench. They were all beat and the body thrashed like a soul in torment from the uncertain grip of the men and their broken steps on the heaving ground. It was their private Calvary and like that vaunted hill some sort of reverence must have emanated from it for after all the anger and violence of the night not another gun was fired.

Although the sleet continued to fall on their abjection they found the road that led back to the trench. A quarter mile on a distant light appeared and grew closer: a speeding car. Joe and Andy carried Mick to the side of the road and Billy readied his rifle. A medical van pulled up. The driver was Davy Rose. There was an injured man in back, his arm tightly wrapped in a bloodied sling. That was Harry Vogeler.

"All aboard," Davy said.

"WHAT HAPPENED TO HIM?" ANDY POINTED AT HARRY AS THE VAN roared off. Joe was still in shock; he felt as if he was in the middle of a nightmare and he was afraid if he allowed himself to be drawn into it by speaking out loud he might never awaken.

"Broken collarbone, I think," Davy began. "Maybe just a separation. I'd have to take a good look at it."

Harry was curled up against the door. Mick's body lay at his feet, covered with a blanket.

"I can talk, you know," Harry said.

At this, Joe perked up. There was a hint of a jag in his voice as he spoke. "What happened, Harry?"

"I don't rightly know, Joe. We were minding our own business according to plan. The shells came out of nowhere."

"I've been on the 'phone all night," Davy said. "The Highlanders said they had nothing to do with it and Warwick said the same."

"It wasn't the Saxons either," said Harry.

"Whoever it was, they woke up the front. I've been pedaling back and forth for hours," Davy said.

"How do you feel, Harry?" Joe asked.

"A little sick, I guess. It's hard to keep my eyes open. Everything hurts. I'm sorry about Mick."

"You're German, aren't you?" Andy asked. "Joe, is he a prisoner of war?"

Joe shrugged. "I guess."

"Right now, he's a prisoner in need of medical attention," said Davy.

"Right now? What does that mean?"

"Enough of that, Andy," Joe said. "Wait—pull over, Davy."

They stopped at a bend in the road.

"We can bury Mick here."

ON ONE SIDE THE WOOD STRETCHED OUT WITHOUT LANDMARK OR signpost; on the other there was a row of abandoned cottages. Someone had planted a neatly trimmed hedge to border their property and the dead remnants of it stood like stark sentinels to the men's bleak task. A slight breeze had risen and the sleet had turned to a cold, steady rain. The water beaded up on the blanket that they used to cover Mick's body and as the men went to lift him it sluiced down to the ground like a wave of tears.

They lit their torches. Andy took hold of Mick's arms and Joe wrapped his hands around Mick's legs and together they swung him out and laid him down on a clear patch of dirt under the spindly branches of a dying fir. They took out their entrenching tools and started to carve a grave. It was hard work due to the layers of frost and entangled roots but after a half hour of digging they had cleared enough space to lay the big Irishman down. Billy was still too weak to do any digging and Harry wasn't in any condition to use tools at all so the two of them stood apart.

Joe removed Mick's identity tag and put it in his own coat pocket. Then he carefully rearranged Mick's shirt to cover the evidence of his wounds. Once Mick was laid in his makeshift grave with his blanket for cover the men moved on to the grimmer task of burying the body. The dirt that struggled to come out of the ground when the hole was being dug seemed to require an even greater effort to go back into it. Each slow shovelful made a dull, indefinite sound as it landed. When the hole was filled, Andy ran the back of his shovel over the earth to smooth it out and Joe laid a cross of white birch branches over it.

"Michael Kennedy, I commend your soul to Heaven," Joe began, making the sign of the cross on his own chest. Harry offered the Lord's Prayer and they all spoke it together:

> Our Father, which art in heaven, hallowed be thy name;
> Thy kingdom come; thy will be done, in earth as it is in heaven.
> Give us this day our daily bread.
> And forgive us our trespasses as we forgive them that trespass
>     against us.
> And lead us not into temptation; but deliver us from evil.
> For thine is the kingdom, the power, and the glory, for ever and
>     ever.

"Amen," Joe said and so said they all. Andy knelt over the grave and prayed silently. Then, one by one, the men extinguished their torches.

THE VAN BOUNCED SLOWLY ALONG THE ROAD. ANDY HAD GRABBED the seat in the front. Billy was sitting up with his back to the cab and Harry was perched beside him, his hurt arm hanging in its cloth cradle like a newborn babe. Joe sat down along the space that had been occupied by Mick. He looked at Harry. Harry had removed his glasses and was trying to sleep. In the darkness it was hard to make out any significant details, but Joe could see Harry's long and unkempt hair hanging down over his forehead and he could see Harry's good arm stretched out along his legs as if in supplication. Harry opened his eyes. He caught Joe's glance and smiled.

Joe knew it was a portentous moment. He felt something holy and heretofore unspoken going on inside him. He remembered Davy and he wondered if he might ever be able to love anyone that instantaneously again. Joe thought about Harry and he remembered their conversation on Boxing Day. How long ago it seemed, that day when his heart was flush with the truce and he turned both of them away. Joe thought of Mick and he remembered carrying his body out of the mud and back to their bunker, the weight lighter for the transmigration of his soul but still full of corporeality. It was the first and only time he ever touched Mick. Not even in anger had he touched him. Now Mick was gone, gone to dust.

All at once it seemed to Joe that the indiscernible patterns in his life were now rising to the surface like a message written in invisible ink. Love was something that was very easy for him to offer but awfully difficult for him to accept and his reticence had made all his emotional investments the poorer for it. Joe made the connection in his mind that he now knew his body had been straining to make all along. He reflected back on his feelings about Mick's body, its weight and his touch and the way that it felt when it was dead in his hands, and he thought: I have never touched Harry, not in the way that people really touch. Harry was always there but I never touched him and never, never really loved him. The chance was handed to me and I turned it away. You can build a life from a touch. The way to build a life is to live and the way to live is to get out of this war. It took a dead man in my arms to understand this. If Harry asks me to go with him again, I will go.

IT WAS NEARLY TWO IN THE MORNING WHEN THEY REACHED THE clearing hospital. The doctors looked at Billy first. He was in mild shock but the effects of it were wearing off and he was cleared to return to the line in the morning. That seemed to spook Billy and he left shaking his head. Harry was handed a set of prisoner tags and sent into the operating theater. Joe took a seat on a bench outside the room and then Davy, Andy, and Billy joined him. Like a rook of sparrows they sat, all in a line at their nesting. Finally, one of the doctors came out. "He'd like to see you," the doctor said, pointing at Joe.

Joe stood up.

"He's fine. Go on in."

Harry sat on the edge of the table. His arm had been splinted and was wrapped in a fresh sling. "Looks like I'll live, Joe."

"What is it?"

"Just a mild fracture along my shoulder bone. It was the pain that was killing me, not the injury. The medic tells me it'll heal all by itself if I don't go getting myself shot at again."

"And how do you propose to do that?"

"You're going to save me."

"How d'ye mean?"

"Do you remember what I asked you to do, Joe?"

"I do."

"Then you still have a chance to be a real hero."

"I've failed so far, Harry. I've failed in my ultimate responsibility to protect my men."

"That's your penultimate responsibility."

"How so?"

"Your ultimate responsibility is to yourself. Don't you remember what I told you? That a real hero is someone who sacrifices himself to save the lives of others."

"Yes."

"Without that self—that real, core self—there can be no hero. Once you figure out who you really are, everything else around you falls into place. But I think you understand. Will you come with me now?"

Joe looked at Harry's bandaged arm and then into the blue of Harry's eyes. He wanted to cry for the pity of it but he held back his tears. "Yes. Yes, I will."

"I am pleased to hear it."

"But how so?"

"Davy knows."

"Davy, Davy—everybody loves Davy. Is that it? Do I need to trust 'Davy knows'?"

"No, you need to trust me. You always have. Don't you remember?"

"I do."

"Then we're set."

Joe asked Andy and Billy to meet him under the flagpole outside the hospital doorway in half an hour. He used the company telephone to ring up another Fusilier section and report. He was honest about Mick but he lied and told them the rest of his section was being reassigned. Then he met with Davy in the office and Davy helped him load their kits with a change of clothes, an extra day of rations, and the sets of papers they would need. Then Joe added two things of his own: a book of Schubert songs and his dilapidated squeezebox, rescued from the boot of the van.

"I'm done, boys," Joe began, digging his hands in his pockets. "I'm suing for peace."

"I knew it," Andy said. "I knew it."

"I don't know how you could be so certain, Andy, if I myself didn't know until now."

"You're nothing more than a deserter, Joe."

"Those are harsh words, Andy."

"What would you call yourself? You're telling me that Mick died in vain."

"No. Tommy Doyle died in vain, because I continued to wage war after he died and I knew I shouldn't have. But Mick Kennedy did not die in vain, because he saved me."

"And me," Billy added. "I'm going, too."

"Billy?" Joe asked.

"If you'll have me."

"Not a problem," said Davy.

"What this all about, Billy?" Andy asked.

"It's time for me to be the M.T.," Billy began. "And it's 'I'll Take You Home Again, Kathleen' that I'll be singing."

"A girl?" Davy asked.

"Her name is Megan Quilty."

"Ah—what a bunch of fools!" Andy began. "Quitting for a principle—that's daft, but at least it's something. But quitting for a girl—that's pathetic. I'd bet you'd all follow that conshie anywhere, wouldn't ye?"

"What does that—"

"Don't tell me you got this bright idea all by yourself. I'll bet you anything that Jew put you both up to it."

"That's uncalled for…"

"I'm not telling you anything you don't already know, Joe."

"You should apologize to Davy at least if not to me."

"I'm not apologizing to anyone."

"Andy…" Billy began.

"Don't get yourself mixed up in this, Bill."

"I'm already mixed up in it, Andy. I told you, I'm going."

"Doesn't a one of you remember what you signed up to do?"

"I think we all remember what we signed up to do. And dying in a trench wasn't it," Billy said.

"But you knew you would die somewhere."

"I intend to die. Just not here."

"And what am I to do about this?" Andy asked.

"You want to fight? Stay and fight," Joe told him. "I can't do it anymore."

"If I told you I would turn you in, Billy, would you stay?" Andy asked.

"No."

"And if I did the same for you, Joe, would you still go?"

"Yes."

Andy put his hands down at his side.

"Then go with God."


Joe addressed the assembly. "I know this is a strange time to be sentimental and this is a strange thing to be sentimental about, but Mick Kennedy was the man who give me my nickname, the Music Teacher, the M.T. Now you know that good old Mick was a Cork man. He might have been a Dub in his khaki but now that's he's back in the earth 'tis a Cork man he'll be. And my ma and my sister live in Queenstown and that makes me an honorary Cork man, too. So I thought before we all forgot about him and went on our way we might just have a bit of 'Nil Na La' in Mick's honor."

Joe led the charge:

> *Nil 'na lá, tá 'na lá*
> *Nil 'na lá, tá ar maidin.*
> *Nil 'na lá, tá 'na lá*
> *Bean a rá, is i ar fhaga.*

And Billy, with a smile as broad as the sun, sang it again in English:

> *I go up and I go down.*
> *I've a rendezvous with the tavern lady.*
> *I put a guinea on the table,*
> *And I drink me fill until the morning.*

Then Joe sang a verse in Irish:

> *Buailim suas, buailim síos.*
> *Buailim cleamhan ar bhean a leanna.*
> *Cuirim giní óir ar an mbord,*
> *Is bím ag ál anseo go maidin.*

Billy looked at a loss for this one, so Joe started it off:

> *Don't send me out into the dark…*

"Of course—" Billy exclaimed. "The bed awaits!" He and Joe sang the verse together:

> *Don't send me out into the dark.*
> *The night is cold and I'll be perished.*
> *But come to bed with me awhile,*
> *And we'll be warm beneath the blankets.*

Billy wrapped his arm around Joe and started to sway with the music as everyone took a shot at the chorus:

> *Nil 'na lá, tá 'na lá*
> *Nil 'na lá, tá ar maidin.*
> *Nil 'na lá, tá 'na lá*
> *Bean a rá, is i ar fhaga.*

Joe brought out a jug of water and four glasses. He poured for each of them. "To Mick," Joe said, raising his glass.

"To Mick," they all came back.

"And to the wish this wasn't water," Andy ended.

THE ENGINE WAS IDLING AND THE BAGS WERE PACKED. JOE STOOD on the running board and looked back at the hospital. A cloud of gray smoke from the kitchen fire was sputtering into the sky. He watched the haze slowly dissipate into the morning air. The sun was out and the skies were clear, that ever-holy shade of blue under which the best blessings are given and the deepest prayers are said. As the wisps of smoke arched and blended with the air, Joe thought about the decision he had made. At each step of his progression, he doubled back upon his own opinions and tried to listen to his warring voices. When he held Mick's body in his arms, was it truly a freedom he felt or merely pity? When he prayed at the side of the grave was it for Mick's soul or for his own? Was he doing all this in the hope of keeping Davy's love or gaining Harry's and was it thus only selfishness on his part? Or did he believe in redemption and will a man who does what his heart tells him to do truly be redeemed?

It was at this moment, conscious of his fate sitting on the balance beam, that he recalled Severin Coole. Despite the agony of self-doubt Joe knew that for every important moment in his adult life whenever he needed to make a decision all he had to do was invoke Severin's prescription and it would come out right. It was Severin who had taught him to trust himself and now he faced the greatest of all tests. If only time flowed backwards, Joe thought—but it can't. He had handed Mick's identity tags to Andy. It was done.

The car drove out unto the new dawn.

# Chapter 18

◆ ◆ ◆

## *Carrickfergus*

◆ ◆ ◆

THE MEN TOOK THE ROAD THAT SKIRTED THE HILL EAST OF GHE-
luvelt and then turned north to Passchendale. Davy drove the van along
frozen creek beds and through low underbrush to avoid any chance of being scouted. A cold wind blew in their faces and Joe was certain he could
smell the sea even thought it was more than ten miles away. Harry was
quiet most of the time and Billy actually slept. Joe looked at the sleeping
soldier and surmised that without human intervention Billy Macready
would snore through a shelling.

When night fell they bedded down in the woods. Davy ran the vehicle
into a little culvert and draped it in sticks and brush in a laughable attempt at camouflage. They rolled a groundsheet on the frosty earth and
laid their blankets on top of it and tried to sleep, staring grimly at the
oh-so-distant stars. When Joe closed his eyes, he heard the sounds of the
forest. Somewhere behind him and to his right a den of squirrels rustled
while another animal—possibly a rat but hopefully only a weasel—made
its own scurrying progress at Joe's feet. Toward dawn, Joe listened to the
ever hopeful chirping of the larks and the sparrows. He asked: What do
you know, little bird? What news have you heard that can make you so
cheerful in the face of such destruction? And have you come at last to
share your freedom with me?

At dawn the men dealt themselves a meager breakfast.

"Have you got anything in your pack other than another tin of jam?" Billy asked. "I never liked the stuff to begin with and now I am sure to have nightmares over it."

Davy wiped his tin with a finger and licked it contemplatively. "We're not going to starve, if that's your worry. The truck is loaded with surplus. But we can't start any fires, not out here. So it has to be cold comfort until we land among friends."

"I swear if I knew peace involved plum jelly I would have opted to stay in the war."

"Now you're just being facetious, Billy."

"That I am. I'm tired is all."

"Hold on now. If we're lucky we should cross the frontier tomorrow night."

At this, Harry raised his hand in the manner of an eager undergraduate making a point. "Gentlemen, gentlemen…I have a plan."

⌒

HARRY WAS DRIVING. EVEN AS IT WAS STARTING TO HEAL, THE fact that one of his arms was still cradled in a sling added an extra touch of realism. He sat alone in the front seat with the three rifles at his side. Davy, Billy and Joe were huddled together in the back with their hands tied tightly behind their backs with strips of cloth. Harry drove straight along the road to Bruges. At the first German checkpoint, he handed over his regimental papers to the guard and pointed to the forlorn British soldiers heaped behind him.

"*Ich habe drei britischen Gefangenen. Ich fing sie versucht zu entkommen,*" Harry began. "*Ich habe Aufträge um sie nach Brügge.*"

The German soldier poked the ersatz prisoners with his rifle as if inspecting a delivery of beef and then waved them on. "*Javuhl.*"

Harry slowly edged the truck along the road. The packs of soldiers marching along side them were staring down at their feet but every now and then one of them would look up and smile. Harry beamed like a general and saluted with his balky arm.

"This is crazy," Billy whispered.

"Trust me," Harry answered.

"Do I have any choice?" Joe asked.

"No, you don't."

"Sooner or later, Harry, someone is going to wonder how one German soldier with a wounded arm managed to capture and tie up three armed British soldiers."

"Yes, but by then we will be on the other side of Bruges."

Harry smiled at another contingent.

"I hope you know what you're doing, Harry."

"I hope so, too."

Halfway across the city, Harry grew even bolder. He asked one of the cheerful and compliant soldiers he passed on the street for the address of the nearest regimental headquarters. Having obtained it, he drove there straight away, parked directly in front of the building, proceeded to walk up to the adjutant's desk and asked for a decent map, some jars for fresh water, and two boxes of cigarettes. In the meantime, his three so-called prisoners sat unguarded and unmolested. It was, Joe thought, an act of stupidity so daring that it was guaranteed to succeed. And it did.

Outside of Bruges the countryside turned wet and flat. The gravel-rigged road laced over sunken fields of melting snow. There were no towns to speak of from here to the sea and thus hopefully no more German patrols to deceive. Davy was back behind the wheel. Both Harry and Davy were being cryptic about their eventual destination but from what Joe could make out they were to cross the border into Holland at a point as near to the sea as possible.

The best time to attempt the crossing was between three and four o'clock in the morning, the hour when all good soldiers who are not fast asleep should be. This in turn required seeking shelter instantly upon the sunset so that a good five to six hours of rest could be obtained before the attempt—and there could be only one attempt. If something was to go wrong and the men were discovered there would be no time to change their story and no position to which they might retreat. In the scheme of battle, the relative safety of the trenches suddenly looked starkly appealing.

⌒

DUSK HAD JUST SETTLED WHEN DAVY PASSED THROUGH DAMME. The road turned toward the sea just beyond the village and there was an abandoned chapel on the side of the road that Harry thought might make for an acceptable billet. They pushed the car behind the building. The old stones bled black in the failing shadows and one whole side of the building was crumbling. Most of the wooden shingle roof was intact but when they climbed inside they saw that a hole had been dug to create a basement, neatly shored up by beams fashioned out of what had once been the pews. At some point early in the war soldiers had camped here but now they were gone with the tides. Still, it was warm and dry and there were casements on all sides for security. Joe and Billy unhitched their packs and heaped themselves into a corner. Davy brought in a box of supplies and helped Harry untangle himself from his sling and try out the use of his arm.

"It's better," Harry said, flexing his arm up and down. "I still feel a little stiffness when I try to twist my shoulder but I should be able to fire a gun."

"Not that we'd want you to be in a situation where you would have to fire one," Davy said.

"Do you even know how to use a rifle?" Billy asked Davy.

"Not really. I'm a medical volunteer. I received plenty of medical training but no one ever asked me if I could fire a gun."

"That's reassuring."

"Listen—in the situation we're going to be in, a gunfight is the last thing you want to see. I know you are a soldier, Billy, and all your learning was in self-defense but now we're playing a different game."

"We did a pretty good job of it with those Germans," Billy said. "But it will be a whole different boys' night out if we have to explain ourselves to ourselves. What do we do if we're challenged by a British patrol?"

"Three British soldiers escorting one German prisoner—I see. It doesn't look right."

"I speak German," said Davy.

"Two and two."

"Perfect."

"If it works…"

"Are the British as dense as the Germans?"

"Look at us and look at where we've been and ask yourself if you really don't know the answer to that question."

The night was coming and Joe put a candle to the dark. As he did so, a shout came up from Billy's corner of the room. "Mary and Joseph, bring that light a little closer, Joe."

Joe walked over to where Billy was standing. At his feet there was a case of beer.

"The previous occupants must have fled in a hurry. Our celebration might not yet be due," Harry cried, "but at least it's complete."

"Is it drinkable?" Joe asked.

"You've asked many stupid questions along the way, M.T." Billy answered. "That, by God, is the stupidest."

SEVERAL GOOD DRAUGHTS LATER, IT WAS NEARLY TIME FOR SLEEP.

"I feel all alone in the universe tonight, Joe," Davy said. "Why don't you play us a tune to cheer things up?"

Davy reached behind and handed the squeezebox to Joe. Joe grasped the bellows and the soft expelled air pushed out a note. "What shall we have tonight?" he asked. Then he answered his own question. "I know." He sang:

> I wish I was in Carrickfergus
> Only for nights in Ballygrand
> I would swim over the deepest ocean
> For my love to find.

"That old song!" Billy exclaimed. "Meg and I used to sing it together."

Davy stood up and, with a sly smile grabbed hold of Harry's hands and danced him around the nave. Billy laughed as Joe kept singing.

> But the sea is wide and I cannot cross over,
> And neither have I the wings to fly.
> I wish I could meet a handsome boatsman
> To ferry me over, to my love and die.

"That's a lovely tune," Davy said as he pulled Harry over. "Could you show me how to play it?"

"It's very simple, really." Joe pulled the instrument over his shoulder and propped it on Davy's chest. Then he reached around and put one hand on the keys and tapped out the notes while Davy pushed on the bellows. "There you have it."

"Now who's next on the floor?" Davy asked.

Harry approached Joe like a shy boy at a county fair. "May I have this dance, Joe Dooley?"

"You may, Harry Vogeler."

Harry took Joe's hand and put his good arm around Joe's waist. Davy lifted up the squeezebox and pushed out the triplets as Billy sang the second verse:

*My childhood days bring back sad reflections*
*Of happy times I spent so long ago*
*My boyhood friends and my own relations*
*Have all passed on now like melting snow.*

*But I'll spend my days in endless roaming*
*Soft is the grass, my bed is free.*
*Ah, to be back now in Carrickfergus*
*On that long road down to the sea.*

As the melancholic notes floated up to the chapel's dark ceiling Joe felt his body under Harry's guidance and he liked it. There was an intimacy to Harry's touch but Joe was not frightened of it, nor did it feel like a mystery that needed to be solved. No, there was nothing unfamiliar about it and that was the strangest thing of all. It was as if he and Harry had been dancing together forever and this moment was a mere manifestation of it, settled to the ground and complete in and of itself. As his feet glided along the floor Joe felt like a bird, dreaming of flight and discovering it was no longer a dream.

Davy picked up the melody and he and Billy continued on, Davy tentatively playing the notes and Billy humming along. What had started out as a lark had turned into something else. Billy sensed this and moved away out of the candlelight, seeking sanctuary in the dim corners of the room. He saw the look on Joe's face as Davy kept playing and the boys kept dancing and it registered as a look of pure and unselfish joy.

If Joe had asked, he would have discovered that Harry, too, was wondering where his own calibrations were leading. Every step he took with Joe under his arm lessened the pain in his shoulder until not only the hurt but even the source of the hurt was forgotten and they were no longer in a stone hut in the cold Belgian night but together and free and in some green place heretofore only imagined. It was not Carrickfergus but it was someplace very much like it. Harry felt no need to speak of it but he knew where they were.

The music ended and Billy and Davy laughed and applauded. Joe and Harry didn't stop dancing but stayed close in each other's arms stepping and swaying to the silence. Then Joe put his head down on Harry's chest and closed his eyes. This was a very safe place to be and he didn't care what Billy or anyone else thought of it. But Billy in his wisdom had already moved along.

"Closing time," he cried, four more bottles splayed in his hands. "Who wants a nightcap?"

⌒

AT DAWN, THE MEN RAN INTO A BRITISH BORDER PATROL. "WHO goes there?" said the first man.

"Two Dublin Fusiliers and two German prisoners, sir," Joe began.

"Excellent. Are you bringing them to Ostend?"

"No, sir. We were hoping to reach Zeebrugge."

"Zeebrugge? But there's nothing but Germans there."

"I'm sorry, sir. I must have received poor intelligence."

"We'll hear nothing further of Zeebrugge. You'll come with us and we'll find you an escort to Ostend. Heroes of your sort are always welcome."

Davy and Harry looked at the rifles pointed in their direction and shuffled a few nervous steps backwards.

"Begging your pardon, Colonel Dooley," Billy began in his most earnest and unctuous tone, "but didn't you say that a party of Highlanders had been expecting us outside of Zeebrugge?"

Joe wasn't certain where Billy was going but it was too late to tack in another direction. "I had forgotten about the Scots. Thank you, Private Macready."

"I hadn't heard of any Highlanders in our neighborhood," one of the other men said, unhelpfully.

"Send them home to Inverness," the first man said, "They won't miss you. You're with the King's Own now and why take an unnecessary risk? Follow us."

There was nothing for Joe and Billy to do but plant Davy and Harry in the back of the van and fall in with the patrol. Joe's mind was racing with a plan. They were heading south again. Every minute was taking them farther and farther away from freedom. The patrol had smartly chosen a route that was relatively secure and well protected by winter shrubbery and what was a boon for the British was also strangely enough a blessing for Joe's party. If they could shake their would-be saviors they might actually have stumbled into a swifter route to the border.

"Wait till the captain sees your pair of trophies," the first British soldier shouted back at Joe. "Under the circumstances I wouldn't be surprised to see him put you in for a medal."

"That's very kind of you to say so, sir," said Joe, his brain going a mile a minute.

Luckily for Joe the King's Own hadn't bothered to commandeer their van, an act of assimilation that they had every right to perform. He wondered if he managed to turn the vehicle around and make a run for it just what the startled soldiers would be capable of doing about it. Just then, a wagon and a team of horses came around the bend in the road. It was the perfect distraction.

"*Allons-y,*" he shouted, hoping the French would confuse the British soldiers for an instant. Joe turned the van around and let the engine out as far as it could go. There was a screech of the tires as they came about on the rough gravel and a babble of confused voices trailing behind as the carload pulled away and rode out in the opposite direction. The sudden noise spooked the horses and they scattered in their traces, blocking the road in both directions. A minute passed and then another and finally Joe concluded that their pursuit had been abandoned.

"I say, that was most unsporting," Davy roared, imitating the upper-crust accent of one of the patrol officers. "We hardly had the time to make proper introductions."

"I hope they don't decide to put us in their report," Joe said. "We might be able to avoid pursuit on foot but I hardly think we're prepared for a race to the border."

"Time is wasting," Billy interjected.

With a groan, Joe said, "Thanks for the tip, Bill. And how much faster would you like me to go?"

"Faster," Billy said.

At the outer edges of a frontier there are no markings. This oak is in Belgium; that hedge is in Holland. The weary men hardly took note of either the oak or the hedge but sometime between five and six o'clock in the morning they crossed the border.

"Do you like John McCormack?"

The old nun's face was so closely swathed in her habit that it made a perfect "O." She gawped at Joe from the porthole window with the concentration of a magus. Joe was startled by the sister's question. *We're trying to find asylum from the enemy, you silly thing—why should we care or even talk about John McCormack?* Then all at once Joe understood the meaning of the question and all that it implied.

"Yes," he answered. "And 'The Minstrel Boy' best of all."

Slowly, the door swung open. "Please enter, gentlemen."

Inside the convent Joe and the others were greeted with a polite nod from the sister. She led them silently down the corridor to another door. The woman knocked and waited.

"Frederika?" came the cry from behind it.

"*Ja.*"

This door opened to a worn stone staircase that led down to the cellar. The sister named Frederika pointed to the steps. Davy went down first, followed by Harry, then Billy and finally Joe. There were three men in the tiny room. One of them was Richard McCormack.

"My God, Richard!" Joe exclaimed when he saw him. Richard was dressed in civilian clothes. He looked fit—exceptionally so, Joe thought, considering what the past months had wrought.

"Joe…Billy…" Richard began. "We've been expecting you."

"Damn you, McCormack," Billy said. "I thought you were gone forever. To come back like a ghost…" He started to cry. Joe put his arm around him.

"That's all right, Bill."

"Strange the secrets I managed to keep from the Dubs," Richard said. "You must understand all the while I was working with Davy and the underground I couldn't tell any of you about it."

"But the battle…when you were captured…" Billy stammered.

"Oh, I was captured all right. The truce was a bonus. But there were men on the German side working in the same direction and I found them soon enough."

Richard looked over at Harry and smiled.

"I'm sorry I couldn't tell you, Joe," Harry began. "It would have compromised Richard's position if I had included you."

"Now I understand a little bit more about what you were trying to tell me back at Plug Street," Joe answered.

"I'm a little bit lost here," Billy said.

"You just took a little jump into a very, very big pool, is all," Richard began. "And I, for one, am very glad you did."

"So am I," Joe added.

"Are there many others?" Billy asked.

"More than you or I could have ever imagined," Richard said. "In every section and in every regiment, at rest or in the trenches, in exile from Lancashire to Kent and from Donegal to Kerry, everywhere I went

I found men full of disillusion. Some were willing to fight on and if they believed in what they were doing I would offer every bit of matériel, money, and support I could muster. In that I am sure we never compromised their bravery or their commitment. But for every man who stayed and fought I found another who was broken or unable to raise his sights to a massacre. These were honest and noble men who feared less for their own lives than for the lives of their friends and their fellows and who thought that it was for their cause we were truly fighting and it was for their freedom and dignity that we had to abdicate our roles as soldiers.

"So here we are. My job is to collect the Irish soldiers from the British lines and arrange their transport back to Ireland. You may note that one of you—Herr Vogeler, you shall remain nameless—is not, by the legal standards of the day, Irish. This I choose to overlook."

"How did you find your way into all of this?" Billy asked.

"I have a brother in Dublin…"

"Donal!" Joe exclaimed.

"…Donal is a solicitor in Dublin and one of the benefactors of our little enterprise."

"I knew Donal was involved in this but at the time I guess I didn't care to know the details," Joe said. "He certainly didn't care to tell me."

"He had the care to tell me," said Richard, "And while I was behind the German lines I was in a position to make certain that when and if you wanted to come over Harry Vogeler would be along for the ride."

"Why did you do that for me, Richard?"

"That's simple enough, Joe," Harry answered. "I asked him to do it."

Joe turned to Davy. "Davy?"

"Yes, Joe. So much of what you ascribed to coincidence was not coincidental at all."

"I am starting to wonder if any of what happens is."

"Now you're getting philosophical."

"The M.T.," said Billy.

"That's me," Joe said, smiling.

"I've arranged for the five of us to drive to Rotterdam tomorrow and cross the North Sea," Richard began. "We'll meet the others in Aberdeen and they'll get us to Cork."

"Five?" Joe asked. "I count six."

"I'm not going to Ireland, Joe," Davy said.

"But surely, you will come to Scotland?"

"My job is here."

"Here, in Holland?"

"And in Belgium and in France."

"But…"

"No, Joe. I have to stay."

"There is a working convent above us," Richard began. "The sisters are up with their morning chores now and part of our consideration is not to interfere with their work and most of all not to expose them should anyone come looking for trouble. So until we are loaded up and on the way out of the village I expect you all to if not stay out of sight at least try not to call attention to yourselves."

"That means keep clear of the pub, Billy," Joe added, smiling.

"I have my eye on the prize, Joe. Kehoe's for me."

"Ah—Kehoe's," Richard said. "Now there's a liquid tone poem. But not until then…"

"Not until then," Billy swore.

"We'll be leaving at five. You all have your papers, and we have room for your kits and that's all. Now, I must attend to our next carload of visitors."

⌒

THAT DAY, JOE AND THE MEN GRABBED THE OPPORTUNITY FOR SOME ordinary freedom and toured Baarle. It was strange to feel so exposed and yet so constricted at the same time, to walk along the narrow passageways and enter the flower shops and cheese markets like ordinary citizens and be constantly aware that you were not like them, that you held a secret which kept you apart and that required your vigilance and even your prevarication. For this point in January and in consideration of the usual Netherlandish weather it was warm and sunny and perhaps this improvement had something to do with the day's optimism. By afternoon they were even able to sit at a café table for their luncheon.

"I feel suspended—" Billy began. "—not able to go back to what I was and not able to go forward to what I will be."

"All in time, Billy boy," said Joe. "Right now I think you'd be better off lingering over your cuppa."

"I am."

"Is it strange that one of the men amongst us most eager to tramp along Irish soil is me?" Harry asked. "Exile is a terrible state."

"Ireland is a terrible state," Billy rejoined. "Do you have any idea what you are going back to?"

"How do you mean?"

"Listen—I was never one for getting involved in politics. This whole thing is personal to me, so don't let's think that I am an Irish patriot or anything of that sort but the war in Europe is only a distraction to get the Home Rule Bill suspended and keep the people of Ireland under lock and key for the duration."

"Whoa, Billy," Joe said. "Where did this partisan streak come from?"

"Dunna know, Joe. But when you get back to Dublin, Harry, I hope you keep your countries straight. 'Tis for Ireland you are now."

"Ever was, Mr. Macready," said Harry. "Ever was."

"I didn't walk out of one war only to walk into another," Joe began. "I have a hard time believing that it will take ammunition to make Ireland free."

"And when has Britain ever relinquished territory voluntarily?" Harry asked.

"I suppose you're right."

Joe swirled another teaspoon of sugar into his tea and sat back in his chair. "This sectarianism has followed me all my life. It nearly flows through my blood. My da was beat for running a printing shop and my best boyhood friend was beat for standing up for his union. I was chased across Belfast for supporting strikers and I've been bullied by Ascendency brats and British officers alike. You'd think I would have formed a definite opinion on it all by now but I have not. Every person I meet seems so sensible to me I have a hard time believing they're not telling me the truth."

"Everyone always tells the truth, Joe," Davy said. "That's the problem. Even when they lie to you, they are telling you the truth. Because what happens is always the truth, and you can only see what is happening in front of you."

"Now you have me thoroughly confused," Billy said.

"That's because Davy is a thoroughly confused person," said Harry with a sly glance at his friend.

"Thoroughly," Davy confirmed.

"I'll drink to that," Joe said, raising his cup.

"Ugh. If only I could switch out this lukewarm tea for a double measure of Power's," Billy cried.

"Kehoe's, Billy."

"Kehoe's—Joe."

THE MEN SLEPT ON BUNKS IN THE BASEMENT OF THE CHURCH. THE mattresses were narrow and uncomfortable and there were only half as many pillows as were needed but it was the first time Joe had slept on a real bed since November and the luxury of it was practically unnerving. He had a hard time falling asleep, playing out his memories like a rope on a spindle. Around four Joe got up and walked out into the courtyard only to discover Davy sitting on a cistern in the corner.

"Couldn't sleep either?" Joe asked, taking a place next to Davy.

"Oh, I was sleeping all right." Davy gazed into the darkness. "I just wanted to sit here for a while."

"I'm glad I found you. I didn't know if I was going to have the chance to say a proper goodbye."

"By a proper goodbye, I assume you mean you want to kiss me and couldn't do it in front of the others."

"Something like that," Joe answered, smiling.

Davy turned to Joe and kissed him. "There."

"I'm going to miss you terribly, Davy."

"Will you now?"

"Don't be hard."

"I didn't mean to be. We're at cross-purposes, that's all."

"To meet someone with whom I am so compatible and then to hear us described as being at cross-purposes, that makes me very sad."

"We love each other, Joe. That doesn't mean we have to want to do the same things or go to the same places."

"When you put it that way, it almost sounds sensible."

"It is sensible. Love isn't a business contract—although I suppose it is enough of one for married people. It's all about the giving. The love you have given me is infinitely more valuable to me than anything else I could ever receive from you. For now I have a measure of it to pass along. Haven't I taught you anything? Don't you understand that the best way for you to continue to love me is to keep giving your love to others?"

"I do."

"That's good."

"I know that you and Harry and Richard have all been working to-gether," Joe said. "Still, I think it was a miracle that you found Harry and brought him to me."

"I didn't bring him to you, Joe. I brought him to freedom."

"You brought him to me, Davy. That is what you gave me."

"How do you mean?"

"I was going to stay on the line. I was sure of it. When Harry asked me to come away with him I turned him down."

"Obviously, you changed your mind."

"Yes, I did, and that was because of you."

"Because of me?"

"Yes. The night the truce broke and Harry was wounded, you saved him. You may have brought him to freedom but you also brought him to me. You did so."

"Yes."

"And now I must go on. With Harry and without you."

Davy stood up and turned to face Joe. "Do you love Harry?"

"I think I do."

"Then you should tell him."

"I will." Joe stood up. He kissed Davy gently on his forehead and then softly on the tip of his nose and then once more on his lips. "Thank you, Davy."

"You're welcome."

The two men stood close together, their breath clouding in the space between them.

"What will you do after the war is over?" Joe began.

"That seems so very far away."

"Still, don't you ever think about it?"

"Actually, I do. And that is because of you."

"How so?"

"I thought it might be fun to be a teacher. I saw the joy that spread across your face when you were singing and the happiness you brought to others when they were singing with you."

"I never suspected you had any musical talent."

"Oh, I don't. It isn't music I'd care to teach. But language—there is the thing that drove the world apart. I think I'd like to teach English in Germany. Try to teach the Germans—and the English, I might add—to love each other a little bit more and hate each other a little bit less."

"Sounds noble."

"Oh, I come from a long line of Stepney nobility. 'Sir David' they call me."

Davy laughed at his own joke and Joe laughed with him. Then the laugh turned into an embrace and the embrace led to a kiss. Joe thought it was sweet and it was sweet and as it was happening Joe also thought to himself: here is the truth.

# Chapter 19

◆ ◆ ◆

# *On the Grace O'Malley*

◆ ◆ ◆

The joke about John McCormack was getting old. It was an idiomatic password to begin with and each time the men utilized it the answering party responded with a merrier and more knowing parry. When the men arrived at their first checkpoint, a house in a small village near Breda, the young girl who answered the door replied by humming the first few bars of the Thomas Moore tune. Their hosts laid out a banqueting table laden with orange cheeses and biscuits so fresh the salt was melting into the crust. Despite the relatively early hour there was a keg of ale to quaff and—even more phantasmagorical—fresh figs. Billy went straight for the beer. Harry eyed the fruit with suspicion until it was pointed out to him that when your entire seacoast is an open port so long as the harbor wasn't under ice every bit of foodstuff from the four corners of the globe could be sailed into your harbor. Joe smiled as he wiped the crumbs with his sleeve and wondered if this was so why Ireland—a seaport in the round if there ever was one—was so inured to its sweet jam and fat bacon.

At their next stop near Dordrecht a fragment of a concert performance answered the question. Just inside the entranceway to a charming if dilapidated townhouse two handsome young men greeted the party with a harmonized rendition of 'The Minstrel Boy':

*"Land of Song!" cried the warrior bard,*
*"Tho' all the world betrays thee,*
*One sword, at least, thy rights shall guard,*
*One faithful harp shall praise thee!"*

The effect of the overly rich breakfast and the onset of nervousness over their imminent castoff had made Joe's stomach roil. He was distracted by the two good-looking boys and found it easy to turn down their offer of extra provisions. Billy too seemed muted as if for the first time since he made his decision to join the party he thought his consideration of it might have been rash and leave him guilt-stricken. But to no one's wonderment, least of all Joe's, Harry seemed to be in his element, joining in the song and laughing at the joy and freedom of it all.

Based on the evidence so far it was true that their mission was not presenting them with a great amount of danger. The drive from the border took less than two hours and the checkpoints were necessitated not so much for security but for the assembling of the documents and supplies the men would need for success. The paperwork required in Belgium had to be exchanged once in Holland and again at the customhouse in Rotterdam and their tattered civilian rags had to be cast aside for more seaworthy garments. The ship would have their provender but anything above the mean requirements of a boat voyage would have to come from their own pockets.

Joe was adamant about his squeezebox. He was like a petulant ten year-old in that no manner of rational argument could persuade him to give it up. When it was pointed out to him that no one else was attempting to drag along even so much as an extra pair of gloves Joe dug in harder. It wasn't until he laid down the threat of a broken superstition that the others eventually gave way: they had made it safely under his guidance so far and his little wooden relic had survived gunfire, a hijacking, a blizzard, and two perforations. After that not a one of them challenged him.

Although Joe held the highest rank of all the soldiers, Richard was in command of the mission and it was he who held the clock in his hand. "Gentlemen, much as I love the boisterousness of our present company and appreciate the care and effort they have contributed to our well-being, we have an appointment aboard the *Grainne Ni Mhaille*."

"The what?" Harry asked.

"Our boat."

"*Grawn-ya nee Wall-ya?*" Harry repeated, sounding it out.

"That's correct. It's an Irish name."

"No kidding."

"*Grace O'Malley* would be the vulgar version. Grace was an Irish pirate who fought the British and succeeded to the point of being offered an audience with the queen."

"Now I get it," Harry answered.

"Who came up with that tongue-twister?" Billy asked.

"Don't blame me—'tis the men who own the boat who are the name-givers. Partisans, apparently."

"Isn't that what we are, Richard?" Joe asked.

"Not yet. We are merely citizens."

"Of what country?" Billy asked.

"Point taken," Harry replied.

"It'll be No Man's Land if we don't get going," said Richard.

IN THE MONSTROUS PORT OF ROTTERDAM THE MEN COULD HIDE IN plain sight. Every thirty yards there was another beat-up wooden dock jutting out into the harbor and along each one an army of stevedores loaded their jute, sides of beef, and bolts of linen. Even the industry serving the industry had its own culture, as the coal barges and iron hulks served the boats laden with stock in the manner of little fish feeding the big ones. Out in the Dutch countryside a glimmer of winter sun had perforated the cold sky but between the haze pouring out from the smokestacks and a change in the weather the whole of the harbor was gray.

Richard told the others that they were under strict instructions to proceed to a storehouse on Schiedamsedijk, one of the smaller side docks where the tramp steamers of the class to which the *Grainne* belonged could move more easily and anonymously. They were assured that despite the appearance of absolute chaos there was no doubt that the business acumen of the Dutch was not going to allow them to board, staff, and store a seaworthy vessel and move it from the port to the open sea without being properly inspected, adjusted and taxed. Apparently the four of them were now local businessmen with interests in the war who were sailing abroad with extremely valuable contracts of great financial benefit to the government and if you would just accept this little honorarium from us we would appreciate your expeditious stamp of clearance.

The storehouse was no larger than a munitions shack and about as well constructed; it seemed as if it was only one squall away from being pushed into the water. It was wood-shingled on all four sides without any windows. Richard knocked on the door and this time it swung open without any password exchange at all.

"Here are our papers," Richard said. "I have the men. Would you like to meet them now?"

From behind the door a man's voice replied: "Yes, very much so."

Richard moved out of the doorway and spoke: "My friends, may I introduce you to the captain of the *Grainne*, Mr. Severin Coole?"

⊙

IN CONSIDERATION OF THE PARTY BEING ENTIRELY COMPOSED OF Irishmen it was decided to spend the last night on European soil in a bar on the Leuvenhaven. Only they weren't all men; among the band was the nurse Joe had met in St. Omer, Sharon O'Connor.

"I'm rejoining the O'Connor clan in Ballymena, boys," Sharon said. "I've enough of extracting German bullets."

"How much experience d'ye have extracting British ones?" Severin asked.

"Not much, yet. They're all the same, though, aren't they?"

"Once they're in you."

"True enough."

Joe lifted his glass. "To the O'Connor clan."

The huzzah that came up from the crowd spread to the tars sitting along the periphery. The breath of it was enough to send the smoke from the cigarettes dancing. Joe's eyes gleamed as he looked at Severin and Severin caught his eye and winked. Through all the planning in the back of his mind Joe had known that somewhere along the coast there was a boat with Severin in it and if he was to cross the sea it might as well be with Severin as with anyone to steer him but he never allowed himself to admit it was a longing. The odds were too great—almost as great, he laughed to himself, as coming face to face, twice, with Harry Vogeler. At times like these Joe was certain in his conviction that the whole wide world was merely an unpaved extension of Sackville Street.

Now that they were together it amazed Joe to think of it but had it been nearly four years since he and his friend last spoke in person? Severin was twenty-six years old now and little of his boyish glow remained; it had been polished like soft marble and smoothed over by care. His stubble had grown darker and thicker with bare patches where scars had been borne and his hair was no longer as curly as a Caravaggio angel's.

Now it swooped in strands across his brow and over his ears like that of the modern artists that Joe remembered seeing in photographs in the papers. With the full thrall of memory Joe glanced at the black hairs on Severin's chest as they twined out from between his collars and remembered how much he had once wished to run his hand through them. For all the years of separation Joe's desire had not grown dim and no gauge of impossibility was going to dissuade it. What was it about this boy—this young man—that inspired such adhesion? Joe was no longer an adolescent and pure sexual desire could not be the final arbiter of these things. He knew there must be something deeper and stronger to ignite such a spiritual connection. Joe remembered all the times over the years when he thought of Severin's beauty and his courage and his dedication and how it inspired him to do what he thought was right and best. It was positively Greek. Severin Coole, Joe concluded, was to him the living embodiment of *kalos kagathos*—the ideal.

"Is that so, Joe?" Harry asked Joe a question that Joe had no recollection of hearing.

"What's that?"

"You haven't had that many, Joe. What is the matter with you?"

"I'm sorry."

"Miss O'Connor and I were comparing war stories. She said your wound was much worse than mine and I grew aggrieved."

"Dooley was shot through his chest, for God's sake," Sharon bellowed. "Your friend Harry got a little dent in his shoulder."

"It was not a dent. It was a hairline fracture."

"A dent."

"I'm out of this argument," Billy injected. "I had a bullet bounce off my helmet and I don't think that counts."

"Where do prisoners rank in this game?" Richard inquired.

"You ended up being friendlier with the Germans than you were with the British," Harry retorted.

"We would have hardly ended up here if I hadn't been."

"'Tis true," Billy admitted.

"Is anyone buying another round?" Sharon asked. "I'd love to sit here all night and listen to you boys argue over who has a hold of the bigger end of the stick but I'm getting thirsty."

Sharon roared at her own joke and her laughter grew contagious.

"I'm buying," Joe said. With exaggerated weariness he hauled himself over to the tap and placed the order.

"I'm afraid I'm out after this," Richard said.

"Oh, McCormack—you were always the first one out," Billy complained. "Must be all that training you received from your wife."

"I am longing to see her so," Richard said.

"Soon, my friend."

The mood turned wistful and the glasses were drained in relative silence.

"Richard, you and Billy can bunk upstairs," Severin said. "I've saved the private room for Miss O'Connor."

"Such a decent lad," Sharon cried.

"Joe, you and Harry can stay with me on the boat. We push out at five."

"Last call?"

"It's time."

⌢

THE *GRAINNE NI MHAINNE* WAS A TAR-WORTHY TRAWLER BUILT IN the 1890s and was in serious need of a refitting. Several of the water-level beams had rotted out and were patched with mismatching planks that in turn looked about to spring their bolts and the engine room was so laden with coal dust that the accumulation could be measured. The entirety of it ran no more than twenty yards and the front bow guard was missing. Joe wondered how much of a sailor Severin really was but this was no time to begin an assessment.

"I've got to load in the coal and run the checks before we turn in," Severin said as he hoisted the men's bags on to the deck and climbed down to the hold. "There's to be no time in the morning and I want to get away without any unnecessary delay."

"Yes, sir," Joe said, clipping his voice in the military manner and smiling.

"Enough of that," Severin shouted back from below.

In the quiet of the night and so close to the water the Rotterdam harbor was actually beautiful. The sky had cleared and the air was cold but pleasantly crisp, much changed from the grime-laden atmosphere of the day. A few men walked up and down along the quay but none of the precariousness of war came near them. Although Joe understood there were grave perils to their voyage he felt strangely calm. Perhaps it was the presence of the sea. The sound of water lapping up against the side of the boat was a tonic. Considering his miserable record as a swimmer it was fascinating to Joe how much his mood improved when the sea surrounded him.

"I can't believe through all the years you and Severin never met," Joe began as he and Harry settled in the cabin. "After all, you are the only friend I've known longer than he."

"Is Severin the friend you made in Queenstown after your da passed?"

"'Tis."

"I believe you spoke of him often."

"I'm sure I have."

"He seems solid."

"He is. That's why we're putting our lives in his hands."

Harry looked up at Joe. "This is an awful lot for you to do for me."

"I'd do it for anyone."

"Is that so? I don't know about that."

"In theory, I meant."

"Am I merely the proof then, Joe?"

"I'm sorry, Harry. It's just…"

Joe tried to finish this thought but he found the words wouldn't come. The boat wasn't moving but Joe felt as if he was losing his balance.

"Come here, Joe." Harry opened his arms and Joe fell into them and held on as tightly as he could. Just then Severin came in.

"Don't let me interrupt your little colloquy."

Severin swabbed a bit of coal dust from his brow and shoved his hands into his coat pockets. Joe jumped up and backed away. "Sev…"

"'S all right, Joe. We're all friends here."

"I…"

Harry offered up his own explanation. "I think the strain is beginning to get to me," he began. "You know—we evaded detection, crossed the border, got our papers, and loaded the ship. That's as much action as I would see in a week's worth of patrols. After all this time handling soldiers who were terrified or wounded or worse, it's an awfully personal thing for me to touch one out of friendship."

"Or love," Joe added.

"Love," Harry said, trying out the word as if looking for a translation.

"Something like that," said Severin.

Harry took off his glasses and rubbed his eyes with the back of his hand. "Would you mind if I went to my bunk now, Joe? I'm exhausted."

"Of course not."

"Good night."

Harry offered his hand. Joe took it but instead of shaking it he held it, the way one would take hold of a lifeline. "Good night."

Harry went inside. Through the porthole window, Joe watched the stars.

"Harry's a good guy, Joe."

"*Cara m'cree.*"

"All that? I thought that was my place."

"'Tis. But you're different."

"I would hope so."

"I mean, we've been over that for a long time now."

"You mean you have been."

"Well, yes. Sorry."

"I will never get over you because I would never get under you."

"Very funny."

"I didn't mean it entirely as a joke, Joe."

"I know."

"Are you and Harry…?"

Joe laughed.

"Did I tell another joke?" Severin asked.

"No. I'm laughing because—as usual—you posed the question to me before I ever asked it myself."

"I don't mean to interfere."

"There's nothing to interfere with. I love him, sure. But where that will lead? I don't know. I think I'd better find out if my story is going to continue or not before I try to fill in the uncompleted passages."

"Your story will continue, Joe."

"You were always so certain of that, Severin, weren't you?"

"Sure as the sun." Now it was Severin's turn to look at the stars. "Do you remember that conversation on the strand at Blackpool, all those years ago?" he asked.

"I haven't forgotten it for a day."

"'Our separate ways at last' you said."

"Yes."

"I knew then that wasn't going to be forever the case."

"I didn't."

"But now you do."

"Yes."

"I've always loved you, Joe. In fact, I can safely declare that there's no one on this earth I've ever loved as much."

For this, Joe uncharacteristically had no response. Instead he turned to look at the face that for so long he had only dreamed of seeing.

"I'm only sorry I couldn't love you more," Severin went on.

"How so?"

"You know. More than this." Severin leaned over and gave Joe a kiss.

"Yes," Joe said.

"I hope Harry is good for you."

"He's not my confessor, Sev. He's not my doctor."

"But he could be, Joe. Just give him the chance."

"The chance?"

"That's all we ever have in this world, Joe. No chance untaken ever proves true."

"Thanks."

"*Codladh samh.*"

"Yes, goodnight."

# Chapter 20

◆ ◆ ◆

## *Maeve's Old Room*

◆ ◆ ◆

THE WATER WAS CALM BUT THE LAND WAS OUT OF SIGHT AND TO the men their isolation was an invitation to all sorts of imagined terrors. The *Grainne's* vulnerability was obvious: they had all the required charts and a radio but no chart could protect them from a U-boat and who were they to call? The happiness the men felt at their getaway had given way to an unspoken fear. Billy was feeling a little seasick and Sharon and Richard kept him company in the cabin. Joe and Harry started the voyage standing behind the nonexistent bow guard and took turns scanning the horizon for a wake or the telltale scope but once they realized that spotting a submarine only meant the boat itself had been spotted and there was no effective means of escape they gave that up and silently meditated under the ice-blue sky.

Severin remained alone at the helm. Deep-sea-trawlers were equipped for crews of up to three men but he preferred to execute the route on his own. Two or three hours of vigilance was nothing compared to the risk that might be taken had an inexperienced or uncourageous second captain been at the wheel. Besides that, he liked the solitariness of it. As in Africa and as had been the truth throughout his entire adult life, Severin's confidence was never higher than when it was self-created. For this particular assignment, Severin held one additional card that was lacking in all his previous sea crossings and it turned out to be his ace. That card was Harry and the trump was a passenger who spoke fluent German.

Severin hoped that by aiming due north toward the Scottish coast he might more easily avoid the detection that awaited the larger, Dover-bound vessels; the *Grainne* was almost small enough to be completely ignored by the virtually blind and not excessively mobile U-boats. But his boat was nearly as blind as the Germans' and there was the constant possibility of an accidental encounter. Somewhere approximately half-away across the sea that was precisely what went down. One hundred feet off the starboard bow a gray mass surfaced like a steel rorqual. She ran up the imperial flag and sent a representative to the top with a megaphone.

"*Alle Mann an Deck, bitte,*" a red-haired officer shouted as the sub rounded the *Grainne's* stern.

"Harry, come up here," Severin yelled. Harry raced up front. "Can you help us out here?"

"*Jahvuhl.*" Harry stretched himself out to bring the most impressive bearing he could muster and shouted back at the Germans in an outraged tone of voice: "*Wir sind die Durchführung von niederländischen Bürgern legitime humanitäre Geschäft. Bitte geben Sie Ihre Absichten!*"

The vernacular response clearly startled the German. He blinked nervously and scurried down into his nest. When he came back up, he was accompanied by a skinny and officious-looking subaltern who was busily scribbling notes on a pad of paper he held in front of him like newspaper reporter. They spoke to each other sotto voce and then the red-haired man shouted back: "*Sehr gut. Lassen Sie uns Bord. Wir möchten, dass Sie Ihre Papiere und Ihre halten.*"

Joe stood next to Harry as Severin slowed the boat. By this point, the passengers below deck had figured out that something was afoot. Richard, Billy, and Sharon came up and hung together near the bridge.

"What's going on, Harry?" Severin asked with the tone of an impatient father waiting for his young son to finish an arithmetic problem.

"They want to see our papers. They want to inspect the hold."

"Good thing I kept the old girl loaded up with a couple hundred second-rate German-issue blankets. Tell 'em we're cloth importers."

"What if they don't believe me?"

"Come here," Severin said.

Harry swung around to the ladder that led to Severin's perch and climbed up. Severin dug into his coat pocket and handed Harry a fistful of bank notes. "If they don't believe you the first time, give them this."

"What is it?"

"One hundred German marks in negotiable currency. With the immediate prospect of a spree in Amsterdam, I hardly think our friends will want to deal with five prisoners."

"They'll take the money and sink the boat anyway."

"Harry…Harry…" Severin began. "Your faith in the martial instincts of mankind touches me to the quick. Here they come."

The U-boat rode up close enough to the *Grainne* to lay out their ladder. One by one, the crew strode onto the little trawler's deck—first the red-haired officer, then his assistant, then a baby-faced *segler* flashing a pistol. Harry handed the officer a leather folder with their false identification papers. The man leafed through them so aggressively that he tore half of the bottom sheet and then handled them back without so much as an apology. He then barked something at the baby-faced boy and the boy jumped down into the hold.

"*Wir nicht der Regel in der Deutschschweiz Geschäftsleute in der Mitte der Nordsee,*" he said to Harry.

"*Dann ist dies Ihr Glückstag,*" Harry replied. "*Außerdem bin ich der einzige von uns, spricht Deutsch.*"

"*Lassen Sie die niederländische, ihre Niederländisch,*" said his counterpart. "*Gott schütze den Kaiser!*"

"*Gott schütze den Kaiser!*" Harry said smartly. Joe did everything he could to keep from laughing. Just then, the boy came back up from the hold.

"*Decken.*"

"*Jahvuhl.*"

The officer handed Harry the packet of papers. "*Ich entschuldige mich für das Eindringen.*" He suddenly turned friendly and put his arm around Harry "*Wenn Sie möchten, dass einige echte Beratung, steuern Süden. Es ist ein großer Sturm kommt auf die Küste.*"

"*Danke, danke.*"

The German officer turned to the others. "*Zeit zu gehen!*"

Nonsensically, he saluted Harry and Harry, trying not to laugh, saluted back. Then the submarine's crew climbed back across their little ladder and ducked into the steel contraption like scurrying church mice. The U-boat slipped back into the murk from which it rose and the others all gathered anxiously around Harry.

"What did he say, Harry?" Billy asked.

"How did it go?" Sharon said.

Joe, who spoke enough German and had been close enough to the entire conversation to follow the gist of it, waited upon Harry's exposition.

"Calm down, boys," Harry said. "I've got good news and bad news."

"It's always better to hear bad news first," Richard said.

"U-boats might be a menace but they do carry proper radio sets. Their captain told me we're headed straight into a storm."

"A storm?" Sharon asked. "But there isn't a cloud in the sky."

Billy regarded her with mocking wonder. "And how long have you been away from Ireland to think this means fine weather?"

"I'll have to take his word for it and hope for the best. We could turn toward Edinburgh but I'm not sure with a storm of this size it would make much of a difference."

"How's the old *Grainne ni Mhaille* on a bender?" Billy asked Severin.

"She's still here, is she not?"

"Good luck, then, Sev," said Joe.

"But what's the good news, Harry?" Severin asked.

"The good news? I nearly forgot about that." Harry dug into his pocket, pulled out a crumpled cache of banknotes, and handed them to Severin. "I saved you a hundred marks."

☁

THE GERMANS PROVIDED AN ACCURATE WEATHER FORECAST. BARELY ten miles out from their U-boat encounter the *Grainne* was overcome by a cloud as black as Hades and covering the horizon. It advanced upon them over the open water with the deliberation of a celestial army. The sea breeze kicked up, then rose to a wind and finally a gale, shredding the flags on the masts. The waves swelled then lashed and curled and within a minute the rains opened on to the deck like a falls. As he grappled with the wheel, Severin shouted orders to his scrambling charges.

"Joe, I need you to close down the coal scuttle. The water will flood the engine. Harry, stick to the inside of the deck and secure a rope around the lifeboat. And Richard, I want you to go below and make sure Billy and Sharon are wearing their jackets. Billy had a hard enough time of it out flat so I'm certain he is quite white now."

Just then the rain that no one aboard could imagine falling any harder did just that, or was the sea itself turning the boat upside down? It was hard to tell. The water rose in sheets on all sides, forming caves of air that to Joe's eye looked like the only safe and dry places available. He longed to leap into the chasm and grab hold of the wet walls as if they were made of stone. Instead, he drew himself hand over hand along the inner railing and swung down into the coal bin, jamming the iron lid of the feeder shut. He was too late—the roiling water had preceded him and blown out the furnace.

"Sev! Sev!" he shouted up at the sky but the roar around him was far too loud for his voice to carry. He thought to join Harry and help him secure the boat which would surely now be needed. He climbed back up to where he thought the deck should be but all he could make out was the side of the cabin. Poor Billy, Joe thought—for him this must be the worst sort of terror. He pushed his forearm across his shoulder to hold back the torrents and pressed his forehead against the glass. There was Sharon playing the angel of mercy, holding Billy upon her lap; he had curled up there like an infant. Richard was moving around the room, placing every loose object he could find into the trunk as the water rose around his feet. Joe crossed himself and said a silent prayer.

He grabbed the rail as tightly as he could and pulled himself around the corner. Here was the ladder to the top deck. He climbed up, one beam at a time, all the while certain the next gust of wind was set to carry him away. There was Severin. He had abandoned the wheel, which was turning of its own volition but to no known compass point. Instead, he had ripped down the extra jackets that had been bolted to the ceiling and was lading them over his shoulders.

"We've got to get to the boat," he screamed at Joe. "Help me with these jackets."

Joe raced up besides Severin and together they carried the jackets down to the main deck. In the meantime, Richard had come up. "Billy's in a panic," he said. "He thinks the boat is going to sink."

"It is going to sink," Severin told him. "Take these jackets and give one to Sharon, and then put one on Billy and get them up to the boat. Joe and I will find Harry."

Just then, Harry came round the stern. "If you need to launch the boat, it's ready."

"Let's go!"

Like a blessing from heaven the *Grainne* chose that moment to slip into the eye of the storm. Although the water kept sloshing around them suddenly it seemed possible to walk from one end of the boat to the other. Joe jumped below and helped Sharon put on Billy's jacket and they carried him up to the side deck where the boat was tethered. They plumped him over and lashed him to the till. Then Richard climbed aboard and Harry jumped in after him.

"Sev!" Joe shouted. "Sev, we have to go."

Joe looked around. Severin wasn't in the cabin. Where was he? They had to lower the boat before another swell caught them. Joe had one foot in the side of the boat when he backed out, swung around the railing on to the deck, and raced around to the starboard side of the trawler.

There was Severin halfway up the foremast. He held one arm wrapped tightly around the wood while his free hand struggled with a leather satchel that he had hitched over his shoulder. The wind and the rain were blowing so hard it was all Joe could do just to see his friend, let alone hear him. There was nothing for Joe to do but climb over to the base of the mast and steady himself against the first peg.

"For the love of God, Severin—what are you doing?"

"Launching a flare."

"You'll fall into the sea."

"If I don't get a rocket up, we all will."

"Let me help you."

Unbidden, Joe tried to climb to the next peg of the mast. He could feel the pull of the wind trying to cast him into the water. Severin had succeeded in removing two of the small rockets from the sack and was twisting off the first charge when he lost his balance. His body spun clockwise around the mast, slamming into Joe's chest one step below. Joe's instinct was to throw out his arms in supplication and by doing so he pinned Severin to the mast and kept him in place.

"Thanks, Joe!"

Joe thought it was necessary to eschew the niceties of polite conversation at the moment so he said nothing and held Severin in place. No sooner had the first rocket been ignited than it fizzled in the onslaught of water.

"Shite!" Severin yelled. He brought out the second rocket and fired it. This time, the flare penetrated the heavens and spread a curtain of blue and white finery across the sky. Severin let out a whoop of joy and turned around to pull out a second pair of flares. His foot slipped on the peg and he fell to the deck.

"Severin!" Joe screamed as he slid down the mast. Severin had landed on one of the steel hold doors and crashed his head against the rail. He was unconscious. Joe reached down and cradled Severin's body in his arms. Even when they were boys, Joe had never been able to lift Severin;

he had never even tried. Now when he went to carry him he found that not only was he able to pick his friend's body up and hold him but he could do so with assurance. It was hard but Joe struggled to his feet and began to carry the unconscious man across the deck to the waiting boat.

As Joe turned the corner at the bow, Severin shook a little and showed signs of reviving. He tried to hook an arm tighter around Joe's neck. Joe turned to where the lifeboat lay and tried to maneuver Severin's body into it. Richard and Harry were cutting the ropes and lowering the boat into the water. Before they could finish the task the *Grainne* lost the eye and rose out of the water and the blow of the water and the wind rushing back against the battered lifeboat set it to spinning. Joe grabbed Severin with all his might and tried to hold on.

Severin opened his eyes.

"Joe?" he asked. He twisted his body backwards. The sudden movement caused Joe to lose his grip and Severin slid away, off the side of the boat and into the sea.

"Severin!" Joe screamed, but already he was gone. Joe had only a fraction of a second to decide whether to propel himself into the water after his friend or turn around and secure himself in the lifeboat. He chose to live.

⌒

EVERYONE MANAGED TO STAY LASHED TO THE LIFEBOAT, EVEN THE semiconscious Billy. The storm was malevolent but it was not relentless and within a half an hour their little boat had drifted into the path of a British light cruiser breaking for the Scapa Flow. A ladder was let down into the water and one by one the survivors of the wreck of the Grainne were led to safety.

Joe was plagued with self-doubt. If, Joe thought, if—that most inglorious and indefensible of words: if Severin had not climbed up the mast to launch the flare, if he hadn't slipped and fallen. Then, if Severin had not regained consciousness at precisely the same moment as the trawler heaved in the churning sea, I might not have lost my grip. And if I could have held my grip on Severin's waist I would not have sent him to eternity.

Joe continued to brood on the boat to Tyneside. While the rest of the passengers gratefully accepted the warm blankets and bowls of broth offered to them, Joe sat apart, Lear-like, allowing the brunt of the weather to buffer his misery. He wanted to hide from the world and he hoped the world would not care to look for him. But he was wrong; halfway between the flow and the port Harry came calling.

"It's not good to sit all by yourself, Joe." Harry put his arm around Joe and tried to pull Joe closer to him but Joe pushed him away.

"There's not a bit of good about any of it," Joe answered. "And it doesn't help me to say there is."

"I know."

"I'm not the best of company right now, Harry. Why don't you go back below?"

"I'm sorry about Severin, Joe. It was God's will."

At this, Joe stood up. "What is God's will, Harry?" he shouted. "What does that mean?"

"Joe…"

Harry took a step toward Joe as a way to embrace him but Joe put out both his hands and pushed him. Harry was startled by the gesture. He lost his balance and fell to the deck. But Joe would not relent.

"What does that mean?" he said. "Am I to think that Severin's life was worth nothing in the balance? Is God so cruel that he punishes only the virtuous and allows sinners to breath free?"

"What are you talking about, Joe? Who is a sinner here?"

"I am. We all are. Everyone who lives. Everyone."

"I don't understand."

"And what did you do to help, Harry? Is that more of your God's will?"

Joe reached back and punched him. Harry had no choice but to defend himself. He landed a blow on Joe's chest. Joe fell back and Harry stood opposite him with his fists raised and readied.

"That's right," Joe cried out. "Back up your malfeasance with violence. Turn against your friends."

Harry threw his hands down to his side. "You're talking nonsense, Joe."

"It's you talking nonsense, Harry. I won't hear anymore about God's will. There's no such thing. God's work on earth is our own—and look… look what a hash I've made of it."

Joe burst into tears, rolling tears of salt indistinguishable from the windblown sea. In his crying he reached out and took hold of the deck railing. His body shook from the effort and for one brief instant Harry feared for him. He looked as if he was going to throw himself to the waves. Instead, Joe collapsed to the deck. He wrapped his arms around his head and gently rocked himself from side to side. "Oh, Harry. What am I to do?"

Harry sat down next to Joe and gently put his arm around his shoulder. This time, Joe let him keep it there.

"You're to do what all of us are to do. You're to live."

⌢

THE ENTIRE RAGTAG CREW OF THE FORMER *GRAINNE NI MHAILLE* WAS being hailed as heroes in Tyneside. Their papers and all their possessions were lost of course but there was no reason whatsoever for the crown authorities to doubt Harry's story, that they had been trying to cross the sea with valuable information that they were supposed to deliver to the harbormaster of the port of Aberdeen and if they wouldn't mind helping them to complete their mission that would be the best thing they could do to serve the King. Joe listened to Harry's tale unfold in wonder before him and was unstinting in his admiration of his friend's ability to convince the world of their own reality.

They hitched from Tyneside to Aberdeen by ferry and from Aberdeen it was a simple matter arranging transport to Ireland. Billy and Sharon had become best buddies by this point and it cheered Joe to see Billy so subsumed by gratitude that he was able to talk to Sharon of Megan, a landscape the heretofore-ungallant Mr. Macready would never have revealed. They decided to head back to the island together, Sharon to her kin in Antrim and Billy to his girl in Dublin. It was a bittersweet departure; Joe and Richard were convinced they were witness to the final break-up of their beloved Dubs.

The rest of the survivors—Richard, Harry, and Joe—continued on with their arrangements as if the little interlude with the storm at sea had merely been an inconvenience. The met up with the Irish nationalists in Aberdeen who had already cleared their way to Cork. Their last ferry ride together was silent. Richard could not serve as a witness to Joe's sorrow because he was not a witness to Joe's soul but he understood the connection Joe had made with Severin and he proved exemplary in providing a portion of the balm Joe needed. But it was not enough.

Queenstown proved no leveler to Joe's emotions. Part of the arrangement that Richard and Harry had worked out brought Donal McCormack to the quay. When Joe climbed off the ferry and saw Donal standing there, for once out of his Westmoreland Street duds and looking completely stricken in his empathy it brought back the ghosts that he had almost managed to stow, everyone from Tommy Doyle to Mick Kennedy to Severin Coole. The two of them stood cumbered in each others' arms for a full minute.

"Thanks for coming, Donal," was all Joe could manage to say.

"It's your homecoming, Joe. *Fáilte abhaile.*"

As Joe looked long and hard into the eyes of the man who once was a boy he had loved he searched for a blessing and for signs of understanding and forgiveness. It cheered him to believe they were being offered.

Still it was not enough.

⌒

JOE AND HARRY TRAMPED UP THE HILL, THE LITTLE CLOTH SACKS that the authorities in Tyneside had given them slung across their shoulders.

"I'm sure my ma is going to think she's seeing a vision," Joe began. "What with me looking like a vagrant and no notice and all."

"If that's what she's going to make of you, what do you think she'll make of me? 'Bringin' home a German now, Joey?'"

"You're as German as Eamon de Valera, Harry."

"Well, he's Spanish, isn't he?"

"Come off it."

The boys were almost boyish in their attitudes. One wouldn't go so far as to say their cares were lifting as they rose farther and farther away from the sorrowful shore but something about the cast of things was growing incrementally lighter with each step. Halfway up Joe stopped.

"If you can stand the climb, Vogeler, I'd like you to come up this way with me for a while."

"If you say so, Joe."

They turned to the right, away from the harbor and the ma's house and made their way to the steps of St. Colman's. From this height and in the bright sunshine the glistening strand at their feet and the wide sea beyond looked almost beneficent.

"This is where Severin and I first met," Joe said, still looking out at the cove. "I was a skinny little preparatory student and he was apprenticed as a glass-cutter for the works of the cathedral."

"From what I can see, you're still a skinny little preparatory student," Harry said, smiling.

"Always will be, too."

Joe turned his back on the water view and looked at Harry instead. "I don't think I'll ever be able to come up here again. There's too much sorrow in the air."

"There's sorrow in the air everywhere, Joe," Harry answered. "We still have to breathe."

"I suppose we do."

THE SHRIEK THAT CAME OUT OF THE MA FROM THE SEEING OF HIM was enough to raise the dead and Joe said so. "The neighbors will be calling the police, Ma, thinking some sort of robbery was taking place, the way you're carrying on."

"Let them call," Mrs. Dooley said. "I want the world to know."

It was Kathleen who had seen them first, standing quietly at the side door and conspiring to plan their approach. Joe spotted Kathleen spotting him and with a shushing gesture and a pat on Harry's back they slid around to the back entrance and planned to take the ma by surprise. A surprise it was, no doubt, leading at first to the shriek and then to tears and stammering before concluding in a suffocating embrace.

"This is my friend, Harry. Do you remember him from Dublin, all those years ago?"

"Harry?" Mrs. Dooley asked.

"Harry Vogeler."

"I'm sorry, Joe—no. But never the mind. I'm overjoyed to meet you."

"I apologize for the difficulty," said Joe.

"Difficulty?" Mrs. Dooley cried. "How on earth can anything involving my boy have any difficulty? I'll make up your room at once, and Harry, you can have Joe's Aunt Maeve's old room."

TRUTH BE TOLD JOE WAS HAPPY TO BE WARM AND SAFE; IT WAS ONE thing to long for the camaraderie of the battlefield when your friends were with you in the trenches but that longing had passed now. They sat up together all afternoon and evening, Kathleen and Joe and Harry and the ma, like a family at a reunion, passing in and out of the rooms with trays and cups and filling the time with laughs and tears and sometimes just plain words.

"I'm done with war now, Ma," Joe said when the discussion returned to the point as it inevitably would.

"Will you stay a while?"

"You know Harry and I have to get back to Talbot Street eventually."

"Eventually is a long time away," Kathleen suggested.

"We'll see."

"I don't like the tone of that," Mrs. Dooley said.

"We'll stay with you as long as you will have us, Mrs. Dooley."

"Why, thank you, Harry. If I could, I would have you forever."

After supper, the boys played whist while Kathleen cleaned up and then they all sat around in the parlor listening to Joe's favorite recordings.

"Anything but 'The Minstrel Boy,'" Joe said in response to Kathleen's request.

"Why so?"

Harry laughed.

"We'll tell you all about it some day."

Kathleen got up and picked out a record and put it on the Victrola. Joe felt a tear rise as the music flooded the room.

> *Du holde Kunst, in wieviel grauen Stunden,*
> *Wo mich des Lebens wilder Kreis umstrickt...*

"'*An die Musik*'!" Joe cried out. "Why did you...how did you..."

"I thought it was the fairest thing to do, considering our company."

Joe sang along with the next verse:

> *Hast du mein Herz zu warmer Lieb' entzunden,*
> *Hast mich in eine beßre Welt entrückt!...*

And Harry joined him for the conclusion:

> *Oft hat ein Seufzer, deiner Harf' entflossen,*
> *Ein süßer, heiliger Akkord von dir*
> *Den Himmel beßrer Zeiten mir erschlossen,*
> *Du holde Kunst, ich danke dir dafür!*
> *Du holde Kunst, ich danke dir!*

Kathleen and the ma beamed as the last notes of the song filled the room, the notes from the horn intermingling with Joe's fervent tenor and Harry's wavering baritone. Joe looked at Harry and thought: Wherever music is playing, I am home.

THE REST OF THE HOUSEHOLD HAD ALL FALLEN ASLEEP BY THE TIME Joe got around to helping Harry settle in Maeve's room.

"The bathroom is just down the hall and the window creaks when it's opened."

"I'm sure I'll be fine, Joe."

"My God, it's spooky being in here," Joe said.

"Well, if it bothers you, get out," Harry put his bag on the floor and sat down on the edge of the bed. "I'm tired."

"If that's the way you feel," Joe answered in mock exasperation. He got up and started to march out of the room.

"No, Joe." Harry reached out and grabbed Joe. Joe turned around and fell in beside Harry.

"So much time has gone by, Harry. What have we done with it?"

"No one planned on the war, Joe."

"It was in the air, always."

"Not the air we breathed."

"You're right about that," Joe agreed. "But there were so many things I wish I could have done differently."

"Wishing won't make them so."

"I mean, with us."

"How so?"

"I wish I could have been a better friend."

"I never had one better, Joe."

"I love you, Harry."

"I know that now. But what I never understood was how you loved me. I mean—it took me a long time to understand. For the longest while I knew there was something you were trying to tell me. I thought you felt too vulnerable or that it might leave you exposed. Or that my world was so different from yours that you would never be able to cross into it. I could never put my finger on it. What a gobeen I was! Here I thought it was too complicated to ever figure out and it turned out to be as simple as anything God ever created."

"How's that?"

"All you wanted to do was kiss me. And all you had to do was ask."

"I thought..."

"I know what you thought, Joe. You never asked me if it was true."

"Is it true?"

"This is." Harry stood up and pressed Joe's face into his belly. He pulled Joe up and took Joe's face into his hands. Then, as if to give words to his actions, he repeated himself. "This is."

Harry kissed Joe.

"I never thought it was possible," Joe said.

Harry smiled. "I knew it was possible," he said, "But I thought you loved Severin Coole."

"I did."

"I'm sorry."

"He…Severin wasn't in love with me. I mean…he loved me but…"

"I understand."

"As long as Severin was alive, I kept dreaming of some great victory. And now…"

"Don't you think love itself can be a great victory, Joe?"

Joe looked out the window but there was nothing to see in the dark. "I always felt I was waiting for Severin. Or waiting for something. But with you…"

"We were waiting for each other, Joe."

"It only took fourteen years."

"Who's counting?"

"You are."

"Ssh…"

Joe got up and shut the door. "Just in case my sister has a sudden urge to sleepwalk."

Harry pulled his army-issue shirt over his head. "No more uniforms for me."

Joe smiled and did the same. He pulled Harry into his arms and pushed him back into the bed. "Forgive me, Maeve."

Then he ran his arm along Harry's chest and down around the small of his back.

"This is how all wars should end," Harry said.

"What a vision!" Joe laughed. Harry rubbed the back of Joe's neck. "That tickles."

"Our war is over," Harry said.

"If only the rest of the world…"

"Let the world alone, Joe. Come to me."

"Yes," Joe said. "I will."

◆ ◆ ◆

Bob Sennett has written two books on Hollywood: *Setting The Scene*, Abrams, 1994, and *Hollywood Hoopla*, Backstage, 1998, and the book and lyrics to two musicals: *Aurora*, 1996, and *At Swim Two Boys*, 2007. This is his first novel.